BEST BUDDIES

JORDAN BACH

CRATER OF THE NORTH PUBLISHING

NOVELS BY JORDAN BACH

Best Buddies

Your son's invisible friend is not imaginary…

Reflected Dark

Are you a killer? Or are you something worse?

Harmony Four

Four murders. Every four years. Forever. Until now.

NOVELLAS:

In the Barn

Even the innocent can only be pushed so far

To my brother
Happy birthday, Graham

PART ONE

BAD BEHAVIOR

CHAPTER ONE

Each morning at eleven a.m., Kate Mallory squeezed the brakes on her workday and visited the men's empty restroom on the 42nd floor. Today was no different, not at first. She ran her fingers over the bank of cool, marble washbasins, overseen by mirrors that somehow remained mist-free after the men performed hot-air grooming sessions. It was also the sole male restroom at Hetherington Brokerage and Bonds in which the scents of cologne and creams hung more sharply than urine.

She pictured the young bucks and would-be masters of the universe shedding three o'clock shadows and refining their skincare routines as they prepared for an evening of shepherding clients around the city. They had to be ready for any taste or predilection, no matter how bizarre—whatever it took to win more business and hit those targets. One day, Kate would be in a similarly luxurious powder room, relaxing from the rush of the New York Stock Exchange and prepping for clients, albeit with a different symbol on the door.

The air hinges hissed open, and a harried Tammy Rhodes

poked her head and shoulders in. "Hey, Katie, got a spill on the main floor."

Kate smiled at her friend. "Welcome back, Tam. I'm fine, thanks. How was your mom's wedding?"

Tammy returned an eye-roll and a brief smile, almost absent of sarcasm. "Moldy Merv's losing his shit over it. Back me up, hon."

"I'll be right there." Kate attacked a translucent stain with a final, vigorous rub with her cloth, then gave up on figuring out which hyper-expensive beauty oil inflicted such a mark behind the lip of the basin, and wheeled her cart to the exit.

Tammy accompanied her through the trading floor, although it didn't remotely resemble what Kate remembered from the movies and TV shows of her youth, where people yelled over one another and gesticulated wildly in some adapted form of sign language. Sleek desks and lumbar-friendly chairs supported on-screen graphs and spreadsheets, several phones to each man—and it *was* still mostly men here —and a buzz of activity churned as money zipped and whizzed between accounts via concealed channels. Kate could practically feel the wealth shooting past her as she navigated to the site of the tragic incident where Mervin Corney was, indeed, losing his shit.

"Don't make me bring back the clear desk policy, Endo." Merv stood with his legs apart, looking down on the culprit, both he and Endo sporting thousand-dollar suits. "We all like our coffee, we all hate taking breaks, so don't fucking spoil it for everyone else, you get me?"

"We're here, Mr. Corney," Tammy said.

"About time." Merv pointed at the floor with a highly assertive finger—so assertive he must have attended a course that taught how to extend a digit in the smuggest manner possible. "This had better not stain."

"No, Mr. Corney," Tammy said.

4

Moldy Merv put both hands on his hips, exhaled through his nose, dropped his hands, and marched off, stabbing a final glance at Endo, the poor MBA graduate who'd committed the crime.

"Don't worry," Kate told him, "the tiles are treated. Even coffee and red wine don't stick around long."

Endo returned to his chair, mumbled, "It's not coffee. It's dandelion tea," and woke up his computer screen with a tap of his mouse. The blueish square danced to life in his thick-rimmed glasses, and he twisted around to face to the two women with the cloths and spray. "What I mean to say is, thank you. And sorry for the hassle."

"No problem, kiddo," Tammy replied. "You worry about all that cash. We'll keep the building going."

Already on her knees, Kate mopped the liquid at the edge of the desk to prevent further dribbles. "Not the worst spill I'll be cleaning this week."

"Ain't the worst I'll be cleaning *today*." Tammy joined her, spritzed the woody-smelling puddle of whatever the heck dandelion tea was, and went at it with a cloth. "So, hey, any gossip while I was away? Any spills worth talkin' about from Aaron's get-together?"

"Not really. His aunt and uncle keep guinea pigs and got a new one for Aaron as a birthday present. They held the party at their house this year, which was nice of them, but I had to have a quiet chat about them buying him a pet without consulting me. Luckily, they're keeping it at their house with the others. To be honest, I think it's so he'll nag me to go around more."

"Nice folks," Tammy said.

Kate finished her part and rose to select a bucket from her trolley, where she squeezed out her cloth. "You want to know what he called it? His new guinea pig?"

"What?"

"Tony Stark. Not Hulk or Thor, but Tony Stark."

"Like Iron Man?"

"Yeah." Kate rejoined Tammy on the floor and used a fresh cloth to rinse the spot she'd cleaned. "Jonathan might be an ass, but hey, he's a rich ass. If he and Jennifer want to provide free babysitting, then I don't need torturing to say yes."

"And the other thing? His offer on the house?"

Kate smiled tightly, then changed the subject. Heating up their chat in the middle of their client's firm would end badly for them both. "I do have some news. While you were living it up in Florida, I enrolled back in night school."

Tammy sat up on her haunches, having scrubbed all she could. "You gonna work yourself half to death."

Kate mirrored Tammy's pose, up on her knees and toes, the job over, the carpet as clean as it had been before Endo's accident. She took in the floor, the money, and the sense of purpose with which everyone peered at their screens. "Couple of years, Tammy. That's all I need. Then me and Aaron'll be fine."

"What, you finish up your degree and just walk into a hundred-K-a-year job at some swanky law firm?" Tammy stood, knees plainly creaking for her. "Or a place like this?"

Kate rose to her feet and hauled the bucket back to her cart. "I can cope with it. I just need four hours or so overtime this week, and I won't have to load up the credit card again."

"And next week?"

Kate sagged slightly. Tammy meant well. She'd never known another life except this one, but Kate hadn't always scraped her weeks together paycheck-to-paycheck. "Aaron deserves a nice place to grow up. A decent life. If I know I can do a job like these guys, what kind of mom would I be if I didn't try?"

Tammy lifted her eyebrows. "A mom like me."

The reply stung in Kate's throat. She touched her friend's arm. "You know what I mean, Tam."

Tammy nodded, but the jab had loosened something in her eyes. Not a massive insult, but sufficient to hurt.

"I'm sorry, it's just… you know Aaron'd be better off if…"

"If what?"

"Nothing." Kate sucked back a sob. If disagreements were frowned upon, bursting into tears at the happy thought of swapping places with her dead husband would lead to a worse situation than she was already in. "You think I should take Jonathan's offer?" Kate asked, switching back to the subject she'd tried to avoid.

"That's your choice, hon," Tammy said. "Might make life a little easier."

Kate stared at Tammy for a moment, and Tammy stared back. A regular impasse between the two—what usually happened when one knew the other was right, but also kind-of wrong.

"Break time," Tammy said, leading Kate from the cleaned spillage. "You got a chance to ask Dev for the OT. See how much of a dick he can be about it."

"If I can handle my brother-in-law and night school, I can handle Dev."

Kate's phone buzzed in her tabard pocket, forbidden in the usual scheme of things, but most of the moms and dads, or those with sick relatives, risked breaking the rule. Dev's one good facet was that he turned a blind eye to it, so long as they were subtle about it.

Kate checked the caller ID and shivered, an icy dread familiar to every parent whenever a particular contact name beamed in their hand.

"I'll catch up," she said. "It's the school."

As per the rule-breaking rulebook, she pushed out into a stairwell where no camera would witness her take the call.

It was the school's counselor, Hester Duval, a gravel-voiced woman who on the phone was frequently mistaken for a man. "Mrs. Mallory, I'm afraid I had no choice but to call you. There's been an incident at the school."

Kate hoped Dev would be snacking in the bare office that served as the cleaners' unofficial break room. They were supposed to travel down to the 30th floor to an overpriced cafe, where they were expected to purchase overpriced snacks or to munch on whatever they'd brought from home. Close to their locker room, management had supplied a couple of banks of chairs, fixed in rows like a doctor's waiting area— hardly a cafeteria designed for socializing. There was a microwave, too, alongside a list of banned foodstuff that included fish, curry, and pretty much anything that stank up the place worse than tomato soup. Since that trek was a pain in all their butts, they kept lunches here, in the office vacated by a junior exec during last year's downsizing, with a view of New York City and a collection of mismatched seats smuggled in by the cleaning company's day-crew.

Kate's perch was the beanbag chair she'd bought Craig for their anniversary two years ago, intended for the reading corner in his planned man-cave at the bottom of their lawn. That would never happen now, though. Each time she sat on it in this place, she wondered if she was disrespecting his memory, saying, *Screw it. What would a dead guy want with an overstuffed scatter cushion, anyway?*

At the moment Kate wandered in, Tammy was occupying the beanbag, legs extended, forking salad and pasta from a tub. "You don't mind, do you? I can move if you make me."

"Dev?" Kate said. "Anyone seen him?"

The other two in the room, Marla and Joanne, shook their heads without looking up from their sandwiches.

Tammy said, "He was just leaving. Doing his rounds, making himself seen. You know what these new kids are like."

Kate did know.

"Anything up?" Tammy asked.

"Aaron," Kate said, low enough so only Tammy heard properly. "He's *never* violent. Never. But he slapped a girl. *Slapped* her."

"Why?"

"That's the weird thing." Kate put her hand on the door but didn't open it. "Apparently, he said he 'had to.' Wouldn't say why. Just that he had to."

Tammy frowned.

"Yeah, I know. But… I have to go in person."

"Just do it, Katie. We'll be okay."

"I know you will. But I need to clear it with Dev."

"Eat first. Did I tell you lately that you're way too skinny?"

"Not for at least a day," Kate said. "You're slipping. But I'll eat on the train home. I promise."

Kate departed, her stomach objecting as she left without opening her paper sandwich bag stored in the mini fridge.

She returned to the floor, heading for the vicinity of Moldy Merv's office, since she figured Dev would be nearby. His goal was to be seen micromanaging the cleaning crew, such lowly humans viewed by those in lofty positions as slackers who'd happily rip off the hand that fed them for a few extra minutes of free time. The term "office" was a loose one, though, as Mervin Corney wasn't a manager with a glass cube, but a supervisor who'd fashioned himself a space out of five-foot-high partition

9

screens, a construction Kate thought of as Merv's "den" since it resembled the forts Aaron and Craig used to build with sofa cushions.

Look out, Dad, it's a mom-ster!

Ah, hide, hide! I'll protect you, my prince!

Merv acted the part of a junior exec, bonused on the performance of the brokers around him. Rumor said he got the job not because of his managerial acumen but his length of service and his willingness to be the first in and last out of the office. He was also impervious to being the least popular guy in the room. At least when senior management wasn't present.

Something he had in common with Dev.

Kate spotted her own supervisor inspecting the door to the brokers' break room, where she and her colleagues were allowed to enter and clean, but not consume food or drink, lest they taint the slick atmosphere with their poorness. As she approached, she heard Merv in conversation with the mildly spoken dandelion-drinker.

"Jesus, that's two hundred grand you cost us."

"I'm sorry," Endo said. "It looked good for it. I—"

"You should've shorted the goddamn company instead of investing."

Not talking about the spill, Kate assumed.

Endo said, "The price didn't drop *that* far—"

"Yeah. It's sarcasm. You know what that is, don't you? How'd you even get this job, anyway? Thought you people were supposed to be good with numbers."

"*Me-people?*" Endo said.

Merv stuttered for perhaps half a second before cartwheeling out of the racial-stereotyping quagmire. "Traders. Math geeks. You *MBA*-people."

"Right, sure."

"Just get out of my office and make up the difference."

Endo stepped out from the divider space, wearing the look of a lost puppy as he shuffled away.

"Hey," Kate said. "Are you okay?"

Endo glanced around, confused, as if Kate's voice had descended from thin air. "Oh, hi. Yes, I'm fine, thanks." Endo added a frown, then walked away at a faster clip.

"Kate," Dev said, loud enough for Merv to hear at the center of his den. "You're supposed to be on a break."

"I am on my break," Kate said. "I need to ask you something."

Dev adopted a pose depressingly similar to Merv's hands-on-hips admonishment of the stain situation. "Yes?"

"Two things, actually."

"Overtime again?"

Kate's head tilted to one side. She softened her eyes. "All the big firms we service are still clean freaks. No one wants to risk being patient zero. So I know there's OT available. Four hours. Six if it's there."

"I need reliable, Kate. If I give you eight till twelve on Saturday morning up on sixty-one, you promise you'll be there?"

"I do."

"On time?"

"On time." She snapped a Boy Scout salute. "Promise."

Dev took out an oversized smartphone and entered her on the roster. "What's two?"

"Two?"

"You said there were two things."

"Right, two." Kate lowered her voice and ushered Dev away from Merv's den. "I need to leave early today."

"Kate…" His reply came out in a warning tone, but ebbed away as if he was too tired to finish the thought.

"It's Aaron, I don't know what happened, or rather, why, exactly, but they want me to go in."

"Is he sick?"

"Not sick, but… They need me there in person."

Dev blinked at the floor a few times, nose-breathing as he pretended to consider it. "You ask for overtime, then drop this on me?"

"It's urgent. Seriously, Dev. Please. Just an hour early."

"You want the OT on Saturday." Dev flashed his big-screened phone. "But you don't want to finish your shift here. Think about it."

Kate weighed up whether begging some more could prove worthwhile, but she waited too long and her cheeks flushed as she bit her teeth together.

"I'm sorry," Dev said, walking away. "It's your choice."

Only when she tried to move did Kate realize she'd grown jittery, swapping from one foot to the other.

Tammy had come along at some point, waited until Dev passed down his verdict before stepping in.

"It'll be okay," Tammy said. "We can cover."

"He'll pull the overtime. If I miss my payment on the car, I'll have to put it on the credit card again or lose it, and I don't want that. Cards are almost maxed already. But… Aaron, he—" She cut herself off. "I need the overtime this week. I *need* it."

"So you're not going to the school?"

Kate swallowed back the urge to shout, smoothed her restless legs and feet, and calculated she had enough time to wolf down her sandwich but not the yoghurt before resuming her duties. "I don't have any choice, Tam. Guess I'll be late for school."

CHAPTER TWO

The Principal of Aaron's school was a wiry man of indeterminate middle age with a widow's peak and skin complexion which, combined, reminded Kate of a sophisticated vampire. Sitting before him as she explained her late arrival, his manner, too, morphed into that of a nocturnal creature appraising its prey.

"I couldn't get away, I'm sorry."

"Becky's mom got here in thirty minutes," Aaron said, perched on the seat beside her, his cheeks rosy, streaked as if he'd been crying. He probably had.

"Becky?" Kate chewed her lip a second. "The girl you hit?"

Aaron dropped his eyes to the floor. His new pose suggested he'd shrunk since she dropped him off this morning. He did a weird pointing thing beneath the Principal's line of sight—his ring and little fingers crossed while his forefinger folded-unfolded on itself. A nervous tic?

"Indeed," Mr. Grimes added without moving a muscle. "Aaron has been waiting for you for some time."

Kate drew her elbows in and met his gaze. "I'm sure

Becky's mom doesn't have to commute to the city for her job, where her asshole of a boss acts like a spoiled prince. Sorry for my language…"

Mr. Grimes opened a file and offered a sheet of paper to Kate, which released a wave of cheap cologne from the man's shirt. Nothing like the crisp scents in the 42nd floor restroom.

Kate reached for it, forced a smile, and perused the spreadsheet mapping Aaron's paltry performance for the school year.

Mr. Grimes laced his fingers together on the desktop. "Because of his father's passing, *hmm*, what was it, two years ago?"

"Coming up on eighteen months," Kate said.

"Yes, yes, we gave Aaron plenty of leeway on his grades, but as we discussed at the last conference, we need him to step up now."

"And he has done that." Kate ruffled the paper. "Three assignments in the last two weeks, two tests. He aced them."

Aaron's head came back up and he almost smiled.

"That's true. Not outstanding, but a, *hmm*, encouraging upward trend." Mr. Grimes glanced between boy and mother, eyes softening as he landed on Aaron. "It was as if his tenth birthday was a turning point. I don't know. Reaching the ripe old age where you have to break out the double figures? Something symbolic to him." Back to Kate. "But this uptick in academic performance has coincided with a decline in his, *hmm*, general behavior. He swore at a janitor. Picked on a younger lad for being—and I quote—*gay*." He made bunny ear air-quotes.

"I'm not defending that," Kate said, summoning all her willpower to balance annoyance at Aaron and her under-standing at why he might act out. While the other incidents had cut deep and caused her no end of embarrassment, they hadn't dropped on days where she'd begged Prince Dev for

14

overtime to make her car payment. "But kids say a lot of stuff they don't fully comprehend. He gets why it's wrong to use 'gay' as an insult now, and he won't do it again. And today was... *What* happened today?"

"Aaron?"

Both adults watched Aaron squirm. He was a small kid for his age—not the smallest in his class by far, but in the bottom five—and he'd always had a mischievous grin. He wore his hair floppy, too, short at the sides, although they'd let it grow out. Since he wasn't like the hard-faced kids who were already rebelling and testing authority, it seemed so out of place when he tried to push back.

"I told Mr. Grimes already," he said. "I told the counselor. I even told Becky. Why do I have to go through it again?"

"Because your mother hasn't heard it from you," Mr. Grimes said.

Kate found guilting kids to be distasteful, but sometimes necessary; how else did you teach empathy?

She said, "Well?"

"I had to, okay?" Aaron said. "I'm sorry you had to come here, and I'm sorry Becky got hurt, but I... I just *had* to."

"What would have happened if you hadn't?"

"I don't know. But it *would* have." Aaron resumed his slouched position. "It would have been much worse than a slap."

Silence followed.

Only two weeks earlier, as Aaron helped Kate hang out the washing, he tripped over the basket, and three towels had tumbled onto the damp ground. He'd said sorry so many times, it was as if he was worried she'd whip him or banish him to the sewer for what he'd done. She'd worked hard at cleaning those, he'd said on the brink of tears, and he'd ruined them.

Today, speaking about slapping a girl, he sounded unrepentant. Almost doubling down. There had to be a reason, but he was unwilling to voice it. Perhaps he'd come clean when they were alone.

"You see, Mrs. Mallory," Mr. Grimes said. "With grades like he's shown recently, he could end this year in the top half of his class. But if his behavior doesn't reflect that, *hmm*, he's going nowhere this summer."

They didn't speak to one another as they departed Mr. Grimes' office, or as they wound through the empty corridors to the exit, and Aaron couldn't shake the notion that Mom would never understand. She wasn't even trying. She seemed to be paying more attention to the trees and lawns as they made for their car, more concerned with herself than him.

"I always promised myself I wouldn't be 'that' mom," she said, although Aaron wasn't sure she was speaking to him. "I would never be the one with the bad kid."

I'm not bad.

Aaron was about to say it, but Mom was talking again.

"Okay, sure, I might end up with no choice in the matter. You choose to behave like that, then I'm already there. But if I'm gonna be 'that' mom, I can't defend my kid being violent."

"I'm not violent," Aaron said.

She tutted, gave his hand a tug to hurry him up, as if they were late for something. "If you get kicked out of here, I can't chauffeur you to the next nearest school."

"I won't get kicked out."

"At least, not one with an above-average rating and a lower mortality rate. You want to go to one of those inner city places? Okay, I can drop you on my way to work."

16

Aaron intentionally mumbled his response, knowing it annoyed Mom. "I don't wanna go to a school like that."

It wasn't the first time she'd wondered things like that aloud. After Dad had died, she'd stayed quiet most of the time. But since school started back up, she'd been pushing Aaron to do better. She said things like she couldn't keep making excuses for him, and that she was working as hard as she could to keep a roof over their heads which made her *tired-so-tired all the time*. But he never understood why the roof would fall in if she didn't work as much.

When she got mad with him, as she often had since he'd turned ten, she'd told him a few times he might have to go to a different school one day, not a nice one, although he'd never thought of his current school as special. But if she would just listen to him, she might see why he'd had to do what he did.

As in the Principal's office, he kept his head down, mumbling a reply he knew he shouldn't say out loud, but she deserved it.

"What?" Mom said.

Aaron frowned up at her. "You should say 'pardon' not 'what'."

"Throwing my own words at me, nice. Can't wait for the teenage years. I asked what you said just now."

"I *said…*" He swallowed, noting his tone and dialing back the annoyance he felt. "I said, at least then you won't leave me waiting so long."

"That's what you're worried about? Me taking too long to come pick you up when the school thinks you're too naughty to go back to class? Just be glad I came at all."

He shrugged, eyes back on the ground.

Mom took one of her big breaths. The ones that made her cheeks red. It could tip either way: Yell at him, or calmly say how disappointed she was. She always talked like that eventually, even after yelling. He needed to feel bad for *what he did*. Not for *getting caught*.

And he did feel bad. Worse than he could say. But slapping Becky had still been necessary. Essential.

Eventually, at the car, Mom paused.

"Aaron, I can't afford more problems. Swearing. Hitting some girl because you, what? Felt the urge to?" She didn't wait for an answer. "How long until you break someone's property that I have to pay for? Until you get suspended and I have to stay home or find childcare? I'll be out of the house even more, making up the overtime."

"I won't do that," Aaron said.

"How do I know that? A week ago, I'd have sworn on a stack of bibles that you'd never hit someone for shits and giggles."

"Mom, you just swore. And I don't even know what it means."

Mom opened her mouth, then bit back what she was going to say, and ran her hands hard through her hair. "I'm sorry for swearing. But it means you did it for the hell of it. For no reason."

"I *told* you, I didn't do it for no reason."

She went on as if she didn't hear him. "I can already barely afford this car, your lunches, the upkeep on the house, all your fish—"

"*Dad's* fish," Aaron said. "We have to keep them. Dad wouldn't want you to sell them."

Kate swallowed. "Yes, right. Your dad's fish. That... *all* that... and everything else I have to do to keep things going... Please, Aaron, just be good." Her eyes glistened, as though she was about to cry, but she blinked a few times and they returned to normal. "Please understand, I can't be around all the time. But things are going to be okay. I have a plan. It'll work out."

"Okay," again, followed by indecipherable mumbling.

"That doesn't sound too enthusiastic. I need you to promise me. Please?"

That seemed to be his chance to put an end to this conversation. But Mom hadn't asked the most important question—or rather, hadn't let him answer it.

She'd asked him why he did it, why he'd slapped Becky, but hadn't allowed him to expand, to tell her the whole truth. If she did, it wasn't likely she'd believe him, because he didn't believe it himself.

If anyone could help him understand things, it'd be Dad, but he wasn't here and was never coming back. Without him, he knew Mom would try her best, but it wasn't enough. Her best, as Aaron had overheard her telling their neighbor, was *never* enough.

At some point, maybe he'd be able to work out how to talk to her about this. For now, though, it was better not to stress her out too much. Keeping this to himself was a kindness.

Aaron's eyes felt the way his mom's had looked a moment ago—damp, raw. "I promise I'll try."

"Good enough," she said. "For now."

No, he couldn't fully explain this to her. Not without hurting her. He could deal with it himself.

Until he worked out what to do about it, he just hoped he wouldn't have to do something even the world's nicest mommy couldn't forgive.

CHAPTER THREE

With Aaron sitting up front, Kate drove, her thoughts jumbling together. How had she let that roll from her mouth?

Just be glad I came at all...

Like she'd leave him alone. Run away. That's something she'd never contemplate, and should never say aloud, not to a boy like Aaron. What if he thought she was dying? Not just leaving him but leaving him the same way as his father.

Still... would anyone blame her for extreme thoughts, fleeting as they were? Any mom would feel like a failure in the face of what she'd heard, wouldn't they? The image of her sweet little boy acting violently toward someone—*anyone*, never mind she was a girl—mixed with her satisfaction at his fine school in their safe district, and dumped out a messy sludge.

She could threaten to sanction him if anything like this happened again, then hope he'd be too afraid to repeat what he'd done. And she would find some repercussions. But she favored something restorative, such as an apology letter, rather than taking the plug off his Xbox for a week where he'd simply serve his sentence before figuring out how to be more careful next time. She'd read kids his age responded better when they had to make amends. Besides, the harsher type of punishment only meant more work for Kate. And she was too tired for more work.

It was only a five-minute journey back home, and Kate pictured herself driving not a Toyota Hybrid but a moving van as she relocated them to a smaller place in a dank, godforsaken neighborhood. Somewhere like—and she hated herself for thinking it—where Tammy lived. That was all chain-link fences and clapboard one-stories with metal detectors in the high schools. Okay, not permanent metal detectors, but they'd utilized them more than once during the previous twelve months.

She couldn't live there.

She lived *here*.

Aaron went to a *nice* school.

Convenient, in their *nice* neighborhood.

For *nice* families.

Ah, White Plains. With what the realtors called a vibrant cafe culture (which she could no longer afford), its eclectic nightlife (which she could neither afford, nor find the time or energy to frequent), and A+ schools, she wouldn't entertain wrenching Aaron away, forcing him to live the way she'd been raised herself. Without Craig's insurance paying off the mortgage and most of her debts, she'd be living in a trailer park, not a four-bedroom house on a tree-lined street with neighbors whose names she knew, so she was already clinging to this life by her fingernails. And they felt so very brittle this afternoon.

"Mom?"

Kate tapped her thumbnail against one finger, then returned her hand to the wheel. "Yeah."

"Sorry you had to come out here."

Finally.

"You want to talk about it, champ?" Kate asked.

"Champ?"

"Uncle Jonathan calls you champ. You don't seem to mind."

He shrugged. A more lighthearted shrug than the *I dunno* shambles from earlier. He was doing that pointing thing again—ring finger crossed over his little one, forefinger extending and retracting.

"So." Kate turned off the 125 and slowed for the lights of a crosswalk. "Do you?"

A teenage boy walking four dogs crossed in front of them.

Aaron asked, "Do I what?"

"Want to talk about it?"

He formed a fist of his pointing-unpointing hand, then released it and snorted in reply. Not disrespectfully, more of an elongated sigh. "I'm sorry I got mad. I know you work hard."

She wanted to believe he meant it, but her stomach swayed at the inkling he was manipulating her, the way all moms felt at distrusting their child without evidence.

"And Becky?"

Aaron said nothing.

On green, Kate set off again.

Silence.

A silence so encompassing that Kate had to fill it. "You're gonna need to talk about it sooner or later, buddy." *Buddy*. Yes. Better than *champ*. "You know I can't let something like that slide."

"I didn't want to," Aaron said. "But I told you, I *had* to."

"Why? You still haven't given me a reason for a nice boy hitting a girl."

"I was confused." He bit his bottom lip, sucking it into his mouth to chew on.

"Confused? Like… scared?"

Kate waited, hoping he'd been picked on, was fighting off some bully and Becky simply got in the way. She'd be proud if that were the case. Or even if Becky was the bully. If she were a bigger kid picking on him, her gender wouldn't matter to Kate. Not for a couple of years at least.

Aaron said, "You won't understand."

"Try me. I've been around a while."

Aaron almost smiled. Almost. "My homework, where I got the A-grades? And the test and the pop-quiz?"

"That's good. Your schoolwork is looking up. You've been working hard. Did Becky say you cheated or something? Was she copying your work?"

"Nothing like that, it's… hard to explain. And I didn't study any harder than usual. That's what's confusing."

"You didn't work hard for the grades?"

Aaron pouted, his finger-pointing tic moving faster. "If you didn't study—"

"I just *know stuff* now."

Kate frowned, taking the right turn that led to her neighborhood. "You… just know?"

"Yeah."

"Without studying or anything? The answers pop into your head?"

"Yeah. Or I know where to look to find the answer, like, online."

Kate thought it through. "That doesn't explain the slap."

Aaron shrugged. "It felt right. The same way I knew the capital of Australia is Canberra, I knew I had to slap Becky."

Kate resisted the eye-roll, held back her groan.

Aaron picked up on it, anyway. "You think I'm just a

dumb kid who got mad at another dumb kid." He stared out the window at the passing cafes and bars. "Forget it."

Kate could humor him or demand he tell the truth. Flip a coin? No, she knew her boy. This was a child who found ladybugs on the grass and transported them to the hedge where they'd be more sheltered from birds or whatever chose ladybugs as a meal.

For the rest of the journey, until they got home and she could threaten his Xbox cable with a pair of scissors, she guessed letting him talk was harmless enough.

"Okay," she said. "You know stuff. Like what?"

The shrug again. "Like, whatever." His face turned slowly to her. The pointing tic had stopped. "Is there anything *you* want to know?"

"What subject?"

"Anything. History. Geography. Math. Sports, if you want."

"So, d'you know about the Comets?"

Aaron screwed up his face. "What's that?"

"Basketball team. Lower league. Me and your dad used to watch the Comets. But never mind."

"You wanna know who they're hoping to sign?"

Kate tried to make her smile genuine. "You know that?"

Aaron blinked a couple of times, held still, then shrugged again. "Yeah. Or should I tell you what the score will be?"

Kate's tongue moistened, as if someone had opened a beer at the end of a tough, hot day. She swallowed it back and the saliva got stuck in her throat before clearing. Her tongue swelled, and an ancient sensation spread from her mouth to her stomach, tingling through her limbs and making her vision tilt.

No—she could not allow that to creep back inside her.

"Well?" Aaron said, an injection of enthusiasm brightening his tone. "Do you want to know the score?"

"Against the Furies tonight? The spread would be plenty, but—" Kate snagged halfway between a laugh and growling at him to ignore her and never raise the subject again. She went for the lighter response. "Well, if you know things like that, I could've done with it before..."

Oh, nope. Not going there.

"Before what?" Aaron asked.

Too late.

"Don't worry about it," Kate said, finding her foot heavy on the accelerator and having to ease off it. "Pretend I didn't say anything."

"Before Dad died." Aaron's fingers curled in his lap, the nervous tic resumed—ring and little finger crossed, twitching his forefinger. "That's what you mean, isn't it?"

Kate rarely spoke with Aaron about Craig. A year and a half sometimes felt as though only weeks had passed. Even now, she always waited for her son to bring it up.

"You argued a lot," Aaron went on. The boy who couldn't remember to tidy his clothes before changing into his jammies but recalled two, three, even four-year-old incidents with perfect clarity. "About sports. I sometimes heard you."

They were almost home, but Kate had opened the can, and now the worms gushed out. "I shouldn't go into sports scores, Aaron. That was silly of me. It's not a joking matter. Your dad, he—"

"It's why he was divorcing you."

Jesus.

She'd had no idea how much Aaron had intuited from back then, or why he was only bringing it up now.

Had he heard them? Or maybe Jonathan and his loud-mouthed, passive-aggressive wife still gossiped and cast blame her way, even now.

Yes, that was more likely. Even when they fought, Kate and Craig kept their voices down. No way to shield their problems from Aaron's orbit entirely. It was *possible* he'd picked up on their more intense chats, but more likely Uncle Jonathan and Aunt Jennifer—the J-Js—had spoken carelessly in his vicinity.

"Remember we talked about Mommy's disease?" she said. "Before Daddy passed?"

"Sure." Aaron's hand stilled, his free one lying over it. "It's why he didn't live with us for a while."

Carefully, annunciating in the most neutral tone she could muster, Kate chose the honest path. "Yes. But we didn't get a divorce, did we? We made up. Because you two were the most important things in the world to me. It was hard. But I made the changes. I beat the disease."

As she pulled into their road, she opened a window, a thunderstorm-like charge now filling the car, despite the AC.

"You get that I'm better, right?" she said.

"Yes."

"And you telling me a score isn't going to make my illness come back. Okay?"

Aaron nodded and his smile peeled into place. "It'd be useful though, wouldn't it?"

"Sure, we'd be mega rich." She allowed a brief laugh as she pulled into their driveway. "Joke. Lame one. Ignore me."

Aaron looked at her in the most serious way she'd seen since the funeral. "You wouldn't have to work two jobs if you could know stuff like that. Wouldn't be late to pick me up. And we could have fun on weekends."

Ah, now they were getting to it.

Aaron, desperate to make life easier without working for it.

Like his imaginary friend from back in kindergarten when he was unable to keep up with the bigger kids' rough-and-tumble. What was it called? Oh, yes, Harold, like an English king or duke. Harold gave him someone to chase

26

who he could actually catch, and an opponent safe to wrestle with, absent the occasional bruise or graze.

But he was ten now, and that was far too old to indulge fantasies like this.

"Okay, buddy, slow it down." Kate turned off the engine and faced him.

"Would you be as rich as Uncle Jonathan and Aunt Jennifer?"

Kate's mouth moistened again, her hunger—not for food —rekindled by a child's desire to magic the world into being better. "Not quite that rich. But, hey. We don't have to be. I work hard, and it's worth it. Two years, and maybe I can take the bar exam. Be a lawyer like I was going to be. Like Daddy was. Remember all the good work he did fighting big corporations? I could do—"

"Six points," Aaron said.

"What?"

"*Pardon*, Mom."

"Sorry. Pardon?"

"The team will win by six points. And it'll be the Furies beating the Comets, not the other way around."

Kate watched him a moment, but grew distracted as her next-door neighbor stood on the property line, the division between her perfect lawn bordered by flowers and Kate's slab of grass. Dorothy, toes to an actual foot-high picket fence, fluttered a little wave.

Aaron said, "When you see the score, you'll believe me."

Kate had promised herself to humor the boy until they got home. Now they *were* home. "Sure." She ruffled his head and opened the door. "But the Comets *always* beat the Furies. Let's see what Dorothy wants."

CHAPTER FOUR

Kate opened the door, stepped out, and turned to Dorothy.

"Oh, hi," the older lady said. "I hate to seem nosy, but thought I'd let you know Sal has been in your place for a while."

"Sal has a key, it's cool." Kate beamed to show she wasn't put out by her absolutely-not-nosy neighbor.

"A key? That's nice. Susan was asking after him earlier. Wondered if you two might be a thing."

Susan lived at the next house down from Dorothy. She was a fitness instructor, a little older than Kate. She'd had children young, married in her twenties, divorced in her thirties, and saw her kids off to college before she'd turned forty. She now frequently pranced about in either yoga pants and a sports top, jogging gear that showed off her muscular thighs and arms, or something that revealed her belly button (pierced) at every opportunity. She was sweet on Sal, but he had shown no interest in a relationship—not just with Susan, but with anyone. He had a sad past and was unlikely to be swayed by a woman just because she was far fitter than she should be at her age.

"He's fixing my porch," Kate said, making a show of helping Aaron out of the car. "No big deal."

Kate and Aaron headed up the two front steps and Kate paused, looking back briefly toward Dorothy, who was still watching them. She waved again and Kate waved back.

Aaron said, "You still don't believe me, do you?"

"We'll talk later, buddy," Kate said, opening the front door.

A faint whiff greeted her, like food starting to go bad. Only mild, though. Probably something festering in the garbage disposal or an apple core left in place wherever Aaron had eaten it.

Aaron shuffled in. "And stop calling me buddy. If you think I'm a liar, don't be nice to me. Just leave me alone."

As he stomped straight up the stairs, bag thumping against his back, Kate couldn't speak. Had her ten-year-old just aged four years? From regressing to kindergarten to fast-forwarding to teenagerdom? All in the blink of an eye?

Was he hormonal? Or was it dawning on him just how badly he'd let her down and was processing it this way?

He'd tried to help by making up a sports result, and the motivation seemed to be so she'd spend more time with him. Maybe acting out at school stemmed from the same intent, if only subconsciously.

She'd have serious words about his teenage dirtbag attitude later. For now, she wondered how much of that attitude was her fault, and how much was to do with the same thing Dorothy was hinting at.

Sal.

She needed to keep the guy sweet without leading him on. Couldn't afford to hire someone to help out the way he did. And if she couldn't keep the house going, she couldn't carry on living here. And Aaron didn't deserve that. No matter his recent spats.

She'd explain later. Properly. A heart-to-heart about how she wasn't interested in Sal. And even if she did one day start dating again, no man would ever replace Daddy.

First, though, she had to put that thirst to the back of her mind. The one jetted to life by Aaron's childish fantasy of predicting tonight's score. She needed to flush it away and leave it there, festering in the sewer where it wouldn't bother her. Leave it for the rats to eat. Because that thirst, that sense of *MAYBE...* she couldn't venture back there again.

Sal.

Perhaps his presence would help. Only one way to find out.

Sal Cantero was a big man, naturally toned thanks to a history of manual jobs, and his half-open shirt attested to clean living. His one vice was the occasional cigar which he would spark with a lighter that held special significance—a gift, Kate suspected, from his late wife. *Suspected*, because it rarely came up. For two people widowed so soon into their lives, they hardly ever discussed their respective losses.

From polite, if stilted, chit-chat over the years, Kate knew Sal owned a construction firm, having worked his way from the ground up. What started as a handyman side-hustle had grown until he'd brought in too much business for one person, and then it had grown some more. But only as far as he was comfortable. It handled mostly residential and small-commercial projects, significant enough to pay for his house opposite Kate's, but small enough to slide by the bigger boys and girls who ruled that world. He kept his hand in, though, and never asked his people to do anything he wasn't able to himself—so he said. Kate had never observed it, of course.

Still, in the eighteen months since Craig's passing, there'd never been a job he couldn't help her with. After shaking her hand at the wake, telling her if there was anything he could do—anything—all she had to do was ask, she wondered if he regretted that.

Wasn't it something everyone said? Something she'd heard countless times since the news of Craig's death broke? Hadn't she also said it to every grieving friend or relative she'd known, and never once had they come to her?

What could she offer, though, if they did?

Kate had tried to learn all the maintenance and home improvement skills left floating in the Craig-shaped void, and she had succeeded in more areas than, say, her own mother would have. For all their modernity, though, Kate and Craig had largely divided chores among what they thought of as traditional 1950s lines. It was her choice as much as his, so she never resented the ironing, the lion's share of cleaning, and running point on school matters. She was more than happy that he took care of unclogging the garbage disposal, resetting trip switches in the fuse box, and replacing blown light bulbs.

Just as Craig would have learned to iron and manage the school run and evade the wrath of the PTA had Kate met her demise first.

She now knew how to wire plugs, change the oil on the car as well as the tires and spark plugs. Last winter, she fixed the boiler with help from YouTube, and knew the garbage disposal inside-out, and there was little the lawnmower could throw at her that she couldn't pivot and resolve. As for the fuse box and changing light bulbs, that was all a piece of cake, and whenever Sal solved an issue with the aquarium, she retained that knowledge and applied it the next time the filter or air pump decided to sputter instead of flow.

But there were limits when it came to more skilled tasks, and carpentry was one of them. That was why Sal Cantero was currently securing a rail along the edge of Kate's deck.

She hadn't called on him for this. He'd noticed it was loose last week after Kate rewarded him for sorting a crackling light switch with a beer, sitting out there one warm evening while Aaron beavered away on his homework—what would become his first A in twelve months. Sal had insisted he pop back and fix it, and Kate saw more in his smile than neighborly grace.

It was clear what that smile meant.

Kate hadn't led him on. Really. Hadn't even considered she'd flirted in the slightest. She'd never entertained the notion of Sal looking at her as anything more than the needy single mom from across the road. If his romantic interest in her wasn't her imagination, she refused to use that to her advantage.

Bringing a new man into her life in that way would not be fair to Aaron, even if she was ready herself. Which she wasn't. Too much... *life* getting in the way.

That was the primary reason she'd given Sal a key. Why she'd asked him to pop over while she was out rather than offering him the chance to display his torso on her stoop like the setup for a ridiculous erotic novel or some porn movie.

The Widow and the Handyman.

Only, she didn't belong in either. Of that, she was positive.

"Hey, Sal."

He paused in packing away the last of his equipment into a steel toolbox the size of a suitcase. "Hey, Kate. Back early."

She'd told him she had to visit someone after school, but the business with Becky pushed the lie from her mind. "It fell through. How's the patient?"

Sal ran his fingertips up the wooden post next to the stairs that dropped into the garden. "Treated wood, good standard. You can leave it to settle a couple weeks before protecting it. But it's still paler than the top and bottom rail and the balusters, and I could do with giving it a finer sanding. I can't tell which oil was used originally."

"We still have some left over," Kate said. "I'll take care of it. Thank you so much, Sal. What do I owe you?"

"Oh, I got it at cost." He patted the post's cap as he stood. "If I got some paint, I could do 'em all. Do 'em nice, classy color. Or sand 'em down, reapply the wood oil—"

"Thanks, Sal. Honestly. I'm just so grateful for that."

Sal bobbed his head, shifted his weight to angle on the four steps down to the lawn. He left his gaze there and fumbled his lighter out of his pocket, and flicked it on. A Zippo-looking contraption, it generated a hardier flame, like a weak afterburner, one he claimed never went out, even in the wind. It had been his habit to fiddle with this item for a few weeks now. A nervous tic, perhaps, like Aaron's pointy finger? He snapped it shut. "Y'know, the bottom step, it's creaking some. Might need replacing."

The step, the electrics, the front door's faintly cracked paint, the roof tiles askew only a few inches—which she hadn't noticed but Sal had offered to mend them.

"Thanks, Sal, but it'll be okay for now."

He nodded acceptance, pocketed his lighter, and picked up his box as easily as Kate would have managed a throw pillow. "Well, offer's there."

His easy smile now seemed forced as he made his way to the side gate which led to the drive out front. Kate walked with him, his sweat airborne in a fine odor.

He paused at the gate. "Y'know…" he said again. A big exhalation, not looking her way.

"What, Sal? Is everything okay?"

He put the box down and faced her. One arm across his stomach, holding the elbow with his other; a curious pose for someone usually so confident.

Oh, no.

33

He was going to ask her out.

"Sal, I—"

"I gotta ask, Kate." His eyes roved up the side of the house, then back to her. "I'm always happy to help. You know that. Never, ever hesitate to ask. You got that, right?"

Kate replied slowly. "Never hesitate. Sure. I understand."

"I mean, I know I got a big house for a single guy. Three bedrooms. But I work out of mine… And I mean, yours was extended to four bedrooms, and it's real nice, but… big for two people. I'm thinkin'…"

Kate stepped forward, light on her feet now she didn't have to reject him outright. A repeat of Tammy's question.

Do you need such a big house?

Trying to help, trying to *be* helpful, but it was a question Kate had considered over and over, and chosen the answer: YES. She would stay until they dragged her out.

Whoever *they* were.

"I might not *need* it," she said, her hand moving to brush his arm but pulling back at the last second, "but moving would be too much hassle. And here, I have what I need. It's better than a gym. I mow the lawn myself, work the garden, and I keep the big ol' house clean."

She cringed internally at the phrasing, partially mirroring Sal's laconic tone.

"*Usually*, I keep it clean, anyway. There's a smell today. I'll figure it out. But wherever I go, it's not much cheaper to live. Nowhere nice, anyway. And besides…" She was rambling, so she changed tack; she stiffened, bit her lip. "Where would I find such great neighbors?"

Okay, right.

There.

She saw it. The flirt. Saw what she was doing as clearly as if she'd been filming it through a Hollywood-standard IMAX camera. And she had no idea how often she'd gone down that road.

She coughed and stepped back, but it was too late.

Sal's posture had relaxed, the difficult subject broached and forgotten. Kate needed to be nice without flirting. Her usual offer.

"At least let me crack open a beer or two. And some Pringles, I think I have half a tube left."

"Listen, Kate…" The arm crossed his body again, the hand to his elbow. "I was thinking—"

"Mom?"

Aaron stepped out of the French doors.

Saved by the bell.

"Yes, baby?" she said.

He bristled at "baby" and stared at Sal. "Is he done? I'm hungry."

Sal waited patiently for Kate to deal with Aaron. Good kid. A bit weird, if Sal was honest, but he liked him. He could have done without the boy interrupting what had taken Sal months to pluck up the courage to ask, but it couldn't be helped. A child, alive and well, interrupting awkward moments, was a problem he'd kill for. Hell, he'd promised so many times that he'd do anything for such a second chance.

No one had replied.

Having instructed Aaron to eat an apple, Kate escorted Sal to the front. If Kate remembered an iota of high school, she probably expected what Sal wanted to ask, and her silence and lack of eye contact testified to this. Sal had to decide: go for it, or let it stew until the next time his bravery gene kicked in.

On the driveway, Kate waved to the ever-vigilant

Dorothy, who watched Sal intently before returning to her flower bed.

"Thanks for your help," Kate said, loud enough for Dorothy to hear. "Please, at least let me pay for the materials."

Sal rubbed the back of his neck, a second sheen of sweat joining the almost-dry first. He didn't want to let the moment pass, but was unsure if Kate's reluctance was nerves or lack of feelings for him. He couldn't have imagined her hints, though, nervous as they'd seemed.

Keeping on subject for Dorothy's sake, he said, "I couldn't take more'n fifteen bucks."

"Oh, okay." Kate's voice rose an octave.

And no wonder. Sal had never taken money before, but it seemed appropriate to the situation; Kate evidently wanted Dorothy to know there was no funny business going on. He didn't need the money, and would have done the same favors for Dorothy or Bodybuilder Bob, the guy who lived in the house next to Sal's, or even—with limits—for Susan, but only if she didn't perform yoga while he was working and ceased touching Sal's chest whenever she came close.

No, these days, he ran a company more than hammered nails, so Sal was eager to get his hands dirty whenever possible, regardless of which neighbor needed him. For Kate, he had rewired the garage, fixed a half-dozen electrical fittings, welded not one but two leaky pipes in the crawlspace under the house on two different occasions, re-hung the door to Aaron's room, re-plumbed the automatic sprinkler system that kept the flowers watered without Kate hosing them down daily, and tinkered with the aquarium's filter, air-pump, and heater—again, all on different occasions. And he'd never needed recompense, even when he was out of pocket.

Kate said, "I'll run the cash over tomorrow if that's okay. I don't have it on me right now."

"Nah, no need, I shouldn't have said that." Sal shook his head, lowering his voice, cheeks flushing. "I mean, it's all part of the inventory, so any I don't itemize to the clients, it's all tax deductible. Really, it's no big thing."

It sounded like the end of a conversation, but he stood there, conscious of his arm across his body. His lips moved, as if rehearsing silently.

Then he dropped the bomb. "Perhaps we should get dinner sometime? No pressure, nothin' like that."

"I…" It came out as an elongated vowel, as if the dryness in her throat tried to drag it back in before she said something that offended him. Then she switched to a happy, almost surprised tone. "I'd love that! Hey, how about tonight?"

Sal jolted as if he'd touched a live wire with his tongue. "Tonight?"

"Sure. Aaron would love it."

"Aaron?"

"Yes. I'll cook!" She had a hand on one hip and a finger in the air. "That's better than a couple of beers on the deck, right? Steak, chunky fries, peppercorn sauce."

She put the finger-wagging hand on her other hip and fired a plastic grin, awaiting the answer.

Sal's neck straightened and his mouth stayed open for a second. "Sure. Okay. Dinner'll be nice. I'll go." He hooked his thumb toward his own house opposite, as casual as a vague acquaintance showing her where he'd parked. Yet his pulse quickened and his face heated up, and he just wanted to get the hell out of there. "I'll scrub up." He brought the thumb back and kept it there, a thumbs-up rather than a direction pointer. He let it drop. "It'll be… nice."

"It will. It'll be on the table at six."

. . .

As Sal departed, his broad shoulders a fraction more slumped than they had been, Kate scolded herself at her obvious rejection, her half-assed attempt at faking ignorance. Of course she knew he was asking her on a date, and there was no doubt he saw it.

Yes. I'll cook!

What on Earth was that?

Hand on her hip, shaking a finger in the manner of a good-old-gal in an old-time musical, about to break into song. The finger wagged to show the audience she had a fan-*tab*-ulous idea, which she worried had made things more awkward between her and Sal, not less.

It had achieved only two objectives: Sal was gone, and the conversation was over. She congratulated herself on temporarily dodging the bullet. Now she just had to explain tonight's guest to Aaron.

CHAPTER FIVE

Sal came over at 5:45 in a white shirt open at the collar, and blue jeans. He'd shaved, and he smelled clean, but hadn't bathed in cologne or presented her with a bouquet of flowers.

Good.

Pretending to misunderstand his offer of dinner had worked out well.

"I still can't locate that stale odor," Kate said, leading him in. She'd given the place a cursory search but hadn't found the culprit.

Sal followed her to the kitchen. "All I can smell is dinner."

When Kate and Craig extended the house a couple of years earlier, they'd knocked through the kitchen to fit a large dining table into the space, allowing Craig to cook up his dinners while chatting to guests. And Craig *was* the chef of the house. Kate cooked more often, especially when it was just the three of them—a fair division of labor. Craig always went the extra mile when friends or family graced their home for an evening, researching more complex recipes to add a bit of zing to whatever they had planned. He even splashed out on a set of ceramic knives in a futuristic-looking block, brightly colored implements that bore too close a resemblance to toys for Kate's liking. But they were sharp and funky, and Craig had loved them.

These days, with the knife block and the multicolored blades stored in a safe corner of the countertop, Kate tried to use the dining table for meals. They chose the same two chairs of the eight place settings each time, but more often lately, she and Aaron ate off trays in the living room. Too often for her liking. Breakfast in the kitchen was never a battle, a routine Aaron appeared to enjoy, although it was normally achieved with the TV on—an older 20-inch model which kept him quiet. Evenings, though, had gotten difficult, and sometimes it was preferable to flop into an easy chair and put the big television on.

"Hi, Mr. Cantero," Aaron said brightly.

Yes, Kate had had words with him, ordering his best manners to the fore, this dinner a chance to say a big, hearty thank you to Mr. Cantero for all the help he'd given them since Daddy passed away. He'd agreed without back talk.

"Hey, Aaron." Sal nodded in greeting, as a man would greet another man in a bar. "Something smells good."

"My mom cooks great fries. I like the thick ones best."

"Me too." Sal glanced Kate's way at this. "Chunky fries're great."

Kate cooked the fingers of potato in an air fryer, another product she'd bought from an infomercial using a credit card and hadn't yet paid for. The salesgirl made it sound like Kate was poisoning her child using a deep-pan fryer for fries and chicken, and whatever else she submerged in vegetable oil to feed him. It took longer, but tasted fine. Unfortunately, she'd mistimed it, so the steak was keeping warm under the grill.

"Hope you don't mind it well done," she said.

He waved her off. "However it comes, I'm good."

"Grab a beer from the fridge."

He did so and offered her one, to which she said yes.

Aaron piped up again. "Can I change the channel?"

The TV was on, as it usually was at breakfast. Before Sal arrived, Kate had flicked it away from the cartoons and muted it to hold a conversation about Becky, but Aaron had deflected with questions regarding Sal. In the end, she'd let it drop and concentrated on not burning the steaks.

"Leave the channel," Kate said. "Tell Mr. Cantero about school." She lowered her chin. "The good stuff."

Aaron watched the TV screen, a news channel silenced, its ticker along the bottom with breaking news and sports scores.

"You want to see the how the Comets are doing," Aaron said.

Kate watched the screen, the ticker showing 0:0 for all games, since there were still ten minutes until the opening tip. The early start in the lower leagues was an attempt to draw in families and locals who didn't want to drag themselves into the city or spend money on NBA games, and she and Craig had enjoyed the local sport. They'd have taken Aaron if he'd shown any interest.

She said, "I'm keeping our conversation going. It's rude to have cartoons on when we have guests."

Aaron half-moaned an, "Okay, Mom, I suppose."

"Your mom isn't interested in sports," Sal added with what he probably thought was a reassuring smile.

Aaron met him with a blank expression.

"Have you washed your hands?" Kate asked, checking the fries.

"Yes." Aaron showed her his hands, flipping them front and back.

"When?"

"When I got home."

She switched off the grill. "Wash them again."

"Why?"

"Because."

Aaron resumed his dead-eyed stare. "Really, Mom? You don't just want to talk about me to Mr. Cantero?"

Kate was about to snap at him, but Sal's presence soothed her tone. "Aaron, you've been in the garden since then. Please wash your hands. I don't need to talk about you to Mr. Cantero."

Aaron slipped off his seat and tramped toward the door, but Sal stopped him.

"Hey, kiddo?"

Aaron stopped and his jaw stuck out, but upon casting a glance at his mom and her returning a "remember your manners" look, he said, "Yes?"

"Call me Sal, okay?"

Aaron looked fully at Kate.

She had hoped Sal wouldn't do that, but she'd be the queen-bitch-mom if she contradicted him.

"Hands," she said.

Aaron folded his ring finger over his little one, then put them back to normal and departed, his attitude unclear. Kate was just thankful he didn't cause her any embarrassment. The finger thing was a concern, but she put it—and his sullen demeanor—out of her mind as she plated up the first portion of food.

Just the two of them.

"So." She used tongs to transfer the biggest slab of beef to Sal's plate. "He really is doing better."

Sal made his way over. Not quite a saunter, but not far from it. "You look nice."

She'd made something of an effort tonight, out of her crappy work clothes and into something more pleasant than

42

the sweatpants she wore most evenings. Not trying to impress. Just as dolled up as she dared without leading to more misunderstandings about her intentions. She liked Sal, but how she felt when he asked her out proved she wasn't in the market for a boyfriend. And she'd never thought of Sal that way, although she had to admit he looked great and had a kind heart.

"Thanks," she said. "You do too."

"Want me to turn off the box?"

"It's okay."

"Sports stuff comes on in about a half-hour. You sure?"

He knew about Kate's issues, had listened when she'd spoken about them on one of those evenings where she'd thanked him with a beer for another odd job that she couldn't manage alone. Only that night there'd been too many beers, three being too many for her, and she'd TMI'd herself so much she woke up with a yawning ache in her gut. She'd been hesitant when she saw him later that week, but he hadn't mentioned it.

Tonight was the first time. Probably the first time it had cropped up between them.

"I'm fine," she said. "I can cope with scores in the background."

"Still…" Sal moved toward the TV remote.

"Please leave it on."

Her words must have landed harsher than intended because Sal held up his hands, a beer in one of them, as if surrendering. "Okay, we cool."

As Kate switched off the whooshing air fryer, she heard a sound like running water. Aaron washing his hands.

She said, "Sorry, I mean—"

"What's that?" Sal asked.

"What?"

"That noise."

Now Kate thought about it, there was no washbasin nearby. "Aw, not another leaking pipe."

Both previous leaks had only become known once a sizeable puddle had formed, and it was audible from the garden or decking. Never from inside the house.

Sal was frowning, roaming the kitchen, following his ear. "Out there."

He wandered out into the hall, Kate keeping up, her own brow furrowed, calculating what it might cost if Sal couldn't fix it using materials on hand. They followed the sound into the living room where Kate found the source of the noise.

"What the…?"

She had to steady herself. Her eyes bugged at what Aaron was doing. Sal stepped back in shock, unable to comment.

Kate didn't blame him.

She screeched, "Aaron Franklin Mallory, what in the name of God are you doing?"

What Aaron Franklin Mallory was doing was standing on a footstool. He'd propped open the 30-gallon fish tank with a copy of Harry Potter and the Prisoner of Azkaban, the tank containing Craig's tropical fish—those Aaron had forbidden her from selling or giving away, and which she'd agreed to maintain despite the cost of food, filters, and occasional medicine. She'd been sure it was a symbol of his father, and hanging onto it was a way of remaining close to the man. He'd done the cleaning and the feeding, kept a close eye on them every single day.

And now he stood over that tank, his winkie in hand, urinating into the water.

The stream of piss ended. He shook himself off, before flipping his shorts back up into place.

Kate steadied herself on Sal. Not for balance, but because it didn't seem real. She was literally struggling to comprehend it. A single question burned from within. One she had to grind out, even though she was still processing the odd scene.

"Why?"

Aaron looked more miserable than in the Principal's office, tears shining in his eyes as he stared back. He switched to poor Sal, who obviously didn't know where to place himself, then back to his mom.

As earnestly as anyone had ever spoken a sentence, he said, "I had to, Mom. I just had to."

CHAPTER SIX

Kate left Aaron in his room, closing the door to the tune of his sobs petering out. He remained under orders to think about what he'd done and could only emerge for dinner when he was ready to explain himself.

As with the episode at school, he had acted like a victim, as if Kate was being unfair by yelling at him and calling him a little vandal. She'd demanded a reason for him pissing into the beloved fish tank—something, *anything* to help her understand. But he'd kept on repeating himself through tears and snot and hitching breaths, insisting he had to do it. He just had to.

Her explosion of fury was now starting to settle like volcanic ash. Lava still flowed as she padded down the stairs and, with it, a pyroclastic flow of regret.

Calling one's child names sat heavy on her. At least she hadn't said "terrorist" which was what had first sprung to mind. And screaming at him. Needing Sal's gentle hand to dial her volume down nagged as a failure on her part.

Moms didn't yell. Good ones didn't, anyway. Not through loss of temper.

She'd always sworn she wouldn't be like that, not like her parents were. Angry at the world for their own shortcomings, blaming the system instead of themselves, and taking it out on their only daughter because—why not—she cost them more beer money than they could afford. A loss of control normally hinted at problems elsewhere in life.

But her actions after calming herself were correct.

Ask questions, don't accuse.

When that fails, change the location.

Give him time.

Listen.

Kate had never believed in bullshit like that until it worked for her. And it had. For eight and a half years, neither she nor Craig had felt the need to physically discipline him, and only rarely did they use sanctions like denial of computer privileges and grounding. They'd raised a good kid.

It hadn't worked right away tonight. He needed a longer pause for reflection, to replay events, and admit to himself what he did wrong. She was sure he'd come around. But she wasn't sure she could last that long. As angry as she'd been at what Aaron did tonight, her overwhelming sensation was of tiredness, of the pull of her comforter, to roll into bed, fold the covers over her head and cry herself to sleep. In the morning, maybe it would never have happened.

Yeah, because that's how life works.

In the living room, Sal was examining the aquarium, using the chemical tests that Kate had learned all about—ammonia levels, pH, nitrates. She could have taken care of this, and would have, but his chivalry saved her a job.

"How's it look?" she asked.

Sal closed the lid, the final check complete. "Okay. It's a big tank. Kids that age don't have much bad stuff in their pee. It should've diluted plenty, but I'll come by tomorrow.

Do a quarter-tank water change. With the little guy. I'm guessin' you want him to fix what he did."

She hadn't thought about it yet, but he was right. "That's a good idea. He's at his aunt and uncle's tomorrow after school, though. I'll take care of it with him. I can manage a water change."

Sal nodded, hands stuffed in his pockets. "Sure. I keep forgetting you can do this stuff now."

His kindness rolled in her chest, sitting in her gut a moment, before she couldn't help saying, "But come by at dinner, anyway. Maybe I can try a replay of tonight's food."

Sal cast his eyes kitchen-wards. "Might still be okay."

Kate hugged herself. "Sure. Maybe. Why not?"

While Kate reheated the steaks and fries in the microwave, Sal washed his hands, then the pair sat opposite one another with the food, the muted TV still on. She'd prepared a salad with Aaron's preferred ingredients of toma-toes, cucumber, and lettuce—absolutely no onions, *ever*—which half-filled the plate. They weren't big steaks, or even high quality, just a means of getting iron and protein into the boy. And now the man. Sal was gracious enough to keep any assessment of them to himself, although even Kate could taste their cheapness and, since they only owned one steak knife, which she gave to Sal, she had to use one of Craig's smaller brightly colored knives to cut hers—this one a lime green.

"Wanna talk about it?" he asked.

Kate couldn't remember how long it had been since either spoke, but she was a quarter-way through her dinner already. "Sorry, Sal. This isn't what I was hoping for."

"Me neither."

Kate detected no malice in his reply. In fact, it sounded light, breezy. Almost… flirty.

Oh, right. That was what he meant.

She said, "I don't know if he's suffering from delusions or stress or some undiagnosed ADHD-like thing."

"Delusion?"

"You know he was a little odd, even before his dad passed, right?"

"He had his eccentricities," Sal said. "But I only saw him a bit, y'know?"

"Eccentricities. Sure. He's a young-acting ten. Isn't always popular at school. He has a few friends, but he's never in the thick of it. Never... involved with the others."

"I was a small kid. Not popular. Not till my growth spurt got me on the football team." Sal gestured to the ceiling in the general direction of Aaron's bedroom. "He'll come good. Craig was a big guy, right?"

"Not huge, but—"

"Yeah, he won't be small forever. Then he'll have to grow up. People notice you more."

Kate hoped he was right. But also hoped he was wrong. She wanted her son to fit in and have friends, but loved that he hadn't grown up too fast, that he'd kept his own personality. The majority of boys in his class were in WhatsApp groups discussing Fortnite, while Aaron had no interest in violent games and had only once asked for a phone last Christmas, then never brought it up again.

"He has this idea that he doesn't need to study anymore. Like answers just pop into his head. He says it's that he knows things. Like he knows he has to do bad things too. Swearing, hitting, taking a leak on the fish." She attacked a sliver of gristle with her knife and thought about buying another proper steak knife at the dollar store, but the fat gave way and she broke the meat free. "I think..." She held the chunk on her fork. "I think he's acting out because of Craig. He wants me around more, so does stuff that forces me to be with him. Don't they have a name for that? Where your personality freezes at the point of a trauma? He's ten, but acting like an eight-year-old."

"Eight's still old for peeing in weird places."

Kate chewed her meat. "He's either lying about not studying, or making up excuses to abdicate responsibility."

Sal gave a subdued laugh. "You sure you wanna go back into the law? Not psychiatry?"

Kate allowed herself to smile. Yes, she was psychoanalyzing her son without an iota of education in that field— just what she'd read in articles and parenting manuals, watched on TV, probably heard from other moms. Besides, Sal had hit a different nerve.

"I'm not sure it's the right thing to do," she said. "Night school. Finishing my law degree."

"Can you change your mind?"

"I can withdraw, but I lose twenty percent of my fee. I saved up for a year, the rest is on credit, and… And I *want* to do it. Long term, it'll benefit us massively."

"You got two weeks to decide, though."

Kate was still chewing the same meat, found the rubbery strand preventing her from breaking it up, and removed it from her mouth as daintily as possible, laying it on the side of her plate. "And in those two weeks, I have to remember everything I stopped learning a decade ago." She sighed and leaned her head on one hand. "Is this crazy? Trying so hard in the hope of… what? A two-year plan?"

Sal glanced at the TV screen. "If anyone can do it, you can."

Kate almost guffawed at the corny show of support. If the number of people who heard that really were capable of the task facing them, the entire country would be far more industrious than it was. She followed his gaze.

Sal asked, "What'd he say the score would be?"

"Furies to win by six." She waited for the ticker to flash

by. "It's half time now and the Comets are up by twenty." She smiled. "I told you. Delusional."

And she was glad. If Aaron had even got close with his prediction… Well, she didn't want to consider where that might have led.

She turned off the TV. "Let's just eat, eh?"

"I'd like that."

Over the next half-hour, Kate became grateful for three things. First, Sal turned off his charm offensive and listened to how there was no way she could afford a psychiatrist, should Aaron get worse, and that she was sure it wasn't covered on their insurance. The second thing was the only bit of advice Sal offered: Talk to the school counselor, who might have a contact who takes kids on pro bono. She didn't need endless streams of suggestions, but that one sounded good. There was no other backup, anyway.

She eventually asked about Sal's business and, in a feeble attempt to dissuade him from viewing her as a romantic option, inquired about anyone special in his life.

All he said was, "Not anymore," and poked at his salad with his attention on the plate. He'd also taken his lighter in hand, flicked on the afterburner-like flame a couple of times, then off again.

Kate had never asked about his circumstances before, and now she had, she wished she'd asked sooner. There was a story there. She'd been so selfish to concentrate on her own needs. As a widow, perhaps she was granted some leeway on that front, a divine decree absolving her of social niceties. She wondered what the statute of limitations was on being self-absorbed after a bereavement.

Now that she'd asked, she couldn't un-ask.

It didn't look like he wanted to talk, but was about to open up. Then the third thing to be grateful for happened.

Aaron. In the kitchen doorway. In age-ten pajamas a couple of inches too big, his arms slunk at his side, so floppy he could have been a marionette held aloft by a sleepy puppeteer. "Mom?"

Kate turned fully to him but didn't get up. Better to let him come to her. And he did. Rushing into her arms and saying, "I'm sorry, so sorry, Mommy."

He weighed less than nothing as she scooped him up and nuzzled his hair.

She said, "You ready to talk, buddy?"

He nodded in her neck.

Sal had finished his meal and was easing to his feet. "Thanks for dinner, Kate. I'll see myself out." He didn't sound put out at all, or even a little annoyed.

Kate set Aaron aside and stood. "Oh, Sal, it's okay…"

He nodded toward Aaron. "Nah, it's cool. Things're tough, I get that. Maybe we'll grab a beer one night."

"It's a—"

She cut off the word *date* and struggled to find a synonym. The pause stretched long enough for Sal to see what she'd meant.

"It's a rain check," he said.

"Right." She pointed a finger gun at him and felt just as ridiculous as she had earlier when acting like a *good-old-gal* with a raised stage finger. "Rain check."

As promised, Sal saw himself out.

Kate prepared Aaron a scaled-back dinner because he said he wasn't that hungry. She didn't push him, didn't bring up the subject, and watched as he ate in silence. Slowly. So very slowly. It took all she had not to shovel it in his mouth for him.

Then when he crossed his knife and fork over the plate,

empty but for a jagged crescent of lettuce and sliver of gristle, he still didn't mention the incident.

She broached the subject gently. "Okay, buddy, you ready to talk?"

Just *talk*. Not about anything in particular. She left the subject up to him.

He looked up at her across the table, his mouth turned down and eyes as large as saucers. "I'm tired, Mom." He slipped from his chair and came around her side, and gave her a feeble hug. "Goodnight, Mommy." He trotted on out.

Kate remained at the table.

He hadn't even asked to be tucked in. He always asked for that. Never slinked out after pretending to be sorry for something.

And she was positive he was pretending.

Stay in your room until you're ready to talk. No food in your room. So you know what that means.

He'd got *hungry*. Not sad, not sorry. He'd feigned regret, and manipulated her into feeding him, then fucked off back upstairs without one solitary consequence for what he'd done.

Well, just you wait, sonny. You'll see there's a price to pay for behavior like that.

She stood so sharply her chair fell back. She got to the TV and was preparing to unplug it and carry it to her room, before taking his Xbox and doing the same, when she stopped dead.

It was still warm.

She should probably wait before moving it.

No, that wasn't it.

She was staring at the blank screen. Remote in hand.

"Aaron! Aaron, get down here!"

She waited.

"*Now!*"

53

She wasn't losing her temper. This was measured. Reasonable. Sure, she was hot and her throat was raw, and she wanted to shake him and scream in his face until the nine-year-old Aaron from three weeks ago reentered the ten-year-old's body. But she wouldn't raise her voice.

She was being a good mom.

"What is it?" Her boy wandered in, performing the worst fake yawn she'd seen in many years.

She punctuated her sentences with the remote control, her finger on the button. "Everything today has been about you, about Aaron Franklin Mallory. And the rotten things you've done."

Aaron stomped a bare foot on the floor tile. "They're *not* rotten!"

"All to make me feel bad about working," she went on as if he hadn't interrupted her. "About putting this roof over your head. So you can live somewhere nice, somewhere you don't have metal detectors on your school gates, where you can play with a toy gun without worrying about a cop shooting you—"

She halted there. This wasn't why she called him back. No need to shame him.

"I want to prove something to you."

"Prove what?"

"That you don't just 'know' things with absolute certainty. You didn't 'know' you had to hit Becky. You had some urge to, and you chose not to fight it. Whatever the reason was, you need to see that you *can* control your decisions. Here."

Kate flicked on the television and found a dedicated sports news channel. It didn't show any games—again, she bit back the slug of depression at being unable to afford such luxuries—but it transmitted a rolling news-channel-type service, rounding up gossip and scores. With live updates in the side-panel, it was more dangerous to have on than the local news, which she'd opted for earlier.

"The Comets and the Furies," she said, pointing.

Comets 64, Furies 60.

Whoa.

That had been some game, clearly. Twenty points down at half-time, it must have been a nail-biting final quarter. Would have been a boatload of last-minute bets filed with various bookies around the city. A heap of money would have changed hands. And been lost.

"You're wrong about the game," Kate said. "This means you were wrong to do those bad things too. Especially hitting that girl."

"The game isn't over," Aaron replied flatly.

She checked the time. "Of course, it is."

"Fine." Aaron shrugged. "Don't believe me."

He was right, though. The scores around the Comets' result were highlighted in yellow to show time was up, but the Comets' highlighter remained blue. The desk presenters were the usual mix, even in the twenty-first century, of a gray-haired, handsome former baseball pitcher and a chesty blonde woman. They chatted in silence, then the side panel scores switched to live footage of an excited man with a microphone, a basketball crowd to his back, most wearing the purple of the Comets.

Kate unmuted the TV.

The man on-screen was wide-eyed and animated, his head and shoulders whipping back and forth as he reported live from the game—no footage; that license belonged elsewhere. He was speaking fast, high-pitched. "I can't believe it. This is turning into the game of the season! Furies, twenty down, coming back to tie."

The score switched up to 64:64.

Kate said, "Still isn't six points."

"Wait," Aaron replied with the weary confidence of someone with a stacked deck.

"And now…" The commentator was all but dribbling into his mike.

The blonde on the desk beside the gray-haired former baseball pro piped up, "What is it, Dave? What's happening?"

"That injury to Martinson added a bunch of time, Gail. And with thirty seconds to go, Comets are panicking. Defense is all over the place. I'm guessing the leg break must have shaken them some because… I've never seen anything like this— Oh my God! It's there! A three-pointer from the Furies! 64 to 67, Furies lead. Only fifteen seconds left on the clock!"

Kate gripped the remote hard. It was going to shatter or slither out of her sweaty palm. She put it down. She stared at the screen. Her fingers worked the air as if playing an invisible piano, tingling with every ounce of hope and dread and thrilling anticipation that she'd jettisoned in the rehab facility that had saved her marriage.

If only temporarily.

Her throat, raw moments ago at the thought of losing her precious little boy, was moist, ready for the cheer, the *ching-ching-ching* of a win bestowing her with the riches she so plainly deserved—

Except, she had no money riding on this. Nothing to gain.

No benefit to her.

"And the ball comes back off the board! The Comets' attack is finished, and Ramirez has the rebound with seven seconds on the clock. Cross court to Jim DaCosta. Into the three-point circle. Back out to Vaughn. He shoots…!"

The half-second—more like a quarter-second—in which

the commentator inhaled lasted so long it was as if someone had hit pause.

"*Scores!* This is unbelievable. It's impossible. Comets 64. Furies 70. And there's the full-time buzzer!" The man's face glowed red and shiny, strung out in a glee only enjoyed by those more passionate about sport than people. "Good lord, what a game, folks. What. A. *Game!*"

They cut back to the main desk, to the gray-haired ex-pro apologizing for any "bad language" during that passionate moment, then recapped what had happened.

Kate stared dumbly, trying to take in both the result and figure out the apology. The only language approaching *bad* that she could recall were some God references. She guessed some folks in the state might still get offended by blasphemy. Maybe the pro on the desk did.

But the *score*.

Six points up in favor of the Furies.

Kate fumbled for the remote and flicked off the screen. "Aaron…"

"Told ya," he said. Then the boy, her lovely little boy in his slightly too-big PJs, turned crisply and exited the room. He called back, "Tuck me in if you like."

And Kate would tuck him in. She wouldn't say a word. She wouldn't ask him anything or push the subject of his behavior just in case she had to discuss the game.

It simply wasn't possible.

And with the sensation she'd once deemed dormant rekindled and smoldering inside her, she doubted sleep would be possible either, not without one of the leftover pills her GP had prescribed after Craig's funeral. If she couldn't sleep, she didn't know what she would do.

Plus, it was preferable to thinking.

Thinking…

What if there were something to this? What if…

No.

She'd take the pill. Then tuck in her son. Then lie on the bed and let oblivion take her.

It would be better in the morning. It would make more sense in the morning.

It had to.

CHAPTER SEVEN

Tammy cornered Kate in the men's restroom on the 42nd floor. "Well? What's up with you this morning?"

Kate hopped off the marble bank of wash basins where she'd been sitting, lost in replaying last night's events. "Just kid stuff."

She snatched up her squeegee and spray and returned to the mirrors.

Tammy carried herself over to Kate and leaned on the wall, setting off the hand dryer. She jumped at the noise, causing laughter to first erupt, then titter, then drain from both women. It lasted longer for Kate, unable to rein it back in.

Tammy placed a hand on her arm and knitted her brow. "You okay?"

Kate's laughing *yuck*ed to an end, morphing seamlessly into tears. Only for seconds, but they fell before she could stop them.

Tammy didn't pull Kate in for a hug or invite her to *get it all out*. She wasn't the touchy-feely type. A firm, reassuring palm to the arm or back or—if she was feeling particularly gregarious—the hands. Today was plainly a shoulder day.

"Is it Aaron?" Tammy said. "This about your call yesterday?"

Kate dried her eyes. "You'll think I'm crazy."

"I already do. Talk to Tammy."

Kate glanced to the door. "You're sure Dev doesn't have you under surveillance?"

"Don't give a rat's *bee*-hind if he does. Gimme your crazy."

Kate relayed what had happened. Quickly, efficiently. She didn't want to split the conversation in two, should Dev come a-knocking to enquire why two of "his" girls were servicing an area designated as a one-person job. She was only half-joking about the surveillance, too. Not James Bond trackers, but he had a keen eye for routines being observed. Or not.

When Kate ended with how she'd ordered Aaron to write an apology letter to Becky instead of watching the TV, Tammy contemplated the events. Both leaned on basins, backs to the mirrors. Tammy actually pinched her chin, like a statue of some ancient Greek scholar. She said nothing for several seconds.

Certain the yellow sign outside the door had been on display for longer than Dev's algorithm suggested a thorough cleanse should take, Kate resumed her spray and squeegee duties.

"Okay," Tammy said.

"Thanks for not laughing."

"We've been here too long. You done the floor?"

"Not yet."

Tammy slogged over to the bucket on wheels and drained the mop, then crossed to the far corner and went to work.

"You know I believe, right? In God, in Jesus, maybe more than that. More'n we got here."

"I know you believe."

"But you don't. That's cool. You did once, though." She swished the mop back and forth, doing a not-so-great job, skimming the stalls.

"I was desperate. The insurance people were trying to say that maybe Craig's death was a suicide…"

"And you got your answer."

Kate dropped the can of glass cleaner in the tray attached to her cart and selected a thicker solution for around the basins. "I got the answer that mediums are horseshit."

"Nuh-uh. That last guy was legit." Tammy had finished the stalls' floor in record time, at which she looked proud.

"It was Craig's *brother* who fought them and got us our settlement, not some psychic. And I haven't done the pans yet."

"I had a quick look. No stains. We can chuck a slug of bleach in there. They'll be fine."

Kate paused in her spritzing to pass Tammy the flowery bleach. "I don't know what he did, but all mediums are frauds. Fact."

"You wanted to believe Craig was at peace and he is. What he told you…" Tammy squirted a jet into the first toilet bowl. "It couldn't have come from anyone else but Craig."

Kate wiped, watching her own reflection. The scratchy uniform and blue tabard marked her as a low-level human being. A cleaner. Not the ridiculously well-organized wife of a hotshot lawyer widely touted for public office. Not anymore.

Soon after Craig died, she'd needed fast money, and with no qualifications, no experience in a professional environment, she'd hooked up with this cleaning agency. The only great thing that came out of it was meeting Tammy. Straight-shooting, no-nonsense, fiercely intelligent, equally quirky Tammy Rhodes.

Yes, Kate had gone to those so-called psychics at Tammy's urging. All those questions, the discrepancies in the circumstances of Craig's demise. Questions he'd answered in ways she'd seen in the mentalist acts in Reno, having dated one and learned several techniques. The final psychic used some of those tricks to sound authentic, but others... Other answers she couldn't explain away.

In their fifteen years together, Craig had never dodged so much as a near miss concerning his shellfish allergy. Always careful. Always planning ahead. That he should ingest some dusting on a bag of chips that did not *contain* seafood as such, but was clearly labeled:

Prepared in a factory that also packages nuts and items made with crustaceans...

The insurance company didn't like that.

The police didn't like that.

And Craig's brother didn't like that. Jonathan had even probed her, interrogated her about why he was spending the night in a hotel less than ten minutes' drive from their house.

We argued.

That was some argument.

He needed to cool off.

Craig was the cool one. You're the one with the temper...

Jonathan had still battled against the possibility of suicide, earned Kate the full payout, but it was clear he remained suspicious.

It's for Aaron. You blow it on anything but raising him right, I'll be on your ass. And I'll have Child Protective Services on your ass too. Count on it.

Kate had been too grateful to take offense at his threat, at the consequences of her slipping back into the old habits that almost cost her her marriage. And yet, she had told no one the truth about that night. About why they'd argued. And she never would. It hurt too much to contemplate.

"My guy told you what you needed," Tammy said, completing her half-assed task with the toilets.

"What I *wanted* to hear," Kate corrected. "Craig didn't commit suicide. He loves me. He's proud of how I'm holding up. Wants me to be happy. Blah, blah, blah."

While Kate packed away her cloths and spray, Tammy rushed the rest of the floor so it at least looked like she'd done her job right. "You wanna know what I think?"

"Yes. I always want to know what you think."

"Either your boy is the luckiest kid out there, and you can sell his handshakes for pocket money. Or he has the sight."

"The sight?"

"He sees the future, like my neighbor, Jemima, before she passed. Only, she had someone talkin' to her from the other side. Whatever it is, your boy's got it."

Kate gave a laugh, a fake one this time, serving as punctuation. "He didn't suddenly become psychic when he turned ten."

Tammy finished the job. Sort of. She returned the mop to the bucket and rinsed it out. "If you don't believe it was some psychic vision, then you only got one option."

"What's that?"

The door opened and Dev entered and stood there, hands on hips. "Ladies."

"Just finished," Tammy said. "Katie's got ladies' issues, so I gave her a hand to catch up." For emphasis, Tammy chopped an open hand at her own groin.

"Okay, but… but get back to it. Now, please. Before the lunch guys hit the snack room."

Once Kate and Tammy headed for the door with the cart and bucket, Dev backed out. Neither woman laughed this time, but their amusement at his flustered attempt at authority needed no comment.

Tammy stowed the bucket in one of the cleaning stations, then joined Kate out on the floor, using the designated route through the brokers' desks to push the cart.

"Where were we?" Tammy asked.

"Apparently, I only have one option left."

"Right."

They passed Endo, the poor sap who'd spilled the coffee substitute the previous day. He wore a headset, stabbing the air with a pen, saying, "I don't care how hard it is. I need to see something in the next hour or I'll be calling your supervisor. You got that?"

Once he was in the rearview, Tammy commented, "So butch today."

"Leave him alone, poor kid."

"Overcompensating only goes so far."

"As do psychic visions."

"Okay." Tammy stopped dead.

They were forbidden from tackling disagreements in the midst of all this class and wealth and money, and there was no three-strike rule. Once you disturbed the powerful bucks in their everyday pursuit of happine$$, you were out. That was why Tammy kept her voice low and smile wide.

"If you don't believe, how do you explain it?"

With the same pasted-on rictus, Kate said, "Not everything that isn't explained yet has to mean aliens did it. Or ghosts. Or God. Or Thor or Apollo for that matter."

"What *is* the supernatural, Katie? Hmm? Just shit that ain't been explained by regular science, right? Like radio waves or gravity was once. The Northern Lights were supernatural at one time. Dinosaur bones were from magical dragons that roamed the land. Get me?"

A knot formed in Kate's gut and constricted in a way that forced her to accept Tammy's point. "I do get it. And I can't explain it yet. I just… I need more than a single prediction and an improvement in his homework assignments to believe in… What is it? The sight? Clairvoyance?"

"Could be anything. Your Craig was a devoted dad, wasn't he? More than the sperm donor who knocked *me* up. Loved his boy?"

"Yes. He was incredible with Aaron."

"Say he sees from beyond that Aaron's got problems going on, wouldn't he step in?"

"I'm pretty sure, even if ghosts are real, they don't get to choose like that. Otherwise, wouldn't every bereaved person with issues have a spirit whispering in their ear?"

"Then speak to the boy." Tammy dropped the faux-grin, softened her facial muscles and offered another rare arm pat. "Be a *mom*. Nothing more than that. If there's an explanation, it'll come. Accept him for who he's becoming. If not…" She shrugged.

"I only hope he doesn't try anything with Aunt and Uncle J-J like he did yesterday. Jennifer's my after-school childcare today."

"If he's playing with Tony Stark, he'll be cool, won't he?"

Kate didn't get the reference at first, but as she leaned on the cart—tired as hell—the image of a black-and-white guinea pig in a suit of armor tickled her humor gland. "If God exists, I think He sees statements like that as a challenge."

"Well, if God's real—and He is—why not other stuff? Maybe Aaron's an angel."

"Or a devil." Kate, too, dropped the fakery and returned Tammy's arm pat by squeezing her hand.

Click-click.

Both looked around and found Dev ten feet away, snapping his fingers and pointing first at his smartphone, then at the break room.

Kate waved to acknowledge him and pushed on to their next destination. Smiling, but at the same time wishing she weren't. Because none of this was funny. Not at all.

After lunch, Dev split Kate and Tammy up, sending Tammy to the insurance company on the 23rd floor, while Kate serviced a different brokerage firm up on 50, before returning to the 42nd to complete her longer-than-usual shift at the end of the trading day—overtime prearranged last week. She floated through the afternoon, convinced it was partially a pharmaceutical hangover from the sleeping pill, and ran a dozen scenarios before concluding that Tammy was right. She had to push the issue with Aaron and push hard. Make him talk to her. Even if she had to threaten and cajole, and risk mangling their mommy-son relationship for a few days. At least there was no phone call from the school.

Once the Stock Exchange closed at four-thirty, most desks at Hetherington emptied out by five. Not to head home, but to press flesh and woo clients in person. As usual, a couple of guys and a lot of the women—scant as they were on the floor—remained behind, either fearful that departing the office without a titty bar to patronize made them appear slothful or less-than committed, or because they wanted a head start on tomorrow's financial feeding frenzy.

One guy who'd remained behind was Endo. His head hung low as he gathered his things, his mouth a straight, thin line.

"Hey," Kate said as she passed.

"Hey." Endo's reply was as flat as Aaron's *told ya* from last night.

Kate slowed, checking Moldy Merv's den of office dividers, and found it empty. She stopped. "Bad trade?"

Endo slapped a thin paper file on his desk and rounded on her, pulling himself up before he raised his voice. Which he was clearly about to. He went back to his open bag, a leather satchel more than a briefcase. A *man bag*, as Craig would have called it.

Endo said, "Sorry. Yeah, bad day. Actually, not terrible. Two good trades, one bad one. I'm still in profit, but— Oh, shit."

He crouched, out of sight of Mervin Corney who was strutting from the break room, a can of something sugary and caffeinated to his lips.

Kate took a duster and flicked it across Endo's desk, stifling a giggle at the schoolboy antics. "He isn't looking."

"I can't believe I did that." Endo repositioned to one knee as if tying a shoelace. He even unlaced the bow, so he'd be seen to be fastening it if anyone busted him. "And now I'm committed." He thumped his own head. "Stupid."

Merv made his way to his den.

Kate said, "Hey, it's okay."

"Move along," Endo pleaded. "You're not supposed to spend this long on the desks."

"It's fine." Kate wiped more slowly, checking the other late-workers' heads remained down, focused on their tasks. "No one notices the cleaners, anyway."

Endo shook his head. "Why are you being nice to me? We'd never said two words to each other until yesterday."

Kate didn't know the answer. She wrote it off as motherly instinct. Although Endo must have been late twenties, possibly pushing thirty, he looked like a child to her—a sure sign of getting old.

Wasn't that what they said? When police officers and doctors looked too young to be proficient at their jobs, you were well on your way to your pension. The same must be true of stockbrokers.

She said, "Does it matter?"

Endo rested his head on his bent knee. "I guess not. Is he still there?"

Merv worked an electric razor over his neck and chin, his tie loose and shirt unbuttoned. Not a thorough job, as many of them performed, but it seemed unlikely he'd be heading straight home.

"He's there."

"Damn."

Kate moved to the other side of the desk, lifting the keyboard, wiping under it, and replacing it before hovering her duster over the rest of the surface. She watched Endo, still amused at him stuck there, unable to come up for air in case Merv collared him. Although the trader's actions in hiding made him look like a coward, it triggered something.

A thought.

She wasn't sure if she should be thankful for the episode distracting her from Aaron, or annoyed that it brought things flooding over her. She couldn't touch sports gambling. That would invite Jonathan and his punitive philosophy, and he'd jump at the chance to exact revenge on the woman he believed drove his brother to kill himself—*I'll have Child Protective Services on your ass.* But what if there was another way?

"Endo?" she said.

Endo sighed in reply.

"What if you knew which trades to make? Like, couldn't lose?"

His face angled up at her. "You mean insider trading?"

"No, that's illegal. Isn't it?"

"It is. Yes. And I wouldn't do it."

"No, no. I'm talking about if I knew for certain that a stock was going up or down, because… I don't know. Maybe I heard something. From a reliable source, or—"

Endo cut her off with a short smirk. "That's insider trading. Using inside knowledge from another firm about their stock price. It's *illegal*."

"Oh." Kate's cheeks flushed hot.

She prided herself on knowledge of the law, of politics, of many things that college educated folks were proficient in. While it would be unfair to label her fellow cleaners stupid, she couldn't get away from the fact that those with whom she shared this job rarely had college degrees, nor did they keep up to date with the issues of the day. And certainly not the finer points beyond those that affected them directly.

Kate checked around again. No one had moved, except Merv, who was striding from his desk toward the elevators without so much as a "goodnight" to those toiling away.

She said, "Just hypothetically, if I figured something out, gave you a cast-iron guarantee… nothing illegal… How much could you make from one trade. Like, a really good one?"

Endo sighed. "I dunno. A thousand bucks for a steady climb, $100K bonus if it's a humdinger."

"Humdinger?"

"Yeah, like a sudden acquisition blows up the price after I buy, or some other rumor sends it up. I sell at the right time, the profit's all Hetherington's and I get a cut. That's if I'm investing the firm's money, not a client's."

"There's a difference?"

Another swift glance around. Another sigh. "We have clients and we have our own portfolio. The client makes a trade, Hetherington's take a commission, and I get a cut. If

Hetherington's investment arm makes a trade, the company keeps all the profit, so the cut is higher. Client commission is less risky. I lose Heth's money, it comes out of my other commissions."

One hundred thousand dollars.

"If you have a dead cert," Endo said, "why not invest it yourself?"

"I don't *have* any money. Look at me." It was true. All the funds they had after paying off the mortgage and their—*her*—debts were tied up in trusts for Aaron. Not even Jonathan or Jennifer had access. "But if I told you where to invest. You'd make a bunch, right? For you and…"

She barely dared say it. But because she'd found no reasoning that made sense beyond Tammy's—*he's got the sight*—she figured why not go for it?

She said, "And for me?"

"You?"

"Like, a mutually beneficial arrangement."

"Is Merv still there?"

Kate craned to view the elevators. Merv slipped inside one and the door closed.

"All clear."

Endo tied his lace and stood, scooped up his man-bag, and squared himself before Kate. "Listen, I don't know what you're trying to do. But you're a cleaner." His tone was steady, and he had to swallow what he must have correctly interpreted as harsh words. "I don't mean that in a bad way, really I don't. I'm sure you're a great person and all, but that's what you are. A cleaner for an outsourced company that services our office. And I'm sorry, but I can't see any way for you to give me a solid tip without having gotten it illegally."

"No, I said *hypothetically.*"

"I know what you said, but my answer is the same. Hypothetically, yes, I could invest the firm's money. When the stock comes good, I get a stinking great bonus which —*hypothetically*—I could share with you."

Kate hunched over the desk, shifting the leather swivel chair to wipe it down. "Okay, fine. Forget it."

He half-turned away, took a step, then turned back again. "I wish I could help, but it's a waste of my time and yours. Even if—"

"I said forget it." Kate shoved the chair back under the desk and returned her items to the cart.

"I—"

"No, I said it's fine." She pushed on. "I was an ass to think I'd be allowed to play with the elites. I'm just a cleaner, after all."

As Endo trudged away without another word, Kate felt like crap. She'd apologize the next time she saw him. Maybe not. He'd cope with a bit of guilt. Besides, Kate had meant it. Dabbling with this notion was ridiculous. There had to be a better explanation for Aaron's prediction than "the sight."

She'd find out what it was, right after she picked him up from Aunt Jennifer's place.

CHAPTER EIGHT

Kate's train was late, then the traffic between the station and the J-Js' place slotted together in a near-solid mass, making her crawl toward Kensington to collect Aaron. When she called to say she'd be late, Jennifer suggested they feed the lad and drop him off on their way to one of Jonathan's work shindigs.

And yes, she used the word *shindigs* without irony.

Seeing the chance to treat herself with something Aaron didn't eat, such as curry, she thanked Jennifer and made a U-turn at the first opportunity. She arrived home, negotiated a brief "hi, how are you?" with a sweaty, tanned Susan from down the street as she returned from a run, then a "coo-ee" from Dorothy herself who was pretend-swooning over Body-builder Bob as he helped move her trash and recycling for collection day tomorrow. Bob—whose surname Kate had forgotten—lived next to Sal, and as far as she knew never went out during the week, so she figured he worked from home and spent several hours in his outdoor gym around the back. He waved a salute toward Kate and called, "How are you?"

"Great, thanks," Kate called back. "Running late, though!"

She rushed inside, and she had time to shower, put on some neat jeans and a clean white tee-shirt, and prepare the ingredients. She'd eat dinner in peace when Aaron was in bed.

With the individual elements prepped, she had enough time to run a vacuum cleaner around before a car horn honked twice. She opened the door, feeling fresh and presentable, then Jennifer stepped out of the Mercedes parked behind her car. She was draped in a full cocktail gown, her hair done up to show off a pair of diamond earrings.

Kate suddenly felt like a troll that'd been dunked in manure.

"Hi there!" Jennifer beamed. "Here she is."

"Heading for the Oscars?" Kate asked.

Jennifer returned a polite chuckle, the rear door closing behind her as Aaron plodded out and shuffled up the path.

Hoping for a hug but settling for him not jerking away as she ruffled his hair, Kate said, "Hey, did you have a good time?"

"No." Aaron continued to the door.

Kate opened her mouth to admonish him, but Jennifer waved both hands in warning. She mouthed, "Can I have a word?" and pointed at the house.

"Sure." Kate led the way inside, where Aaron was removing his shoes. She noted his clothes were streaked with dried dirt, and guessed he'd been playing somewhere in a garden six times the size of Kate's, dreading the "word" Jennifer had requested. "You okay there?"

"Fine," he mumbled.

"Oh, it's nothing big," Jennifer said, coming in behind. She took a long look around, wrinkled her nose, and shone

one of her thousand-watt smiles at them. "He's a bit down, that's all. Don't worry, we took care of it."

Kate watched the gargantuan effort it took for Aaron to carry his shoes to the rack under the coats. "What happened, buddy?"

"Playing with the guineas," Jennifer answered for him. "A couple got out of the pen, including Tony."

"Tony Stark," Aaron said.

"Ah, the birthday pig." Kate understood. "Did you get them back?"

"All except Tony," Jennifer said. "That's why he's a little bit…" She mimed crying the way a clown would.

"You didn't find him?"

"Oh, he tried his absolute best, didn't you? But let's not worry. They're domesticated. They come home for food. Unless a cat gets them. Which it won't. Obviously." Jennifer's smile hadn't faltered since she slinked out of the car—and it *was* slinking, a slender woman who moved like a mountain lion. Her lipstick reflected the light, so red it must have cost more than the car payment Kate was struggling to afford.

"He was very upset when we found him in the crawlspace."

That brought to mind Kate's own crawlspace, the one with the leaky pipes. "I didn't realize you had one."

"What? Of course we— Oh, no, not under the house. No, we have a cellar. But the shed has a crawlspace. For the heating."

"Right."

By "shed", she meant what they'd nicknamed a granny flat, a fully serviced one-bedroom apartment—more of a cottage in Kate's eyes—used for guests staying over who didn't want to use a hotel. Although not quite a mansion, the J-Js' house was far nicer than a Hilton, and they'd even offered Kate the apartment if she chose to sell up here and get back on her feet.

"It was a bit of a shock, wasn't it, champ?" Jonathan said, appearing in the doorway. He was wearing a tuxedo and looked weirdly taller and more square-jawed than usual.

God, where did these people get ready? How long must it take? And what kind of midweek "shindig" demanded they turn out in full Academy Award regalia? Even Jonathan's gray hair looked more like silver, while Jennifer would never allow a single strand of hers to lighten.

Kate made a mental note to check her own roots later.

"Lost you for a while, didn't we?" Jonathan added.

"I was looking for Tony Stark," Aaron said glumly.

"I know, champ, and it's all cool." Jonathan ruffled his nephew's hair. "Hey, why don't you go wash up for your mom?"

"I already ate at your house."

Jennifer patted her husband's chest. "I made him spaghetti and hot dogs."

Kate's stomach looped. He'd be hungry again soon, which meant a later night than she'd planned. It didn't matter. She was still determined to enjoy a meal alone in front of whatever child-unfriendly dross had been squatting in their DVR for weeks.

"Go put your pajamas on," Kate said. "We'll have some cereal on the deck."

Reluctantly, Aaron tramped up the stairs.

Jonathan leaned to check the boy wasn't eavesdropping and settled back beside Jennifer. Neither made a move to leave.

Chit-chat time. Kate hated small talk.

"I'm going to night school," she said, purely for something *small* to *talk* about.

Jonathan's head tilted. If he were wearing glasses, he'd be

staring down his nose at her. "Oh? Good. Very good. And you have it all worked out?"

"I found a regular sitter I can afford. High school kid. Recommended by another mom."

"What are you studying?" Jennifer asked.

"I'm going to pick up my law degree."

"Really?" Jonathan's down-the-nose look snapped into a frown. "I thought you bailed on that. Got too hard for someone without a… without an academic background."

"I didn't bail. I was pregnant. Craig and I made the decision together."

"Of course." Jennifer glanced at her watch. "How wonderful."

"It's not as easy as taking a few classes," Jonathan said.

"In a year, I'll have enough credits to work in a law firm. Paralegal or secretary. Something that pays better than scrubbing floors."

Kate heard her own voice. Her desperation to impress this couple.

Why?

Because they'd always deemed her an unsuitable wife for Craig? Or that they had always looked down on her for nothing more than her upbringing?

"After that," she said, unable to stop, "I'll be able to fund something higher. Maybe even take the bar in three years. Possibly four or five, but…"

She ran out of steam, petering to a halt under the gaze of two people who plainly saw her plans as the fantasies of a tired woman dreaming way too far above her station.

"What's the occasion?" she asked.

The J-Js looked down at themselves as if surprised to find someone had dressed them this way.

"Oh, a work thing," Jonathan said.

"Don't be shy." Jennifer again leaned into him and his

arm snaked around her shoulders. "The firm wanted to throw a party in honor of Jonathan making partner."

An ambition he'd been talking about ever since Kate had known him. Something Jennifer had chattered about too. Always "almost there" according to her. Now, having finally achieved that lofty goal, Kate hoped perhaps Jennifer might shut up about it. Huge salary bump, shares, voting privileges at a firm that serviced what Jonathan called "high-value clientele" and whom Craig had referred to as "people too wealthy to have accountability."

Craig was the kind of lawyer equally comfortable digging a non-fee-paying client out of a hole installed by some wealthy bastard to trap them in poverty as he was fighting truly negligent companies for millions in damages. From this, he earned a healthy income without being ostentatious. But his motivation was never money. It was one of many things Kate adored about the man. He'd also told Kate already about how Jonathan had made partner in his swanky upscale firm after proving himself with an allegedly unwinnable case, having uncovered a paper trail relating to a bribe. It led to a slew of money saved for his client *and* a counter-suit. But Jonathan hadn't mentioned it since Craig passed, so Kate had assumed it was either on hold or Craig simply got it wrong.

"Didn't they already decide on the partner a while ago?" Kate asked.

Jennifer said, "Well, they made the decision shortly before Craig passed away. Jonathan felt he needed a little space before taking up the post, and they concurred. A slow, steady transition."

Kate noted the bob of Jonathan's throat, but Jennifer did not.

Jennifer added, "We agreed to postpone the official party

after… Well, none of us had the appetite for celebrating at the time."

"I wasn't going to say…" Jonathan scoffed in an *aww-shucks* way. "I mean, I don't want to brag when you're… you know."

He wafted his free hand around.

"When I'm what?" Kate said.

"Nothing," Jonathan said. "It's fine."

Jennifer hadn't picked up on the veiled dig at a house which, by most people's standards, was still a damn nice home. She added to the non-showing-off: "He's been on the brink for years, but we couldn't let that Jamal Preston character beat him to it, could we? It was such a big win, our last case tipped him over and, well, he deserves the party, don't you think? After all he's been through?"

…our last case tipped him over…

…our…

Because Jennifer was more than "just" a housewife, as she reminded everyone who'd listen after a couple of gins. Whenever she spoke of Jonathan's promotion, the delay between the decision and enacting it, Jennifer usually hinted that Craig's death was a terrible inconvenience to her and, more importantly, her social climbing project. How awful that her husband hadn't felt like a big celebration. Life went on. He continued working as was expected, but Jennifer must have insisted on a coronation of sorts. Once it was tasteful to do so, naturally.

"What's wrong with my house now?" Kate asked Jonathan.

"Why, not a thing," Jennifer said, still oblivious. "It's a lovely little place. I mean, it could do with a visit from an interior designer, or maybe just a decorator, but you're doing a fine job."

"A fine job," Jonathan said.

Kate stuffed her hands in her jeans pockets. "Except…?"

Jonathan made a point of looking at his watch. "Time we were going."

Chit-chat accomplished.

"Okay." Kate held the door for them. "Thanks for watching Aaron again. You know I really appreciate it."

Jennifer hugged her and broke away. "Anytime. We adore having him. Don't we, Jonathan?"

"Anytime," Jonathan agreed.

At the doorstep, Jonathan paused, inhaled, and let it out in a long, single breath. "There is one thing."

Here we go…

Jonathan turned on the spot, Jennifer already halfway down the drive before she realized he wasn't on her heels. He said, "It's a buyer's market out there. And with this new position, I can afford an investment. Like this place. I'll give you market value, no haggling, and you'll have plenty of money to set up somewhere more… manageable. Especially with your, *heh*, night school starting up. It will get harder for you."

"Christ." Kate ran her hands through her hair, holding what she wanted to say in her lungs. "What is it with people this week? First Tammy, then Sal, now you. Did you all get together like some sort of intervention?"

Jonathan frowned. "Who are Tammy and Sally?"

"What makes you think I can't cope here? It's a big house, but I've done a decent job, haven't I? It hasn't fallen down yet."

"The carpet needs replacing. There's faded paint everywhere. And it smells, Kate." Jonathan circled his finger. "Your house smells bad. You clearly can't cope. And I'm being very generous in offering to help you out. Again."

Kate searched for an excuse, for something that might justify what Jonathan had pointed out. Because nothing he'd said was untrue. It wasn't a perfect home, and there *was* a faint odor that she hadn't yet identified. She'd had plenty of those, though. Most people had, especially busy parents who couldn't afford cleaners.

"What time did you say your shindig started?" Kate asked.

"Fine." Jonathan scratched the side of his face as he resumed his route back to the car, which—Kate now saw—had a driver at the wheel. "But remember I offered."

"It's some old fruit," she said to his back. "Aaron's always leaving things where he shouldn't."

He waved without turning, crooked his arm, and Jennifer slipped hers into it, smiling back with her redder-than-red lips shining as she went.

From his room, Aaron didn't hear everything the adults said downstairs, but he was sure they were talking about him. Did they know? Did they know what he'd done?

It wasn't his fault. It was his mom's. His super-busy, won't-listen mom.

She thought Aaron had little understanding of the world, and how things worked, but he knew lots. He had access to the internet. Even with parental controls, plenty slipped through. Information he needed. Stuff on educational sites for school, for extracurricular activities, camping, hunting, physics, chemistry, engineering, and more. Even some naked ladies and men in biology texts.

Things his mom would not approve of.

Aaron hugged his schoolbag, listening to the voices rise and fall, of harsh words spoken, then cut off, lowered—he suspected—to keep his tender ears from knowing Mom and Uncle Jonathan didn't get along. That Uncle Jonathan thought Mom was somehow to blame for Dad's accident.

Aaron could know the truth if he just wished for it. He could tell them and settle it once and for all.

But the price had gotten harsher recently. The bigger the question, the worse things he had to do.

And he hated those favors.

Really, truly, hated them.

And yet, he also hated letting his mom down. Hated his teacher giving him bad grades and instructing him to "step up" and "try harder." Hated that he felt like he was constantly failing, and that even the bullies and slackers did better than him without caring so much.

He *was* trying.

It literally hurt in his stomach and behind his eyes to think people didn't believe him. Maybe he was just stupid. Maybe that was why he needed to do these favors.

Favors for favors.

He hugged his bag tighter, wishing so hard for things to be different. One day, maybe, when he got ahead a bit, if Mom didn't work so hard and could spend more time helping him with his schoolwork, then he wouldn't need to summon those facts from…

Well, he wasn't sure *where*, exactly. One thing he was sure of, though, was he couldn't have pulled himself up without them. Or without delivering his return favors.

Weird thinking of them as favors, though. He didn't know what to call them otherwise. An urge? A need?

He wasn't so dumb that he couldn't spot a pattern that obvious. Use the gift, fight the urge, lose, then perform the task.

The door downstairs closed, and a car drove away.

"Aaron?" Mom called up the stairs.

This was it. He was about to find out.

Do they know?

Could they have guessed or discovered how bad things have gotten for him? He'd never have believed himself capable of such things before he needed to do them. And now he knew he could live up to the other children, it was difficult to let go.

Yet, he couldn't keep on committing acts that made him cry and ache with guilt. His mom would hate him if she found out. She'd be even more disappointed than when he flunked a math test.

"Aaron, can you come down please? I have something I need to talk about."

She knows.

Only, she didn't sound mad. Just that weird tone she used when she was upset but trying not to let on.

They didn't know. They couldn't. He'd been so careful.

No, he was certain they didn't know what he'd done.

But was that because he'd worked it out himself, or because it had filtered it into his brain from… his… *buddy?*

Mom had called him "buddy" so maybe that was as good a name as any. A friend, helping him through life, gifting him knowledge in exchange for bad deeds. Perhaps, if he explained it that way, Mom would understand better. If he had to. Like, really, really had to talk about it.

And after getting that score right, the awful price he'd had to pay, it might be best to come clean.

Aaron carefully set his schoolbag aside, summoned all his courage, and ventured downstairs, keeping all his fear and anger at his mom inside.

Do they know?

Let's find out.

CHAPTER NINE

Kate saw little point in putting off the inevitable. She had no answers of her own, and speculation wasn't helping her mental state. If she didn't solve this tonight, she'd have to drug herself to sleep again, and would spend another day staggering through her shift in a daze.

There had to be more to this than simply Aaron pulling the answers to tests from thin air, boosting his homework achievements, and predicting unlikely basketball scores. More likely Aaron had sourced the academic step up from within himself. Her little boy was simply smarter than she had realized.

Okay, his father's death had held him back emotionally, so he was all mixed up. Kate's job was to unravel that tangle of emotions. She'd worked on that with his teachers, getting him to knuckle down and pound out the academic necessities. He'd worked so hard, dammit.

The only thing improved focus couldn't be responsible for was the basketball game.

And while she was grasping for a logical explanation, luck seemed the only factor she hadn't considered.

Out on the deck, with the repaired post staring back, Kate invited Aaron to join her on the cushioned wicker couch that formed part of a set with two chairs and a glass-topped table. He didn't seem sure at first, as if she were a stranger trying to tempt him into a van to go cuddle some puppies at an as yet unspecified location.

"Okay, Mom," he said as he climbed up and accepted the arm which she curled around his shoulders and squeezed. "Mom? Is something wrong?"

It struck her too late that this was the same place where she'd informed him of his father's death. They'd snuggled up like this. That day it had been sunny and warm, whereas tonight the sun was setting off to their left, but otherwise it could have been a rerun.

She chose not to draw attention to the similarities. "No, nothing like that. I just want to talk to you about the stuff that's been going on."

"Like losing Tony Stark?"

"If you like. Why don't you tell me about that?"

He shrugged, his shoulders digging into her waist. "I lost him. I was looking for him under the crawl space of that place where Grandma stays sometimes."

"Right. You know that's not a great spot to play, don't you?"

"But I had to find him."

"There are pipes. Hot and cold. And if things haven't been maintained properly, you might get an electric shock."

"Uncle Jonathan always hires someone to fix things right away. He doesn't need to get a neighbor in to do stuff."

Kate couldn't allow the conversation to drift into Sal territory. It wasn't about him. It was about the man Aaron might worry he was replacing.

"Your dad would be proud. About your schoolwork. About how much you care for your guinea pig."

Aaron said nothing. Didn't move. Not even a shrug.

Kate pressed. "Even if you have some help."

"I know."

"And you know I am proud of you too, don't you?"

"I guess."

"I'm just worried."

Aaron pulled back, stared up at her with wide eyes that reminded her of a kitten watching her open a carton of cream. "I cause you problems. But I don't mean to. I'll try to do better on my own."

On my own.

As Kate feared, he was constructing his efforts into a force outside himself. A power. Like a superhero. She needed to speak to the counselor about this, perhaps take Tammy's advice about looking for pro bono psychiatric evaluations.

But who was she kidding? She couldn't stop at slapping a classmate.

"That basketball score," she said. "How did you know?"

Aaron's kitten eyes clouded over and his whole face changed, the kitten realizing the cream had gone bad, but was still expected to lap it up.

He said, "I just did."

"Like, it fell out of thin air? Into your lap?"

He nodded. "I don't get it, not really. That's why I don't want to talk about it. It's like… a friend helps me when I need it. He does me favors, and—"

Kate hated to cut him off, but she needed to voice her thought. "A friend? Like, you're hearing voices?"

"No, not like that. It's hard to explain. It's—"

"So it's *like* a friend helping? Not a person sat beside you, feeding you the answers?"

"Yeah. A buddy who knows the stuff I need to know."

Relieved to cross *schizophrenia* off her list of amateur diagnoses, Kate readjusted her position, tucking one leg under the other. She took both his hands in hers. "Do you believe me when I say I'm not angry with you? That I want to understand?"

He nodded, but his eyes were watery and his bottom lip had begun to quiver.

It wasn't easy keeping up the affectionate, soft expressions that she needed to soothe him, or to maintain her cordial tone when every fiber inside her wanted to yell in his face, *Tell me, kid, tell me the truth.*

She said, "You need to know that you don't have some... *buddy*... helping you. Understand that you're just being super smart. On your own. I'd like to help prove that to you."

"Like..." He sniffed, although he wasn't crying. Yet. "Like we should do an experiment?"

"Like an experiment, yes."

"How?"

"Well, let's look at a control sample."

Kate took out her phone and checked the sports news for what games might be on later. This wasn't planned. The plan —if that was the right word—was to steer clear of this. But with a nick in the wall Aaron had erected, here was a chance to prove he was being smart through hard work. She could not resist a chance to boost his self-esteem, even if it meant dipping her toe into dangerous waters.

She said, "I'll pick a few games, you pick one."

Kate found four NBA matches, plus a couple of minor league baseball games, including one locally—the White Plains Wanderers. Legend had it that the name came about for their ability to train up promising talent and have them *wander* to the majors. But Kate and Craig had met the owner, Phil MacNemeny, at a charity ball three winters ago on an upstate retreat, where he said the Wanderers' name came from a UK-based soccer team. MacNemeny never learned the provenance of the soccer team, but he'd liked the alliteration and it stuck.

"Okay, Aaron, the White Plains Wanderers are playing the Washington Night Cats. Do you want to go with the score or the spread?"

"Doesn't matter," Aaron said.

"Okay, so score."

"Are you sure? You won't get sick again?" The boy had converted from teary-eyed and quivering lips to a child learning to ride on two wheels.

You won't let go, will you?

No, son.

Don't let go.

I won't.

Promise you won't let go.

I already let go. You're doing it all yourself.

"I went to that institute," Kate said. "I've been to meetings where people help me keep a lid on it. And even if I wanted to go gambling, I don't have any money. Except, maybe a little reserved for the car payments. But you know I can't cope without a car, and I'd hate to make you ride to school in an old scrapheap. I wouldn't risk losing that."

"Which games are you going to guess?"

"I'm going to write my four down." She opened a notebook app and listed the teams as she spoke. "And then I'm going to write your one down. See if I guess right. See if you guess right."

"Okay, if you're sure you won't get in trouble."

As she entered her own predictions, based on nothing more than random numbers and a knowledge of how baseball scores were formatted, her stomach fluttered. Like yesterday, her mouth moistened—a hamburger dangled before an obese person on a strict diet.

"Wanderers win nine to four." Aaron's chin dipped, his throat bobbing. "Is there anything else?"

Kate noted his forecast, and the hunger in her gut demanded the hamburger. She struggled to recall the mental exercises dished out at the rehab center.

Picture the hurt it causes your loved ones.

Craig, in the car, leaving her. Again. He'd been patient, funded her rehab. Trusted she'd follow the plan. And she had. Except once. Once—when she'd maxed out her card on a can't-lose tip which had somehow, mysteriously, won.

Aren't you happy? Why aren't you happy?

He'd explained why he wasn't happy, then left.

Then died.

So much hurt. All her fault. From her weakness. Her selfishness. It'd be even worse if she brought that down on Aaron.

"What if we steer clear of sports?" Kate suggested, her hand shaking as she placed her phone on the wicker chair to one side. "How about some card tricks?"

"Like, you pick a card and I tell you what it is?"

"Would that work? Would you just know?"

"Yes, but you could do it with a number in your head."

"Okay, fine."

Kate glanced at her phone, sat dark and motionless on the padded seat. Calling to her.

Look at me. Look at the lovely baseball game. Check off the scores. Get rich!

She asked, "What number am I thinking of?"

It was seven.

"Seven," Aaron said.

"How about a harder one?"

He pulled his chest in, withdrawing himself from her. "I don't want to."

"Why not?"

"Because."

"Just one more. Okay?"

She thought of a random big number: 832.

He said, "I don't *want* to." Again, his eyes were damp, and that lip came out.

Kate was pushing too hard. It wasn't worth triggering another episode in which he might act out. Peeing in the fish tank when Sal came for dinner was one thing. What might he do if he got even more stressed?

She pulled him in and gave him a huge hug. "It's fine, baby. It's fine." She stroked his hair. "No more tonight. Maybe I should've asked you the stock market question instead of baseball ones."

Although she couldn't see him, the way his body tensed, the way his fingers curled in and his breath changed, she knew he was crying. She just knew. Like he "just knew" things. His homework, his test answers. Because the input was there. All he needed was a push to access it.

Kate kissed the top of his head, content to sit here.

The sun was now an orange glow behind distant houses and trees, the light breeze cool on her skin. If they waited like this, they might see bats swooping, hunting the late-evening insects. It'd mean her eating even later, missing out on her treat of a dinner, which could tempt that other hunger back.

The phone remained blank.

Look at meeeeee...

"What is the 'stock market' question?" Aaron asked, wiping one eye without lifting his head.

"Oh, I'm being silly. I wanted to show some mean guys where I work that I can do more than clean. Don't worry about it."

"People are mean to you at work?"

"Sometimes. But not super-mean. Not like bullies hitting me. But when you do a job like mine, people think you aren't worth much. It's nothing you need to worry about. I'm a big girl. I can handle it. I can handle anything. I promise."

She stroked his hair some more. Thick and soft. It needed cutting, but she liked it long. It kept him looking young.

He said, "Go short on Villiers Media Group within the next forty-eight hours."

He sat bolt upright, her finger snagging in a lock of hair as her heart raced and stomach sank. Aaron frowned and seemed genuinely confused.

"Mom, what does that mean? 'Going short?'"

Kate's jaw was working with not much coming out. As her pulse steadied, dots of sweat pricked on her forehead, and she retrieved her phone.

"It could be good news," she said. "A fresh start."

I won, she'd told Craig that night, beaming from ear to ear as she showed him the three thousand dollars in cash. *Why aren't you happy that I won?*

The answer was simpler than she'd ever considered. Why wasn't Craig happy?

Because winning once in a while made her forget all the times she lost. The occasional big win set the endorphins skyrocketing, and they never settled.

Even when she flushed that three grand down the toilet —and Craig had been certain she would—she'd ride that wave like a champion surfer. But instead of sinking and calling it a day, she'd paddle right back out in a lagoon of debt, clawing at the prospect of the Next Big Win.

She'd slipped. Just once. Once in three months of sobriety. Because her sponsor—her *sponsor*, of all people—had given her this tip. He'd called her because he'd been tempted and was feeling weak. It was her responsibility to dissuade him. Instead, they'd headed out together to place the accumulator. Three horses, all to win in an afternoon. Ten bucks. What could it hurt?

Nothing.

Ten bucks to predict three winners in three different races. All or nothing.

Ten bucks became three thousand.

Oh, what if they repeated that success? With three thousand as the seed? *900K*. Almost a million smackeroos.

"You okay, Kate?" Sal asked.

She'd called him as a last resort. Even with the curry beckoning, a greater hunger grumbled, pulled at her. The one trying to convince her that her late husband was wrong to leave her. That going for the million bucks was the right thing to do, the sensible option. After all, who couldn't use a million dollars? And when that didn't land, surely spending more on credit to get back to even was a reasonable course of action.

Gamblers' logic.

She couldn't go back there.

As annoyed as Aaron might be at her, she needed this.

"No. I don't think I am okay." Kate's throat was tight. Her phone hot in her hands. Pressure swelled her tongue. "I need to go to a meeting, Sal. I'm sorry, but I don't have anyone to watch Aaron."

"You're struggling?"

She nodded, although no one could see. "Please? There's a place on my commute. I go to it sometimes. They run sessions whenever there's a game nearby. Will you watch Aaron? Please?"

"Of course. I'll be right over."

CHAPTER TEN

Unlike many things in life, addiction meetings were very much the way they were depicted in movies and TV shows: a circle or, in this case, a semi-circle of people with a history of addiction—be it alcohol, narcotics, or gambling—sharing their thoughts, their feelings, their fears. Standing tall, meeting the others' gaze, receiving no judgement, no advice, no grumbles about how dumb you were being. The one big difference to the movies and TV here was that the group favored a podium of sorts, like politicians used to make speeches, rather than slumping in a chair and moaning at their peers.

Every time she stood up there and told them her name, confessed to being a gambling addict, and the room greeted her in tired unison, Kate cocooned herself in a giant hole, as if she'd been sucked down and no one could see her.

"Hunger," she said, her hands either side of the lectern. "That was the thing. Whenever I got an inkling, I thought I was going to die of hunger. Or thirst. Something."

Nods from the circle of seven near-strangers. She knew

some first names, but had met none of them on the streets or the train, or at the school.

"And that's what sets me back sometimes. I look at a sure thing. A big team taking on a small one. I mean, obviously I know the minimum spread, right? We all do."

The nods intensified, a sprinkle of *been-there* chuckles. It was one reason these sessions helped. A person up front, telling you what they did wrong, and you recognize it in yourself. And for the addict relaying the story, vocalizing it, the room responding with affirmative murmurs, confirmed you were right to think this way.

Kate held up a finger. "One score. That's what I always need. What I know is being served on the next table. If I upgrade, move seats, tell the waiter I'll have what they're having. And when that one big score comes in, it's mine. All mine. Because isn't that what we all think is right around the corner? One. Big. Score."

The nods were back.

"Yeah. And then I'm drowning in debt, maxing out my credits cards online. A VPN masking my location so I can pretend I'm in Vegas or the UK where I can gamble to whatever levels I fit inside that bit of plastic. My husband's Amex card, for one month at least."

A ripple of understanding from around half the nodders.

"But the debt doesn't matter, because that one big score is due. All that bad luck I had, it's got to turn sometime, hasn't it? One BIG score. The notorious B.I.G. score. And then I'm back to zero. Or even a little ahead. And those wins, those itty-bitty tiny wins along the way, they keep me coming back. And if I keep upping the ante, when the next win lands…"

She petered out. Shook her head.

"Sorry, I'm rambling."

This session, out of a community hall in the grounds of a

Catholic church, was run by a priest so handsome he could have dropped from a Swedish wall calendar. Nearby, he reassured her, "It's fine. There are no time limits."

She smiled her thanks. "It doesn't help that I used to be a mean-ass poker player. Out West. I was raised in a trailer park by trailer trash parents. My mom was a waitress, my dad a sometime bartender, coffee shop barista, a gun enthusiast—"

A tender memory surfaced, a sidebar she considered keeping to herself, but these sessions were for sharing. Bad and good.

"He used to take me to the range. Soon as I was old enough. I wasn't sure he really enjoyed it that much, like it was an obligatory pastime to stick it to *the libruls*. I was good at it, and it was the rare time he'd praise me. Rifles, pistols, whatever. I loved working with my mom and shooting with my dad."

She juggled her sweet words in her mouth for a moment, but reality turned them sour.

"Other than that, my dad was mostly a grifter. One of those rip-off artists you get on the street. Follow the lady, that kind of thing. It helped me learn the town. Reno, not Vegas, nothing big like that. The little brother. I was young, tagging along with my mom because at first she couldn't afford childcare. Then when I was older, she didn't trust me to keep my legs together and didn't want no grandbaby to support."

Kate noted she'd regressed to that odd drawl her parents spoke with. She corrected that with a cough.

"I learned guns with Dad, cards with Mom. I played blackjack and counted cards and soon progressed to poker. Taking on all comers. My mom was proud, but she took her cut. Every week, I won more money than I lost. I guess that made me a pro. It's how I met my husband. He was on a bachelor party, and I was part of the private game scene, and took him for a thousand bucks."

Warmth bloomed inside her at the memory. Later, in his suite, both of them naked and panting in a post-orgasmic stew, he'd confessed he found losing to a firecracker like her the hottest thing he'd experienced in years. Much hotter than any stripper or sorority house on Halloween. She chose not to share that, though.

"It wasn't until I had my first kid, and moved here, where they're not as lenient on the casinos as they are in Nevada, that I realized I couldn't leave it behind. And online, where you can't look at your opponents... it's not right. You can't build a career on that. So I found sports."

Blank stares returned. She'd overstayed. No one would say, but she'd been on the other side of those stares. Bored to death, waiting for the next person to bare their soul; to *be* the next person.

"What I mean is, those card games never scared me. It didn't feel like gambling. It felt like... competing. When you throw a fifty down on a ten-point spread, that's a risk. So many variables. And when they come in... Oh, man."

More nodding, heads and shoulders swaying, the chucklers recognizing themselves in her, as she had seen herself in others who'd shared.

"But there's always a price before the reward kicks in. Before that big score lands. Lots of costs. Too much overhead. And pretty soon, you see how you never deserved a family in the first place. There's only the thrill of winning. And when you don't win, those around you... well... maybe you shouldn't have infected their lives in the first place."

She hesitated here. Pushed away that sense of worthlessness, of worse than worthlessness, of making life horrible for Craig... and now Aaron too. But she could put things right for him, for her. This was why she was here. She had a question to ask. A thirst she feared was festering not-so deep inside her, a thirst hadn't dissipated since standing up and announcing her name the way it usually did. If anything, it had grown.

"What if you couldn't lose? What if you *knew* you couldn't lose? And I don't mean the strong feeling. I don't mean the hot tip from some pro who's never been wrong that fills you with confidence and hope. And not some syndicate that claims they've cracked the bookies' algorithm, and all you need for a buy-in is a thousand bucks. I mean, absolutely cast-iron certainty. What if you could not lose?"

Silence.

She blinked. Gave it a three count.

The thirst, the *hunger* inside her withdrew a touch. She'd vocalized her troubles, her concerns. She felt better for it. Not cured of the urge, and she'd need a pill again to sleep, but that was a price worth paying. She couldn't let Aaron down the way she had Craig. Plus, if Jonathan got wind of it, he'd be on to social services in a flash.

"Thank you," she said, and stepped down to the smattering of applause.

She walked back to her seat as Father Handsome moved to the podium where he would, as usual, ask if anyone else wanted to share.

A man in a baseball cap and denim jacket interrupted with a single barking laugh. "If it's a cast iron certainty, ain't no fun in it."

Kate paused in place, the others laughing at the gallows humor.

"Yeah, I feel that," said a woman with her arm in a cast.

"But hey," the first guy added, "if God himself comes down from Heaven with a hot tip, like some Alpha and Omega shit, cause he knows everything… that ain't even gambling. Right, Father?"

The priest at the lectern stuttered a couple of, *Ah, ahs* before shaking off the potentially upsetting declaration and getting his usual line out: "Would anyone else care to share something?"

The woman with the broken arm made her way to the front. But even as she announced her name was Carla and affirmed she was a gambling addict, and all of them including Kate said, "Hi, Carla," the echo of the denim-jacketed man reverberated around the tiny community center.

...that ain't even gambling...

...that ain't even gambling...

Right, Father?

CHAPTER ELEVEN

Kate drove away from the meeting, calmer and less confused than she had been. She'd gotten out what she needed, expressed it to her peers, and now it all looked stupid. The hot tip. The can't-lose.

And yet.

Ten bucks magically turning into $3000.

That had been a hot tip. A near certainty.

Near.

She had in her phone a real certainty. Or as close as she'd ever gotten. Because Aaron was right yesterday, was right with his number seven guess, so he must be right today. Her little boy, the clairvoyant.

There was no schizophrenic delusion here. He just knew.

He has the sight.

And if he has the sight, and he's right about the score, well…

THAT AIN'T EVEN GAMBLING.

Is it?

"Don't be stupid," she said to herself.

One basketball result didn't mean Aaron was clairvoyant.

A guess at the most common think-of-a-number-between-one-and-ten didn't prove he had some mystical sight. Kate didn't believe in that sort of thing. Except when she needed to.

Like putting down money from Craig's Amex card to pay off the previous week's losses.

Okay, that was another wound she didn't fancy opening tonight. Way too many scars cutting away at her, and each of them felt like grief.

She shoved it back inside her mental box and focused on tonight. On whether she'd shipwrecked herself on an island of fantasy, or if there might be some way she could justify the notion she'd contemplated since leaving the house.

The difference here was that she hadn't seen those *can't-lose* tipsters personally, hadn't witnessed an impossible result. This meant the only thing keeping her straight wasn't the meeting, but her own self-worth. Because if she'd been trying to squeeze another *can't-lose* tip from Aaron, not help him to boost his self-esteem, then she hadn't been momming at all. No decent parent would do that.

No. Here, in the cold light of night, she accepted the truth: She'd been milking her son for a tip that she knew—deep down, *knew*—would come in.

Kate was driving, but not home. Her autopilot had guided her to the route that took her through Queens, and she only had ten minutes to turn around.

Specificity.

It was why the rewards were greater in those complicated depths of prediction. And it was why bookies were richer than gamblers. Forecast the winner of a two-team game with no spread, you got shitty odds. Put in $50 and win, you get $60 or $70 back. The bookie takes the cash from folks betting on the other team and is happy as a pig in muck to pay out the insignificant percentage of winnings.

Odds went up with more teams, more options, like horses.

Like predicting three winners in three races was a 300-1 gamble. If she'd gone for four winners, it could have been 600-to-1; for five, she'd have seen 1200-to-1.

She was so thirsty tonight. A woman dragging herself through the desert toward an oasis, getting there, and finding it filled with Evian. Only, this oasis was named Buckeroo Brandies, and her throat wasn't in the mood for beer. Or brandy.

She parked in the lot down the alley and behind the bar, recognizing the battered lime-green Trans Am with a black and white stripe bisecting it down the middle, spoiler to grill. It was an ostentatious classic which the owner seemed to think made him more attractive to the opposite sex. He was wrong, but no one seemed interested in disabusing him of the fact. Still, nobody touched the anachronistic muscle car. They knew who it belonged to.

"If I go in there," she said aloud, "I'm not gambling. It's science. I'm testing a theory against a control group. It's just…"

She fumbled her purse open and poked around. A five, a collection of coins. This was all she had left until she got paid on Friday. There were enough groceries in the house, and she had a season pass for the parking lot at the train station as well as the train itself, and enough gas to see her through. Aaron's school snack money was in place back home, and he took his own lunch.

The money in her purse was "spare." She could afford to lose it. If she did, she wasn't letting anyone down, except maybe the guy who sold her candy once in a while in the 30th floor cafeteria.

"Ten bucks," she announced to the rearview mirror,

where the shadows under her eyes bore deep into her skin. "I can handle a measly ten-dollar bet."

She gripped the five-note and assorted coins and stepped out of the car, her feet heavy as she approached Buckeroo Brandies. At the door, her left palm clutching the last of her money had sweated. She switched the contents to her right hand.

"Ain't even gambling," she said.

And pushed open the door.

The inside of Buckeroo Brandies was much as she remembered, although there'd been a minor paint job on one wall. A pool table dominated the rear, with a dartboard off to the side, and she wound through the worn-out tables and chairs hosting couples and singles with the same confidence she always did. She resisted looking up at the three TV screens, two showing baseball games and one NBA match she'd thought about testing.

Science. This was *science*.

She made her way along the bar, one bartender on duty —a skinny, black-haired girl sporting a nose ring, dragon tattoos down each arm—whose eye-roll followed Kate when it was clear she wasn't here to drink. On the same stool he'd pretty much owned for the last six years, Ollie Swag looked up from a physical newspaper and squinted Kate's way.

Ollie's actual name was Oliver Smith. They called him Ollie Swag because he was the bag man for a muscle-bound creep who grew up in the neighborhood but had since moved to a more luxurious zip code. Ollie accepted protection money and banked it through various fronts, but never got down and dirty with the rough stuff himself. His primary job, though, was to take illicit bets, offer odds, and turn a profit. Rumor was, they split the profit eighty-twenty, and not in Ollie's favor. It was enough to keep Ollie from regular work, and it kept bars like Brandies, a number of fast-food outlets, and a handful of not-too-fussy hookers in business.

"Katie-Kat!" he bellowed, opening his arms but remaining seated. "She's returned! As usual. Few pounds lighter, too. Lookin' good. Oh, shit." He feigned worry. "It ain't cancer, is it? Just good living?"

"Hey, Ollie." Kate swapped her money back to her left hand, now dry, unlike her right, which was as damp as her back. She pulled up short. No way was she hugging the fat, curly-haired extrovert.

"Took a while longer to wake up and smell the good stuff this time," Ollie went on, lowering his arms without a hug.

Kate uncharitably wondered if anyone had ever hugged him without a down payment—as a man or a boy. If he'd received more affection, maybe he'd have chosen a different career. Despite his jovial personality, Ollie had access to some serious muscle, and more than once he'd meted out retribution on people who'd done something as innocuous as dinging his precious automobile. Accidental or with malice, no one got away with that.

"White Plains Wanderers," she said. "Washington Night Cats. How am I set?"

Ollie grimaced, a man swallowing a sour fruit. "They started already, Katie-Kat." He lifted his phone and flicked it on. The same sports news app Kate used showed a list of scores. He scrolled down from the majors. "Third quarter just started."

Kate's jaw extended, jutting forward. She hoped to exude a confidence she wasn't quite feeling. "What's the score?"

"Wanderers six, Night Cats three."

"Wanderers win nine to four," Kate said. "What'll you give me?"

Ollie sniggered. His teeth were foul, more stained than

the last time Kate saw him. It was as if the gaps were spreading, although only their dark color, not their size. She hadn't seen a mouth like that since back West, in the public park that was home to more than a few meth heads.

For all their faults, at least her parents hadn't succumbed to that.

"Three," Ollie said.

"Come on," Kate answered. "For a score? I could get twenties for an exact score in Manhattan."

"Then go to Manhattan." He picked up his paper again. "Of course, game'll be over by then, but good luck with it."

Kate stood there.

Ollie lowered one corner, his eye catching hers. "Okay, five-to-one."

"Fifteen, Ollie. Come on."

"Eight. And no more, or I'll need you to add a little sugar, you get what I mean." He made the universal jerk-off gesture.

Maggots crawled under Kate's skin. "Eight, then. Here."

She passed him the five dollars and change that made up her ten-dollar bet. He weighed the collection in one hand, pulled the kind of face a reasonable person might adopt thinking about administering a hand job to a rotten-toothed asshole in the men's room, and laid the money on the bar.

He pushed it back toward her. "Buy-in is fifty."

"Since when?" Kate demanded.

"Keep it down, Katie-Kat."

Kate sat two stools away from Ollie Swag, hands in her lap. "Fifty?"

"Times are changing. What can I say? Gotta make it worth my while. Worth my boss's while. About a year ago, he did some online business course, and now he says shit like, 'Go big or go home.' He's had it with pennies. Fifty's the minimum. Take it or leave it. Make it worth my while, or don't."

Again, Kate shuddered.

Ollie laughed. "Relax, I don't mean that. I mean... are you good for the fifty bucks?"

Kate looked at him. "I get paid on Friday."

"Keep your panhandling money." He wafted the small pile of cash away and slid a seven-inch computer tablet from under his newspaper. "If you're certain you wanna go for it, I can spot you a line of credit."

Fifty dollars.

If she lost, she'd have to work a night shift in some client's deep-clean add-on. They were okay, and paid more than fifty dollars even after tax, but because they were supposed to help ward off diseases and viruses, the managers over Dev's head made everyone suit up in full PPE—personal protective equipment. It was a pain in the butt and everyone hated it, which was why they paid so well. The downside would mean asking the J-Js if Aaron could sleep over. Jonathan would want to know why, but she could lie to him convincingly. She had done for the past eighteen months, after all.

"It's been a tough year, Ollie," she said. "You know I'm a widow now?"

"I didn't." His expression remained disinterested. "Condolences. You in or out?"

She set her bitch-face, the one from a former life that she'd use to bluff tables full of poker players into folding. "I want ten-to-one if I'm risking fifty."

Ollie sighed, checked his phone. "Night Cats got one back. It's tight. I guess I can do ten-to-one."

"Deal." She hopped off her stool and scooped up the money—five in one hand, the coins in the other, so she wouldn't have to shake hands with Ollie.

God, when did she become such a snob?

"But Katie-Kate?" The bookie used a stylus on his tablet computer, pecking away at it. Presumably, his fingers were too fat. Or greasy.

"Yeah?"

"Interest is compound, you know? You don't pay me by Friday, on Saturday it's sixty. On Sunday, it's a hundred. By Monday, it's two. You get that, right? And the guys I work for, they don't fuck around askin' nicely."

Kate stared at the stylus, poised over the final peck.

If Aaron had the sight, she was $500 to the good. If he'd simply got lucky yesterday, and her disease was mutating that one freak event into a sign from God, or an omen that a million gamblers all over the world mistook for *can't-lose*, she was in the hole with a hoodlum who would not hesitate to hurt her.

"Do it," she said.

...ain't even gambling.

CHAPTER TWELVE

The next morning, with $480 in her purse, Kate pretty much skipped into work. She'd spent $20 on a strong coffee from one of White Plains' "vibrant" cafes after dropping Aaron at school, followed by a breakfast of pastries and a bacon sandwich, then a second overpriced coffee in Manhattan.

Keeping last night's success from Aaron was the right thing; hard, but momming was never easy. Besides, how could she be truthful with him when she hadn't got it straight in her own head? Better he kept it a secret from everyone except her, until they worked out what to do with it.

She'd needed half a pill to drift off to sleep. The craziness of Aaron pinpointing such a precise score had cartwheeled her brain, then ramped it up onto a rollercoaster that only sped up in the dark. Fantasies of the crazy's potential ruled one minute, the next she'd slap herself mentally and order her rational side to get a damn grip.

You can't exploit your son like that.
But it's for him.
Is it? Is it really for him?

Is it even true?

She'd always told herself she'd keep an open mind about things beyond conventional understanding. But having witnessed it herself, she was, oddly, more determined to prove an earthly conclusion. She'd need more proof before accepting it wholesale.

What was it he'd said? *Go short on Villiers-something* within two days. Kate had heard the term but only got that it was a high-risk, high-reward transaction.

How about the Lotto? She should have asked him for the numbers instead of a stocks tip, but she must have been tuned in to the notion of sports gambling. The next step up, in her mind, was the stock market. Crypto, maybe. That was meant to be the next big thing, wasn't it?

Shorting, though, sounded like something she should avoid, since she didn't understand it the way she understood cards, horses, sports.

Changed, ready to mop, Kate stepped out of the cleaners' area with her trolley fifteen minutes early to avoid confessing to Tammy what she'd done. Or lying yet again. Until at least lunchtime. She normally started on the 40th, working her way up to the 42nd where she'd enjoy a moment in the quiet of the "nice" men's room, but today she'd swapped with Mikka.

Her first stop was the women's powder room at the opposite end of Hetherington's trading floor, which meant crossing it via the designated route, taking her past the one broker who gave her the time of day. And she had to do it before last night's winning high petered out.

"Endo." She paused at his desk.

"No." He kept working without looking up. There was a spreadsheet on his primary screen, color-coded. His second screen displayed a line-chart with what seemed like all the colors of the rainbow zigging and zagging. "I'm in the middle of something. Come back after the bell."

"I'm not working late tonight. I need to speak to you."

"Later."

"If I give you something," she said, "and it blows up. What will you pay me? Half?"

Endo sighed, tainted with the humor of a parent patronizing a child. "I can't accept a tip without a ton of due diligence. To make sure you don't service one of those places on the side."

"How long will that take?"

"Days. If I have time."

"I don't have days," Kate said.

Endo lifted a bored eyebrow. "If you're so confident, take the risk yourself. But not here. Not today."

Money. She had none. She could borrow, she supposed. "Tomorrow is my day off. Can I do it by phone?"

"I'd have to open you a brokerage account. You'll need to show me ID."

"Right, I can do that. One question. What does 'shorting' mean?"

"Oh." He turned away from her. "That's a hard no. Especially for a newbie."

"Please talk to me. I'll be gone quicker."

"Look, I'm sorry. Moldy Merv is coming in late because he has a 'breakfast meeting' but we all know that means a whiskey or coke hangover, or both."

"Then meet me at lunch."

"No."

"In that case, I'll make sure I'm sitting on the end of this desk when Merv struts out of that elevator looking for an excuse to yell at someone."

Endo sagged in his chair, made a decision, and straightened, going back to work. "Fine. Garbo's. Twelve-thirty."

. . .

Garbo's was an eatery and bar on the 20th floor that served
light snacks and cocktails. At 12:25, Kate took off her tabard
and put on a coat, but in the sedate lounge-type bar, she kept
the coat on to hide her working-joe clothes and ordered a $5
Diet Coke. It came with too much ice and zero free refills.

Endo got there at 12:32 and opted for a fruit juice and a
Caesar salad. Kate ordered the same food without worrying
about the cost—if it was less than $475, she'd be okay—and
they waited on an outdoor patio seemingly carved into the
side of the building.

Endo watched her, waiting for her to speak.

"Shorting," she said.

"Yeah."

"I don't get it. I looked it up. But it's… I know it's more
common to make money by buying a share and hoping it
increases in value, but shorting is saying a company will lose
money. I read people in your line of work make a fortune out
of it. But… it makes no sense."

"Okay." Endo wearily made fists on the table. He flexed
his left: "Broker." He flexed his right: "You."

"With you."

He showed his hands as he explained. "You want to profit
from, say, Failing Bank Inc. We'll work it with one share
worth $100 to keep it simple. You call the broker and say,
'Hey, let's short this bank.' The broker has to find a share to
lend you. You're not *buying* it. You're *borrowing* the share
from the stocks available through the company, or one of the
broker's other clients, or even other brokers."

"Borrowing, not buying," Kate said, grounding it in her
brain.

"Let's say the broker finds a share in one of his client's
existing portfolios. He borrows it. The broker sells the share

on the market for $100. That $100 goes to your brokerage account. Are you with me?"

"I'm with you." Kate had been filling in the narration with flashes of numbers and stick men swapping them, and her stomach looped at the similarities between this profession and that of a sports-betting junkie. Only, this game, with vastly more zeroes, was a career that propped up economies. "I still can't see where the profit comes from."

"Soon." He lifted his right fist. "You got it right. Yay. Failing Bank Inc's stock value falls to $70. You have $100 in your account. You call your broker and tell him to cover Failing Bank Inc's share. The broker uses the brokerage money to buy one share of stock from the market at the current price of $70. Then he returns the new discounted stock you purchased to his client's portfolio."

Kate reviewed her stick-man cast. "So, the borrowed stock got sold for $100, you bought a new stock for $70, then replaced it in the original account like it was never missing… and I pocket the $30 difference?"

"Minus the broker's commission, yeah. You make, like, $27."

"For investing nothing?"

Endo's fists opened, palms-up. "Thing is, if I was gonna short something, you'd need enough to cover the trade in case it goes bad, unless you've got a history of big-money transactions. If you had, you could get a bank to cover you. But then you'll owe them."

"You're a broker."

"I am."

The food arrived, and they stopped talking. Kate sat up straight, only just realizing she'd slumped, leaning her head on one hand as she used to in high school when trying to ingest dense science. She'd always been more detail oriented, hence her introductory years at law school, following her minted boyfriend in the expectations they'd be a well-known New York power couple within ten years. If Aaron hadn't happened along, maybe that's how it would have turned out. But those years hadn't been big on advanced math.

When the waitress left them, Endo said, "But that's not the end. The risk on shorting versus long-trading is huge."

"How so?"

Endo again slackened, as if he'd been grilled too many times. Kate supposed it was the equivalent of a doctor being asked at parties, *Would you have a quick look at this rash?*

He said, "With a long trade, it's about profit. You jeopardize the investment you make and nothing else. The stocks tank, you go home empty handed. They go up, you go home rich. Shorting, by its very nature, can land you in the hole for unlimited losses."

Kate thought about it, then snagged on the reason. "Because I can't sell the borrowed share at a profit anymore. I owe the person I borrowed it from."

"Exactly. If that hundred-dollar share doubles, you have to pay out the cash you made in your broker account, plus the hundred it's gone up by. If it triples in value, you're in for an extra two hundred."

"I risk being cleaned out."

"Yeah, and then some. If I was your broker…" He scanned her up and down. "It'd be unethical of me to give you bad advice. Or run something if I suspect you're pulling an insider."

"You wouldn't make a short trade for me?"

"No." He talked as he ate. "I don't know you, and I could end up ruining you. Even if it's a good tip, I'm still suspicious of the intel."

Kate stabbed at the chicken and secured some lettuce with a drip of sauce. She should perhaps have ordered a burger. Tammy was right; she was skinny, and had lost weight lately, but then she hoped to one day populate a world that paid well, and those places didn't find excessive meat on the bones particularly desirable.

She said, "It's my risk, isn't it?"

"You really want to go there? You want to be my client?"

"Why not?" She ate the forkful, and it was the most flavorsome, succulent chicken she'd tasted in months. Nothing frozen here. Nicer than a fast food burger. Even the lettuce was crisp and light, and the dressing was tangy without making her lips pucker. "I could do well here. And you could do well off the back of it."

Endo exhaled through his nose. Closed his eyes. Slowly opened them. "To sign you as a client at Hetherington's, you'd need to look… different." He indicated her outfit. "No offence, but…"

"I own a suit. But I have to place the—" She almost said "bet," but this was a sure thing. *Ain't even gambling.* "We need to make the short trade by tomorrow."

Endo chewed his next mouthful, mulling over the decision. "Which company?"

"Villiers Media Group."

Endo half-smirked. "You think they're going down?"

"I know it. How much can I make from $450?"

Endo's smirk almost resurfaced, but it dropped into a frown. "Do you mean $450,000?"

"No, I mean $450. That's all I've got."

"Shit." Endo put down his fork and glanced at the folk on the next table, who gave no hint that his curse had put them out. "Kate, the max you can make on a short is whatever you put in. You want to put in $450, the most you make is $449.99, minus my commission, and that's if the share price drops to a penny. Villiers…" He pulled out his phone. He must have had a share-price app handy, as he came back with, "They're at ten bucks a pop. And twelve cents. That's forty-five shares. They tank completely, like liquidate, you're looking at doubling your money. They go down to a dollar, you make $400."

"After your commission," Kate said, already wondering where she could get her hands on more money. "It's shitty odds."

"Yep, two-to-one. Profit comes from volume. And value."

"It's not two-to-one, it's evens. You count your original stake when calculating odds. Put in ten bucks on evens, you get ten bucks back plus your ten you put in."

Endo returned a blank stare, but she wasn't bothered if he lacked interest. She was working out the implications, her diminishing options.

She'd all but maxed out her cards, and she still owed on the car. She could sell it for cash, some place they didn't check on outstanding credit, or borrow against the house. There was no mortgage. This was a long game play, in on the ground floor. Prove herself with this, stay away from addiction triggers like sports betting, and she was set for a better life than she'd imagined working herself to the bone with two jobs and night school to contend with. All she'd need was a bank willing to spot the cash to her in time to make the trade tomorrow.

"*If* I took the trade on," Endo said, virtually reading her mind.

"Why wouldn't you?" Kate asked.

"Because I don't want someone of your means to lose four hundred bucks that you clearly need. Again, no offence, but… am I wrong?"

"I can afford it." She made her face as hard as possible. "But you said you invest the firm's money too. You get a big cut. You'd go fifty-fifty on it—"

Her phone rang. She ignored it.

"Fifty-fifty on your bonus of—"

Endo put up a hand. "One step at a time. First, I see how you go. Second, I need to be confident there's nothing illegal going on. Third—"

The phone started up again.

Endo said, "You want to get that?"

"What's third?"

He waved her off. "No. Forget it. It's too dangerous. I am not risking Heth's money with this. Plus, if it's illegal, like a cleaner friend overheard someone at Villiers talking layoffs—"

"I have more friends than the cleaning fraternity."

She wasn't sure why that had caused her offence. More snobbishness? She thought of Tammy, who'd been a better ally to her this past year than anyone in White Plains. Except, maybe, Sal.

Endo raised a hand in apology. "Doesn't matter who. If it came from within the company, it's dodgy. If it's a guess, someone from outside, it's risky. Very risky."

Her phone rang yet again and this time she pulled it out. She'd guessed the caller from the first trill, but hadn't wanted to interrupt her flow. It was both their futures. Hers and Aaron's.

The school.

"I have to take this."

"And I have to go." Endo stood and signaled the waitress, pointed at the table and then at himself. "If you still want to go ahead, leave your number and email address on my desk but don't chat to me. I'll text you what I need, and I'll send you some paperwork. But make sure you want to take the risk. Because I'll be playing it safe all the way."

He departed and Kate answered the phone. The words from Hester Duval, the school's counselor, were almost identical to those earlier in the week: "Mrs. Mallory, I'm sorry to call you. Aaron is fine, but we need you to come in…"

Endo signed something on the waitress's pad. Kate hoped it was the check. But what followed on the phone was lost on her. She was already doing math in her head.

Gambling math. The sort professionals could perform on instinct.

"I'm sorry," she said at a pause in the other person's speech. "Could you repeat that? There's some background noise."

"We need you to come in immediately, Mrs. Mallory," the counselor with the gravelly voice said.

"I'm at work."

"That may be the situation, ma'am, but the Principal is a hair's breadth from calling the police this time. Please. How soon can you get here?"

CHAPTER THIRTEEN

This time, Kate had no qualms about slinking off early. Dev withdrew her overtime shift from the weekend, but she didn't much care. She almost quit on the spot. Almost. Convinced she'd be wealthy within a matter of weeks, she didn't need the friction until that boat came in. At the same time, she wasn't ready to dance out the door. She'd be cordial until the home-stretch dawned, but no longer saw a need to kiss the prince's bejeweled ass.

As she rode the train out of the city, she distracted herself from speculating about Aaron's offence by calculating that to double her money on something other than gambling was an acceptable return on investment. If Aaron were seeing the future, as she was starting to accept was impossible to deny, how many trades would she need to short through this one amount?

Exponential growth was fast, which was why accumulators rarely used that method. But it was a famous system at the roulette table.

Keep doubling your bet and you eventually come out ahead.

A dollar on black?

Whoo, you have two dollars.

Now put those two dollars on black again.

Whoo! You have four dollars.

Four dollars on black, please.

Red.

Boo. You're out a dollar.

But then here's where the beauty comes in. You take a further *eight* dollars of your own money—what you would have won on the last roll—it makes your outlay a nine-dollar bet in total, and you place that all on black.

Black comes in, you're up eight whole bucks.

Red, and you invest $16 to win $32. That's a $7 profit. Next, $32 on black...

Keep doing that—putting your bet on black or red, sticking with it all night long, covering your losses, then doubling what you lost—get lucky often enough and you double your money, or even more. Depending on your nerve. And a smattering of luck.

The key is knowing when to stop. If you're not lucky at least half the time, sure, you can lose money. But with a binary choice, it's sometimes worth the risk.

Shorting clearly wasn't like that. The risks were much bigger. But not with a sure thing. And although Kate's brain was still reluctant to accept Aaron's gift as reality, her gut ran with it free and clear.

Not quite doubling your money each time, minus a small commission.

Let's say 75% profit with every short trade. As discussed in Garbo's.

She was not great at complex math, but gambling math was something else. Multiplying, division, addition, subtraction. Get the algorithm right and she'd be sailing.

In her head, as the city outside her train sped by, she calculated the can't-lose profits:

$450 at low odds. A 75% profit on that left her with approximately $775.

With a $775 investment, it'd give her over $1300.

From $1300, she'd be looking at $2200.

She kept on going up to the point she broke the million-dollar mark.

"Fourteen trades," she said, then clamped her mouth shut. The train wasn't busy, but there were enough passengers around to stare at the crazy woman talking to herself.

Fifteen trades to touch two million.

Could she be home and dry in less than a month? Never have to work again and still live in comfort? Free to attend law school if she chose, without the baggage of holding down a job?

Assuming Aaron's talent didn't fade away.

No, that was too optimistic. She didn't believe there'd be one company every week unfortunate enough to shed 75% of its stock value. Not unless a new financial crisis or pandemic came hurtling around the corner.

Only, why stop at shorting? Why not go for the winners instead of the losers? Spread the money around. Go positive. That was where the "unlimited" profit came in.

She reined herself back.

One trade. Concentrate on that. Get this right. Be sure Aaron's gift doesn't suddenly run out of steam, but first…

Aaron.

…the Principal is a hair's breadth from calling the police this time…

What had he done? Was it him, an incident of his own making, or this notion he had to act out when the urge took him? That he was so taken by this gift that delivered knowledge on tap that every urge seemed to him like permission, a delusion his mother could not allow him to buy into.

Nothing she could do about it now. She had to be patient. Try to analyze it objectively. Once she saw the full picture.

She disembarked at her stop and headed for her car with feet that had trotted along as light as clouds this morning, now sucked down into mud. Her journey to the school was swift, and she was shown into the counselor's office—not the Principal's—less than an hour after hanging up the original call. Here, Aaron was sitting, dressed in his gym kit, hands in his lap, head bowed.

"Mrs. Mallory," Hester Duval said, rising from behind her desk.

The Principal, Mr. Grimes, was standing to the side. The whole setup seemed staged. They'd probably been made aware of her arrival and readied themselves for her.

"What is it?" Kate asked as she rushed over to Aaron and put her arms around him. He didn't acknowledge her. Barely moved. She noted both hands were curled into that weird ring-little-finger tangle. "What's wrong with him? What have you done?"

"Mrs. Mallory, we've done nothing," Grimes intoned. "But Aaron has gone too far this time."

"Too far? What do you mean 'too far'? He's ten. I'm assuming he hasn't stabbed someone or sparked up a crack pipe."

"Please sit down," Hester Duval said, her voice softer than normal. "We'll explain." As Kate found the chair beside Aaron, keeping hold of the boy's hand, the counselor added, "Or perhaps we should let Aaron explain."

Aaron maintained his coma-like position. Staring. His forefingers slowly pointed, then folded back, pointed again.

He was conscious, not drugged, as Kate had worried about for a fleeting second. The school couldn't do that.

Was he high?

Grimes didn't have the patience for an interrogation. "Mrs. Mallory, your son smeared his own, *hmm*, excrement on the bathroom walls. With his hands."

Kate's fingers tightened on the chair. "He what?"

"He strode into the girls' restroom, where he—in front of five female students—pulled down his, *hmm*, pants. And undergarments. He then squatted in the middle of the floor…"

Grimes bent his knees slightly.

"Reached around the back…"

Grimes mimed the motion, both hands forming a scoop behind him. Kate found it faintly ridiculous, almost humorous.

"Where he ejected a significant quantity of feces into his hands."

He bobbed in place and his hands jerked as if he'd caught a log. Kate had to physically restrain a smirk. He straightened and turned to the window overlooking the sports fields.

"Then, without pulling up his shorts, Aaron waddled over to the wall, and smeared said deposit on the walls and mirrors."

Again, Grimes mimed what he was describing. Then he faced Kate, hands clasped before him, dripping with imaginary poop.

"As you can imagine, Mrs. Mallory, *hmm,* those poor young ladies are quite traumatized."

"We got him to clean himself up in the showers," Hester said. "Luckily, he had his gym gear available. His soiled items are in a bag which you can collect or leave with us for disposal."

Kate's face warmed, but the rest of her iced over, killing

the nervous laugh that Grimes had stirred up. She fumbled for the right words. There were none. She could only look at her son, seeing not her sweet little boy, but a stranger wearing his face. A stranger that performed hideous acts whenever he exceeded expectations in class or at home.

"Were he more mature in the, umm…" Hester Duval struggled for the word.

"Pubic region," Grimes finished for her.

Do not smirk at that man.

"Yes," Hester said. "Were this a senior incident, we could be sitting here with the police, and Aaron might be facing an indecent exposure charge." Hester shaped her hands into a triangle, resting on the desk. "As it stands, we may still have to report this. *If* any of the girls' parents demand further action. Currently, we have no choice but to suspend him until we can be reasonably sure of this never happening again. My chief concern, though, is what led to this…"

Kate zoned the words out until the counselor sounded as if she were speaking from a box submerged in water. So far, Aaron had instigated some awful things, but they'd obviously been the kinds of urges all kids experience when stressed or upset. Slapping a classmate, tormenting precious pets when your mother entertains a daddy-replacement in the dining room, swearing at a grownup… But this? This took some serious thought. Planning, even.

How could he think it was something he had to do?

It signaled an escalation in terms of scale and the thought required. What would the next thing be? Smashing up a car with a bat? Setting fire to something?

Aaron plainly couldn't deal with the power he'd inherited.

And Kate couldn't handle the fallout. It'd be a disaster for their already tenuous living situation.

"I need help," she blurted out, cutting off whatever Hester was saying. Her throat had dried, almost closed, but as the confusion between Mr. Grimes' comedic earnestness and the shock of learning what Aaron had done started to ebb, her fingertips tingled and she needed… something. She had to *do* something. "I need a psychiatrist. Someone professional. No disrespect, but I think it… you know…"

Mr. Grimes nodded sagely. "It goes beyond the brief as well as the capability of a school counselor. Our feelings precisely. And I am glad to hear you are taking this seriously."

"Do you have a recommendation? Anyone who takes on troubled kids for free?"

Hester dropped her triangled hands and straightened her back. "Free? No, that's not something I can help with, I'm afraid." She slid a business card across the desk, evidently prepared ahead of Kate's arrival. "Dr. Parnell Patel is an excellent specialist. Normally, he deals with children who are a little older, matters of depression, anxiety, and other typical problems. But I have contacted him and he will see Aaron this afternoon for a discounted first session."

Kate accepted the card and held the little white rectangle in two hands. "Discounted? How much?"

"He typically charges $300 per hour, but he would speak with Aaron for two."

Kate almost said, "Two dollars? Bargain!" but refrained. She also withheld the hysterical jackal laugh brewing deep in her chest. Instead, she stood on legs that wobbled, pocketed the business card, and took Aaron's hand. She yanked him to his feet. Again, he didn't resist.

Kate bent at the waist, cupped Aaron's face in her hands and demanded, "Why?"

He blinked, flicking his fingers loose. Shook his head. His bottom lip quivered as it had the night of the fish-pissing.

"Why?" she said again, more forceful this time, dropping her hands to his upper arms.

"Mrs. Mallory?" Hester said.

Kate ignored her. "Just tell me, Aaron—WHY?"

"It's your fault!" he cried. "Making me say those scores. It's all *your* fault!"

"*Mine?*"

Aaron dragged himself away. "Ow! You're hurting me!"

Kate's right hand remained a flint-like claw, grasping for him. Her stomach sank. She'd been gripping him. *Too* tightly.

Aaron rubbed his arm.

Hester said, "Are you okay, Aaron?"

"Mrs. Mallory, if you cannot handle this without, *hmm*, physical discipline…" Mr. Grimes' implication was plain.

Kate shook her fingers loose. "No, it's okay. I'm fine. I… never use that. I…"

What could she say? What could she *do*?

"I'll take him to Dr. Patel," she said. "Would you let him know I'm on my way?"

CHAPTER FOURTEEN

The psychiatrist's assistant, who serviced three doctors in the prefab building, treated Kate's $200 in cash like a rare insect —both gross and on the verge of extinction. She emphasized what a massive favor Dr. Patel was doing in seeing them at such short notice, and advised her that most clients came outside of school hours, before sending them right on through.

$275 and counting.

They entered another waiting room. This one had two armchairs, a TV, and a corner full of colorful blocks, wire toys, figurines, and a bookcase stocked with reading material for younger kids. The next door opened, and a man in a suit with a squashed-looking face and square glasses stepped out. He appeared to squint as he greeted them, and spoke in a light Indian accent, evident only at the ends of words.

"Hello, I'm Dr. Patel." He peered down at Aaron. "You must be Aaron."

Aaron nodded.

Kate introduced herself and confirmed their appointment.

"You know how this works?" Dr. Patel said.

"No. I'm sorry, I've never been to a place like this."

"Okay." Dr. Patel ran through his method for this initial meeting, the first step being for him to chat with Aaron alone, while Kate occupied herself in the parents' room. To maintain confidentiality, she couldn't linger in the waiting area in case the next patient's family arrived. As in many places, there was a way in and a different way out.

She understood and told Dr. Patel to go ahead, reassuring Aaron it was okay to tell the nice man anything.

Aaron's dad once instructed him to have pride in himself, to search inside his soul for things that made other people happy, and to cling onto them. It wasn't showing off, Dad said, but truth. Acknowledging good parts of your own self was important. And Aaron had always been an honest boy. It was only in the past three weeks, since facts and answers started popping into his head, that he'd needed to lie.

White lies.

They're okay, Dad said. Like lying to Mom when they prepared a surprise party for her, or telling her she looked slim in a new dress when bits of her stuck out more than they did the previous time she wore it, or saying you couldn't remember why you smeared poop on a wall when you knew perfectly well why.

Telling her the truth would crush her. She was already on the verge of tears. If she knew exactly what Aaron was doing, and why, she'd lose it completely. She'd try to help, but that'd make things worse.

Was that last one a white lie?

Aaron wasn't sure if he was keeping it bottled up to protect her or himself.

"You can tell the nice man anything," Mom had said.

"Anything?"

"Even if you don't feel comfortable, or you're worried how I'll feel, it's okay. You won't be in trouble. It's his job to fix things like this."

Aaron wasn't entirely sure why he was here. He wasn't the one with the problem. It was Mom who pushed him to say things, so it was Mom's fault he'd had to do what he did. He just didn't want to make her feel bad about it. He wished he hadn't said it back at the school.

Now he was stuck.

He just hoped she didn't use the other things he'd revealed to her, otherwise she would be back here again pretty soon.

"So," Dr. Patel said, offering Aaron a place on a comfortable armchair. "What would you like to tell me?"

Aaron remained silent. But Mom had been adamant. This was Dr. Patel's job.

If it was his *job*, he would have to open his ears and take it in. And if he *could* fix things, that'd mean Mom wouldn't have to overreact and ruin it all…

"You really want to hear it?" Aaron said. "Like, all of it?"

"Everything that has happened at school lately, how you feel, what you think will happen next. Or anything else you wish to say."

So Aaron chose to take a risk. He opened up and told Dr. Patel everything that had happened at school. The only white lie he would use today was to be sure Mom didn't get into trouble.

Once alone, flicking through an interior design magazine without reading it, Kate replayed the image of Aaron smearing excrement across a bathroom wall on a constant loop. Occasionally, he'd turn to her and say, "This is *your* fault, Mom."

It was as if the prospect of her newfound luck had come up against a steel door, then been snatched away. The universe was trying to remind her, "Stop trying to better yourself. You're trailer trash and you always will be. Remember how hard law school was? How the other students treated you?"

No. I'd have seen it through. I could handle it.

"Was Aaron even an accident, Kate?" The universe's voice sounded like Jonathan now, things he'd only ever hinted at but was clear he meant. "*Was* he? Or did you diddle with your birth control? Was it an excuse to force your meal ticket to marry you and put off your education indefinitely?"

It wasn't like that.

"Mrs. Mallory." Dr. Patel was stood in his doorway alongside Aaron. "We're ready for you."

Aaron padded out and hugged her, and his smile seemed bright and genuine. But then, hadn't his regret appeared real when he manipulated her into letting him out of his bedroom? She didn't want to think he was acting again.

"We'll be quick, Aaron," Dr. Patel said. "Help yourself to books and magazines. Can I get you a juice?"

"No thank you, Dr. Patel," Aaron said.

Kate kissed him on the top of his head and entered Dr. Patel's office, where she took a seat on the couch as directed —not opposite the desk as she'd expected—and the psychiatrist opted for an armchair nearby.

He had no notes, or none he referred to. "Your son believes he has a friend. A 'buddy.' He cannot articulate the substance of this friend, but he believes he has to do things to appease him. Favors in exchange for help with certain problems."

"Yes." Kate recalled Aaron had tried to explain it that way

to her the previous night but had treated it like a metaphor. She didn't mention that, though. Didn't want to speak too much. They were on a clock here. "I just don't understand why."

"Tell me about Aaron's father."

Kate folded her arms over her stomach. "His father?"

"Aaron said he died. An allergic reaction. But there's more there, he says. He isn't sure it was an accident."

If she didn't need them so badly, Kate would have marched out of here and punched Jennifer in the face, then stomped on Jonathan's balls. She had never voiced such things around Aaron, not even with Sal, and only with Tammy when at work or on their way to a visit a psychic con artist.

"Craig was highly allergic to shellfish. It happened when we'd argued one night about... I'd been a gambling addict, and I slipped. He'd been ready to divorce me, fight for custody of Aaron. I'd begged him for another chance. Like, literally, on my hands and knees."

"You loved him?"

"Of course, yes. He took me back, but made it clear it was my final chance. If I went back on my promise, there'd be no more warnings. He paid for my rehab, took time out to look after Aaron while I was away, and said he'd give me whatever time I'd need. I went to meetings once a week at first, then every two weeks, and now it's every month, or... or whenever I feel the need."

"The need. To gamble."

Kate nodded. Wet her lips. Crossed her legs.

Dr. Patel took in each movement.

Kate fell still, motionless, wondering if she'd conveyed something in her fidgeting. Perhaps she should mention Aaron's odd tic, the finger thing, but he should have noticed that if it was important. Plus, it might suggest to him she was deflecting on her own body language and—

Damn. She hated analysis like this. People always over-thought shrinks.

"Anyway," she said, "when Craig took me back, things were good. Until, three months after rehab, I gambled. The bet landed, and I was so happy, he knew something was wrong. He got it out of me and walked straight out. Stayed in a hotel a few miles away. I was sure he'd be back, but he died in his room."

Kate withheld the tears, a knot in the middle of her throat. If she hadn't done what she did, Craig would never have been near that vending machine that supplied the tainted food. But this wasn't about her. This wasn't her session.

She elaborated to fill the silence. "It was a bag of potato chips with a tiny warning on it that he must have missed. 'Prepared in a factory that also handles seafood.' It must've got contaminated."

Dr. Patel had nodded throughout. "Aaron is aware of these circumstances. The details. Did you know that?"

"I talked it through with him. Explained how the accident happened."

"But there's speculation, no?"

Kate took a deep breath. "His life insurance thought it might have been suicide. Or even that foul play was involved. They tried to push that so they wouldn't have to pay out. Craig's brother fought them and won. We got the mortgage paid off, along with my credit card debt, and set up a trust for Aaron. It's not millionaire trust fund level, but it'll see him through college and maybe a few luxuries. A down payment on a house. I can't touch it."

Dr. Patel remained silent, still nodding as if she hadn't

stopped talking. When he ceased nodding, he asked, "Has Aaron ever brought this up?"

"Not with me."

"And this friend of his. What 'favors' do you understand him to be doing for Aaron?"

"Homework," Kate said, growing more concerned with the notion of Aaron turning his gift into an imaginary friend. "Test answers. But I just thought it was him. Inventing a reason for something he'd worked hard at."

Only now, Kate had two examples of unbelievable prediction. Was a spirit whispering to him more far-fetched than Aaron's brain mutating into a prediction portal?

"It is what we call imposter syndrome, Mrs. Mallory. When someone succeeds in a chosen field, it overwhelms them with fear. They don't believe they deserve it. Very common when, say, a struggling actor lands the lead role in a major movie. They've achieved something but worry they're not really good enough, that they don't deserve the success." Dr. Patel let that sink in. "The tests Aaron took, the schoolwork, yes. He passed them on his own. This imaginary friend, his 'buddy' as Aaron calls him, has been giving him answers, because Aaron doesn't consider himself worthy."

"Could it be Craig?"

"The boy's father? I don't believe so. If he were to be inventing the ghost of a deceased relative, he'd be more specific about it. No, these favors he does for his 'buddy', they manifest as feelings. Like he knows he has to do something, and that it results from the information. But he isn't hearing voices."

That jibed with what Aaron told Kate. Not a voice, but "like" a friend helping him.

Dr. Patel said, "It is a compulsion to act out. Because he doesn't want to disappoint you, he has to find something—or someone—else to blame."

Kate stared at the floor. It seemed Aaron hadn't mentioned the sports scores. "This is confidential, isn't it? Both me and Aaron?"

Dr. Patel spread his hands. "You can say whatever you choose."

Kate bit the inside of her mouth. "There's more."

"More?"

"He… His 'buddy', whatever it is, predicted a basketball game. We were talking, and he said it. Then he—"

Dr. Patel held up a hand to stop her. "Ah. Yes. He was rather proud of that."

So Aaron *had* spoken of it. Dr. Patel was waiting on Kate to bring it up. A test of sorts.

He stood and paced as he explained, "This is a more common delusion than you might expect. Psychic phenomena." He picked up a newspaper from his desk and folded it back to the sports section. "What was this prediction? That a team will win by X or more?"

"Yes," Kate said. "But—"

"Here." Dr. Patel showed her the paper, a local one with the victorious White Plains Wanderers pictured. "Take any ten games. Let's say basketball. I could tell you that every one of these games the home team will win by ten or more. In around half of those instances, I'll be correct. Drop that to *one* team. Aaron picks one at random. Say this one."

He tapped a fixture that Kate couldn't read.

"It's a fifty-fifty bet. Okay, a one-in-four chance. Either the home team loses by more than ten, or less than ten. Or, since a draw is almost impossible in basketball, the home team wins by more than ten or less than ten."

Kate saw the doc had precisely *nada* experience running the odds, so was waffling to make her feel better. Something to justify the impossible.

She said, "There were two games."

"Fine." Dr. Patel put the paper back on his desk. "What Aaron did, with two games, is a one-in-eight chance."

Actually, the odds are compound, so it's a one-in-sixteen, but that's only if the original supposition is true, and it isn't. Also—

Dr Patel said, "If he is really able to predict such things, why not the Lotto? Or the next Bitcoin?"

Forget it. Kate couldn't argue about odds or gambling. It was already whetting her appetite. Already making her yearn to get Aaron home, to access this buddy's bank of psychic energy and get stinking rich with minimal effort. If Aaron couldn't use his gift—if that's what it was—without resorting to abominable "favors" in return, he'd need a tutor to get through school. For that, she'd need money. And there was no extra money without access to that gift.

"I have seen imposter syndrome in many children," Dr. Patel said, retaking his seat. "But rarely in one so young. I can't determine with one session if it is to do with living up to the pedestal on which he has placed his father, or if he's just lacking confidence. I would like to see him twice a week, if you can manage that, Mrs. Mallory."

Kate uncrossed her arms, folded them again. "Twice a week? At $300?"

"For twice-weekly, we can work out a small discount. Perhaps $500 in total?"

"Two grand a month?"

Dr. Patel squint-smiled at her. Confirmation. "If Aaron is in therapy, it is possible the school will look more favorably on him returning to class."

Kate remained stoic, or thought she did. As in most situations where money was concerned, she said, "That should be okay. I'm sure I can arrange something."

. . .

On the way out, hand in hand with a more relaxed boy than the one she'd arrived with, Kate spun numbers around, forming a paradox. To get rich quickly, she needed Aaron to keep predicting things. Yes, she'd accepted the psychic gift as real, even if she needed a big dollop of faith to do so. But as a responsible parent, she had to forbid him from using his gift due to the appalling behavior that ensued. He couldn't handle the weight of it pressing from within, causing more problems than it solved. Curing him might cost more than facing the consequences.

After paying for that one session, she had enough to make a single car payment without scrounging more overtime. From here, to cover the doctor's bills, she would have to swallow her pride and ask Jonathan for what she would phrase as a loan, but would in fact be a handout—one he wouldn't expect her to repay—and Aaron would get the help he needed. Either from Dr. Patel or someone Jonathan insisted upon, which wouldn't be a bad thing.

Could she trust a man who bullshitted about gambling odds like that?

If she set Aaron on a steady keel at school, she'd work like a dog for the next two years, get a decent job, then work some more and, finally, take the bar. She'd be on a par with Jonathan and repay what she was sure he'd lend or give her in the short term.

After she made this month's car payment, she was already back to even, that holy grail of a drowning gambler, and that was only because she'd stepped over the precipice once. Easy to pull herself back in. All she had to do was remove the temptation.

At the car, she picked Aaron up and sat him on the hood, angled so their eyes were level. "Aaron."

"Mom."

She wasn't sure if he was mocking her or just being his

cute self. No matter. "Aaron, it seems obvious that you can't accept favors without you doing something bad."

"Yeah, but it was you, Mom. I tried to tell you—"

"Yes." She stayed calm. The calmest momma who ever lived. "It was my fault for pushing you. And I'm sorry for that. But if we can agree, me and you, that you will stop getting answers from… wherever they're coming from… then you won't do any of these awful things? No more incidents like today?"

Aaron said nothing for a long moment. "But if I fail at school, you'll be mad."

Kate summoned more patience. "What you have, it's like a superpower. And you must not use this power until you can stop doing bad things. Until you can resist those urges. Promise?"

He gave that shrug again, the one that infuriated her because it was such a non-answer.

Still, the world's calmest momma kept her cool. "Nothing bad will happen. *I'll* help you not fail. How about I study with you? I'll be your buddy instead. And I won't make you do bad things."

He thought for a moment, then broke out into a grin. "Okay, I can try."

"Great." She helped him down and opened the door. "You have another letter to write, though. Five, actually. Plus one to the Principal."

Not that she expected a letter would lift the suspension. It might fend off an appalled parent reporting him to the police, though.

Aaron pouted as he secured himself on his booster seat.

Kate closed the door and pressed her hand on the roof. Her forehead rested on the hand.

She'd been here before. Swearing off her vice. Meaning it. Completely and utterly meaning it, but…

One more. Just one more to top herself off. Then it was over. Then she'd be done with it forever and ever, amen.

Aaron had promised never to use his gift, not until he got it under control. And since she'd already pried one more prediction from him, one he'd voiced so couldn't take back...

This last gamble. But it had to be worth her while. And $275 would not cut it.

PART TWO

AIN'T EVEN GAMBLING

CHAPTER FIFTEEN

The morning saw Aaron dropped at the J-Js' house at eight a.m., where Jonathan had already departed for the city. Jennifer expressed to Kate what a lovely suit she was wearing, although it was hard to tell if Jennifer was pleasantly surprised or if it was a *good-girl-for-trying* pat on the head.

"Interview," Kate told her, rushing to kiss Aaron goodbye.

"Well, the best of luck," Jennifer said. "I'll be at your place when you're home."

There was no need to explain the circumstances again. Last night, after a fortifying glass of wine (the grape: "white"), Kate had jumped on a video call with the pair and trudged through the issues concerning Aaron, playing up the notion of family being key to his recovery. His shocking behavior was "a delayed stress reaction to Craig's passing"— that was Kate's line. They accepted it studiously and without obvious judgement, far more understanding about Aaron than they were about a faintly stale smell in Kate's hallway. Kate attributed their sympathy to the fact Jonathan had suffered similar grief triggers of his own.

She didn't tap them up for the loan-gift just yet, instead dropping a further lie about the Principal waiting on the psychiatrist's report before he'd allow Aaron back on school property. In truth, she had no idea when they'd lift his suspension, but she needed to show them—Jonathan in particular—a plan of sorts.

She'd lied a bunch of times lately, trying to stay afloat in their eyes. Too many lies. She hoped she wouldn't have to continue much longer.

On the morning trek to Manhattan via car and rail, she felt different. Lighter. Not lighter like yesterday, driven by the euphoria of beating the bookie. But with her hair down, makeup applied, and a loose-fitting designer suit, she met the eyes of her fellow commuters, sitting tall in her seat. Someone even held a door for her on the way into the tower block housing Hetherington Brokerage and Bonds.

On 41, she texted Endo that she'd arrived, and he told her to walk up to their floor. Once there, Endo gave her the same up-and-down look she'd received from Jennifer, bobbed his eyebrows in approval, and ushered her to what the staff here called a "pod," which amounted to glass sheets walling off a table and three chairs, a computer, and the words *Consultation Zone 4* stenciled on the door. This was number four of eight such pods.

Inside, Endo positioned her with her back to the through traffic, although Kate doubted anyone other than her own colleagues would recognize her. Endo sat opposite and called up the prep work they'd put in, having set up her account information last night via Kate's phone. "Just need your ID for scanning."

Kate presented her driver's license, passport, and two utility bills, which Endo placed flat on the table. He used an app on his cell phone to scan each item.

"Better than the flatbed scanner," he said when Kate's

brow furrowed. He tapped the phone a few times and the .jpg files ported over to the computer. After checking the quality, Endo hit confirm. "We're good to go."

"Villiers Media Group," Kate said. "We short it, we make some money."

"Kate." Endo laced his fingers together and pulled his chair in closer. "We do a credit check on all our clients. You have an outstanding car loan of $12,000, four canceled credit cards with zero balance and one low-interest one almost maxed out, and therefore no reliable credit history. And you only have $250 and change in a checking account."

Kate had deposited the money into her account; Hetherington's didn't take cash. "Yes, but that's still a lot of cash for me."

"Heth doesn't mess around. I'm doing you a huge favor here, and I'm not even sure why."

"Because I'm nice?"

"Probably, yeah." He slouched, eyes averted. "But there are things I can't skip out on. Our commission is two percent or $50, whichever is higher. You're investing $200, not two-fifty. And if Villiers doesn't tank in a few days—"

"It will."

Endo pushed his glasses up his nose. "How can you be certain?"

Kate watched him a moment and caught a flicker of curiosity. Before, he'd been adamant it was a bad idea, and downright suspicious of her. "What's changed?"

"What do you mean?"

"I mean, you rejected this idea yesterday. Now you're interested, I can tell."

Endo hunched over again, fingers tapping. He thinned his lips, seemingly reluctant to share what he was thinking. "Okay. I made some calls. You remember how we start out a short trade? We borrow from either our existing clients, another broker, or the company's available shares."

"Right."

"I looked at borrowing from the market. Forty shares. Just probing about the possibility. And they were... weird about it."

"Weird how?"

"Like the guys I spoke to... they knew something. Like you know something."

Kate crossed her legs and squared her shoulders. "I have no contacts that can be traced to the firm, or me. None of the information I have is proprietary. It's my decision. $400 might be a meal or a cheap shirt to you, but it's a car payment, a month of frozen food, or a whole new wardrobe covering the next two growth spurts for Aaron. My son, by the way."

"Fine." Endo worked the computer, pulling in files and some accounting program. He opened four new windows and spent the subsequent three or four minutes setting up the trade.

"That's more work than I expected," Kate said, growing bored.

"Yeah." Endo stared at the screen, his finger on the mouse.

"What are you waiting for?"

"I must be crazy."

"Why?"

Endo craned to see the trading floor, then resumed tapping the mouse—a fidget rather than clicking anything on the computer. "It's worse than I let on." Perspiration dotted his brow. "I'm hanging onto this job by a thread. But a big win like this would pull me back in."

Kate saw his dilemma. "And a loss will tip you over the edge."

142

"Screw it." He clattered several keys, then hit the mouse. "Ten million bucks. Gone."

Ten million…

"Of your money?" Kate asked.

"Hetherington's. The short comes in, it's a 10K bonus." Endo sat back in the chair, exhaled as if he was about to light up a cigarette. He laughed—a touch hysterically.

He was desperate, Kate realized. She'd taken advantage of a drowning man, and he'd trusted her word based on nothing more than the confidence with which she delivered it. If she had been willing to bet her entire minuscule net worth on this, why not a final Hail Mary to end or boost his career?

She didn't have the heart to tell him she'd bet far more than a career before, and lost.

The computer made a dull beep.

Endo's nervous, clown-like smile turned into a frown. He sat forward and hit some buttons. Clicked the mouse. "Oh, no. No, no, no." He craned again to see into the main floor and groaned. "Oh, crap, no. Keep facing me unless you can't help it."

"Why?"

The pod's door opened and a plume of cologne wafted in. Mervin Corney stood behind Kate. From the corner of her eye, she saw he'd chosen his usual hands-to-hips stance.

"Ten mil? Really, Endo?" Merv said.

"It's a safe trade," Endo replied, standing to even up the eye lines. Some power play, no doubt, learned on one course or another; don't be smaller than your opposite number. "The traders are skittish, our new client is putting her own money in. I'm confident."

Merv said nothing for several loud, nasal breaths. "Client?" He came inside and assessed Kate. His eyes narrowed. "Have we met?"

She felt like Clark Kent without a set of thick-rimmed

glasses, only for her the disguise was a mop and tabard. "No. And I was busy."

Merv held up his hands. "Sorry, madam, but Endo is one of our junior brokers. He's on something of a probation. We don't let him play with funds over one million."

"Why wasn't I made aware?" Endo said.

"I took the decision last night when I saw your numbers. Anything over a mil flags for approval. From me." Merv had a swagger about him, half-nodding to every sentence he uttered. He turned his hips to Kate. "Endo should introduce us. I'll take care of anything in this territory."

"She is my client," Endo said. "I brought her in."

Merv patted the air, the universal "calm down" gesture. "And if this bears fruit, I'll trust you with our prime clientele again. For now, calm your tits and I'll take care of... I'm sorry, I didn't get your name."

Kate blanched, cold sweat pressing from under her skin. It hadn't broken through yet, but soon would—a bad bluffer at the card table realizing she was about to lose the farm.

Confidence. She had to show confidence. *She* was the client, after all. Her poker bitch face should suffice.

"Actually," she said, "I'd prefer to deal with Endo. He impressed me enough to bring my business here."

Merv's head tilted. "And where are you bringing your business from? Which firm?"

Shit.

"I'd rather not say," Kate answered curtly. "It's not your concern and, frankly, if you don't let Endo complete this transaction, I'm of a mind to go elsewhere." Her cheeks flushed, hearing her own voice, a faux-Britishness inflecting her tone. "Now, please, do what you have to do, and—"

Merv did a weird shimmy and suddenly, he perched himself on her side of the table, his smile so slimy he could have pulled it from a fish tank with a damaged filter. He grinned. Reached for Kate.

She pulled back.

He said, "Ah-ah, gimme one second." He put both his hands on her face, then swept back her hair. "Ah, man!" He laughed, full-on and throaty. He let her go and hopped down, pacing a circle. Jabbed a finger at Endo. "This is why you're hemorrhaging cash, is it?" He hitched his trousers up over what Kate was sure was the start of a gut. "Banging the cleaning staff instead of your hot boyfriend?"

Endo fired a quick, annoyed glance at Kate. "I'm not banging anyone. Just— She was asking me something, and I was being polite. It won't affect the Bolton thing."

Merv gave Kate a short, sharp sneer and tilted his head in the direction of another member of the cleaning personnel, heading into the ladies' room. "How about you get out of here and get on with making our toilets look nice? Leave the real work to the professionals."

"I have money to invest," she said, "and I aim to invest it. And if you listen to Endo, your company will make a mint."

"No." Merv strutted toward Endo, and nudged him out of the way, ignoring the junior broker's "hey" and signing onto the computer with his own credentials.

"What are you doing?" Kate said.

"It's a good call," Endo insisted, his voice a little whiny. Almost pleading. "I'm sure of it."

"Villiers is trending up," Merv said. "You're not shorting it with Heth's money. In fact..." He grinned, fingers clattering the keyboard with a flourish. "I just blocked your stupid-ass punt. And disabled Mrs. Mallory's account. Now get out. No one is playing dumb-fucks today."

Kate sat there for a moment. When Endo shuffled for the door, she stood. Kept her face neutral. She wouldn't give

Merv the pleasure of seeing her defeated. She turned crisply and strode for the exit. But Merv had one final dig.

"Endo?"

Endo paused. Kate waited beside him.

Merv said, "You got until the end of the week to get back the right way up, or I'll be recommending to management they let you go."

Kate wanted to help Endo more than she wanted the $200 investing. "Will one million help? You can play that yourself, without this asshole blocking it."

"No," Merv answered for him. "Because *this asshole* put the ten mil on a long trade with Villiers. You couldn't short your minimum hourly wage against them now."

Endo let the door close behind them, heading for the elevators.

"Is that it?" Kate asked. "It's over?"

"No one at Hetherington's can make the trade." Endo's jaw had tightened, his pace stiff and quick. "I might know a way around it. And you can keep your two hundred bucks. But this just got a *lot* riskier."

CHAPTER SIXTEEN

"I know a firm who'll take us on," Endo said, leading her out of the elevator and across the lobby floor, and pushing through the revolving doors to the street where he waited for Kate. "I'll use my money. I have a couple of hundred thou from a good run last year. But I need to see something from you too."

"What like?"

"Like more than $250. I need to be sure this is real, and not some punt. I want you to take the same risk as me."

Kate wondered if she'd been speaking Swahili for the past half-hour. "I told you I don't have that kind of money. I'd have to re-mortgage the house for—"

"I don't mean the amount," he said, patting the air for calm. "I mean, an equivalent risk. Because if this fails, I'm out of a job and out of a place to live."

"Seriously, Endo, you don't have to do this."

He pointed up in the approximate direction of Hetherington's. "He's hobbled me on purpose. Only way I can get back on top is with some serious stakes. A lot of them if I'm going to win with million-dollar trades, which is nothing in *this* world. Pocket change."

They speed-walked, dodging pedestrians, and once they arrived at a spot Endo decided upon, seemingly at random, he held out his arm for a cab.

"Where is this place?" Kate asked.

"Five minutes by car."

"*What* is it?"

"Smaller firm. My college roommate set up on his own. Wanted me to join him. He had a bunch of us interested from back then, so he's probably got less than ten guys working with him. But I figured it was safer going with a big organization and a 401K."

The first cab glided by without slowing.

Kate said, "What's the minimum buy in? Because I doubt I can come up with that much by lunchtime."

Endo twisted the top half of his body to her. "I dunno. Usually 10K. Plus, if you're committed to it, I'll cover it. You'll get a cut of my profit on top of your own."

Kate recalled when she'd originally spoken to him this week, how he'd seemed so timid, so broken. He'd been all but cowering. Later, he'd cowered for real, hidden behind his desk, and appeared ready to run for the hills at any hint the authorities might sniff an impropriety. Now he was bracing to burn down his once-secure job, to trust a woman she barely knew. He was going to make a fortune, and he'd promised to share it, except...

He didn't have to. He could withdraw that offer at any time, and Kate didn't know this guy, not really. If he'd transformed from a dripping beta player to this alpha dog go-getter in mere days, what would several hundred thousand dollars look like to him? Especially if his conservative, safe job got blown to dust. Bringing her own capital didn't just sound inviting suddenly; it sounded essential.

She said, "I'm assuming your friend won't spot me credit?"

"He doesn't know you and, no offense, but I don't either. I can't vouch for you without some goodwill." Endo rubbed his finger and thumb together, the universal gesture for money. "He'll need you to have cash in the broker's account."

"Ten thousand?"

Endo nodded. "Honestly, now. Do you have something hidden away? Something you can use?"

"No. And I only know one way I can get it fast enough." Kate stepped out into the road, almost into the path of a yellow cab. It halted, and the window wound down. She leaned in. "Can you take us to Queens?"

"Queens?" Endo said, climbing in. "What's in Queens?"

Ollie Swag. *That's* what was in Queens. Along with something, some*one*, a glow inside Kate she'd thought had blinked out forever. There was no hesitation in her actions here. No doubt. It was perfect.

On the verge of financial freedom.

One bold investment.

Couldn't lose.

She found Ollie Swag at Buckeroo Brandies for early hours, where they served sausage and egg on the approximation of a muffin, dripping with cheese and barbecue sauce, a popular choice with the half-dozen patrons. He'd taken a bite from the second half of the concoction with surprisingly little spillage, pausing when he clocked her marching ahead of Endo toward him. Having been dropped on the street, at least she didn't have to view his gross, lime-green car in the lot; she'd make do with his gross face instead.

"Katie-Kat." His smile contained shreds of sausage as he

149

lifted his coffee mug. "Gonna gimme a chance to win my pride back?"

"You do loans."

"My *boss* does loans. I do the admin. *They* collect on folk who don't repay on time."

He dipped his mug toward two men with shaggy hair and shiny tracksuits, one with a chunky gold watch, the other playing a game on his phone. They looked exactly like characters who broke legs in lieu of keeping up with repayments.

"Why, Katie? Whatcha need from ol' Ollie?"

"Ten grand. Now, please."

Ollie's face lit up, mouth forming an "O" ready to chortle and slap his thigh like an ostentatious vaudeville player, but Kate stepped into his personal space.

"I'm not in the mood and I'm on a clock. Can you get me the cash or not?"

Ollie's humor died, and he nodded behind her. "He pressuring you, Katie-Kat? Because I got guys who don't like that sorta thing."

He meant Endo, who hadn't stopped glancing around since they entered. It was like he'd shrunk in the minutes after leaving the cab, insisting on accompanying her. She thought it was sweet, although if anyone in here tried something physical, he'd be as much use as a lump of butter against a blowtorch.

"Well?" Kate said. "Can you or not?"

"You better be sure, Katie." Ollie took out his little computer tablet, called up an app, and pecked at it with his stylus. "And we're electronic these days. Blockchain, digital currency, borderless accounts. It's all the rage."

"I get it today?"

"Seconds after you sign."

Kate studied the offered pad—a simple agreement, Ollie's transaction merged into a form stating the loan and the interest payments building over time.

"Read it carefully," he said. "I mean it. Carefully."

Ollie Swag was predominantly a good-natured drunk/slob/sexist pig, and although he came across as cantankerous with the tact filter of a caffeinated toddler, he wasn't usually violent by nature. His transactions with Kate spoke to that. It was well known he only resorted to collection agents after all avenues were exhausted, but one rumor stood out.

A man in his forties, a military veteran of two conflicts, had borrowed money to pay for an operation on his back. When his recovery lasted longer than expected and he lost his job, Ollie had no choice but to dispatch people to remove goods of equivalent value from the vet's home—a mistake the pair would long remember into their own convalescence, a period of time notably more prolonged than the injured military man. The loanee, it turned out, wasn't just some grunt, but a Navy SEAL who, even operating at 25% physical strength, handled himself laudably and with justifiable force. Once he returned to 50% capacity and the loan had ballooned to 700% the original amount, he paid Ollie a visit to hand over his initial stake and negotiate the interest owed. It didn't go well, and in the scuffle, Ollie's Trans Am suffered a broken window and a scratched wing.

No one knew precisely how Ollie wrangled it, someone suggesting he took on the debt himself, but after a second appointment to his home, this time by four heavies visiting from Florida, the military veteran was reduced to a worse state than before his operation and, as far as anyone knew, would never leave his wheelchair.

As Kate put the rumor mill to one side and read the terms—carefully—an electrical charge flowed through her.

The thrill. The old tug of certainty. About to hit it big, big, BIG!

Sure, it was at Endo's insistence that she shared the danger of losing everyone, but the faith in her son's ability only strengthened. $10,000 to bring home a bounty. Enough to last several months, even if Endo stiffed her on his bonus. If he didn't go back on what was ultimately a verbal agreement without witnesses, she'd be good to quit. Able to concentrate on her studies for a year or so. No need for Aaron to access his gift, not until he wrangled that other compulsion under control, and Kate would revisit her meetings and never, ever gamble again. This was it.

The big one.

Ten big ones.

She didn't have to do it, though. She was already back to even.

"Katie-Kat," Ollie said, offering the stylus. "Repay quick, or you won't be able to afford it. I promise."

Her fingers accepted the stylus, unable to hide the tremble.

"I won't enjoy takin' your car," Ollie went on. "Plus whatever else the interest builds to." He waited. "*Katie.*"

Kate looked up at him.

"Katie-Kat, you know I like you. Not in a sleazy way." He made the jerk-off gesture again. "I mean, yeah, in a sleazy way, but not *just* in a sleazy way. You're a good woman. Whatever you need this for, it ain't worth losin' everything over. Sign, and you owe 12K next time we speak."

The floor tilted. Kate's head swam, then swooped like a fairground ride, and she couldn't have said where the grin that broke on her lips came from. Gun to her head, she'd have translated it as pure pleasure; the danger, the prospect of greater reward, the nostalgia for winning.

"You don't pay that back in full, it's fifteen the week after.

Then it gets serious 'cause the week after that, you're in for thirty-K, and your car's ours. Then sixty after that. Keeps on building, Katie-Kat."

"I'll have it for you Monday," Kate said, and signed her name.

CHAPTER SEVENTEEN

As promised, Kate's banking app showed her $10,000 to the good less than a minute after Ollie transferred the funds. He'd done so with a gray tinge to his skin, as if he were certain Kate had dug a grave in which she'd lie, rotting, by the end of the month. Maybe he really did like her in a non-sleazy way.

Didn't matter. Mission accomplished. She had her seed money.

Relieved at her demonstration of faith in the short trade, Endo again promised he'd share his return, adding the usual condition "if" it came in. It would, she'd assured him. She wouldn't have signed Ollie's contract if she'd had any doubt.

They returned to Manhattan and proceeded to a low-rise office building full of insurance firms, tech startups, and Marcus LaRoe's fledgling brokerage on the fifth floor, Versatile Ventures.

It had a staff of two in a space large enough for twenty, so empty it looked like this whole level was prepping for a refurbishment. They crossed the linoleum floor toward four well-equipped desks, much like Endo's, in a squared-off section near the corner made to look like a professional setup. It reminded Kate of a film set, where the camera would frame only a small section of the stage. Once in this alcove, she noticed TV screens covering one wall, full of financial channels from around the world.

As they entered his radius, one of the two workers—a bald black man with shoulders as wide as a minivan and hands like shovels—jumped to his feet. "Endo! So great, man!"

Endo took a step back as the bear hug loomed. "Geez, Marcus, you've…" He waved a finger up and down at Marcus's impressive physique.

"Two hours a day," Marcus said, slapping his abdomen. "Cardio for one hour before I start, weights for an hour when I get done. And keto." He pointed at Endo's gut. "Look up ketogenic diet when you go home. In a month, you'll thank me, seriously."

Endo put a hand on his own stomach and looked down. "Umm, this is Kate. We're hoping you can help us with a transaction."

"What are you standing there for?" Marcus lunged and wrapped his arms around Endo, and the pair bro'd it out with backslaps and some weird fist-bump-handshake combo and a healthy portion of bonhomie laughter. Then Marcus led him toward what he plainly expected to be the seeds of an empire—significantly fewer than Endo's estimate of ten guys. "That's Chuck," he said, meaning the skinny kid working a station. "Intern. Works good. I throw him a bonus now and then."

"When a big one comes in?" Endo said.

Marcus shrugged in reply. "We started trading in penny stocks too. Building up slow but steady. You ever trade with crypto? Virtual currencies?"

"Sure." Endo scanned the setup, lips parted, thoughts

whirring behind his eyes. "This is it? You were expanding last time."

Marcus clapped Endo on the back. "Slow, but steady. Profit every day. No matter how small, it's a win. Right?"

"Sure."

Kate kept back. It wasn't easy to stay silent, not when ten grand smoked and smoldered in her account, begging to be spent, to be *invested*. This wasn't her world.

"All these virtual currencies," Marcus said, showing Endo an oversized screen full of line charts. "Look at 'em. Up, down, up, down."

"That's worth thirteen cents," Endo said.

"Yep." Marcus sounded proud. "Find one with an upward trend in the morning, like this one at 0.001135 dollars." He pointed at something called SafeGalaxy trending at +22.56% with a green wavy line. "It moved up two decimal places last week, that's over 1000%. Lotta guys like me got rich on that one. I missed the big leap, of course, but I'll slap half a mil on it now it's steady, then sell before the bell. Most times, we pick up a few thousand dollars. Might play it again the next day, too. But, man, pump-and-dump crypto, it's pretty safe. Small potatoes compared to Hetherington's, but it keeps me in hookers and cocaine."

Big laugh between the pair.

Marcus focused on Kate. "Joke. I'm clean. And not an asshole."

The intern, Chuck, glanced up at that. "He's right. He's not an asshole." Then he went back to his work.

"So what do you have for me?" Marcus asked. "Sounded very secret agent. You thinking of jumping ship? Joining me on the ground floor? Because I gotta show you my five-year plan. It's awesome. This is just the start. I'm investing in tech and app startups, too. You see the change in name? Versatile

Ventures. Great alliteration, and I already found a couple of beauties—"

"I need you to open two brokerage accounts," Endo said, an injection of assertiveness blooming. "We'll drop some capital in there right away, and then I want you to short Villiers Media Group before noon. Can you do that?"

"You want to be a client, not a partner?" Marcus emanated a sad aura, the bro-ness seeping from him.

Endo took in the screens, the intern, the view of a city in shadow. He smiled at his former roommate, body language already relaxing yet pumping up—a shark with a full house trying to underplay his hand. "I'm thinking of making a change. Taking a few chances."

Marcus looked past Endo to Kate, studying her for a moment. "Shorting a big company like that… It's…"

"If I hear the word 'risk' again, I'll barf," Kate said.

Marcus wasn't deterred. "You need to think about it."

Kate placed her hands loosely behind her back. "I have."

"I'll set up the account, add your money as collateral, but… take twenty-four hours. Both of you. A cooling-off period. Something as risky as that. It's making *me* nervous. I'd hate to—"

"Do this for me," Endo said. "If the horse comes in, we'll talk about me leaving Hetherington's and buying a stake here. Me and you. Together again."

Marcus beamed and stood and pulled Endo into another bro-hug, before breaking away. "In that case, let's get to work."

After Marcus took care of business, transferring her ten thousand into the brokerage account as collateral and executing the trade, Kate didn't know what to do with herself for the rest of the day. She was too tense to go home and relieve Jennifer of her sitting duties early, knowing she'd ignore Aaron in favor of scrutinizing CNN financial bulletins and wherever else might report the plummeting share price of a major digital media company.

With Endo at a similar loose end, she'd asked him to show her around, educate her a little about what to expect. He said he didn't have that much access, so it'd basically be a lecture while they munched sandwiches on a park bench. And, besides, he'd promised to do lunch with Marcus. He invited Kate to join them, but she detected such scant enthusiasm she put on a brave face and said she'd prefer to play tourist within the Wall Street district.

"I've lived in New York so long," she'd declared in a chipper tone she didn't recognize, "I never have time to do the fun stuff."

She tagged onto a Wall Street tour, along with a small but diverse group of foreigners, for a service she'd been vaguely aware of since getting her job in the area, which promised to disclose "many inside secrets of the world of preeminent financial institutions." There wasn't exactly a slew of "secrets," only a brief history of the financial crisis of yesteryear, how the coronavirus pandemic decimated stocks before the government somehow created money out of thin air to prop them up, and Kate tuned out much of the aftermath. She helped several people take photos next to, and draped over, the iconic bull statue, and also on the steps of NYC's Federal Hall under George Washington's watchful eye.

While she got to see plenty of the history and functionality of the district, little of interest, or anything that empowered her to decide the future, cropped up.

She sloped off early and found Endo had already arrived at their rendezvous: Goldilox, a cocktail bar popular with what Endo called the "less affluent" employees of Wall Street.

The prices on the specials board and the plush decor made her wonder what "less affluent" meant in this world.

Endo was perched on a barstool, much like a hygienic Ollie Swag, and when he saw her he raised a glass of something milky and brown and full of ice. His grin was a drunk one.

"Where have you been?" he called over the sedate music —inoffensive pop tunes. Kate hadn't caught the artist.

She now noticed Marcus lounged next to him with an identical drink and an equally inebriated happy face. "You guys been here since lunchtime?"

"You haven't heard?" Marcus sounded astonished.

"No," Kate said, checking her watch. "It's not even three-thirty."

"You were waiting for the bell?" Endo said, and the pair chuckled at her obvious stupidity. Alcohol, it seemed, turned Endo into a bit of a dick. "No, no, it's all happening. Look."

He gently bumped her at the elbow, pointing with his drink at a TV screen tuned to a news channel.

"It's not just a stock tumbling," Marcus said, signaling the bartender. "It's a massacre."

The program wasn't simply a finance channel with a ticker tape of + and - next to long numbers, but a main news bulletin. People in suits and ballistic vests were leading smartly dressed men and women in handcuffs from a building somewhere in New York City. Crowds lined the route to the waiting vehicles, gawking at the operation. The strap line at the bottom of the screen read:

FBI Raids Villiers Media Group

Beneath the headline, the details kept changing. Currently:

Villiers board arrested in international money-laundering scandal

"I don't know how," Marcus said, presenting Kate with a fresh brown, milky drink, "but you did it. The prices dropped like a stone, and I covered the losses before the lawyers came in to shore it up."

Kate sipped the booze; creamy, heavy on Kahlua. "Does that mean…"

"It means you're up almost $9000," Endo said. "Plus ninety from my cut."

Kate couldn't take it in. Not yet comprehending the math, but she knew that was short. "You're giving me ninety dollars? That's—"

"Ninety-*thousand*, Kate." Endo leaned on her, eyes wide with glee. "What we agreed. As soon as my funds clear, you earned *ninety-thousand dollars*."

Marcus slung his arm around Endo. "And I get a new partner." He added quickly, "*Junior* partner."

This was it. Finally. The **ONE BIG WIN** she'd always dreamed of.

Despite her car waiting when she got off the train, Kate took a long, slow drink, and joined the boys in celebration.

CHAPTER EIGHTEEN

Home. Unsure of her blood-alcohol level, Kate pulled into her driveway beside Jennifer's compact SUV. Only two drinks, and she'd sobered up—or felt she had—with a large coffee on the train.

Ninety-nine thousand dollars. So close to an even hundred.

What would it take to top that off to five zeroes? Achieve that milestone? Could some of Marcus's penny stocks or those volatile virtual currencies pull her up?

It wasn't necessary. With *almost* one hundred thousand dollars, she wouldn't be buying a yacht, but she could quit her weekend gig, and maybe even her main cleaning job. Live off the windfall while she pursued full-time study. Once she had enough credits and some interning, she'd land a part-time paralegal or secretarial position to prop up her living expenses.

After tax.

She was sure there'd be tax to pay.

Until she found an accountant to minimize that, she'd

play it safe. No more investments. No risking Aaron's delicate grasp on reality, using his gift to feather their nest.

It was enough.

Inside, Jennifer was waiting with her bag and coat and a red, bee-stung smile. Kate had texted to say she'd be home early. Jennifer seemed shorter today, the makeup unremarkable.

"Aaron is playing out back," Jennifer said. "How did your interview go?"

The chit-chat zone.

"I got somewhere," Kate said, holding her distance in case the alcohol tinge overrode the coffee. "I won't be cleaning toilets much longer."

"That's *won*-derful news." Jennifer reached and touched Kate's hands but took them back without the full-on hug which seemed about to land. "What's the job?"

Telling the truth wasn't possible. Not yet. Too many questions. Too close to falling at a bookie's mercy. Another lie wouldn't hurt.

Kate said, "I'm going to be a trader's assistant. A bit of admin, some auditing, that sort of thing." She did not understand what that meant and hoped Jennifer didn't pry too deeply.

She didn't, preferring to pretend she'd just remembered something. "Oh, and I gave it a quick spruce up in here. Couldn't find Aaron's apple core, or whatever it is, though."

Kate hadn't realized, but the place did look cleaner. Some of the clutter from Aaron's toys was gone, too. The musty smell remained. A deep cleaning company would sort that, now she had the funds.

"Thank you, Jennifer, that's very kind." Kate opened the door for her. "Hopefully, I'll have a little more time after I settle into my job."

Jennifer patted her again as she passed. "Yes, me too.

Now Jonathan is officially a partner, I won't have to work quite so hard, either."

She didn't need to remind Kate. Everyone who knew the couple had heard the story: A big case won shortly before Craig died; his firm successfully counter-suing thanks to Jonathan unearthing documents that proved a bribe to an elected official; a deferment of his coronation due to Jonathan's loss, because he figured celebrating was in poor taste. In the end, he probably did deserve it.

"He has *three* secretaries," Jennifer added. "Did you know, I was like his paralegal when he worked from home?"

Kate did know. Everyone Jennifer met knew. She rarely failed to mention something along those lines. Kate hoped Jennifer enjoyed her semi-retirement.

"It's like *my* big break too," Jennifer said with exactly the amount of humility Kate expected: *Kate delivers good news for a change and Jennifer has to bludgeon her back into place with a better slant on her own life.* "It's like we've both made partner."

Okay, you win. You're still way better than me. Congrats.

Kate nodded absently. "Aaron's out back, you say?"

"Absolutely, yes, you must be itching to tell him the good news."

Looking out of the kitchen window over her garden, Kate poured herself a glass of water. She had never lost the glow inside when she watched Aaron playing, unaware of eyes upon him. There was something so pure about it as he fiddled with something, his back to her.

She wondered if a gardener would cost too much. No need to rely on Sal anymore. But as she gulped her water, she worried he might see it as a rejection, should she cut him off completely. He was a friend, after all, not merely someone useful to keep around.

She wasn't a person who'd use another for the sake of using them. Not at heart, anyway. However, she was unsure about maintaining a platonic friendship with a man who'd asked her on a date. It was unclear if he'd invested himself in her that way, or if he was just probing.

She'd wondered *what if* plenty of times with a few men since Craig, including Sal, prospects who weren't floating her boat at that moment but might, if given the chance. She was too old for love-at-first-sight nonsense.

Perhaps Sal deserved a chance.

Aaron stood from where he'd been playing, trying to control a sheet of black plastic—an empty garbage bag. Kate's first instinct was to worry; a child messing with a plastic bag always flashed a danger sign. But he was ten. He knew how to handle an object like that without suffocating himself.

Still, he struggled to get it under control in the breeze as he jogged toward the house. Kate rinsed the glass and made her way out to the deck.

Halfway down the stairs to the lawn, she noted Aaron wasn't headed back inside. He crept on all fours beside a length of lattice wood that he'd pulled from the side of the building. It gave him access to the crawlspace.

"Aaron?"

He stood in a hurry and cinched the bag tight. "I'm okay." He faced her, holding the sack by his side. He was dirty, his hands black with mud, face and hair dusted.

"What are you doing?" she asked, keeping her voice even. No accusation. "Can I help?"

"No. I'm okay. Go back inside. I'm nearly done."

Kate approached. "Let me help."

He backed away. Shook his head. Held the bag behind him. "I said I'm fine."

"Show me the sack."

"No."

Aaron turned from her and got back on his hands and knees, scrambling for a hole in the barrier designed to keep out bigger animals, like racoons and skunks and whatever mega-rats evolved this year. Kate snagged him around the middle before he made it under and hauled him back.

He screamed, the pain-filled sound of a boy being burned with a hot poker. Kate was so stunned she almost dropped him. But she hung on. When she grabbed the garbage bag, he screamed some more and kicked her in the thigh, firing dull pain through her leg. Perhaps, if she'd listened to Tammy and got more meat on her, it would have hurt less.

"Aaron! Stop it."

She wrapped both arms around him, pinning his arms and his upper legs, for once thankful at his underdeveloped stature. He writhed and struggled.

"Aaron, it's okay, I'm not hurting you. Calm down."

"Get off me, get *OFF* me!" He squirmed harder.

And the black liner shuffled.

Mother and son fell still. Kate couldn't move, processing what could have made such a movement. Deep down, she knew, but it was so deep it didn't make it to her consciousness, and only mystery fogged what she was seeing.

The thin black plastic jerked again, like a popcorn kernel had silently burst.

"Mom…" Aaron ceased struggling and went slack. "Please don't open the bag."

"I have to, baby."

As his muscles gave him a little room, he bucked again. "Don't open the sack." He cried out again, as loud as she'd ever heard him, then yelled, "If you open that fucking sack, I'll kill you!"

Kate reeled at the outburst. She had never been afraid of her son. Even when she learned he'd slapped a classmate, caught him pissing in a fish tank, and after he wiped handfuls of his own shit on a wall, she'd simply believed the "real" Aaron was temporarily blocked, a blip in the road to being a far better kid than most of his peers. Because kids were horrible. Not all kids. And certainly not hers. Other kids, the nasty ones, had negligent parents, parents who didn't care, who never showed an interest.

Kate wasn't one of those.

"I'm not letting you go," she growled in his ear. "Calm down, or you are spending the rest of the night in juvie."

Craig had used the "juvie" ruse once, when Aaron refused to come in for dinner because he was busy playing on his new bike in the street, the kid's sweaty exercise giving him a sense of immortality. When Craig dropped the juvie-bomb, which Aaron only knew translated as "kid-jail", he couldn't sprint inside fast enough. Kate hadn't wanted to use an empty threat like that. Couldn't stand to be called on it.

But it worked.

The lad ceased fighting her. As she set Aaron down on the deck stairs, ensuring there was no bump as he landed, his rage slipped into terror—the level of terror usually reserved for being cornered by an angry rattlesnake.

"Please, Mom…"

"Wait here," she said.

The bag popped from within again.

Keeping watch on Aaron, Kate kneeled and reached for the liner, reading in his eyes that he would gladly carry out his threat.

"You don't understand," he said.

"I will. In one moment."

"No!"

He launched at her, a battle cry on his lips, rising to a scream as he raked at her with his fingers. Kicked at her. Uncontrolled, a panic reaction—fight or flight set firmly to fight. More ferocious than before. She couldn't respond, couldn't defend herself without hurting him, so cowered beneath his attack, arms over her face.

"Don't do it!" he yelled. "Leave me alone. I have to—"

Then Aaron was floating. Rising above her.

She blinked, lying on her back, unable to move even as the onslaught ceased.

Sal was holding him. Aaron fought back, but Sal was big enough for the blows to hurt the boy more than him.

"What's going on?" Sal said, struggling to restrain Aaron. "I heard the screams."

Kate sprang up on her knees again. "Grab his arms and legs."

"You can't *do* that!" Aaron cried.

Sal did, wrapping him up as Kate had done moments earlier.

Kate snatched the garbage bag and ripped it open. A blackbird tumbled out onto the grass.

Kate stepped back, glancing at Aaron with her hand to her chest and a million questions begging to be released. She'd yell those questions, though, so she held onto them.

For several seconds—two, ten, fifteen, Kate had no idea —the bird lay motionless. Then it twitched. Jerked upright. Finally, it spun up onto its legs.

"Must've been in shock," Sal said.

"You can't let it go," Aaron whined. "Please, Mom, put it back."

The blackbird spread its wings and tried to take off, but only the left extended fully and immediately fell back to the ground. There was a tiny length of wire around the damaged wing.

Kate plucked up the courage to touch it, but as her fingers got close, the bird hopped aside. "Is that... a snare?"

She glared at Aaron as Sal set him upright.

"I had to." Tears streaked Aaron's dirty cheeks. "And you messed it all up. Both of you."

"Why...?"

"It's *your* fault, Mom," he said. "You made me get that shortie thing, and now I have to do this. But... *catch it!* It's getting away!"

Kate looked for the bird, but it was hopping along, one wing disfigured to the side, almost at the hedge. Then it disappeared into the undergrowth.

Aaron wailed in despair, a melodramatic, "Nooooo!" like he must have seen in a movie.

Kate didn't point out that the bird was as good as dead anyway. A bird that couldn't fly may as well shoot itself in the head.

But there was another problem. One that dawned on her in slow increments as she dabbed at her face and examined her arms, checking for scratches. The problem grew, one plodding footstep at a time. At first, as light as a cloud, the pressure amplified with every damp cog that fell into place.

She stared at the broken lattice where Aaron had attempted to escape. For a time, she couldn't blink, glazed over, asleep with her eyes open.

Knowing she had to, but unable to traverse that final stretch, she willed herself to move. But the truth was, she wanted to confront this even less than the doomed bird.

"Kate?" Sal said, leaning his head toward Aaron, still wrapped in his arms.

Kate snapped out of her trance, unsure how long she'd drifted from reality. Now it came slamming back to her in full HD, like a slap clearing the fug. "Can you hold onto him a minute longer?"

Sal shored himself up, clearly uncomfortable. "Okay. Why?"

"I hope I'm wrong."

Kate lowered herself to her hands and knees, pulled more of the lattice border from the gap between house and ground, and steeled herself to go under. She heard a moan from Aaron, which she took to mean she was not mistaken, and tried to ignore the fact she was still wearing her best pantsuit. Sure, she could have changed in under two minutes, but that would be two minutes where she'd continue to speculate.

She was not a parent who didn't care.

She was one of the good ones.

She refused to let things slide.

The ground was bare and outside the daylight, it was dark and cold, but not pitch black. She had to belly-crawl under a heating pipe, daubing her in dusty earth.

Screw it. She could afford a premium dry cleaner. Or a new suit. Or three new suits.

When she'd crawled under, she didn't know what she'd been looking for, but pretty quickly the adage *follow your nose* took on a more literal meaning. She had enough room to take out her phone and activate the flashlight, then shone it around the increasing dimness in the direction of the strongest smell.

There.

At the back. Well, the front of the house, really. Right under the entry hall. Where the smell had first materialized. The rotten fruit, she'd assumed. The odor Jennifer hadn't been able to purge with her quick spruce.

Nearing the accumulation of garbage bags, at least four

of them, Kate patted around, locating a short piece of wood —a twig that had blown under. She was too big to sit upright, so propped herself on one elbow and snagged the first plastic bag with her makeshift probe. Dragged it toward her.

The stink made her stomach clench. Meaty, rotten, like chicken left in the sun.

She ripped it with her fingers, then shuffled back, gagging at the stronger cloud of decay blooming forth. Pulling her blouse up over her mouth, she parted the torn flaps to reveal the contents.

A cat, fully formed, but stiff and crawling with something beneath its skin. It was a tabby she didn't recognize, but it had been dead for over a week. There was a wire around its neck.

And this was one of four bags.

"Oh, Christ." Kate couldn't decide if this was blasphemy of the sort the sports presenter had worried about the other night, or if she meant it, pleading with a higher power to deliver a reasonable explanation.

Someone else did it.

This wasn't Aaron. A bad child planted it here. Aaron was trying to save that bird. Or he thought it was already dead, and this was a graveyard, honoring the deceased.

A graveyard like his dad was lying in right now.

She had to know for sure.

Using the stick, she pulled another sack forward, picking a smaller package this time. Not wanting to see, dreading the truth. But it made sense. One thing, to be certain, to rip any chance of motherly denial from her.

She tore the plastic and leaned back, allowing the initial haze of rotting funk to disperse minutely before edging it open using her stick.

And there it was. All hope that someone else had done this vanished. Aaron was one sick little bastard.

With its stomach sliced open, its pink innards almost blackened, a guinea pig lay on its back. A *black-and-white* guinea pig.

The remains of Tony Stark.

Kate wasn't sure when she started screaming, or when she stopped.

CHAPTER NINETEEN

Once Kate threw each bag out from the crawlspace, she emerged on her hands and knees, numb yet shaking and all but hyperventilating. Sal saw what was in the bags and assured her he wouldn't say anything to anyone. She remained seated on the floor, tears dried and dirt crusted on her cheeks.

Aaron stood before her like a penitent monk. "I'm sorry, Mommy."

He wasn't sorry. Kate was sure of that. It stabbed her in the heart to perceive her son as manipulating her, playing the cute card to stress his innocence.

"You're not innocent," she said.

At this, his eyes flared to life, his mask dropping. "I knew you wouldn't believe me. But you *have* to believe me."

"Why?"

"Because I'm your little boy."

She looked up at Sal, who shuffled in place, a swallow, and his gaze drifted from her.

"My little boy doesn't murder innocent animals," Kate said.

"I *have* to." Aaron's little fists clenched. His foot stamped. "Don't you *get* that yet?"

Kate pushed through her numb body, stretching her nerves to feel the air around her, then the pins and needles rushing through her made her regret dispensing with numbness. Numbness was her friend. Now, attentive and aware, she wanted to shut down, curl into a ball, and sob. Her biggest wish was to reboot her son, restore him to the kid he was before... Before when? It seemed as if this had swirled through her life for weeks, when it was really just days.

Only, it wasn't just days, was it?

He'd worn one face to show how good he was being, how much he'd improved at school, then another to slap a girl, to kill several small animals, and get creative with his bodily waste. She simply hadn't seen it. Hadn't been present enough to detect the change in her son.

"It ends. Now." Kate stood and, with a firmness she thought had ebbed away under the house, faced Sal. "Thank you for your help. Really. I don't know what I'd have done, but I can handle it from here."

Sal stuttered a couple of platitudes, but Kate's stony new attitude zoned them out. He gave her and Aaron a sympathetic smile. "You two got some things to talk about." He padded toward the side gate, adding, "You need anything, you call. Got it?"

"I will," Kate said. "And, if I do, bring a cigar if you like. I don't mind you smoking it on the deck. It's the least I can do."

Sal nodded a sincere *thank you*. "I'll take you up on that."

After Sal left, Kate changed her clothes and located two of the heavy duty masks—from New York's coronavirus era —in the back of her wardrobe. Instead of going mad at Aaron, she ordered him to help remove the plastic-wrapped carcasses. Neither spoke much. She felt no need to voice her satisfaction that at least they had discovered the odor pene-trating the floorboards, and relief that Jennifer had left before the screaming began. No way could she cope with explaining this.

Not yet.

She'd have to, though. And soon. If Aaron let it slip and Kate had said nothing, there'd be more judgement, more hints that she was a terrible mother.

As they buried the fifth and final animal—a decom-posing pigeon with another of those wire snares around its neck, which Aaron explained he'd learned about on the internet—she sure as hell felt like a terrible mother. Worse. The mother of a future serial killer.

"Now, please," she said to Aaron.

Aaron put his hands together and—again, for the fifth time—recited the Lord's Prayer over the grave. "Our Father, who art in Heaven…"

Kate paced with her back to the funeral, rubbing her face to cling to a semblance of sanity. She wasn't religious, but some form of ritual might help Aaron see what he did was wrong, that there were consequences.

Once Aaron finished praying, Kate needed a few deep breaths to face him.

He was gone. She searched around and found he had moved to the edge of the garden, rummaging through the hedge. Obvious what he was doing.

Kate closed her eyes and breathed.

There were kids out there who'd stabbed classmates, intending to kill; twelve-year-olds with rape convictions; sixteen-year-olds on pedophile registers. Families got through that. Dealt with it. But were they ever happy after the dust settled? Did those parents truly love their offspring, or did they convince themselves through denial, out of duty?

Kate opened her eyes and strode over to Aaron. "Looking for the bird?"

His movements seemed sped up, as if on fast-forward, frantically pulling back twigs and leaves, rushing along the border and ducking low to see if the escapee was hiding in the soil under the leaves. "I have to find it."

"Why?"

"You know why, Mom."

"I want to hear you say it."

"To kill it."

A calm, cleansing breath. At least he was being honest.

She said, "Because you have to?"

"Yes."

"Why do you have to?" She'd asked that so often, she could predict the answer without clairvoyance, so she rephrased. "*How* do you *know* you have to?"

Aaron let a branch snap back in place, paused for a moment, then sat on the grass cross-legged. "I don't know. It's just that… it'll be worse if the bird lives."

"It's injured. Can't fly. A cat will catch it. Or an owl later."

He shook his head. Sad rather than angry. "It has to be me."

"Why?"

"Because I'll end up with something worse."

"Worse than you killing a bird? Painfully?"

He nodded. "Whatever you think about this, it's true. I don't like being naughty. But if I don't do what my buddy wants, something terrible will happen."

The buddy again. Making sense of his clairvoyance by manufacturing an imaginary friend.

Kate said, "Your… buddy. It's like…?"

She hated this. Hated sympathizing. If it were someone else's kid who'd done all Aaron had, Kate would write it off as bad parenting, that all the kid needed was discipline. *Stop mollycoddling and do something about it*. That's what she'd say, what most moms would say, plus a lot worse online.

But this was different. Aaron was different. Troubled. Not evil.

Kate said, "It's like going back on a deal? There's a price to pay if you don't follow through?"

He nodded again, this time with a thin smile and something approaching genuine warmth in his eyes. "You *do* understand."

"I'm trying to. If I had a magic wand, I'd wave it right now and take what's happening to you away. I'd carry it myself if it'd help you. So, please believe me when I say I'm *trying* to understand."

"Okay, that's great." He scrambled back onto all fours and recommenced his search of the hedge.

Kate's heart creaked, ready to break. "That's not what I meant, Aaron. I'd rather a cat hunted down a meal than you eviscerate an innocent animal."

Aaron froze in place. He turned his head to look back at her over his shoulder, bearing a sneer that reminded her of a coyote interrupted in its roadkill feast. That hateful flare was back. "Then my buddy will make you sorry. You'll see. And it'll be all your own fault."

After a brief spell of reflection, waiting on him to melt back into the picture of innocence, Kate banished Aaron to his room under threat of him losing the privilege of all his electronics, including TV, for a month should he step out for anything other than the house setting on fire. She instantly regretted putting that idea in his head because, judging by the killing field in the crawlspace, he might consider it'd be swell to burn the place down.

Once he was ensconced in there, and Kate gathered all the matches and anything able to produce a flame, she asked Sal to come back over, "for a beer or something."

He came, of course. She had beers waiting, and they drank them in the living room. On other nights, they'd chatted on the deck, allowing Sal to spark up a cigar as she'd suggested, but tonight Kate needed to keep an ear out for Aaron.

"Dorothy was good enough to say she'd seen me leave earlier," Sal said. "Asked about the noise."

"What did you tell her?"

"That Aaron was playing. Got spooked by a raccoon. Then found he'd busted himself up with a couple splinters."

"I'll have to remember that. She's bound to ask."

"And she was interested in why I was coming back." Sal gave an amused half-frown. "Only because she wonders if Aaron's okay, though. She wouldn't pry."

"Oh, no, she hates to pry." Kate almost smiled.

They drank. Their lips smacked, loud in the room with no background noise—no TV, no Aaron—but they found a way to sip quietly.

A quarter down her bottle, Kate said, "You know what it means. Killing animals early in life."

"I don't think that's always what happens." Sal was halfway through his. He held it to the light, watching the liquid sway and foam. "I seen the films, the TV shows, but it's just shortcuttin'. Convenient plot twist. Someone sounds clever saying serial killer stuff, then everyone moves on. Ain't a big thing."

"It is a big thing, Sal."

"I didn't mean it like, no big deal. I mean, you got this. You're trying, right? Got him to a shrink?"

A wave of tiredness swam behind her eyes, trickled to her

chest, then flowed to her arms and legs, ending in her hands and feet. They all felt so heavy. "I can't handle it."

"Expensive?"

"No, I—" She was so weary she almost blurted out today's windfall, a euphoric climax that was snatched from her and rendered almost meaningless by the discovery that Aaron hadn't left an apple core or some orange peel to rot behind a shelf or in a coat pocket. "I've got it covered."

"You think it's..." Sal angled his bottle toward a photo on the mantle. One of Kate, Aaron and Craig, arms raised as they screamed down a log flume. "Suppressed stuff?"

"When Craig died, we had some problems." Kate had slumped without realizing it, her limbs weighting her down, too tired to lift them. Sal knew about her stint in rehab, her past addiction, so she didn't repeat all that. "He'd filed all sorts of documents with his brother relating to my lapses, my broken promises. Personal statements, journaled and referenced in real time. I wouldn't be able to deny any of it."

Both Kate and Craig used to keep journals, mental health breaks in which they could write whatever they were thinking, and which the other swore never to read. It had helped for a while, and she'd kept it up even in the year after Craig left them. But she'd quit using it. She no longer found it useful. Perhaps she should take it up again, given all the shit that was going down around her.

She said, "He'd taped some of our conversations, too. All the ones involving the deals we'd made. About my gambling. How I wouldn't do it. He even documented the rehab. He had power of attorney when I was inside, and only he got to decide when I was safe to be discharged."

Sal just listened. Sipped. Listened.

"I agreed to his terms, but I slipped. The bet came in. He announced he was leaving me. Or, rather, I had to leave. So, to spite him, to show him how wrong he was, I did it again."

"Again?"

She'd only ever told Sal the abbreviated version of that night. "It hurts to talk about. I mean, literally. It hurts inside me. Because I know, if I hadn't done it, he'd still be alive. It's my fault he's dead."

Sal worked his mouth, searching for words of comfort. There were none. Kate had accepted this already and sworn to use the pain to keep herself sober. Now, with Aaron's gift, she was at risk of submerging herself in that hole again.

She said, "It wasn't only one bet. It was the only stake that won. When he caught me, and hated that I'd won, it triggered something inside me. Like a mental breakdown. I wasn't thinking, not even debating with myself if it was right or wrong. I just did it."

"Did what?"

"I went ahead and placed a ton more bets online. All using his card. I reinvested the winnings, too, all high risk, high reward. One of them had to come in, right?"

Sal continued listening.

"I'd spent forty-thousand dollars trying to prove it wasn't a fluke. And guess what?"

Sal sipped. Lowered the bottle. "Turned out to be a fluke?"

Kate no longer felt like drinking beer. "He wasn't even mad that I did it. Spent forty-grand in an hour. He calmly told me it was over. *We* were over. He'd give me the night to pack my things and say goodbye to Aaron, but in the morning he was calling the cops. What I'd done was a crime. Stealing his credit card, spending all that money."

She was staring at the log flume photo.

Sal focused on it, too. "You think he woulda called the cops on you?"

"He'd have to, if he planned to claim with Amex for

fraudulent activity. We were well off, but not so well off we could afford to lose 40K."

"Craig wasn't no shark," Sal agreed.

"No, he was a talented lawyer and a decent guy. Not a common combination. He didn't deserve someone like me. And I don't even hold his threats against him. I deserved it." She sniffed, breathing back tears. "We'd have lost the house, probably more than that. If he hadn't had me arrested."

"That's why the insurance companies thought it might be suicide?"

Kate nodded. "Yep. They called it 'money troubles'. Jonathan snagged on it too, and he was Craig's executor. He saw all the charges. He guessed what happened."

"But fought your corner."

"For Aaron. Not me."

Silence again. Sal was waiting for her to resume.

"I think Aaron somehow knows what I did. Maybe overheard Jonathan and Jennifer, and blames me. He never talks about the specifics, but if he's seeing an illness as responsible for my destructive behavior, it could be he's doing all this for the same reason. Finding something to hang it on and hoping we believe him."

Sal closed one eye and peered into his empty bottle. "Could be."

"You understand," Kate said. "You understand why this is so hard? It's like I killed my husband, and now I'm losing Aaron too."

Sal held the bottle in two hands. Contemplating. Again, Kate could envisage no comfort in any words that he might bring forth. Because there were none. She held the guilt and pain at bay by concentrating on the immediate issues, on maintaining the standard of living Craig had toiled so hard to give Aaron, to share with *her*. She flushed it away. Her weakness destroyed everything.

"I blamed her for killing my daughter." Sal's eyes rested on Kate. "When my wife died, I was angry."

Kate knew he was once married, that there was a tragedy in his past, but they'd never talked about it. It wasn't for her to bring up.

"I hated her. I wrote a speech for her funeral, telling her family how stupid she was for drinkin' in the afternoon, thinking a nap and a coffee was enough to sober up before collecting Bella from pre-school. It wasn't."

Kate's turn to listen. Hoped he had a point beyond bonding over death.

"I never recovered," he said. "Didn't give a eulogy, neither. Couldn't say those things, but couldn't say good stuff in God's house, 'cause they'd be lies. Maybe if it was only her, just Maria, who died, I could get over it. But she took Bella, too. Stole my little girl from me."

"I'm sorry," Kate said, taking his hand. "I can't believe I just unloaded like that."

"Nah, it's fine. I'm glad." He tried to smile, but it wasn't happening. "Haven't celebrated Christmas in eight years 'cause it's too painful. Never gets easier for me. But you don't have to live like that, Kate. Whatever you did, however you think you're to blame, you still got Aaron. You love him. What happened with Craig, it don't matter right now. Maybe he thought dying was better than choosing between having his son's mother arrested and losin' the house. Maybe he was so messed up he forgot to check the bag of chips, or didn't care. I don't know. You don't know. We never will."

Kate squeezed his hand.

"You and Aaron," he went on. "I wish I'd been able to catch Bella killin' animals under our floorboards. I'd do anything, anything at all, for a chance to see her again, to hold her and tell her I love her. Don't matter how bad she behaves. Because you can fix behavior. Can't fix dead."

She didn't know where it came from, but it felt right. An instinct, a sudden yearning. She leaned over and kissed Sal on the cheek, and whispered in his ear, "Stay."

He held still. His lips inches from hers. She could taste his breath, the remnants of a cigar he must have sparked up at home, resurrecting memories of smoky rooms in Reno, the hint of beer playing on the back of her tongue. She leaned in closer, her lips connected with his. But he pulled away, her hair falling over her bowed head.

Sal eased his hand from hers and stood. "Not tonight, Kate."

Her cheeks burned.

"Fix things with Aaron," he said. "Then, maybe, if you still feel the same way, we pick this up another time."

Kate could not find the words. Instead, she nodded like a mute and wrapped her arms around herself, stomach churning. He must have realized there was nothing more to say, as he departed without attempting any platitudes, no final goodbye.

She was half-glad of the rejection, but she'd wanted him to stay too. She couldn't tell if she was angry or sad or just a silly woman who'd made a huge mistake with a good man's feelings. All she knew for certain was he was right about Aaron.

He was still here. And he wasn't beyond hope.

CHAPTER TWENTY

Kate lit a slow-burn log in the chiminea on the deck, added some dry wood to catch, then set up blankets and pillows, along with a plate of chunky marshmallows and wooden skewers. Inside, she cooked hot dogs and prepped the buns, then put them outside by the fire.

Once ready, she called Aaron for dinner.

She had tried yelling, she'd tried talking calmly to him, and she'd tried shaming him. Nothing had worked. She now accepted there was no easy fix. Her son had a gift—psychic sight, or clairvoyance, miracle, or whatever word science employed for predicting answers—but he could not understand it. And nor could she.

If he was hearing voices or conversing with some apparition, Kate would have to admit to some presence from the hereafter guiding him, thus offering her the proof she needed to adopt Tammy's certainty of an afterlife. If that spirit then made a deal with him, threatening him, she could even accept that level of malevolence in whatever was haunting him.

But from the snippets he'd revealed, it wasn't like that.

Not a ghost, no disembodied voice ordering him around. Just horrible acts to offset the good stuff.

To fix this, to get his imposter syndrome under control, if that's what it was, she needed him on her side. And if it meant twisting his manipulative cute card back on him, fine; she was all ready to play her *I'm-your-mother-and-I-love-you* card.

"Hot dogs! Thank you, Mom."

At the sight of his favorite food on the table outside, he regressed to his former self. Joyful and grateful, digging in with the enthusiasm of a person lost in the desert happening upon a three-course meal. He squirted ketchup on the hot dogs and Kate added mustard to the ketchup for hers. She missed onions, but Aaron didn't like them, so she hadn't bothered tonight. This was for him.

With the fire crackling, Aaron ate like a little boy, like the child he was. Smeared with ketchup, catching some crumbs but not many, chomping more processed meat than was healthy, and washing it down with diet sugar-free cola.

Afterward, the pair snuggled. They watched the stars take form, and soon the usual influx of bats swooped in, an occasional fluttering black mass snatching a bug before flying away.

Aaron pointed at the plate. "Marshmallows?"

Kate sat him up and retrieved the plate, stabbed one skewer into a white blob of candy, and held it up. Aaron reached, but she took it away.

"I am sorry," she said. "I didn't realize the burden you were carrying around. I want to help you, and Dr. Patel is a good start. What do you think?"

Aaron frowned, eyes on the marshmallow. "I think I want to toast that."

"And I want you to toast it. But I also want to understand, as your mommy, how you got into this. Before we see

Dr. Patel again, before you toast this marshmallow. How did you start…" Her mouth fuzzed over, and it physically hurt to finish the question: "Killing animals?"

He stared at the stick in her hand. "I tried to say, but you kept cutting me off."

"I'm listening now."

Aaron thinned his lips. His left ring finger bent over his little one, the forefinger pistoning faster than usual. Kate recalled other tics he'd had since he was a toddler: the stretching of his mouth, a widening of his eyes, popping eyebrows.

She'd read a lot of kids had them, and it was best not to comment or the child could grow self-conscious and the tic can become more severe. They were common in low-level autism and Asperger's, and similar learning disabilities, giving Kate another reason to deny there was anything wrong; once even a mild case of limited mental capacity got diagnosed, the education system labeled the kid forever.

Kate lifted his hand at the wrist, the back-and-forth pointing coming to a stop, but the crossed fingers remained in place. She used her "concerned" voice. "What is this? Is it something to do with what's been happening?"

"No." He took it back and watched his own finger point, fold, point, fold, as if he wasn't controlling it. "I don't know what it is. Makes me feel better sometimes."

"That's okay." She lowered the hand and made no move to stop the tic. "Did this start when your other problems started? Is that what makes you feel bad?"

He fixed on his folding finger.

Kate pushed, but not too hard. "I mean what I said before, baby. If I could take this from you, I would. But I can't. We have to deal with it together. I promise I won't be mad. I'll listen. But talking is the first step."

The finger raced faster, although Aaron's concentration

wilted, and his intensity dulled. "My teacher told me to grow up."

Kate didn't like that. Teachers didn't speak to kids that way, or shouldn't. She stayed quiet, though. Let him talk.

"Mrs. Pinkerton. She said I was acting like a baby and needed to buck up my ideas. I made a wish on my birthday, and then I started to know things. Okay? Can I have my marshmallow?"

"Your birthday?" She pictured another kid sneezing on him, coughing, spreading the power of foresight like an infection or virus. "Are... any of the other kids misbehaving? Were they? Before your party?"

"Nuh-uh, I wouldn't have invited bad kids."

Kate could not recall gossip regarding other "problem" kids. She'd ask around, but it didn't matter that much. It was more important that they handled it rather than worrying about its origins. And yet, she couldn't help hoping some other kid was to blame. Some bad influence taking her loving boy from her like this.

Aaron tapped her leg. "Can I have my marshmallow, please?"

Trust. He had to trust his mommy, so Kate let him have it. She'd said to answer the question, and he had.

That's how bribery works.

He ceased his twisty-pointy fingers and used one hand to hold the proffered marshmallow on a stick, the other to steady it, and toasted it as she watched. Fire danced in his dark eyes as he glooped the mess into his mouth. There was a fear-tinged moment when it looked as though he'd burned himself, but he recovered and survived.

Kate selected another wooden spike, breaking a pink marshmallow skin. "Another?"

"Mmm." Aaron nodded, grinning.

No more finger-curling, his anxiety now occupied by more important matters.

"Tell me what it's like. How it goes for you. In here." She touched his chest. Then softly tapped his head. "And in here."

"Fine." Aaron huffed toward the promised reward, out of reach for now. "It's... I need to know something. Like a test answer. Or where to find some cool stuff to write about for a project. And I know it."

"It just pops into your brain? You suck it in out of thin air?"

"Not a pop. More of a... I don't know. Starts small, gets big. And I don't pull it in. It's sent to me. Like an email. Or when a spy steals secrets onto a thumb drive."

"Like it's downloading into you?"

"Yeah. Can I have that now?"

"No." Kate kept the skewer near her leg. Thought about how to phrase her next question. Or the same question, part two.

A scratching noise sounded, Aaron getting restless about his marshmallow.

"I asked how it goes," she said. "I mean all of it. What happens next? After you learn the answer?"

"Well... it's after I *use* the answer. My buddy sends me these things all the time. But if I use them, that... *data*, I suppose they call it on TV, I'll have to do something in return. Favor for a favor."

"How do you know what to do?"

Aaron shrugged, focus returning to the stick. "Same."

"The same? It just comes to you?"

Another nod. More scratching.

"It downloads?" she said.

"Not exactly the same. It's more... Creeping. Like there's a tickle in my tummy." He touched his stomach. "Then, it's getting stronger, and I get all scared, like when I used to think there was a monster under my bed."

And Daddy would go grab one of his pastel-colored kitchen knives, lie on the floor, and say he was a knight who would protect the fair prince, and Aaron would laugh, and in a few minutes, forget about the monster and go right off to sleep...

"I remember," Kate said.

"It's like that. Then, when I see the thing, I know."

"It's not a voice? Not a command from the sky or inside you?"

"No. I just notice when it's time. Can I have my marshmallow?"

Kate handed it over.

Deal's a deal.

As he cooked it, Kate noted he was motionless, but that damn noise was back.

Skrit... skrit... skrit...

"Have you ever refused?" Kate asked.

Aaron checked the marshmallow's charring and put it back to the fire. "No. That would be bad."

"How do you know?"

"Same as the other stuff." He withdrew the marshmallow, blew out a tiny flame and appeared satisfied. "It's a certainty."

"Nothing bad happened after I let that bird go, did it?"

He chomped on the gooey treat and, as always, Kate prayed the sugar and gelatin didn't transform into napalm on his chin or the roof of his mouth. He was fine.

She said, "And the bird was the thank you for my stocks win, wasn't it?"

This was the first time she'd run the timeline, compared it to what Aaron said moments earlier.

...it's after I use the answer...

How had he known she'd banked the intel he gave her? Another facet of his gift?

He said, "I guess, yeah. You did something with it. I had to catch and kill the bird." Matter-of-factly, as if talking about lacing up his sneakers, he added, "I was supposed to rip its wings off."

The *skrit... skrit... skrit...* got faster. Scratching, scrabbling.

She looked around for a branch caught and shifting in a breeze she hadn't detected, sheltered in the corner. It was too dark beyond the orange glow of the chiminea and the artificial light from the kitchen.

"How about this?" Kate said. "We refuse to do what this... *buddy* or whatever it is wants."

Like the peck on Sal's cheek, her urging him to stay, she did not see her next words coming. As they spilled from her, she felt they were boiling up from a deep well, a place where impulse control was as tangible as fog.

"We'll fight him, Aaron. You and me. You see what you see, and it's yours. *Your* vision. Your gift."

Aaron sucked the stringy remains from his stick. "You're still not listening."

This is for him, she told herself, the instinct from this dark place not quite words, not quite a voice. She wondered if that was how Aaron felt before slapping Becky, and as his warm, stinking log curled out into his hands. Was it a genetic memory, the seeds of addiction sown into his very being?

"I am listening, but... please do this. Give me one thing." She stuck another marshmallow on a spike. "Lotto numbers?"

"No. No way, not the Lotto. That's too big. Too much. I can't. I don't know what it'll want from me."

So, if he was giving up a marshmallow, he really thought of it as a sliding scale.

"Something less than the Lotto," she said. "Okay, another tip, then? A company like you did yesterday. One that goes well, not badly. And I'll show you there's nothing to be afraid of."

This was for *him*. A test, an experiment. She wouldn't *use* the intel. She'd just *tell* him she did. Or punt with pennies, like Marcus's regular investments. She wanted to see him react. Prove he was delusional, handling his clairvoyance in a self-destructive manner, before going back to Dr. Patel.

She held the skewer out.

"Now?" Aaron said.

She smiled her mommiest smile. Handed over the marshmallow without emphasizing conditions. It gave her a morsel of deniability. She wasn't bribing him. She was helping him.

He accepted the treat and stuck it into the fire. This time, he displayed no glee, no joy at the popping flames gathering around the outer skin. "You should invest in a startup called Whale Ride-On Sports, floating tomorrow."

Instead of creaking, her heart jumped, then settled, and pooled into a puddle of loving warmth. He'd trusted her. Trusted her ahead of this buddy delusion. Proof, she thought, that he was going to make this work.

"Thank you." She hugged him.

He dropped the marshmallow on the deck, splatting the melted feast over the wood. However, where he'd normally reach down and attempt to recover the bounty, he didn't react. At all. Just froze in her arms.

"Are you okay?" Kate asked.

The scratching grew louder. If it was a branch, it had moved.

And it started fluttering.

Kate let him go and stood, followed his eye line. "What is that?"

"You should have listened to me," Aaron said. "Now, my buddy will make you sorry."

CHAPTER TWENTY-ONE

Kate placed one foot closer to the deck's edge, one hand on the post Sal replaced this week.

There was a bump, a scratch, another flutter.

At the bottom of the four stairs, abutting where the lawn met the concrete path, a dark object the size of a tennis ball juddered side to side, creating that *skrit-skrit-skrit*.

Heart pounding, Kate took the first step down, gripping the guardrail. Surely nothing that small was a serious threat.

When the black tennis ball bounced, a bladed shape snapped out to the side, causing the flutter sound.

A wing.

It was a blackbird.

Kate descended another step, then glided away from where it repeatedly battered itself against the wood.

Not *a* blackbird. It was *the* blackbird.

The bird had a broken wing, and its eye was bloodied and seeping pus. It tried again to rise, to flap its wings, but only got its beak on top of the stair before *skrit-skrit-skritting* its claws against the front, unable to find purchase.

"Aaron, go back inside."

"I can help, Mom."

She had to put it out of its misery, but couldn't tell Aaron that. He'd interpret it as the buddy winning. He needed to see that this, and his Whale Ride-On Sports prediction, would carry no consequences.

Through gritted teeth, she hissed at him, "Go back inside."

He turned away.

She trod a careful path onto the ground, planning to grab a spade from the small store cupboard she and Craig had bought from Ikea as a temporary solution six years earlier. She had left it open, only a set of edging shears, a roll of netting, and a garden fork handle having been put away. She'd left the spade and trowels on the lawn—not lazy, she told herself, too exhausted, physically and mentally, to tidy up.

As soon as she moved away from it, though, the blackbird screeched.

Aaron rushed back to the top step. "Mom?"

"Stay back!"

The bird hurled itself at her, its high-pitched *caaaaw* sounding like a terrified child—like Aaron had before Sir Craig saw off the monster under the bed with a kitchen sword. Where before it couldn't muster the means to ascend one step, it somehow flew up, its intact wing fully extended, its broken one half-out, straight at Kate's face.

Its beak opened. Talons bared, like a hawk snatching a field mouse.

It collided with Kate. Squawking, scratching, pecking at her. She cried out, but refrained from a scream, even now conscious of the ruckus from Aaron's commotion earlier.

She batted at it, covered her face, but it attacked her hair, pulling strands out at the root, its bill surprisingly painful for a small creature as it pecked at her. Up, down, as if dive-bombing her with a handicapped wing.

"Mom!" Aaron shouted.

His feet pounded on the stairs, running to help.

Kate yelled, "No!" and cleared her mind.

This was, she suspected, how animals defended their young. A total sense of peace, of understanding what must be done. She was serious about showing him he was not cursed, that he had no friend or guardian demanding favors for favors, and that he—and she—were in control.

For just a second, she lowered her defenses. She pinpointed the feral bird's position. And her hand shot out and snatched it from the air. It keened and squawked, and puffed up its chest in her fist, but she did not let go.

She didn't know what, exactly, to do with it, so she improvised.

Put it out of its misery.

She carried it to the flower bed where they'd founded a pet cemetery, and gripped it tight. The idea of breaking its neck, as she'd seen valiant heroes do on TV, ran through her nerves and turned her stomach. Weirdly, the caveman approach gave her less of the willies than cracking bones with her hands. It took a few seconds to locate a sizeable rock, then had to fumble the bird around so it sat snug in one hand before picking up her bludgeon.

She then checked that Aaron was still stood on the deck, and shouted, "Back inside. Now!"

He sighed, turned his back, and trudged into the house.

Then Kate brought the rock down on the bird's head. It didn't get up, but nor had it stopped moving, writhing in the spatter of its own blood. Kicking. Weaker, but still alive.

She tossed the stone aside, dislodged the spade from the soil where she'd left it, and repositioned the blackbird on a stone. It emitted a faint squawk.

Kate raised the shovel. And slammed it down harder than she had the rock.

The bird crunched under its force. Its beak fissured and hung open in a death-smile. She spent over ten seconds staring at the corpse before realizing the wet taste in her mouth was blood that had sprayed from her first strike.

She dropped the spade and sat back hard on her butt. Glanced back at the house where Aaron was watching from the kitchen window.

"Fuck," she said, and dug a sixth grave with her fingers.

PART THREE

JUST KNOWING

CHAPTER TWENTY-TWO

Kate showed up for work as usual, except she wore a long-sleeved top to cover the scratches to her wrists and forearms, had applied Band-Aids on two of her fingers, and she smelled vaguely of antiseptic where she'd treated the pecks and talon marks on her head.

It was preferable to write the encounter off as a feral bird stuck in its territory, then defending itself against the humans —the creatures who had wounded it in the first place—but the inkling it was something more kept whispering to her.

What if he's right?

What if it really is some... entity... tagging along with him?

What if there are consequences?

After all, she'd accepted the notion of Aaron possessing a psychic gift readily enough, when it benefited her. When it benefited them both. Was it so wild a theory that the scales needed balancing? That there was a price to pay for every transaction?

She was tempted to quit the job rather than show up and make enough to tide her over, but the stocks money hadn't cleared and she was still amply cautious to wait until she cashed her chips before buying the champagne. By the end of today, Marcus had told her, he'd have the funds ready in her brokerage portfolio, which he'd transfer straight into her checking account. She'd pay Ollie Swag back, then luxuriate in handing Dev her notice.

Soon.

Patience.

After deflecting Tammy, then performing her rounds up to and including the men's room on 42, rather than stopping at Endo's desk, she slowed, moving in a constant forward motion to camouflage her side-mouthing to him, "I want to go longer on the next one. Just a small amount. I need to test something. Something positive."

He, too, wanted no one seeing them interact, especially Merv who was at his desk-den, so kept staring at his screen. "I'll set it up. You should come intern with Marcus. Maybe you're a natural."

"I'll think about it."

Then, unable to resist a spreading smile, she was gone, sorting her cart as she went. She met Tammy at the break room, lacking her usual relaxed demeanor.

She jerked her head back behind her. "Dev's on his rounds. You might wanna start with women's problems again."

"Too late," Kate answered, spotting Dev coming their way. "I'll handle it. Don't worry."

Dev didn't slow as he passed them. "A word, Kate, please. Now."

Once he was out of earshot, Tammy said, "Ooh, that's one assertive individual."

"Executive material," Kate added, and followed him.

He led her into one of the rarely used stairwells, suddenly turned to her, and made a show of how hard this was for him. Big sigh, a false start, a smaller sigh.

"Kate."

"Dev." She wasn't being rude, either. She just didn't know how else to respond.

"What you do on your day off is not my business. I get that. It's part of the company philosophy."

"Great." Okay, now she was being rude. She knew exactly what he was getting at.

"I'm annoyed your personal life has intruded on my world."

She folded her arms. "Your world?"

"You know what I mean. Hanging out with a broker. Playing cozy clients." His voice was rising, so he lowered it to a hush. "Look, if you make enough money on the side to jump in with these guys, I'm happy for you. But I'd barely get through the door, and I'm management."

He wasn't management, he was a supervisor, but Kate didn't bring that up.

"Is that what you're doing, Kate?" Dev asked. "Or is it... Something else?"

"What sort of something else?" If Kate hadn't already folded her arms, she would have now. She settled for pulling them in tighter. "What's been said?"

"Mervin Corney. The boss-man out there? Says he sees it a lot. Low-wage girls trying to land a rich sugar daddy. Or, in your case, a boy-toy."

"What?" This time, her arms unlaced and she came in close to Dev. "Are you insane? I'm old enough to..." She didn't want to consider what she was old enough for. "You believe that?"

Dev backed up against the wall, pulling back his shoulders and squaring his chin to avoid looking frightened. "It's not what I think. It's what *he* thinks. And if he thinks a cleaner is throwing herself at his staff, distracting them from their work, I can't keep that girl on."

Kate's entire head glowed with heat. She could easily reinvest her windfall from the short investment. Three Hail Mary calls from Aaron had been right on the money, so she was sure she could manage this. Go all in. And then she'd never need a job again.

"I quit," she said.

"Now?" He glanced side-to-side like a cornered fox.

"Fine. Two weeks. But not because you're desperate. I don't want to land my friends with extra work they might not want. Are we done here?"

"Sure. Thanks for the talk."

"You're welcome." Kate strode away, opened the stairwell door to the trading floor and stopped. Watched as people darted back and forth. "What the hell is this?"

She stepped out, searched around, and when she found the source of the commotion, her heart dropped through the floor.

It was a blur. A juddering, gasping blur. Kate waited for maybe thirty seconds, maybe a minute, before her legs worked again.

She backed away, unable to turn from the sight, seeking refuge in the stairwell. But Dev had emerged and was eager to view the source of the gasps and rummaging. He blocked her way. Kate had to remain here, on the edge of it all, powerless to help.

Two men in suits bent Endo over his desk, one holding his head firm while the other cuffed him. Each had big yellow letters *FBI* stenciled on the front of their ballistic vests.

Beside his den, Moldy Merv leaned jauntily against his partition screens. He seemed as amused by his colleagues' shocked reactions as he was at Endo himself being straightened up and turned by the burly FBI agents. As they marched him for the exit, Merv clapped his hands and climbed up onto a desk.

Attention fell on him and he called everyone round. "Thank you for your cooperation. It's a sad day here, but if there's one thing we don't tolerate at Hetherington's, it's breaking the law."

At Dev's nudging, Kate floated toward the group, hanging at the back, hoping no one noticed her.

"This is Andrea Ruiz." Merv opened his hand toward a tall woman in a tan suit across from the desk on which he stood. "*Special Agent* Andrea Ruiz. When I discovered what Endo was doing, I had no option but to call the SEC, who sprang into action."

The mood in the room frosted over, not one face suggesting they believed him.

"It was a simple investigation," Merv said. "And if I spotted his obvious maneuvers into insider trading, I expect there are many of you who probably suspected too. I would like you all to give Special Agent Ruiz your full cooperation. Point her to any of Endo's high-risk trades you've witnessed, while I go back through his records. Special Agent Ruiz, do you need to say anything?"

The woman had held herself straight and still throughout the self-aggrandizing speech, waiting patiently. She refrained from standing on a desk but edged closer to Merv. "Mr. Corney told the SEC of his suspicions, and when they looked into another transaction performed outside this office, I'm sorry to say it was clear Mr. Shunji got information from somewhere. I'd like to know where that was. You are obligated to tell me if he had ever approached you before, asking you to help him make a trade he either wasn't authorized for, or needed to conduct on the down-low. Doesn't matter if you didn't report him at the time, but it is imperative you notify us now. If it comes out later, we may have to make more arrests."

She cast her eyes over the assembled group.

"No one wants to snitch on a friend, but what Mr. Shunji did endangered all of you. Your jobs, your livelihoods. If we'd picked it up on our own, if he'd conducted this trade before Mr. Corney stopped him, Hetherington Brokerage and Bonds could have faced unlimited fines. As it stands, I'm recommending no action on that front... As long as you all cooperate. Clear?"

Mumbles and nods rippled through the group.

"For now," Andrea Ruiz said, "go about your work. Agents will be along soon to talk to all of you."

"Thank you," Merv said, final-wording the FBI agent as he climbed down. "That's all, folks. I'll be watching."

The meeting ended, mumbles rising in volume, nods becoming head-shakes. Kate picked up several expressions of disbelief, a handful of pragmatic murmurs declaring it must be true if the SEC acted so quickly, and many more silent, shellshocked wanderings. It was a slow, steady parting of bodies, as if someone had turned out the lights, making them find their way back to their desks by touch.

Dev said, "Wasn't Endo the guy you were trying to land?"

Kate avoided crumpling in a heap by morphing shock into anger at Dev's comment. "I wasn't trying to land him, you prick. I was—"

It wasn't a noise that cut her off. Not even a movement. Just a cold, definitive fog forming out of the corner of her eye. Only not a fog, but a pair. A pair of humans, people in suits. A man and woman. She could barely see them, but she was certain they were staring at her. The man pointed.

She turned her head.

Moldy Merv and Special Agent Ruiz observed her.

Merv was the pointer. Ruiz nodding.

"Kate?" Dev said, picking up on her fear.

Ruiz led the way, Merv coming up behind. The FBI agent slowed, said something to him, and he stood rooted to the spot, face like thunder for half a second before regaining his composure, hands on his hips, as if whatever she said to him had been his idea all along.

Ruiz arrived at Kate and Dev.

Kate's face felt drawn, bloodless. She was sure she'd turned pale.

Ruiz didn't quite smile, but she wasn't being hard either. A look of sympathy, as she'd received for weeks and even months after Craig's funeral. The soft hand on Kate's arm smarted as she caught a scratch, but again reminiscent of someone offering condolences.

"You're Kate Mallory?" Ruiz said.

Kate could only nod.

Ruiz's gentle touch strengthened to a grip. "I think we need to have a chat too, don't we?"

CHAPTER TWENTY-THREE

They handcuffed her, then bundled her into a plush minivan and sped to an FBI field office only four or five blocks from Hetherington's. She saw neither hide nor hair of Endo. They processed her by taking her fingerprints and DNA, and reading her Miranda rights again, this time recording her affirmative answer that she understood.

Kate couldn't remember when she'd last blinked. Her eyes hurt. Dry.

"I'd like a lawyer, please," she said.

Craig had drilled it into her that no matter how innocent she was, she should never speak to law enforcement without one.

"Got a number?" the gruff agent asked, getting ready to lead her to an as-yet unspecified room.

She only knew one lawyer, and no way was she calling him. "I'll need a public defender."

"You're lookin' at five hours. You okay with that?"

No, she wasn't okay with that. She had to get home, relieve Jennifer, who was watching Aaron for the third day this week. The more time Aaron spent with the J-Js, the happier he seemed with them—from his birthday, to the guinea pig, to the freedom they gave him, freedom Kate thought of as not enough supervision. But she couldn't afford to be picky. If she wasn't careful, and Aaron got pissed at Kate for being late again, he might confide his troubles in them. Might let slip the awful things he'd done.

She had to be the one to explain all that. In a grownup manner. Doing so on the same day the FBI grilled her was unacceptable.

"Then I'll waive my right to a lawyer," Kate said, the recording still going. She searched, found a faint glow deep inside herself, and snatched it, imbuing her with a voice that no longer cracked, no longer sounded frail. "I've done nothing wrong. Ask your questions. I'll answer."

It took another half-hour to set up, and it was Special Agent Andrea Ruiz who faced her across the table. The room was plain—a camera and several mikes, four chairs to the only table. Kate wasn't cuffed to a steel ring, just left to sit on the uncomfortable plastic seat. Ruiz had a stack of papers and a computer tablet before her. She once again confirmed Kate had rejected an attorney, and Kate agreed, but emphasized her right to change her mind.

They got into it, Ruiz perusing notes as she spoke.

"Yesterday, at 10:54 a.m., you and Mr. Shunji entered the building in which Versatile Ventures trades, and met with its owner, Marcus LaRoe…"

She then laid out, step-by-step, their entire day. The process by which Marcus borrowed the shares and sold them on the open market shortly before noon, how two hours later the FBI launched a raid classified top secret for almost a year, and how the shares plunged to almost zero as evidence of Villiers Media laundering money in their overseas operations hit the airwaves. On the tablet, she showed Kate what they called "covering the trade" in spreadsheet format, and presented her and Endo's brokerage accounts chock-full of cash. She even outlined the places Kate, Marcus, and Endo had been spending on their personal debit cards that afternoon, despite it being irrelevant to the criminal matter at hand.

"Yes," Kate said, composed and firm. "That's exactly what happened. Why was I arrested?"

Ruiz showed her another set of printouts. "If you'd pulled the seed money out of savings, we might not have looked at you so hard, but you don't have any. You received ten thousand dollars from an offshore account, then immediately made a ten thousand dollar short trade. That indicates you received a leak about our operation against Villiers, needed capital, and either accessed a stash of money you never declared to the IRS, or you went to a loan shark for instant cash."

Kate said nothing. There was no question in there. She wasn't unfamiliar with this process, so followed her rights and remained silent at Ruiz's probing.

The agent waited long enough. "We've requested intel from Organized Crime and NYPD's fraud squad. We'll find your loan shark. We'll piece together where you got the intel. And if it's some cleaner friend who overheard—"

"Oh, Christ, really?" Kate said, again triggered by the assumption. "I have more friends than people who scrub toilets."

"—or if you have a boyfriend," Ruiz continued as if Kate hadn't blown up at her, "or girlfriend, in the bureau who tipped you off, whoever your source is, they will go to jail. You, making this trade, will land someone in jail, even if you somehow remain free."

"You're trying to guilt me," Kate said.

"Is it working?"

"No. Because I did nothing wrong."

"That isn't true, Kate. You're guilty as hell, and so is whoever tipped you off. Tell me about Endo Shunji." Ruiz rested one hand on a closed manila file. "What's your relationship with him?"

"I'm a cleaner in the office building where he works. We know each other's first names. I'd never even heard him called Mr. Shunji before today."

Ruiz leaned forward an inch, tightened her eyes. "This will go easier for you with less attitude. You made nine thousand dollars and change. Mr. Shunji made two hundred thousand. Mr. LaRoe took home half a million."

Kate's brow rose at that figure. She hadn't realized Marcus had gone in so hard. She was more concerned with getting out of here without heading to jail overnight, clearing up the misconception that she'd committed a crime, and gain access to her money. She still had a car payment to make, and the cash in her checking account wouldn't cover it, not to mention her impending deadline with Ollie Swag. Her broker account contained every penny she owned, and it was frozen, locked up tight, and the woman across from her held the key.

"Okay. What do you need from me?"

Ruiz let out a breath. "Was it Endo or Marcus who approached you, or did you approach them?"

"I approached Endo. He introduced me to Marcus."

"Why?"

"I had a feeling something bad was happening at Villiers. I wanted to short it. I thought I could make a bunch of profit."

"But why?"

Kate looked off to the side, panning back and landing on

the camera. Back to Ruiz. "What do you mean, why? I'd heard shorting was a good way of making money."

"No." Ruiz put her palms flat on the table, then turned them over. "We get a tip from someone who observed a brand new client—that's you—confabbing over a speculative trade. A sudden transaction like that flags, and it leads to Endo Shunji, a broker whose record is as spotless as any I've investigated in my two years embedded with the Securities and Exchange Commission."

They wanted Endo. They wanted Marcus. Not her. But she wasn't about to sell Endo out for her own benefit.

"I never told Endo where I got the tip off." Kate interlaced her fingers, mirroring Ruiz in her micro-lean forward. "But I'm reluctant to share, because you won't believe me."

Straightening, Ruiz said, "I've heard some odd stories in my time. Try me."

If there was a name to give, she'd give it. An insider. But there wasn't. And she couldn't name Aaron. That was selfish. She had to take the crazy on herself.

Kate said, "It was a dream."

"A dream. Like, when you're asleep, or like a big ambition?"

"The sleeping kind." Kate was gambling again. A different type of gamble. "I dreamed Villiers was going to go belly-up. I swear. No matter how much you dig, no matter what forensic analysis you do of my communications, if you open my skull and scoop out my memories, you will find no contact with an FBI agent, someone from Villiers, or anyone who might have had foreknowledge of it. I dreamed it. I gambled. I won."

"You risked ten thousand dollars of a loan shark's money… on a dream?"

"Maybe I absorbed it during the course of my duties, maybe it drilled into my subconscious."

Ruiz held still for a beat, thinking, then leaned that inch forward again, as though they were girlfriends sharing a Bellini over Sunday brunch.

"Talk to me, Kate. A cleaner doesn't pick up this sort of tip by osmosis. No one does. It wasn't a trend or a hint of legal proceedings. It was a confidential federal operation. You got intel from somewhere. You tapped up a previously scrupulous but desperate young broker, and he trusted you to help dig him out of a hole."

She fixed another of those funereal head-tilts on Kate.

"You can get off lightly. If you tell me the truth. If not, you're looking at jail time, and a criminal record for life."

Kate wasn't going to jail. With no evidence of an inside man, they couldn't make it stick. It was all supposition. All they could do was drag it out, keep her money in place, and Endo's too. They could also hold her without charge for longer than she was comfortable. She needed a different tactic.

She couldn't drop Aaron in this mess regarding psychic phenomena, but she could use him another way: Sympathy.

"My son's name is Aaron."

Ruiz frowned. "Is it?"

"Yes. You're doing a thorough job of examining my life, so you'll discover a few things. I'm having problems with him. Bad behavior. Like, suddenly. Really bad. I'm taking him to a shrink. But as you're all so fond of pointing out, I'm nothing more than a cleaner."

"You don't talk like a cleaner."

"I wasn't always." Kate stayed on track. "But Aaron, he's suffering PTSD over his father's passing."

"I'm sorry to hear that."

"He's hurt a classmate, conducted a dirty protest in the bathroom... You know what that is?"

"I know what a dirty protest is, Kate. What does this have to do with a very suspicious trade?"

"I'd been stressed about Aaron. About how I'd afford the psychiatrist's bills to sort him out. It isn't covered on our medical insurance, so I needed the money. Then I had that dream. It felt so real. Like... God speaking to me."

She was laying it on a little thick, but Ruiz listened intently.

"I appreciate it seems implausible at best, irresponsible at worst, but my troubles with Aaron, and that dream, and when Endo called his friends and asked about shorting Villiers... he said they were acting odd. I knew then. He knew, too. Something was happening. It was worth the risk. It came in. I did nothing wrong, so I'd like my money unfrozen, please."

Ruiz stared at her, expressionless, as if waiting for more.

Kate hadn't worried about mentioning Endo calling up friends or colleagues to check out Villiers. It was a fact they'd establish—if not now, then eventually. Endo would probably have used that part of the narrative to explain his actions too.

"I'm sorry about your son," Ruiz said, although there was something else going on there. A glimmer that she'd listened hard and had processed Kate's version of events. "Are you sure you want to stick to that story? You being psychic?"

"Osmosis," Kate corrected. "A subconscious deduction."

"We have you cold on this, Kate." Ruiz tapped her pen on the word *Aaron* on her pad. "There's no way out. You won't get your money for a long time, if ever. And when we prove collusion, you and your friends are going to prison. This is your last chance, Kate. If I stand up and leave, I stop playing nice."

It wasn't working. They weren't buying any of it, determined to prove what wasn't true. There was no insider, no illegal leak. But the only way she'd get from under this was by stretching it out until they concluded there was insufficient evidence to prosecute.

Once again, as so often in her life these days, she saw no other choice. It dug in her gut to say it, but if she didn't reach out now, she risked alienating the one person who could help.

"Jonathan Mallory," Kate said. "He's my lawyer. I'm not saying another word until he gets here."

CHAPTER TWENTY-FOUR

Andrea Ruiz had been an agent for twelve years, embedded with the New York Securities and Exchange Commission for the past two. In that time, she'd received more threats, mocking laughter, and disrespect from suspects than she ever had chasing terrorists and mobsters during the previous ten combined. The people of this world saw themselves as above the rest of humanity, as if laws didn't apply to them. When the law did apply to them, they saw it as unfair, a blip in the true order of things. Their lawyers soon negotiated more lenient treatment with sympathetic DAs who moved in the same circles, and lobbyists set to work getting the law changed. It made Ruiz sick, so interviewing Kate—compliant if still in denial about her crimes—made a pleasant change.

Until she mentioned her son.

Waiting personally in the lobby for Kate's lawyer—to hurry the process along—Ruiz drank her fourth coffee of the day and found it hitting her harder than expected. She should have gone with water. Perhaps if she worked a less sedentary assignment, she'd drink less coffee, eat fewer pastries, and run off the part of her ass she'd never planned on growing. An hour at the gym three times a week just didn't cut it. She needed to get back in the game. And soon. Before she got left behind forever.

She had good reason to be stuck here in the SEC, though, and understood why it was her only option given her state of mind after the accident. But, for the past couple of months, she'd believed it was time to get out. Return to the real job, to the terror suspects and mobsters. She was ready to pick up her life where it had sunk without a trace after Julietta died.

Julietta.

Letting Kate Mallory's sob story tug on an emotional nerve made Ruiz question if she really was fit for a return to the knife-edge units assigned to the worst crimes her country faced. Maybe the SEC was her limit. Trigger her in this environment, and all she'd do was overindulge in caffeine and sugar. Out there, analyzing the movements of an Islamist recruit or monitoring a white-power group's firearms activity, if she got sluggish or distracted, it'd cost lives. Here, it was just data, pretend money filtering through accounts, making rich assholes richer than they needed to be.

There was more to that story. To Kate Mallory. She had stirred something in Ruiz, something she'd heard, like—ironically—a dream, half-remembered.

Was it the son? The notion that a cleaner pulled off a mega-trade from nowhere? Or the innocent-seeming stockbroker, whose version of events matched Kate's without sounding rehearsed? She'd listened to enough statements that were near-enough word-for-word identical to see through pre-arranged witness accounts.

A tall man in a suit entered through security, surrendering to a search with the weary manner of someone who knew the routine inside-out. Ruiz guessed this was Jonathan Mallory, the lawyer Kate asked for.

At least now, they might get to the bottom of the matter, and Ruiz might have time to work out why Kate's story sat so uneasily with her. With everything they had uncovered so far, with more to come, she hoped the lawyer would get her to cooperate—because with what they had on her, the last thing Ruiz wanted to do was send a single mom with a troubled son to prison.

"It's not as simple as them lacking proof," Jonathan told Kate over a similar table to the one at which Ruiz had interviewed her an hour earlier. This room, naturally, had no cameras or microphones. "It's about there being no other rational explanation."

"How can that be?"

Jonathan had a legal pad out, a silver or possibly platinum pen poised over it as she recounted her story, but he'd made no notes. Sticking to what she'd told Ruiz for now, she would talk about Aaron's issues later. They needed to keep this incident formal.

"Kate, I'm a partner now," he said, unnecessarily. Perhaps he was compelled to keep saying it, so Kate remained in awe of his brilliance. "But I worked the trenches. And let me tell you, whenever an accused person swears innocence, short of clear and unambiguous recorded footage of a person committing a specific crime, all evidence is circumstantial. To a point. DNA on the murder weapon? Yes, my client touched it, but that was after the crime took place. Witnesses? They're lying or mistaken. My client's pubic hair on the victim? It was consensual, your honor. Do you understand what I'm saying, Kate? Even with what looks like hard evidence, if I can convince a jury of a more reasonable explanation, or simply reasonable doubt, my client goes free."

"Not really, no. They don't just have dicey evidence. They have *no* evidence."

Jonathan set the pen down. "They have you, a cleaner in a trading firm, shorting a massive trade in league with a second-rate broker. You're struggling for money, he's struggling to stay afloat in a very competitive field. That's a powerful motive."

"Motive isn't evidence."

"Oh, you did listen to a few classes before quitting. Good. Then listen some more. You scored big, because of a secret operation involving thousands of man hours and—literally—hundreds of agents from the US and other countries, following a massive media corporation's dealings around the world, for over a year. This is a company that has only ever gone up. And you decide, on the day the FBI executes the warrant, to bet against it. Your friend, Endo Shunji, he's down the corridor singing loud and proud about how you hassled him, begged him to help you make the trade."

"I don't deny it. I approached him."

"With a hunch. A dream you had. What was it you called it?" He over-pretended to think back to what she'd told him. "Oh, right, you've been around so much of this business that you absorbed it into your subconscious and dreamed something so real you just had to visit a loan shark and grab yourself ten thousand dollars as collateral."

"It's what happened."

He tapped the pen on the pad, up, down, *tap-tap-tap*, waiting for Kate to speak.

Jonathan broke the silence first. "Fine. You're sticking to that. But here's how this will play. The FBI will tell the jury what you did. What you admit to, and what they have in black and white. You shorted a strong stock on the same day a raid sent it tumbling. They will say the only way you can do that is with inside information. We will say you dreamed the whole thing and borrowed money from gangsters to cover the trade."

Kate extended her hands, fingers tense, as if looking for someone to throttle. "But there's no evidence."

Jonathan tutted as if she was being intentionally obtuse. "This is the equivalent of a man being arrested over a dead body, covered in the victim's blood, holding the knife, and with witnesses recounting how the accused argued with the victim, then pulled a knife and attacked them. All that's missing is the video footage. But the prosecution doesn't need video footage. You know why?" He paused just long enough for Kate to open her mouth. "Because any explanation other than 'the accused did it' is not *reasonable*. Now, high finance isn't my area of expertise, but following your actions, any explanation other than 'Mrs. Mallory was tipped off by either a Villiers employee or someone on the FBI task force' is not reasonable."

Kate stared at her hands.

"Well?" Jonathan said. "As family, we won't charge you billable hours, since you count toward our pro bono quota, but there's a limit to how long I can sit here waiting for the truth. And remember, this is a privileged conversation. We can't use it against you."

"You're doing this pro bono?"

"Yes, but don't think that makes you special. The last client we took on was some hobo accused of setting fire to another hobo's tent. Couple of them, actually. Burned the poor bastards alive. In the end, they ruled them misadventure."

"Did your client go free?"

"Hammered them down to negligent homicide. Couple of years. But let's not dwell on that." Jonathan sat forward, the way Ruiz had positioned herself when trying to elicit a bond with Kate. "They don't really want you. You could end up with nothing more than a suspended sentence. If you name the people who engineered it."

Kate frowned. "But I did it. I—"

"Lying to your lawyer is dumb. So let me lay on a different scenario." His tone lowered, softened. "You over-heard something. Endo discussing a trade, for which he'd received intel. You demanded they let you in, and—we won't call it blackmail, but you know what I mean—and he relented. Because you, Kate, single mother, working as a cleaner and occasional barmaid, striving to make ends meet, are not someone with connections in the FBI or a major international media group. Endo might be. Marcus too. Could've come from either of them. They have to be the ones to give up the mole, the insider."

Kate's head thrummed. Pressure behind her eyes. She blinked it away. "You know, another of those lessons I attended at law school... before I 'quit,' as you put it... It talked about how a lawyer should never propose a lie to a client. That the lawyer can never be the one to invent a story. If they steer the client toward an alternative scenario, it's unethical but not illegal. Just about. We had a big debate about it."

"And how did that conclude?"

"Doesn't matter. But you're here, a *partner* in a presti-gious law firm, feeding me a lie to get me out of here."

"I don't believe it is a lie, Kate. It's how I honestly believe this shitshow went down. You all agreed it'd be you who takes the fall because, hey, who would believe a woman like you would have the connections to pull this off?"

"A woman like me..."

"Uneducated, undisciplined, desperate. An addict, Kate. Don't think for a second I don't see the similarities between

Villiers and what you did to my— What you did the night Craig died. 'Hot tip.' 'Can't lose.' *Gambling* with someone else's money."

And there it was. The closest he'd gotten to outright laying responsibility on her.

"The bottom line is this," he said, ruffled but undeterred. "I'll sell them that story. You don't have to rubber stamp it today, just promise cooperation at the next interview while they needle it out, and I can get you out on a bond. They'll need your passport, but you'll be free until Endo or Marcus breaks first. Once that happens, you're unlikely to be needed except to plead guilty and accept the suspended sentence. Clear?"

Kate had read about miscarriages of justice, of how law enforcement and prosecutors pressured the accused to confess to a lesser crime so the bigger threat of incarceration went away. It cleared up a statistic, buoyed the defense lawyer for keeping them out of prison, and the client accepted the lesser option, albeit with a criminal record. And that, along with lying about Endo, was the sticking point.

With this hanging over her, Kate would never be a lawyer. Never even work as a paralegal.

"Sell them whatever it takes to get me home today," she said, but promised herself she would not confess to wrongdoing, especially if it landed someone else in prison.

Jonathan picked up his pen and pad and slipped them into a leather satchel with his initials on the corner. "Good enough for now. We'll cross the next bridge when you've had a chance to think about it some more." He stood and made for the door, knocked, and it opened. He was halfway out when he turned to her and said, "I need a word with you when we're out of the building."

"I have to get home."

"I still need a word. I'll drive you. Make the time, Kate,

or take your chance with a public defender. You want that? Because if it comes to cutting a deal, theirs won't be as good as mine. And if you choose trial…"

Kate heard the omitted words as surely as if he'd said them. She'd go to jail and lose everything.

"Fine," she said. "Get me out, and I'm all yours."

CHAPTER TWENTY-FIVE

The first ten minutes of their crawl north out of the city was as slow and cordial as the Bentley that Jonathan drove, insulated against the engine noise, not a single bump felt through the suspension. It was new, likely bought this week off the back of his promotion, and he bragged by failing to even mention it, like it was normal, like... *Oh, you don't have a Bentley? Really? How strange.* The chit-chat zone surrounded them, with Kate dragging out the subject of Aaron's feces art but omitting the animal slaughter, then bringing up the prospect of therapy for Aaron. Jonathan begrudgingly agreed it was for the best.

Kate then raised the request she'd been putting off for days. "I hate to ask, Jonathan, but I need a loan. Until this is all cleared up. I can repay you, I—"

"A loan? Seriously?" The man's mask of civility dropped so fast it was as if it had burned him. "What for? Another bet? Another trade? What'd you do? Dream a horse is going to romp home at fifty-to-one?"

"No, I—"

"A dream, Kate? Really? That's your defense? You're,

what, a fortune teller now? Is that what they teach at night school these days? Fucking card reading? Jesus, I thought for one second, maybe you'd turned a corner. Ready to do something with your life, but instead you do this."

"Does it matter how it came about?"

"You saw *the future*, Kate. That's what you're saying. It's ludicrous, and you'll be laughed out of court just hard enough to look like a liar, but not enough to appear insane. *Please* don't think that's a reasonable defense."

Kate chewed over the rebuke. If the position were reversed, would she see an explanation like that any differently? Probably not. There was still no chance of her revealing the true source, though. That would be far worse.

"What if it was possible to prove to a jury?" Kate asked.

Jonathan sighed, humoring her. "It'd change a lot, and not just in your case. Can you imagine?" He barked a humorless laugh. "If this is real, why not other supernatural bullshit? 'It wasn't me, your honor, it was a ghost,' or, 'I couldn't help it, I was possessed by a zombie vampire from Venus.' Besides, it throws up a bunch of other stuff, too."

"Like what?"

"Like the prosecution finding holes in it. Like posing impossible questions that make a jury think even worse of you. Not to mention the judge who's likely to slap you with the maximum sentence for insulting our fine legal system."

"Like what?" she repeated. "What holes?"

Jonathan dropped his brow, concentrating as if he were taking it seriously. "If I went in and demonstrated your masterful powers of fortune-telling, a decent counter-witness would be a professor of... I don't know, whatever field covers this crap. Quantum physics, probably. Whatever field, he says that you see the future, fine. In a dream, through a wormhole, or a crow whispers it in your ear. Doesn't matter. As soon as you look at the future, you have power over that future. You must have known you'd be arrested, for example. You know the outcome of the trial. If that's the case, you understand the prosecution's arguments and can counter everything they throw. Since you haven't done that, you are lying."

"But I'm not lying."

"If you can't convince me, Kate, how will you convince a jury?"

Kate replayed his argument to herself, seeing his point, but unable to explain why it didn't work like that. If she came clean, he'd snatch Aaron away without a second thought.

She said, "So because knowledge of the future changes the future, there can be no clairvoyance? That's your legal stance?"

"I wouldn't put it as crudely, but that's the basic crux, yes. If you saw your fate, how did you end up caught and boxed into a corner? That's only one reason to come up with a better explanation."

"A dream won't cut it?"

"No, Kate. A dream will get you five years."

Kate watched the road through the panoramic window—even the view looked bigger from the Bentley. "It's true."

"It's not true. And let's not forget the other side of it. The high-interest loan. Even a junkie like you wouldn't risk ten grand from a loan shark on a *dream*."

He slapped the wheel and lapsed into another stretch of silence.

Again, he broke first, this time in a more conciliatory manner, almost tenderly. A pleading tone, hoping she'd go for it. "You got a tip off from an old scumbag gambling friend, or heard something on one of your cleaning jobs, or… I don't know. Insider trading, Kate? *Seriously*?"

She was about to object, but she'd said all she could already.

"This is another form of gambling." His hands left the wheel, thrown up in despair. He returned one hand to grip it, the other waving as he went on. "If you drop back into your old habits, I'll be straight onto Child Protective Services. I'll do what's best for my nephew, no matter how hard it is on him. Whatever's for the best."

Kate didn't think a simple accusation of gambling addiction would get Aaron removed, not unless she was bringing her *scumbag friends* around to party with booze and drugs. Those dark days where she was driving along and thought ploughing into a bridge support would land Aaron with a decent payout on her life insurance—an auto accident, not suicide like his dad—were always ripped away when she realized her son would more than likely end up with Jonathan and Jennifer. Plus, she wasn't there yet. And she certainly wasn't there now, not if she could haul herself up financially. No, those thoughts of losing Aaron to the J-Js kept her both sober and battling through the constant tiredness and challenges.

Besides, Jonathan was only venting here, a long-repressed need to lash out at the person he saw as responsible for his brother's death. But today, she saw something else. More focus on Aaron.

"You can't have kids," she said. "So you're gearing up to steal mine."

"Don't you dare bring up Jennifer's—"

"Is it only Jennifer's? I didn't pry. But you seem mighty keen to get Aaron away from me."

Jonathan gritted his teeth and his waving hand clenched and pointed. "I told Craig he was nuts taking you back. He knew you couldn't keep it up, couldn't stick to the program. You would always relapse."

Kate was about to emit a, "Ha!" but it died in her throat at what he said next.

"If I find you had anything to do with his death, I could get his case reopened in an instant." He clicked his fingers.

"Me?"

His comment suggested more than her bearing responsibility, more than driving him to suicide. More like…

"You actually think I'd *hurt* him? Kill him myself?"

Jonathan's lick of the lips, the shoring up of his calm exterior, lasted just long enough to serve as his answer. "I don't know. It makes more sense than suicide. But even it was by his own hand—"

"It wasn't. He'd never do that."

"If it was, and I got that case reopened, you'd have so many lawsuits. People suing you for the insurance money, the bank taking the house, and you in jail for insider trading."

Kate's stomach curdled, confusion swirling in her brain. "Why? What could make you think I'd ever do something to harm Craig?"

Another facial tic showed he was composing himself in the stop-start traffic. "I was handling the divorce, so I know everything. Or my firm was. It's not my area, but I'm still covered by the privilege. And they were more than happy to do it since they'd already decided to make me a partner."

You had *to get the mention of partner in there. Again!*

He said, "Craig sent it all through me, copied me in on everything. It was as though he was worried. About himself. And I have paperwork that would have shone a different light on the coroner's investigation. But I didn't bring it out. I kept it quiet. For Aaron, and for Craig."

Kate's churning stomach clenched. "What paperwork?"

"Not literally paper. A voicemail."

"From Craig?"

They were at a stop point in the stop-start traffic cycle so

Kate could easily open the door and run. It was tempting. But she was rooted to the seat, Jonathan safe to glare at her.

"I never said anything because I didn't want to believe it. Didn't want to risk you and Aaron left destitute. *He* wouldn't want that. But the night Craig died…"

Kate pointed to the front, traffic moving. She didn't want to listen. Yet needed to hear it so badly. More than anything.

Jonathan set his hands at ten and two, and drove on. "He called the house that night, drunk. We could tell he was drunk, but… Let's just say he was concerned about the divorce. And he was definitely going through with it this time. No more rehab. No more chances. But he saw it so often. That the courts usually side with the mother, and you'd do enough to convince them Aaron was better with you. He knew first-hand how manipulative you can be."

Manipulative. Was she that bad? Was this where Aaron got it from? From her?

"He didn't call the cops on me," Kate said, "because of you?"

"Jennifer, actually. She called him back for me. Pointed out doing that would make him look vengeful or something. I came on the call too. Agreed we could put that off until later. But you knew. You knew he'd threatened it."

"Yes."

"That's motive."

Kate's jaw tightened. She looked out the side window. "Again, it's not proof."

"I'm going to be completely honest here." Jonathan pulled to a stop light. "I don't think he killed himself. If he was going to do that, anaphylactic shock isn't what he'd choose. And I'm pretty sure you don't have the brains to concoct a murder so perfect. But remember, I can drop those hints. Get his case reopened. I could destroy you, and I would, if it keeps Aaron safe from his junkie mom."

Kate bit back her revulsion at the threat, at the power Jonathan held over her. She knew what he needed to hear. "I'll step up my meetings. But about what I said before you started ranting."

More manipulation?

Jonathan set off on green. "The loan? Forget it."

"Not for me. You had your big break in that losing case, the big push that got you to partner. And yes, yes, before you say it, I know, I *know* it was your own effort, not luck. But you also had backup at home. I don't have anyone helping me. *Aaron* doesn't have that. All I want is to take him to therapy again. And I still maintain I did nothing wrong yesterday. When that account gets unlocked, I will pay you back, but... We're struggling. It's important."

He was clearly mulling it over as they pulled onto the expressway.

She laid a final plea on him, unsure what she'd do if he refused. "You'll do what's right for your nephew? Well, yeah. That's good. And I will do whatever it takes to keep my son well. Even if it means embarrassing myself by asking my brother-in-law for a loan."

Yep, manipulative.

What a bitch.

"If you really care about what's best for him," she added, "*I* go to meetings weekly instead of monthly, and *he* goes to Dr. Patel."

"Fine," he said. "But I'll be watching."

What Kate hadn't voiced yet was her concern over the loan from Ollie Swag. If they didn't get the brokerage account unfrozen—with or without the shorted windfall—she'd be $12,000 in the hole with no way to climb out. Enclosed inside a moving vehicle was not the right time to discuss that, nor was it right when Jonathan dropped her at the train station to pick up her car, or back at the house after he followed her home.

There, with Jennifer simpering at his sheer manly decisiveness and generosity, he called Dr. Patel and arranged a standing order to cover Aaron's treatment. Kate managed to schedule a session right away.

It was partly to get moving on Aaron's troubles, but equally to free herself from Jonathan's orbit. And the things he'd said that still echoed.

If the case were to be reopened, if he carried it through and took Aaron...

If he went even further and accused her directly...

He had no proof. Not of Kate doing something intentional. Perhaps more proof of Craig's fragile state of mind, of being stuck between calling the cops to prove what his junkie wife did and hanging fast, hoping—*gambling*—that things swung his way in court... Maybe that was enough.

The half-hour she spent pacing in Dr. Patel's family waiting room took her from one extreme to the other and back again, then on another ride entirely. From donning an orange jumpsuit, convicted of murdering her husband off the back of hearsay, to losing her house as a cackling insurance executive turfed her out; from strutting proudly out of the FBI building, all charges dropped and her trade endorsed as lawful, to a judge sniggering as she presented her "dream" defense to the jury; and the smaller, more choking scenarios, of Aaron escorted from her home by CPS workers, into the waiting Bentley and Jennifer Mallory's oh-so-sincere condolences and promises that they'd take care of him until Mom was back on her feet, and Ollie Swag's tracksuit-clad freaks dragging her into her garden and setting about her with baseball bats—

"Mrs. Mallory?"

Dr. Patel. He'd said he needed to do a deeper analysis, get some more details from Aaron, before consulting with them both.

This time, he invited her to sit before his desk on a surprisingly comfortable metal-framed chair beside Aaron on an identical seat. The boy was smiling and held his mom's hand as she lowered into position.

"We've had a good, long chat," Dr. Patel said. "Aaron still believes this is an outside force. Don't you, Aaron?"

"Because it is," Aaron mumbled.

"Yes. And you, Mrs. Mallory, you've not witnessed anything to corroborate this?"

"She can't," Aaron said, clearer this time.

"Remember, Aaron. We agreed certain ground rules for this part of the conversation."

Aaron nodded glumly.

"I believe it is a delusion," Dr. Patel went on. "And you believe it is, too, don't you, Mrs. Mallory?"

She glanced at Aaron, who averted his eyes.

A delusion. Did he mean the predictions, which could not be faked, or the behavior after? She played it safe.

"He's under a lot of pressure at school," Kate said. "And with his father's passing still hurting, I hope we can all work to—"

"Liar!" Aaron blurted, snapping to her. His face was drawn, tight, not full of hate but perhaps fear. Confusion. "You got the scores, and you made money. You got that shorty thing, and you used that too. You saw the bird. It came for us because we didn't kill it. And you asked me about the Whale shop thing, and you'll see. When that comes true, you'll see."

Dr. Patel watched, his bushy eyebrows raised. "There have been more predictions?"

Aaron's chin dipped, eyes stuck on Kate. "Sorry, Mom. It slipped out."

Kate scrambled to find an excuse, but Dr. Patel was already on it.

"I hope nothing was held back," he said. "I need complete honesty. If you're telling Aaron to keep things from me, this isn't a very auspicious start to our process."

"I didn't," Kate floundered, words stuck in her throat. "I mean, I told him not to mention it to people, but I didn't mean you. I meant his aunt or his friends or teachers." She addressed Aaron. "You can tell Dr. Patel anything. *Everything*. He's not allowed to reveal it to anyone except me, and only then if he tells you first that he'll share it. Okay?"

"Okay." Aaron still sounded downbeat.

Dr. Patel took it in and carried on as before. "Aaron's mind is pressing on him so hard, he has made it feel like an external force. He can get through this, though."

"If I don't use the things I get given," Aaron said.

Dr. Patel focused on Kate. It was her cue to fill in the blank, but she didn't know how. The psychiatrist took the initiative. "Have more of these 'psychic' predictions come true?"

Before Kate could lie for him, Aaron said, "Yes."

One eyebrow lifted higher than the other. Waiting.

"A share price," Kate said. "I don't know where it came from, but he got a stock market prediction right."

Dr. Patel returned his eyebrows to their resting state, exhaled portentously, and steepled his fingers under his chin. "Aaron, might I have a moment with your mother? It won't take long, and I'm not going to say anything bad about you. I promise. And I'm not allowed to lie. Okay?"

Aaron hopped off his chair without a word. Dr. Patel offered a lollipop from the plate on his desk, but Aaron shook his head and mooched out to the family room.

"Did his predictions really come true?" Dr. Patel asked. "Which ones? And what did you do with the information?"

"What if it's real?" Kate countered, eager to avoid discussing what might become a criminal case. She thought, maybe, doctor-client confidentiality flew out the window if it was leading to a crime, or covering one up. Not that it was a crime, but still not worth risking it. "What if he is psychic? If he's seeing these visions? If he is, is it beyond the scope of possibility that he's right about the bad things too?"

"Mrs. Mallory, after millions of dollars, possibly billions in today's money, the best scientific minds in the world have found no conclusive evidence whatsoever of psychics or fortune tellers having any credibility. Nothing they cannot write off as statistical coincidence."

"I know," she said. "But *what if*? Ask that of yourself when you're treating Aaron. *What if* he's right? How much more damage are we doing by denying it?"

He remained blank for several seconds. Processing something behind the glasses resting on his squashed nose. Eventually, he put his hands down and opened his drawer, pulling out a pad. "This is for a weak medication—"

"Oh. No." Kate held out a hand—*stop*. "I don't want him drugged up."

"It isn't anything serious, just a very gentle mix to help calm him. Focus him on the real world a little more. We normally use it for children on the lower end of the ADHD spectrum." He tore it off and handed it to her with a flourish. "It's temporary to get his behavior under control, and we'll wean him off it as the sessions develop."

Kate stared at it.

"If he takes this," Dr. Patel said, "the school might be willing to allow him back into class. If I assure them we are progressing."

Kate nipped it with her fingertips, holding it away from her like a rotten fish.

Dr. Patel gave a satisfied nod. "You have to accept this is not an easy process, a means to an end, not a definitive answer. But it will alleviate his stress and, perhaps, allow you to take a step back yourself."

"Me?"

"You are clearly very upset, Mrs. Mallory. You want to see your son as having nothing wrong with him. In fact, you're elevating his misbehavior to a supernatural entity. Like many parents, a child's mental health challenges can have a knock-on effect to the adults. Through stress, anxiety, depression. It's important to not let it get that far." He took a card from the same drawer as his script pad and slid that to her. "I recommend speaking to a colleague of mine. Dr. Herrera. She is very good with suburban matters. I send a lot of parents her way."

Kate lay the prescription in her lap and took the card.

"You take the kids, she gets the adults?"

Dr. Patel opened his hands, as if miming the word *book*. "It is beneficial to both children and parents. She will help you come to terms with your troubles."

Instead of arguing, trying to prove Aaron's talents were real, Kate flattened the card to the prescription, held onto them both, and stood.

"Thank you. I'll be sure to give it some serious thought."

But she and Craig had always been against medicating children out of their problems. Always. She needed to try something else first.

CHAPTER TWENTY-SIX

Unlike pretty much every kid in the neighborhood, Aaron preferred Wendy's over McDonald's, although he'd also never turn down a meal from the latter. Driving back from Dr. Patel's in the rain, Kate chose the former, even though it took five minutes longer to get home with the bounty. Today, though, she'd also needed an excuse to pop into a pharmacy "for something" before picking up dinner, which she did without Aaron questioning her. In fact, he initiated no conversation during either detour, responding in monosyllabic non-sentences and shrugs and sighs to Kate's chit-chat questions.

And they weren't specific questions about the session. Nor about the situation that had escalated to where Kate fully accepted Aaron's seemingly supernatural gift as fact, yet denied the possibility of retribution if he didn't assuage that feeling he got afterward. Given the nature of the raid that sank Villiers, it was natural for the SEC to find their trade suspicious. Merv reporting it was in line with his personality and merely escalated the timeline on an investigation. No supernatural karma or whatever. Besides, Aaron said killing the blackbird was the price for using the short-trade tip. Something *he* initiated.

The notion of favors for favors still seemed so silly to Kate.

Sillier than a ten-year-old wishing for psychic powers and being granted them?

She had no theories about the origin of his gift and did not want to probe that. Mainly, she thought, because the answer was obvious to her. Tammy had offered the best explanation days ago.

"I wanted to talk to you about some ideas I've had," Kate told Aaron as they unloaded the burgers, fries, and milkshakes in the kitchen.

"Is that what this is for?" he asked, suspicion clouding his face.

"No, this is a treat for being such a good boy in the doctor's."

"Right."

Although Kate preferred the deck for difficult conversations, the rain was coming down, and she thought a different type of junk food might loosen Aaron up a little. She vowed, too, that the next meal they ate together would be healthier, packed with veggies and minimal meat.

Approximately halfway through the feast, Kate raised the subject she hoped would lead to him accepting the medication willingly. "Where do you think this gift came from?"

"Why did we go to Wendy's?" he asked, munching, focused on the burger in his hand.

"I told you, a treat after the doctor's. But I was hoping you had an idea about where you got this. When it started."

"I blew out my candles, wished for help to be good at school, and then I could do stuff."

"The next day?"

He nodded, his mouth full.

Kate sucked at her milkshake. "Okay. What were you thinking about? Jesus? God?"

Aaron swallowed his food and held still.

Kate rested a hand over his. "It's okay, you can tell me."

He shrugged. "Dad, I suppose."

As Kate had suspected. "You were thinking about Dad on your birthday. You were surrounded by family. Isn't it possible that if there's an afterlife, whether it's the Christian one, the Jewish faith, or any of the others—"

"Like Thor?" Aaron said.

"Thor, Apollo, Allah, Krishna…" She struggled to remember the Mormon prophets or another version of Christianity, but came up blank. "Whatever. If there's a soul, and the people we love who pass on can watch over us, wouldn't Dad have been at your party? With all our family?"

"I guess."

"I think your father gave you this gift to help you. It might only be temporary, but it's your gift. Doesn't that make sense?"

Aaron put the burger down. "I could ask the buddy."

"No, please don't use the gift yet. When we've got it under control, and you don't have to hurt people or animals, maybe we'll pick it up again. For now, don't ask it anything."

He shrugged and picked up his burger and took a bite. Chewing, he said, "Okay. How?"

She was glad he asked that. It made what she had to do next appear as a seamless part of their conversation. She produced the bag picked up from the pharmacy—the prescription paid for on Jonathan's standing order. "This is medicine."

"Why do you need medicine?" His expression dropped into fear—an innocent about to be given terrible news. "Are you sick? Are you going to die? I don't want you to—"

"It's *your* medicine," Kate said.

Aaron waited a beat, eyes darting as if expecting an ambush, then settled back on her. "But I'm not sick."

"You're seeing the gift as something you don't deserve. Other people don't have it, so you shouldn't be able to use it. Not without consequences. But you deserve it. You don't need to be ashamed of it. This…" She scrunched the top of the bag with the bottle in the bottom. "It'll make you calmer."

His face fell into another confused frown. "It'll take away the bad stuff?"

Kate removed the bottle from the bag. She pushed the corners of her mouth out, tried to remember how to soothe herself into a picture of comfort, to get her little boy to trust she knew what was best with only a smile. "Baby, if I could take it from you and hold onto it myself, I would. But I can't do that. This is the next best thing. I promise."

"Will pills stop my buddy making me do things I don't wanna?"

Opening the bottle, she sensed every contour of her skin, the crinkling around her eyes, tight at her mouth, her head tilted a little too far. "Yes, I think so. Will you trust me?"

She tipped one pill out onto the burger wrapper.

"Will you try it?"

Aaron stuffed the last of his burger into his mouth and emptied his remaining fries into the wrapper next to the pill. He picked up the tiny white caplet. It was smaller than an Advil, white, with a symbol Kate couldn't make out—the drug company's logo, she figured.

"If you say it's the right thing, I'll do it." Aaron popped the pill and swallowed it back with a slug of milkshake, then opened his mouth and waggled his tongue to show it was gone. "Can we watch a movie next?"

. . .

235

They sat together on the couch. Upright. A glass of water each to counter the salt and sugar from dinner. On the TV, Kate had selected a movie from the 1980s, a big kids' block-buster from that decade, but she couldn't remember the name now it was a quarter of the way through. Boys disobeying their parents, alien technology, questionable gender roles, inappropriate humor for a ten-year-old; par for the course with these things.

Aaron's eyes seemed heavy. Drowsiness was a possible side-effect, but the pharmacist said he should develop a resistance to it after the first couple of days.

"Did it work?" Aaron asked, his voice as laden as his eyelids.

"Did what work?"

"The Whale shop."

"Do you want to know?"

"Yeah."

She checked for "Whale Ride-On stocks" on her phone and, as well as the share price, found a smattering of news stories. Whale Ride-On Sports had floated that morning at $0.52 per share. At ten a.m., a major Hollywood action star with vocal liberal politics endorsed them on Twitter, which prompted several alt-right types to jump on and call for a boycott of the "socialist" company—ridiculous, since no government controlled that company or its means of production—and that pushed it into the headlines of CNN, Fox, and MSNBC, followed by the other majors on a slow news day. The attention meant a frenzy of trading activity, which closed the share price out at $5.43, a surge of over 1000%. If she'd invested $10,000 this morning, that'd have given her over 19,000 shares. Selling them right before the bell, she'd have netted around $105,000. With access to the money held by the FBI, the full $99,000…

She calculated it at a round 100k for ease, and it came to over a million dollars in revenue.

For one day.

If she'd given this tip to Endo and he was able to gamble up to a million at a time, he'd have been set for the month. And that was without it climbing more the following day.

Damn. Should've tapped up Ollie again.

Yeah, right. The same day they arrested her for shorting a company using her son's foresight? For which she might still serve jail time if they didn't come to their senses?

"And I didn't use the vision, did I?" Kate said, biting back the regret, the anger at losing all that money. "Just like I promised."

Aaron sipped from his glass and let Kate take it from him. "Who's Endo?"

Kate's fingers weakened, and she had to put down her water. She felt her face flush. "Where'd you hear that name?" Had she said it out loud?

Aaron tapped the side of his head. "In here."

"You can't have. Why would you? I didn't use the information."

"You did." His voice had diminished, eyelids all but closing.

"No." Kate shook her head, conscious her eyes had gone wide, that she had shuffled back from Aaron. "I promise, I didn't use it."

He retrieved his glass, drank some more water, his jaw working afterward as if he remained thirsty. "But that's okay, Mom. I took the pill. I won't have to do it."

"Do what? You shouldn't have to do anything, Aaron." She was still in shock. She'd denied the need, the compulsion, to offset a favor for a favor, but it seemed so unfair. As though her son was about to slide into something she couldn't pull him out from.

"I didn't use it."

"You *did.*" He set the glass back on its coaster himself, then snuggled into her as if her concern was unfounded. "You used it to make me feel better. And it worked. But the medicine will make it go away."

"Make what go away?"

"You know." He said it like the most obvious thing in the world.

Kate hugged him tight. She couldn't imagine how awful it might be, the sensation to hurt, to damage, to kill, when it was against his every instinct. That was one thing she'd picked up from this. It was a compulsion to balance the good with a bad thing, but he didn't enjoy it. He wasn't taking anything for himself with the death of his guinea pig or the birds. No glee in daubing shit on the walls.

He was nevertheless a good kid at heart.

"I wish someone would give me that magic wand," she said, her mouth in his hair, drinking in his scent, his clean, flowery hair. "I'd snatch it from you and stop it without a pill."

"But you can't. Can you?"

"No, honey. I'm sorry." She was stroking his hair like she used to when he was a toddler, something that had soothed him in the days before he could speak. She still remembered his form, his little face, from way back then. His hair was the same—soft and shaggy, like a pint-sized surfer-dude.

"But then you'd have to kill Endo," Aaron droned, voice fading toward sleep.

Kate's heart literally ached to hear him speak this way. But it wasn't him. He didn't *want* to hurt anyone.

Aaron yawned, barely able to stay awake. For the first time in days, he looked at peace. No, he looked… *serene.* As if he had no more troubles.

"I hope I've helped today," Kate said. "The pill will fix all this."

"You have helped me, Mommy…" Yawn. Eyes closed. "I don't need to kill Endo."

Kate threw up a prayer of thanks to the god of all things medical. It was working. She had fixed her boy.

Certain he was asleep, she kissed his head. "I'll do anything for you, baby. Anything at all."

She slipped aside, picked him up as gently as she could, carried him up to bed, and tucked him in. At his door, she watched him sleep. His steady breaths, the tiny dimple at the corner of his mouth. Then she closed him in, and headed downstairs for a glass of wine, which she sat down to enjoy slowly, and block out the world of problems she still had to deal with.

The FBI.

Unfreezing her money.

And getting Aaron back into school now his troubles were behind him.

She switched out the 80s movie for a murder mystery series, grabbed a pack of Doritos and dip to supplement her wine, and made it through one and a half episodes before her phone bonged.

A message from Ollie Swag:

You owe 12k from tomorrow, Katie-Kat. Make the payment. Please.

CHAPTER TWENTY-SEVEN

The medication worked in more ways than one. Besides Aaron getting a good night's sleep and waking up refreshed and bright, Kate received a call from the school office at 7:55 to say they'd welcome Aaron back now he had made progress. Dr. Patel had followed through with them as promised. Kate was happy to relieve Jennifer of her kind offer to sit for her again, dropped Aaron at school, and he practically glided away from her—Atlas, relieved of his global burden. She'd monitor his finger-crossing tic, too, see if that eased along with his anxiety.

Kate found her commute a breeze. She might not have had a job to return to, but until they made her dismissal permanent, or her two-weeks' notice elapsed, she saw no reason not to head in. If it took more than two weeks to unfreeze her funds, she would get desperate soon. Every little bit would count until then.

And there was Ollie Swag to worry about.

Already, her debt to him was $12,000 and even her original $10,000 stake was on hold. Staring out the train window, she mused that she could fold on Endo, lie to get out of the situation, and demand her money in exchange for her obedience.

That was what they did in this game, wasn't it? Made deals?

She couldn't be sure if that was too bold a move. At the very least, if she decided to go that route, she should be able to access the 10K.

There was another option, though. Which she saved until she got to work.

"What is it?" Tammy asked, after Kate unloaded on her in full.

They were in the break room, Tammy having grabbed her as soon as she came in. She told her Dev had already announced that Kate's arrest meant she wouldn't be working again and had divvied up her roster between everyone else. Kate's account skipped a few steps, such as the animal mutilation, but she managed to babble everything else. She didn't hold back, either. Of all the people she could confide in, Tammy was the one true believer in Aaron's clairvoyance—be it Craig bestowing help from beyond, some unheard-of spirit, or even a scientific explanation, burrowing deep into quantum physics.

"Endo," Kate said. "That's my backup."

"You're not gonna snitch?"

"It wouldn't be snitching, Tam. He's the innocent party. *I* approached *him*. He trusted me. I just need him to help me out until the FBI lets us go."

"But you'll tell 'em what they wanna hear if you got no other option."

"I don't want to threaten him. But I can't go to prison. And Ollie's people will take everything I own."

Tammy wiped a hand over her face. "Endo ain't gonna be here. I'm guessin' he ain't answering his phone."

"Voicemail. But I can go out at lunchtime. Can you cover for me if I'm late back?"

"You know where he lives?"

"I…" Kate checked her phone. The address had come with Endo's contact card the night before the trade. "Yes, I got it."

"If he's your only shot, go now. Dev thinks you're toast already, and we can deal with it. Lemme know how it goes."

Before Kate could hiss Tammy's name to call her back, she rushed out and closed the door behind her.

It was annoying, but she was right. Kate's problems with the FBI shrank to a pinprick in comparison with the freight truck bearing down on her in the form of Ollie's soaring interest. The only choices she had were to lie to the feds about her source, borrow the cash from Jonathan which threatened her standing with any future charges from CPS, or hope against hope that Endo helped her out; a loan, a plan, something.

Endo wasn't answering his phone, even when Kate left a voicemail to say she was slipping out of work. On the Metro, with little to do but think, she entertained the possibility that he was still under arrest and being grilled by Special Agent Ruiz or her contemporaries, although that was soon put to rest when she emerged from her journey and buzzed his apartment from the street.

"Yes." It wasn't a question, just a tired word spoken from the intercom.

"It's Kate," she said. "Please, let me in."

No reply.

"I have to speak to you, Endo, please."

A pause, but the line was open. Breathing. Then, "I'm not supposed to be in contact with you."

"Do they have a court order to that effect?"

Another spell of dead air. "No."

"Then buzz me up. If you don't like what I have to say, you can kick me out." Kate's turn to pause with her finger on the button, letting the sounds of the street resound through the comms. "It's not like either of us has anything to lose."

She released the button and waited. Waited a little longer. Then the door gave a grating *hnnnnnng* which only stopped when she opened it, walked through, and closed it behind her. She navigated up in the elevator to the tenth floor and followed the apartment number plaques on the wall. It was like a hotel, only with plush linoleum instead of carpet and more rules posted every few feet, relating to waste management, recycling, personal hygiene, and noise limits.

Endo's door was open a crack. She knocked once and pushed inside.

"Hello?"

The apartment was dark, as if the drapes were all closed, and it smelled funkier than whoever posted the personal hygiene advice would approve of. To Kate's left, a kitchenette had several plates and pans in the basin, Chinese takeout cartons and a pizza box piled beside it, and mugs and glasses lined up to the side. The counter nearest her stuck out over the lower section, with tall stools beneath it to serve as a breakfast bar. She could detect the Chinese food, not rotten or old—a recent meal. According to her watch, it was only noon, although it wasn't unreasonable to think takeout delivered this early.

It had only been a day since their arrests, but it seemed Endo had become a depressed frat boy in that short time.

"Hello?"

No answer.

A vision flashed into Kate's mind of her advancing into the dim space and finding Endo on the floor, his torso sliced vertically and his body flayed like a ragged autopsy, her son crouched over him with a bloodied machete, saying, "I had to, Mommy."

Kate found a light switch and flicked it on, illuminating the apartment ahead of her: open plan with tan floor-to-ceiling drapes drawn, a huge TV on the wall, U-shaped arrangement of couches and chairs, a crescent bar area abutting the kitchenette on one side, a bookcase on the other. It screamed BACHELOR PAD. Other than the kitchen, it seemed clean and well-organized, not a single corpse to be identified.

To her right, a short passage held three doors—bedrooms, a bathroom, maybe? Under one of those doors, a light shone.

A faucet turned on for five or six seconds, then shut off.

The door with the glow opened and Endo came out, rubbing a towel over his face and hair. He was dressed day-off smart in jeans and a long-sleeved top, and Homer Simpson slippers. He fished his glasses out of a breast pocket and put them on.

"Great, you found the place," he said. "Just freshening up. I don't get many visitors."

"Have you been okay?" Kate asked.

"Sure. Bit of a headache. I drank too much wine last night. They grilled us for hours."

Kate pivoted to keep him in sight as he passed her and started fiddling with the mess in the kitchen. Filled the reservoir for his Nespresso machine.

"What did they ask you?" Kate said.

"Oh, probably the same as you. They seem more interested in the leak than putting me and you in prison." He made a serious-sounding huff, lips pinched and his manner so heavy it was as though someone had bound him with rope. "But they will charge us. They said you'd laid it all on me, but I didn't believe them. If I can bring them your source, they'll cut me a deal. No jail time."

"They repeated the same to me." Kate was here for a favor, the hope of a loan to fend off Ollie Swag, assuming only the brokerage accounts were frozen. She wasn't sure how to broach the subject, though. "They said it couldn't have been me. They didn't believe me when I said it was my psychic powers."

Endo gave a chuckle and resumed his water-filling operation. He noted Kate's gaze hit the cartons, the dirty plates, and seemed embarrassed. "Sorry, I turn into a slob when I'm stressed. And Merv was stressing me already. The feds just pushed me over." He set the water tank into the machine and passed a wire rack full of coffee pods to the counter nearest Kate. "Coffee?"

Kate perused the selection, panicked at the array of choice, and said, "Cappuccino?"

"Sure." He set the pods in place and took a clean, glass mug from a cupboard, and set to work. The machine was louder than Kate expected. "I already ate, but I'm still hungry. Slobbish and starving."

He smiled, although it seemed forced as he took a loaf of unsliced bread from a different cupboard and arrayed it on a wooden board. It gave off a fresh aroma, as if bought or baked that morning.

When the coffee process ended, Endo passed her the mug. "Can I get you a sandwich or something?"

Kate declined with a polite shake of the head. She hadn't

been around drug users for years, not since her Reno days, but she recognized the manic behavior of someone who'd taken a supplement to their usual habits. She didn't peg Endo as a big coke user, but suspected he'd have a stash for those rare times he entertained a client with tastes that stretched to the chemical as often as booze and rich food.

"So, what's with the urgency?" Endo asked. "My lawyer says the feds will be watching my building, so they'll think we're colluding."

"It's about the brokerage account," Kate said.

Endo slouched in place. "Right. Yeah, I've been trying not to think too much about it."

Kate sympathized, but had no right to judge his way of dealing with it. She'd had other things to worry about—a son, a debt to a loan shark, judgmental in-laws. "I was wondering how long it will take to unfreeze the assets."

A nervous laugh burst from Endo. He turned to the refrigerator and retrieved butter and a packet of cooked meat that looked like he'd got it freshly sliced from a butcher or specialist section of the grocery store. Kate wondered if she'd be able to buy that kind of quality cut soon, not the water-infused processed crap she resorted to from the pre-packed aisle.

"Can I get one of those?" she asked.

"Sure." Endo lay the butter and meat beside the cutting board and selected a bread knife from a block nearby.

A flash blinded Kate. Not her imagination this time, not her guilt at Aaron's animal murder-spree. This was a physical burst of light, like a camera snapping her picture. When it faded, a swarm of red, blue, and green blotches danced before her.

Endo rushed from his spot, came round to her side. "Are you okay?"

She'd gripped the countertop, spilled the coffee somehow. She blinked hard and fast. "I…"

He eased her onto one of the high stools lining the breakfast bar. "When did you last eat?"

Endo cupped her face in his hands, his own face pulled away, as if searching her features for an answer. Kate stared back, her balance restored, but she hadn't regained her breath. Her heart yammered.

What the hell was that?

"You're pale," Endo said. "I have something of a pick-me-up if you need it."

Kate filled her lungs. Expelled the air slowly. As she found a cloth and started mopping the spill, she assured him, "I'll be okay. Maybe that sandwich will do me good. And another coffee if you trust me not to spill it."

Endo removed his hands, concentrating on her. And a half-inch below his left eye, a ripple blemished his skin.

Kate wondered if it was a tic of some sort, a nervous reaction. But then it happened again, closer to his jaw. He didn't react, and this time it lasted longer. It was as if there was something inside him, crawling around.

It disappeared, and he returned to the kitchenette and his unsliced loaf.

"You should see a doctor." Endo took up the serrated bread knife. "Stress does some weird things. Me, I binge." He made another self-deprecating gesture toward the debris in the sink, then started cutting the bread. The knife's teeth bit into the crust and sawed back and forth. "If I knew the source, I'd tell them."

Kate watched the blade—in, out, in, out. The fresh bread aroma bloomed stronger as crumbs dusted the cutting board. "You know the source. It's me."

The slice fell to the side and Endo made a notch to cut a

second, but hesitated and twitched the knife like an orchestra's conductor. "You're *my* source. Not *the* source. I mean, for a while, I wanted to believe you. I even convinced myself you might be psychic." He returned the knife to the bread and went to work on it. "But deep down, I knew you must have someone else. That Ruiz woman. She'll be fair, I know it."

The blade—in, out, sawing, grating the crust into crumbs —mesmerized Kate. She couldn't stop looking at it. "I'm not lying. I was the source."

Her brain turned to mush. She was struggling to think.

"I came here for a reason," she said. "Something important."

"Yeah, I guessed that. I was kind of hoping you wanted to go in together, make a deal. Hey, if we go to her, say you revealing the real source is conditional on all three of us getting the light deal… that'd be something, right? No one having to betray the other?"

Kate glanced from the knife to Endo. His face and neck were crawling, wormlike creatures bulging under the skin, writhing, and he hadn't flinched, hadn't noticed. Or didn't care.

Back to the knife.

"Kate?" Endo said. "Do you need to lie down?"

Another burst of light assailed her. This time, at the center, a ghostly image faded into view, a blackbird with a broken wing, its beak open in a razor-sharp attack, talons bared. Then it was gone, replaced by those blotches, floating in her vision.

Endo lay the knife aside and ran the tap. He came back to her, presenting a glass. "Drink this."

Kate could hardly breathe. "What is it?"

"Water. It's water, just have a sip."

She did so, but it was vile. A slimy texture coated her

tongue and throat. Rotten. Like fluid that spilled from a garbage bag left to fester too long. She spat it out.

Endo jumped back. "Whoa!"

The knife.

Kate leaned on the countertop, her hand close to the handle. She was sweating, panting, struggling to stay upright.

Endo kept his position. "Kate, please lie down. I'll call a doctor. If you're not sleeping, not eating, it's—"

"NO!"

Kate's fingers brushed the knife's handle.

There was something wrong with Endo, that was for sure. The creatures burrowing into him were trying to trick her, to make her say what he wanted to hear, something to appease the FBI. He aimed to cover up the truth. This man was a betrayer. A man who would sell her out, let her rot in prison.

He was a threat.

He needed to die.

"Kate…" Endo came forward one step, a hand extended, voice shaking. "What are you doing with the knife?"

She was clutching it. Yet didn't remember picking it up.

He sidestepped to the edge of the breakfast bar, hands out, a cop placating a drunk. "It's okay. I can help. I'm sorry I pressured you. We just need to—"

"Shut… up!"

Kate was standing. No longer faint, no longer gasping for air. Her lungs were fine and her head was clear. The man before her posed a serious threat. To her and Aaron. And who would believe she'd murder him? He could have attacked her.

He *was* attacking her.

A destroyer of truth. Demanding she lie to the feds. What kind of psychopath would order her to lie like that? And if she didn't do as he said, he would cut her down as easily as he did that loaf.

One motion.

That was all it would take.

He'd be out of their lives for good. She could tell Ruiz she begged him to tell the truth, but he wouldn't. He took the secret of the mole to his grave.

Self-defense was such a delightful option for a woman in her position.

Then the blackbird shimmered before her. Not like before, not the burst of light, but something inside her. Her own memory.

An audible clip, as if edited on a voice app, filled her mind. No, she summoned it. Aaron, telling her:

Like there's a tickle in my tummy…

Then, it's getting stronger, and I get all scared…

And, last night, so many times, she'd told him she'd take the burden from him if she could. She'd tried. She'd tried so hard. The magic pill had done it for her.

You have helped me, Mommy…

Kate blinked away the images, the sounds, but one final nugget wouldn't drift away with the others.

I don't need to kill Endo.

Kate, in the apartment, with Endo glancing around, more so at the door than anywhere else, grinding her teeth. She lifted the knife, the gleaming blade flashing from the lights overhead. Then she caught her own reflection: her entire face had contorted into a snarl.

That line from Aaron: "*I* don't need to kill Endo anymore."

Was she imagining it? That emphasis? She hadn't perceived it last night, but there it was. In this memory. Or in this invention of a memory. This corruption.

As if Endo was corrupting her. He was a corrupter.

I…

But was it an invention, a corruption?

Rephrased: *I'm not the one who needs to kill Endo.*

Rephrased further: *You have helped me, Mommy. Now you have to kill Endo.*

"No." Kate threw the knife away. It clattered on the countertop and sluiced through the coffee. She edged toward the door, her face aching from the exertion. "I'm sorry."

Endo moved aside, his breath hitching. He clearly didn't trust that she wouldn't go psycho on him again.

"I'm sorry," she said again as she reached the door. "I thought you were going to hurt me."

"No." Endo shook his head, terror still frozen over him. All but the insects, worms, whatever they were, rippling his skin. "I just want this over with. I can't go to prison."

In that moment, Kate wanted nothing more than to drive a blade into the man. To stop herself lunging for the knife again, she fled into the corridor and ran. She didn't even bother with the elevator, banging out into the stairwell and running.

It didn't help.

As she ran, the urge to kill Endo only built in her chest. She cried out, doubling over, her stomach retching the farther she descended.

Out in the street, she stumbled into a parked car, setting off its alarm as she staggered along. She must have looked drunk or hurt, but she couldn't think of her appearance. All she knew was that if she returned inside, as every fiber of her body was telling her to, she'd kill Endo. She'd stab him and remove his innards, and play in his blood and entrails, and as she tried to get farther away, there was even a tingle between her legs.

Not a mere tingle.

She was *moist.*

Down there.

The idea of gutting a man turned her on so much, she

could have dropped her drawers right there in the street and just—

"Mrs. Mallory?"

Kate spun at the voice. Two men, clean shaven, with nice but boring suits. She recognized one of them.

"Mrs. Mallory, are you okay?"

Kate snapped upright. Calm. As if a wave had crashed on a shore, leaving only a foamy residue. Every desire to commit murder leached from her, an odd feeling all that remained— like the rare occasions she'd overindulged and wasn't sure what she'd gotten up to the night before, but was certain that when she found out, she'd be embarrassed.

Embarrassed.

About wanting to kill a man?

It was like they had woken her from a deep sleep with water on her face.

"Mrs. Mallory?"

He was an FBI agent. One who'd been there at Hetherington's. The man with him had been at the field office.

"Hi," she said, leaning on another car. "I'm… I was feeling faint. I think I'm okay now—"

"Holy—!" The lead agent dove for Kate and tackled her around the waist, tumbling them both to the sidewalk as an almighty crash rang out.

The air around them swelled, as if a breeze had gusted up from one direction, but a second car alarm had joined the one Kate set off. She didn't know which way was up for several seconds, until the strong, ever-so-polite agent helped her to her feet. He wasn't looking at her, though.

Nor was his partner.

Kate zeroed in on the source of their shock: the car she'd been leaning on.

The roof was crumpled, a crater of blood and mangled limbs partially hidden from view, but not so much that it wasn't clear someone had fallen from a great height. The car's side windows had been blown out, the windshield caved in. And two legs were slung over the side.

On the feet, in the exact spot where Kate had been leaning, were a pair of Homer Simpson slippers.

CHAPTER TWENTY-EIGHT

The cops did not arrest or Mirandize Kate; she was a witness. Throughout her interaction with NYPD—as a stockbroker plunging to his death on the street was their jurisdiction—they treated her like an upstanding citizen who'd been in the wrong place at the wrong time, and even, tacitly, as a victim. A solemn female officer took her statement a suitable distance from the scene, with a younger male cop bringing her sugary coffee and water and the bonus of a donut.

She couldn't bring herself to eat the donut.

After a short, numb time perched on the back step of a police wagon, alternating between staring into space and replaying the car smashing under Endo's body, Special Agent Ruiz arrived and badged her way through. She spoke with the two detectives who'd assumed responsibility for the scene. They responded by pointing up at Endo's apartment, then down at the vehicle now screened off while the CSIs worked, and finally at Kate. They spoke some more, but Ruiz trained her gaze on Kate and didn't turn away until she thanked the NYPD for their courtesy, and approached her.

She stood over Kate, who rose from her perch on the

back of a police van, her knees and muscles creaking, having been immobile for so long. "I think it's time we reconvened our discussion."

"Do I have a choice?" Kate asked.

"Sure. Between handcuffs or no handcuffs."

"Here?"

"Call your lawyer on the way."

First, Ruiz reminded her of her rights, then she and Kate's savior—whose name it turned out was Richardson—drove her to the same field office as before. Kate said nothing, as advised by Jonathan on the phone before departing, but once they disembarked and were escorting her to the interview room, Kate stopped.

"Problem?" Ruiz said.

Kate touched Richardson on the arm and waited for him to face her. "Thank you. For saving me."

"That's okay, Mrs. Mallory." His face remained set. No emotion.

"I'm sure he would have hit me if—"

"Please keep walking," Ruiz said.

The coffee and water swished heavily in Kate's stomach. She wasn't convinced the donut would have weighted it down better, but was more concerned—mortified, actually—to remember she'd left it at the van where the nice kid who'd brought it for her would see it and think she was a horrible person for rejecting his kind gift. As they showed her into the room, she wanted that donut more than a lawyer. More than freedom. More than the money she needed to fend off Ollie Swag and his tracksuit-wearing leg-breakers.

"We'll get started as soon as Mr. Mallory arrives," Ruiz said.

For a fleeting moment, Kate thought she meant Craig, but she snapped back to sobriety, her daze swept away. "Okay."

"But…" Ruiz glanced at Richardson and the man read something that encouraged him to back away, out of earshot. "Can I ask you something? Off the record?"

"I'm saying nothing without Jonathan."

"Not the SEC investigation. We're waiting on their forensic accounting to pull through everything you and your partners have done in the past five years."

"Why am I here?"

"Because one of those partners fell to his death moments after he attempted to record you confessing to insider trading."

It's a trick. She's making this sound informal, but it isn't.

That felt like intuition, an obvious ploy Kate had seen on TV. Yet, there was more to it. A certainty she was right. As Aaron said, it wasn't coming from within, but as though the knowledge had been delivered to her.

Kate sat, producing a show of looking comfortable. "I'll wait for my lawyer."

Ruiz nodded and shifted to leave, then paused. "Do you mind me asking something about Aaron?"

Kate all but forgot where she was, that she was to remain silent until her lawyer dropped whatever he was doing and rushed to her aid—a lawyer whose name she'd blocked out in favor of drilling her stare into Ruiz. "What about Aaron?"

Ruiz turned fully, propped on the doorframe with one shoulder. Her mouth closed tight, eyes studying Kate. She tapped her phone on her leg.

The camera is on. So are the microphones. You've been Mirandized. This conversation is admissible, no matter how informal she says it is.

Again, that comprehension landed with her—a message. Only, it wasn't words. It was insight. She knew it but hadn't heard it or read it or seen it.

"I thought your story sounded familiar," Ruiz said. "I did some digging."

"Familiar?" Kate held herself straight, hands in her lap, body language she hoped conveyed her as *haughty*. Superior. Not falling for her trick.

Ruiz bit her bottom lip, then relented. "Your son, he's acting out. Behavioral problems at school?"

"Yes."

"Doing gross things you're ashamed of?"

"Yes."

She's getting to you. She knows more than you realize.

Still not a voice, just an instinct. Clear, unambiguous. Kate simply... *knew.*

Ruiz said, "Animals killed?"

At that, Kate stumbled over her words, but managed, "No. Of course not."

"Okay."

She doesn't believe you. She knows you lied.

"Why are you asking me this?" Kate said.

"Because I think there's more happening here. To you, to Aaron. More than an inside trader." Ruiz put one foot inside the room then reconsidered, holding her spot. "Ever heard of Brian LaPaul?"

Kate leaned to one side, trying to see out, hoping Jonathan was here to advise her on how to answer. She settled on the truth. "No, not that I can recall. I may have met him through my late husband, but... no. Right now, I—"

"It's okay, I'm not testing you." Ruiz again tapped her phone, lifting it briefly before slipping it into her pocket. "He went to jail in 2007. Ten years for the same thing you, Marcus and Endo were here for."

Kate picked up that the pause was for her to speak. "A ten-year sentence? He must be a free man by now."

"He killed himself two years in."

"Not to sound callous, but how does that concern me? And Aaron?"

Jonathan is here. He will be ready to help you in minutes.

"My predecessor ran the case," Ruiz said. "And it's long resolved. But there aren't many bizarre cases for agents embedded at the SEC. It's pretty boring compared to national security and smashing drugs rings. Figures and spreadsheets, proving connections, figuring out how to convince a jury someone is guilty when the defense ties laymen in knots with jargon. But this one… It's a similar thing."

Ruiz angled to check the corridor. Finding nothing to bother her, she came back to Kate.

"So, yeah, 2007. About six months before the big crash. A loser broker starts coming up roses at work by flinging risky trades around, capitalizing on overvalued firms biting the dust. But, at the same time, his kid is going off the rails at home. It got so bad, it involved the cops."

Kate refused to see the similarities. "Is my lawyer here?"

"We're just chatting, Kate. If you want me to stop, I will. You only have to say the word."

Kate worked her jaw, but made no reply.

"I heard about it when I first took over. An oddity. That's why it dawned on me as familiar. When I looked into it some more last night, after we got done with Endo, I found out the kid—Victor LaPaul—ended up institutionalized."

Kate remained silent.

"From what I've dug out, this kid, he said he had to do nasty stuff. Started small, pranks that got increasingly mean. Progressed to vandalism, and then smaller animals. A neighbor's pet poodle disappeared, but the neighbor saw Victor swipe it on a yard camera, then caught him in the act of disemboweling it. Called the cops."

Kate gave nothing away, maintaining her haughty bearing.

"It was a few months before the markets crashed, so we weren't in the midst of a panic. We were already on Brian LaPaul's case, and after his son told the cops he was doing the animal stuff because he was helping his dad at work, the investigators figured he was lying to help his dad out." Ruiz let the implication hang, then added, "Anything familiar here?"

She knows.

"No," Kate said.

She's a threat.

"The child got worse. That institution he ended up in, they called him a psychopath. Highly intelligent, intuitive, but incredibly disturbed. Violent. He'd attempt to hurt staff, other residents, even himself. At the age of fourteen, he succeeded in committing suicide."

The same day as his father.

Kate stiffened in place. It was the closest to a whisper inside her brain that she'd sensed so far. Still not quite a voice, but there was an intelligence behind it. A presence she felt as surely as Ruiz remained standing before her.

"The same day as his father," Ruiz said.

Before Kate could react, guess at some earthly reason for knowing what Ruiz was about to reveal, footsteps clomped outside, growing louder, shutting off Ruiz's "informal" chat.

Jonathan appeared beside the woman. "I was listening with Agent Richardson. Interesting, Special Agent Ruiz. Interviewing my client without legal representation."

"We weren't discussing the charges against Mrs. Mallory," Ruiz said.

"No, you were trying to coerce her after she witnessed a traumatic event. You're conflating the suicide of her colleague with that of a parent experiencing similar child-rearing challenges as she is."

Kate hadn't seen it that way, but couldn't deny it. If psychic abilities like this really existed, she couldn't have been the first recipient to use it for gambling big on the stock market.

Jonathan shouldered his way in and placed his briefcase on the table. "I'll thank you to leave us alone and switch off all recording equipment."

Ruiz obeyed, backing out, but Kate called, "Wait."

Jonathan gave her a hard-eyed, subtle shake of the head.

Kate responded with a firm nod—*I know what I'm doing.* When Ruiz came inside, in view of the camera, Kate said, "What if this was the same thing? What if it really is some psychic phenomenon?"

"Are you making that your formal position, Mrs. Mallory?" Ruiz asked.

"No, she isn't," Jonathan answered for her. "Kate, what are you—?"

"Hypothetically," Kate said. "If I were sitting drinking my one glass of wine after dinner and some Jacob Marley-type ghost popped out of my fireplace and told me to go short on Villiers… how the hell is that insider trading?"

It isn't. She knows it.

No one spoke.

Kate said, "Unless someone from Villiers or the FBI, or anyone with proprietary knowledge gave me the information, it's not a crime. It didn't happen. You even brought me a story that says it's happened before."

"That's not the point, Kate," Ruiz said.

"Then why tell me about Brian LaPaul?"

"Because," Jonathan said, his knack for answering other people's questions continuing, "she wants to show you that a defense of using psychic powers doesn't wash. No matter how bad things are at home." He arched an eyebrow Ruiz's way. "Which she will not be repeating." Back to Kate. "And you will not fall for such blatant intimidation again. Clear?"

Ruiz said, "I wasn't trying to intimidate—"

"Nope." Jonathan didn't even look at her. "Please leave us. Nothing she said to you is admissible in court. You were out of line."

He wants you alone. He is manipulating you. He will hurt you if you let him.

"It was a vision," Kate said to Ruiz's back.

The agent halted in place. Jonathan fired up his hard eyes again.

Kate added, "It was me. I saw it in a dream, and that's the end of it. Prove otherwise, then you'll have a case. But you know I'm right. Please..." Kate's voice cracked.

There was something at the back of her head trying to make itself heard, but she didn't want it. The things she knew, the information she'd received but hadn't yet used, such as the child killing himself the same day his father did the same, extinguished any lingering doubt at Aaron's ability. The difference was it was no longer Aaron's. It was hers.

Ruiz faced Kate again. "Then what am I thinking right now?"

She wants to believe you. Because she doesn't want you to go to jail. She's desperate for proof of an afterlife because her sister died three years ago and it still hurts. It hurts her so much.

Again, not quite a voice in her head, but seeing it through Ruiz's eyes, feeling her grief, her desperation, concealed by a job that demanded stoicism. Like Sal, this woman had lost someone dear. Had she lost a husband as well as a sister? Grief can torment relationships in multiple ways.

Divorced...

Knowing this, seeing the hurt and desire in Ruiz, all Kate

wanted to do was hold the woman's hand, to say she didn't know, *couldn't* know for sure—all despite the special agent attempting to lock her up. Using her to get to a mole who didn't exist warmed Kate to her further, saw it as a side-hustle, her professional duty, while proving the existence of the supernatural was her prime concern. Hoping, in the execution of her job, she might learn the fate of a lost sibling.

Jonathan's expression remained unchanged, and Kate felt Ruiz's loss even more deeply. If she could use this connection to offer her comfort, perhaps Ruiz would become an ally, someone who could help her, who might find a way out for her and Aaron, but—

Kate recalled the consequences of Aaron's predictions, how she'd felt compelled to kill Endo, to see him as a threat. Then, when she hadn't done the deed, he dove out of a window, aiming—if she wasn't mistaken—for her.

What price would she have to pay for voicing this? For bringing Ruiz onto her side?

"I'm going to consult with my lawyer," Kate said.

"About time." Jonathan sat, annoyance still oozing from him. "Close the door on the way out, please."

It didn't take long to get Kate released. They'd wanted to ask her about a conversation Endo recorded during her visit, but they hadn't pulled it off his phone yet. It wasn't available for Jonathan and Kate to review, and the FBI prosecutors and SEC investigators needed to go over it first to assess whether there was anything they could use. Kate recalled little of the exchange, vaguely aware that Endo encouraged her to give up a name more than once. But she was overcome with terror. Her overriding memory was Endo looming as a monster, a beast that needed slaying.

She opted not to mention the worms beneath the man's

skin. Only his manner, stating that he seemed erratic, certain they'd find drugs in his system. She couldn't be sure what she'd said, so implied she'd cowered from him, and fled before raising the subject of a loan.

With the FBI unwilling to release the recording, and since the cases of Endo's suicide and his alleged financial crimes hadn't yet been synced into one investigation, there was nothing more to hold her on.

After release, Jonathan bought her a drink in a coffee shop a block from the field office, the quietest seats being in the corner on a counter by the window. He didn't show her to his own firm for the meeting, she noted, but didn't mention it. Perhaps pro bono clients didn't require special treatment.

"Visions?" Jonathan said. "Still going that route?"

"Any reason I shouldn't?"

"Because it's nuts."

"Is it?"

"Even if it was true, you can't use it in court."

Kate believed him. Concentrated on what he was saying, trying to block out a niggle in her head, like an itch, another morsel of information coming to her. If she let it in, she'd have to decide what to do with it.

"Mental health is complex." Jonathan's manner dialed down a gear as he talked. "I give you a hard time over the gambling because of how it hurt Craig. And Aaron. I keep on your back about relapsing because I don't want to do what I promised Craig I would do."

"What was that?"

"Watch out for Aaron if anything happened to his dad. Take him from you if you were a danger to his wellbeing."

The hairs on Kate's arm bristled. "He said that?"

"In a roundabout way. If he weren't there anymore, he

worried you'd slip." Jonathan's WASPish features softened. "Have you?"

"Have I what?"

"Slipped."

Although they'd had their differences, Kate never believed Jonathan acted in any way except what he thought was right. However, he decided what was right through his own blustering sense of self-importance. He was *always* right. His first instinct was *always* right.

Only it wasn't.

But even when he was wrong, he never seemed downright malicious. More… afraid of what could befall her and Aaron if he didn't manage her properly.

"I didn't slip," Kate said. "This was a business transaction. I haven't been to the track. I haven't taken part in a card game. Okay?" Not a direct lie.

He fixed his eyes on hers.

He doesn't believe you.

Was that whatever had been haunting Aaron? Or her own intuition?

"I was tempted, okay?" Kate said, relenting, forming plausible excuses and platitudes in one part of her brain while another section controlled her mouth. "I've been having these ideas, and I figured I could make some money. Something to help me study. To better myself."

That phrase sparked a twitch in Jonathan, but he let her speak.

"And yes, I admit it, I needed a meeting to keep myself on course. But this thing with the stocks… I'm sure it wasn't a gamble. I didn't get anything from anyone."

"If you're struggling, I can help." His hand hovered over hers, but he elected to wrap it around his coffee instead of touching her. "Endo Shunji is dead. He is who we blame for the insider tipoff. As long as you didn't confess to a crime on tape."

"I didn't." She wasn't sure, although she could find out by letting in whatever was trying to access her consciousness. "There was no insider."

Jonathan again looked as though he wanted to resort to his usual know-everything *obey-me* manner. "I'm sure you've convinced yourself of that. But I want to make a deal with you."

"A deal?"

"This *was* gambling. Whether or not you want to admit it. There's no psychic power. All this is on the record, you claiming to be a fortune teller, gambling with stocks, and all the rest. That means, combined with the affidavits Craig filed when he was preparing to divorce you, there are more than enough grounds to remove Aaron until they can perform a full mental health check."

"No, wait—"

Jonathan talked over her. "I will hold off with that on three conditions. One: you attend twice-weekly meetings for the next month. Then weekly ones for the subsequent six. No repeat of this. No gambling of any kind, even if you dream it. Clear?"

"Twice-weekly, sure." She didn't know what else to say. Affidavits, FBI interviews, bizarre claims. Claims she could only prove if she succumbed to the buddy's favor in return for knowledge. "What's two?"

"Two, you go to a therapist. Private. One I'll pay for. You choose who. And it's a gift. Not a loan. It's for my peace of mind. And there's a sub-condition attached to this."

"A sub-condition?" Kate said.

"Don't tell Jennifer I'm funding your therapy."

"I can live with that."

"Three." He sipped his coffee and set it down. Deep

breath. "Between you and me, no one else, did you know anything about Craig?"

Kate jolted, replaying to herself what he said, and her throat closed.

"About his death, I mean," Jonathan said. "I don't mean, *Did you do it?* Not, *did you kill him?* But… promise me you're being straight. Did he kill himself? No repercussions. He was my brother. A wife would see it, regardless of how things were in the relationship. You would have known. And I deserve to know."

I could tell you.

"No," Kate said, although she wasn't sure who she was talking to—Jonathan or the source of her foresight. The knowledge.

"No…?" Jonathan said, expecting more.

"No, I don't know any more than you. I swear it."

You could learn for sure. You just need to ask.

They weren't words. Not a voice, but an inkling. A feeling. No, a certainty: she could receive the truth by opening the gate.

Where before it had filtered through on autopilot, she'd now become aware of it. With that awareness, she'd gained an element of control. It required permission to deliver its predictions.

"I promise," she said, firmer. Dedicated. "I had no idea, no hint that Craig might have been thinking about…" She couldn't say suicide, Endo's shattered corpse drifting through her mind. "Drastic action. If I did, I swear I would have tried to stop him."

Jonathan nodded, his stiff posture relaxing somewhat as he raised his coffee. This was unlike him. So masterful most of the time, now conciliatory, exhibiting warmth and understanding.

"I have a counter-condition," she said.

"Oh?"

"That money from the trade is legit. It's mine. I want it."

"That might not be possible. If we hang it on Endo, it's still illegal—"

"We try. At the very least, I need my stake back. I can only put off repayments for so long."

Jonathan nodded. "You'll get it eventually. Not yet."

"Then it's time I was going."

"Where?" He sounded put out, as if he'd been enjoying time with her.

She gathered her coat and bag, and told him not a *lie*, because she had no clue what she was doing next, not exactly. But she knew it was a half-truth before she uttered a word: "I'm going to a meeting. That's a good start."

CHAPTER TWENTY-NINE

"Let's talk about a common story. A fable, really. The fable of the One Big Score."

Unfamiliar faces watched her from the floor. Some were different, anyway. Some were the same, as they always were. A smaller group than last time. Early evening tended to be thinner on the ground than later when the games commenced. She wanted this, though. Needed it.

With Aaron collected from a non-eventful day at school (non-eventful except no one would speak to him at breaks or lunch) and doing his homework in his room while Sal kept a vigil in front of the TV, Kate was free to keep her promise to Jonathan. She also needed some alone time. Without the stimulus all around her, it was easier to fend off the temptation trying to crawl inside her. To furnish her with knowledge.

You could know if he killed himself.

As enticing as it was to learn what he did, why he failed to check that packet of potato chips, Kate wasn't sure she wanted the truth.

"One big score," she said from the lectern. "A sure thing. When you know it, you know it."

Nods all around.

"I've been in that situation so many times. Just one more race, one more bet, one more game. Then I'm free. But even when the One Big Score comes good, there's always another One Bigger Score sneaking up on me."

More nods. Some eyes downcast in shame; the newer attendees who still hated themselves.

"The sad thing is, I always meant it. Always believed it, in the moment, when I said those words: *one more*. A sure thing to get me out from under that rock, to dig myself out of my hole, or, hell, pick your own cliché."

Polite chuckles.

"But we all feel it, deep down. It's not about the result. It's never about climbing out of holes or buying a jack to lift that rock. It's about the moment. That one moment when you experience your score romping home."

Kate hadn't known what she was going to do today. Unable to retrieve her funds, unable to ask Jonathan for a loan without revealing she'd gotten the money from worse than a pay-day loan shark, but mobsters, what choice did she have?

"I've been a liar all my life. Lying to my friends, my family, to myself. But I believed it was the truth. Even when I was scrambling around for cash, for credit, to gamble with, I meant it. One Big Score, and then I'm done."

Kate scanned the faces. She found the guy from her previous meeting, the one who answered her hypothetical question about placing a bet when you knew the outcome. The *that ain't even gambling* guy.

As if speaking to him directly, she said, "I mean it. I'm telling the truth about the One Big Score. It just never works out that way, does it?"

. . .

Buckeroo Brandies was transitioning from evening to night, a mix of casual and hardened drinkers swapping places. The TV switched from music videos to various sports, and Kate felt as though she owned the place. She'd been here so often this week, armed with foreknowledge, that she was ready to rumble from the second she clapped eyes on Ollie Swag. She pulled up a stool beside him.

He looked up from his computer tablet, then back down again. "Please tell me you got a payment fixed."

"Better," she said.

Ollie snorted. "No chance, Katie-Kat. You're twelve in the hole, and it's fifteen in a couple a' days. You wanna hand over something of equivalent value now, like that car, I reckon it could pony up nine or ten grand."

"That's a thirty-thousand-dollar car."

"Not with outstanding credit, babe. It's maybe ten at a chop shop if you're lucky. Ain't what we need, but it'll keep us from your door a while longer. Thirty-thou? Not even close."

Since leaving Jonathan, Kate had contemplated all that had happened. She understood what Aaron had been going through, the need to act out following an upload of knowledge. It was real, not imposter syndrome. And Kate had beaten it.

She hadn't killed Endo in reciprocation for the Whale Ride-On info. She had refused. And sure, Endo's suicide might have been a direct attack on her, but more likely it was a demonstration, showing her the reality of its power. What could happen if she disobeyed.

The difference was, she was an adult. She analyzed these feelings, these urges, and resisted them better. No way would she kill anyone. If this force, this rebalancing of favors for favors attacked her in response, she'd have to handle it.

"One bet, Ollie," she said. "Yeah, I got in a little over my head, but I can get out."

"Listen to yourself." The bags under Ollie's eyes deepened, growing darker. "You got any idea how many assholes I hear that from every week?" He adopted a whiny voice. "*Spot me a thousand, Ollie, I'm good for it. I got a hot one today, man.*" Back to normal. "Katie, hand over your car, and I'll take it as 10K straight. Better you go to court with a finance company than have my pricks show up one night. I can put off the interest payments for a week, but that'll be five thou if you go over seven days. Another five days, you're back to—"

"I'm back to owing ten. I get it. How much do I need to put down to net the full twelve tonight? Gimme a number. Gimme a game."

"No."

Kate looked up at the TVs. The bartender—the same overly tattooed girl as the first night she came here—flicked through the remotes so the screens showed different channels.

She asked Ollie, "What's on tonight? Something I can go with a multiplier?"

Ollie tapped his fingers on the bar, swigged from his soda. Either a mixer, or he hadn't started on the hard stuff yet. "You got a couple small baseball games here, you got some NFL games down Florida, Texas, and Californ-I-A. Or I'm takin' books on soccer now, too. Major League or the Mexicans, some Brazilian friendlies playin' if you're up for that. Or you got dogs."

"Dogs?"

"Yeah, dogs. Greyhounds."

"Good for accumulators. If you lend me a thousand, what does that get me?"

Ollie shook his head, his mottled teeth on show as he smiled. "Gets you a fuck-ton of trouble, Katie-Kat."

"Then spot me a fuck-ton of trouble. How many races?"

"No races. No credit."

Kate had exactly $204.65 in her checking account. That was everything until she got paid, then she'd blow it on Ollie's interest payment. "Two hundred. How do I turn two hundred dollars into twelve thousand? Can't be that many races."

"For twelve? Averaging four-to-one, you need to get three races bang on. If it's the favorites all the way, that'll leave you up two grand."

Okay, time to test how much control Kate had over this thing. How much she could let in. How much she could allow herself to see without learning the return favor first. It might be awful. Or nothing. Something she could live with. $200 at 4-to-1 would give her $800, then putting the $800 into another 4-to-1 got her $3200, followed by one more left her at $12,800.

It was her risk now. Not Aaron's. She could think of no reason to stop.

"Four races," she said. "Multiplier. Compound odds."

Again, he shook his head. "You're killing me, Katie-Kat."

"For a creep whose job it is to take money from vulnerable people, you're either great at acting like a reluctant gatekeeper or you think I'm dumb as shit."

Ollie opened his tablet and tapped to the correct screen. "Or maybe I prefer customers who can come back to place more bets over those who're gonna be homeless by the end of the month. Here."

She input her debit card number and handed the tablet back.

He asked, "Which races?"

I need to know how to win my accumulator, she thought.

Win the accumulator. One transaction with the void, with the entity feeding her brain. Not four. Four would be bad.

The experience was similar to how Aaron described it. An upload. Not linear, though. One second, nothing. Then, a pinprick of clarity, swelling, brightening, blooming like a flower, until she knew all she'd solicited.

Race one: Devine Pup 2-1
Race two: Leprosy Walking 4-1
Race three: Woman's Best Friend 3-1
Race four: Grandpa 5-1

Kate tapped the winner for each of the races Ollie presented to her.

"Last chance," Ollie said, his stylus over the final stage.

"Do it," Kate said.

He did it. And he looked in physical pain as the bet went through.

CHAPTER THIRTY

Kate called Sal to ask him to stay on a little longer, and he was curious but didn't probe why. In two hours, Kate was more than happy.

With the accumulating odds, as each dog romped home, every part of Kate burst and tingled. She whooped and swore and pumped the air, jigging and running a circuit of the bar at the final win, her $200 transformed magically into $24,000.

Ollie sweated more and more profusely throughout. This being a slow evening, he'd made a loss for once. The laughter he emitted as he signed over the money was not full of mirth, but disbelief.

"I'm deductin' the loan," he said, pecking at the tablet, "and you got $12,400 waitin' in your account first thing in the morning. Congrats."

Kate grinned. "Nice doing business with you."

"Yeah, and that's the last business you're doin' here. I don't know what kinda juju you got going on, or if you're in with some Ay-rab syndicate or whatever. But ain't no one got luck like that. I'm cuttin' you off. Have a nice life."

It was like being barred from Vegas for card counting; nothing against the rules, but they didn't like it. Plus, there were other places to spend her money if she was so inclined. But she wasn't.

This was it—her One Big Score fable come true. She was out. Done. *Finito*.

She trotted out of Buckeroo Brandies into the back lot where she'd parked a sensible distance from Ollie's vulgar Trans Am, the loud gas guzzler waiting proudly in plain view. It struck Kate how much better the lime-green muscle car would look if it were on fire.

She giggled at the thought. Pretty flames, dancing over the paintwork, fed and powered by the conflagration from inside. All those manmade fibers combusting, spreading, breaking free, reaching for the stars. Yummy smoke.

Yeah, that'd be cool. And Ollie would be so happy.

Kate reached her car and popped the trunk and searched for her spare gas canister. She found it and jiggled it. Empty.

Damn.

She closed the lid and contemplated the Trans Am. It really needed burning, didn't it? But how to achieve that without appearing to some nosy cop that she was doing something wrong.

Alright, there were fewer and fewer cops these days. In fact, she couldn't recall seeing one in this neighborhood unless someone called 911. Patrols were few and far between, and the local muscle kept the peace better than anyone in uniform, anyway. Which was fine, as long as you fell on the right side of them.

Kate drove her little Auris hybrid to the nearest gas station and filled the tank, then the can, and went to pay, picking up a disposable lighter along the way. She swapped the plastic lighter for a heavy Zippo sold from behind the counter. This one had a pirate skull and crossbones on it, and she'd look very cool tossing it into the Trans Am after applying the gas.

Just like a movie.

She reversed her journey, pulled into the lot a good twenty yards from Ollie's pride and joy, and skipped around to the trunk. She hefted the gas can and unscrewed the lid, inhaling the sweet scent of future fire. The fumes trailed up, stinging her nose before filling her lungs with its odor.

Kate coughed.

She screwed the lid back on and coughed some more, stepping away from the noxious air to scold herself for treating a can of gas like a fine wine.

Her head spun and her vision blurred. She bent at the waist, hands on her thighs, and coughed again. When that bout ended, the lime-green Trans Am lay in a halo of light, calling to her.

What the actual hell was she doing?

The spotlight faded, rising to encompass the whole parking lot, and Kate's vision returned to normal. A regular slab of tarmac with a smattering of vehicles, where one in particular stood out.

One that should be burned to the frame.

But Ollie surely has cameras out here, Kate thought. How else did he know what car she drove? He'd know who set the fire.

Doesn't matter. Worse will happen if you don't.

She wasn't sure if the story she'd heard about the military veteran getting crippled for breaking Ollie's window was true, but there was no doubt Ollie's ebullient demeanor soured when anyone so much as insulted the vehicle. During her first illicit trip to place a bet here, she'd made the mistake of joking about the color. He'd cut her odds in half as punishment. She'd thought he was kidding, but in the absence of love or affection in the man's life, this machine was undoubtedly his surrogate.

You have to.

With feet planted, Kate twisted her body toward the Auris. The gas can's nozzle poked up from the open trunk. Back to the Trans Am.

It really would be great to set it on fire.

She shuffled off to her car.

The risk was too great. Not only the cops, but Ollie Swag. No matter how much he liked her, this was the one thing that turned him psychotic. He might even kill her for it.

And yet, as she arrived at the Auris, picked up the gas can, she could not help thinking of what would be worse. What *was* worse than a murderous chump seeking revenge for torching his mommy-substitute?

She had to.

"Damn it, what am I doing?"

Kate thudded the canister into the trunk and closed the lid. She strode back to the driver's door and reached for the handle.

Fear clenched her chest, her stomach, her throat. Her legs shook like a cartoon character's, and she had to sit on the ground. Propped against the car, she pulled her knees up to her chest and thumped her forehead on them. Willing the creeping, spreading terror to release her.

It wouldn't stop. Wouldn't let her go.

Burn the car.

She had agreed with Aaron that they'd resist it together. Take the knowledge, use it, make it their own. She hadn't begun to contemplate how hard it would be. Harder than giving up smoking, stronger than the instinct to recoil from a spider or snake, and even more inviting than a *sure-thing-big-score* bet that couldn't lose.

Burn the car.

Worse will happen if you don't.

Worse than a bird attacking her? Worse than a man leaping from a building? Worse than a group of musclebound sociopaths breaking every bone in her body, and possibly even worse than that too?

Ollie had already expressed an attraction to her. What if his retribution delved into places where he fulfilled that fantasy?

Kate pressed her hands to the asphalt, firmed her legs, and stood on shaking muscles. The Trans Am still needed burning, still demanded the flames, but she would not bend to that demand.

Worse will happen.

"I guess we'll see," she said to the night, then climbed behind the wheel and drove home, checking the rearview mirror all the way.

CHAPTER THIRTY-ONE

By the time Kate got home, the influx of fear over not burning Ollie Swag's gross automobile had transitioned into pure adrenaline. Her shakes were not from worrying about the bookie or whatever punishment awaited her, but from the new chemical coursing through her. The first thing Sal said as she entered her home was, "Are you okay? You're completely white."

The evening must have piled more on her than she'd realized, as she collapsed into tears right there in the hall. Thankfully, Aaron was in bed, so he didn't witness his mom needing help to get to the living room, to be placed on the couch where she shrank into a sitting fetal position. Her hands were claws, her arms blanched twigs, elbows pinned against her ribs.

"Kate?"

Sal sank onto the seat beside her, as tentative as a bomb disposal officer, unsure which wire to snip.

Kate accepted the glass of water offered, surprised at how steadily she held it to her lips. That act of control helped her focus, regain command over the functions she felt sure she was losing.

She handed back the drink. "Thank you."

"You gambled," Sal said. "Didn't you?"

Kate stared ahead, seeing nothing in particular. The fish tank burbled and trickled. Sal put the glass on the coffee table. Next to an unlit cigar and his never-go-out lighter, she noted. He'd been hoping for one of their evenings on the deck, another hope she'd dashed thanks to her idiocy.

"I was trying so hard," she said.

"Talk to me."

"I can't. It's impossible to understand."

"Try me."

She shifted her body to face him. "How much do you believe in beyond this life, Sal?"

He stiffened the way he did when he spoke of his daughter and wife. Deep breath. Released it gradually. "I believe in more. My mother saw to it. I don' see how a book written by men hundreds of years ago, then rewritten a bunch more times over the centuries, can be the literal word of God. But if I didn't feel my daughter's spirit somewhere in my life every damn day, I'd go crazy."

"Maybe that's why we got religion in the first place," Kate said. "To stop us going mad with grief."

"Man invented God instead of God creatin' man. Yeah, I get that. But what's this about, Kate?"

"It isn't God or Jesus, that's for sure."

Sal's rigid posture remained as he shuffled closer. "Not much is, Kate. But whatever's goin' on, I'll believe you. So hit me with it."

"Okay, don't say I didn't warn you."

Kate unloaded. For the first time in what felt like forever, she regaled another human being with the unbridled truth of all she'd seen, learned, and experienced in the past week. She jumped back to Aaron's birthday, how it all seemed to stem from that one childish wish to be better at school.

"Like a genie," Sal said. "Tricking you into wishing for something you want, then putting a bad twist on it."

Kate had never thought of it that way. She'd been so caught up in the "how" it happened and "what to do next," she had not yet seriously considered the nature of it. The "what is it?" question.

"When he first did it," Kate said, "I thought it was a gift. Like a power. You know, like a comic book thing? That he was offsetting it with a psychological impulse. But you might be right. What if it's conscious?"

"How does it feel to you? Is it talking? Is it in any way a voice?"

"No, it's… like it's me. Like I'm the one initiating it. I mean, I can tell it's twisted, and false, and not me at all, but… I've spent so much time on self-reflection, getting out from Reno, trying to be the sort of person who fits in with Craig's family, in and out of rehab…" A cool wave spread through her. "If I hadn't been that way, forced to understand my own mind and subconscious urges… I probably would have fallen for it. A child is like the perfect canvas."

Sal inhaled deeply, then exhaled with a thoughtful nod. "Maybe why it picks children. It can hide itself inside bad behavior. Then when the host becomes aware, it leaves."

Kate felt both good and guilty for burdening Sal with it. Good that she didn't have to censor herself, guilty that Sal took it all seriously, without a hint of disbelief. He'd kept his promise. Now she had to allow Sal to process her disintegrating life.

"I don't know what I can do to help," he said. "But I'll try."

"It can't be my mind playing tricks. It has to be… something. Something with an intent. Consciousness. Now you've said it, I'm sure."

"If I know my little Bella ridin' beside me on a lonely journey ain't a trick, then I got no right to think what's happening here is." His words resounded in the beats Kate had seen with Ruiz: loss, consumed by grief, salved by hope. "I seen Aaron, I seen what he's done, and I can't pretend to have some insight into him. Hell, I'm just a neighbor. But if I gotta choose between him flicking some switch and turnin' into a crazy boy, and some creature that prays on the wishes of children… I'll pick the second option. You're a good mom, Kate. And you've tried to fix it, even sacrificed your own health—"

Kate kissed him. Not some friendly thank-you kiss, but arm around him, hand on the back of his neck, her breasts to his chest. He responded, too, his hand around her back, not roughly but firm. An exploration, unsure how far to go.

She helped him with that. Her hand landed on his thigh and headed north. He intensified the kiss, their tongues meeting.

Then he pulled away, legs together. Embarrassed.

"I'm sorry, Kate, I…" He rested his head in one hand.

Kate readjusted, sitting prim and proper with her legs closed. "No, it's fine. It was me."

Silence. Neither met the other's eye. Kate wasn't sure what brought on his sudden change of heart, but it was up to him to explain.

"Do you really want this?" Sal asked.

"Yes."

"I mean, a week ago, if I'd tried to kiss you… Would you have let me?"

Kate had been honest with him about everything else, so she plowed on with this. "No. I mean, I don't know."

His head eased around, viewing each other side-on. "That's what I thought. Right now, you're high. On fear and worry. I'm a safe guy, though, so… I guess I'm just worried. If we go further with this, you gonna regret it?"

More honesty: "I don't know, Sal."

"Then we should put this on hold, yeah? Or do we scratch it completely? Because if you never considered me a prospect before, that might be for the best."

Kate looked away, gathered some zigzagging thoughts, then risked voicing them. "I *have* thought about you. About me and you. And I use you sometimes. Lead you on in a way. And you're right, you're a safe bet…" She stuttered at the word *bet*. "You're a good man, Sal. Someone I want to care for in that way. Maybe even love. But I'm not sure I can."

He nodded, confirming something he'd known a while. "I figured I'm permanently in the friend zone here."

"A date," Kate said.

"A date?"

"I'm sorry I came on so strong. You're right. I'm hyped up. My son was carrying around some supernatural entity that has somehow passed to me." She barked out a laugh at how absurd it sounded. "Who wouldn't be looking for something more significant to numb all that? I'm sorry it was you who got on the end of it. And yeah. A date, Sal."

"You and me? When we get this figured out?"

He said *we*, which made Kate want to kiss him again.

When did gratitude and horny get all mixed up?

"Yes," Kate said. "You're a beautiful man, Sal, so that's the physical side taken care of. A kind man, so you're good to be around. You take no crap, you're honest, you make me laugh when I need it. Perhaps you came along at the wrong time, and I treated all that like a checklist instead of considering another man in my life."

"Can't date by having a robot checkin' off your positive points."

"No. But we can explore the other side. Just people. Talking. Ignoring the other things. A reset. Treat love like a destination, not the journey."

Sal considered it, and the tension in him melted away. "Love, huh?"

"We're both too old for that youthful love-at-first sight crap."

"Speak for yourself."

Kate laughed. Like unloading on Sal, her neck muscles loosened, her smile relaxed.

Sal mirrored her and sat back on the couch. "And, hey, we're *mature*, not old. If it doesn't work out, we'll be mature enough to be friends. Okay?"

"Deal."

The living room door crept open. A small body wedged itself in the gap.

Kate frowned at Aaron, his eyes still narrow through sleep. "What are you doing up so late?"

"It's Sal," Aaron said, groggily. He glanced back into the hall before trying to blink himself awake. "Out there."

"What? How long have you been out of bed?" Kate stood and reigned back her instinct to be harsh with him. "Were you listening to us? Spying?"

"No." Aaron rubbed his eyes, and Kate could tell it wasn't fake. "Sal…"

"What is it, kiddo?" Sal asked.

"Your van."

Sal sat forward, perched on the edge of the couch. "My van?"

"I can see it out my window." Aaron pointed in the street's general direction. "It's on fire."

"Fire?" He shot to his feet and swung open the door,

slowed to get past Aaron without knocking him over, and rushed to the front.

Kate followed, patting Aaron as she went, meant as a comforting gesture, but it may have been too fleeting. The hall was empty. Sal had run outside, leaving the door open. She hurried out after him, the orange glow already visible before she made it out of her driveway.

Sal's Ford Ranger pickup blazed in an all-encompassing rage, a furnace blasting heat as far as Kate's property. No wonder it beat Sal back, unable to get close. Neighbors speckled the sidewalks, and a couple of the more helpful ones dashed toward Sal with domestic fire extinguishers. Sal accepted one and galloped forward, but again, the blasting heat drove him back.

Kate pulled out her phone, dialing 911, even though others in the street, including the nosy Dorothy from next door, were working their own. As she listened to it ring, she tried to keep her lips from compressing at the corners. She failed, but she kept her mouth from curling upward.

She was looking at the consequences of refusing to burn Ollie Swag's Trans Am. A burning car for a burning truck. It was over.

It's not.

Kate was caught off guard by that. A sudden injection into her brain, overriding the operator picking up, asking her what service she required.

Look to your right. Not an order, but an instinct. As though she had to turn her head to the right. Had to.

She obeyed, scanning the street, squinting through the smoke and the hellish orange glow.

There, four houses away, parked on the side of the road.

Although she couldn't see the color, she made out the black and white stripe bisecting the car front to back, and the model was plain.

A Trans Am.

Better check on Aaron.

Kate didn't even consider the consequences, the need to offset using the warning. She sprinted back up the drive, screaming her son's name.

CHAPTER THIRTY-TWO

Instead of barreling inside, Kate pulled up short on the stoop. She stepped in, hyper-aware of the fact Ollie Swag had shown up in her street. If the buddy-thing could persuade Endo to jump from his apartment, what would it take to force Ollie to harm her? Or Aaron?

She crept along, her back to the wall.

"Aaron?"

The fish tank burbled as she searched for a weapon. Nothing came to hand.

"Aaron?" Her voice sounded shrill, mouselike.

She was not an imposing woman. Far from it. She'd always been slim, and birthed Aaron young enough to regain her pre-pregnancy weight within a year, but today she was smaller than even twelve months ago. In that sense, she wished she'd listened to those telling her she was "too skinny" instead of smugly fobbing it off as having room to spare should she feel like bingeing one evening.

"Hello?"

She had never been in a proper fight, hadn't been struck for many years, not since before she met Craig. There'd been violent men in her life, although never any sustained abuse. She'd been slapped, choked, and punched in the stomach. As a young woman, she'd been conditioned to accept that as normal for a trailer-trash gal working the card tables in Reno; *gamblin' and shootin' and tryin' to land a man who didn't lay hands on you.* Weird how it took breaking free of that world, looking back upon it from afar, to undo such acceptance.

Still, even though she knew in her head that no one was to blame for getting assaulted, she declared herself *stupid* for returning inside her house alone—a *dumb* victim about to be picked off. If the entity had tipped a man whose life was dissolving around him over the edge to suicide, it must be simple to take someone for whom violence was an occasional —if necessary—tool and point them at a woman or a boy and say, *Do harm.*

She couldn't defend against Ollie alone. But she couldn't back out. What if the difference between life and death was the few seconds it would take her to convince Sal to abandon his truck and come running with a chainsaw or something to use as a weapon—

"Mommy!" Aaron cried from within the house.

Kate's good sense vanished. Before she realized it, her legs were pumping. Past the open living room, to the kitchen from where the voice had emanated. She managed a quick head-bob around the door in case an axe descended. But when the space appeared empty, she delved straight through, arrowing for the open French doors.

"*Mommy.*"

The call came from outside, Kate's instinct spot on. And it *was* instinct. She wasn't following instructions, not gleaning intelligence from the ether. She knew her house, knew how sound carried.

It wasn't until she was out in the night air, tainted with smoke from the street, that she realized she'd played the dumb victim routine with all the gusto of a cheerleader with access to only half a brain cell.

Here she was, alone, following the fearful voice of her only son. The lights failed to come on automatically, too, making her wander to the deck's edge in the dark.

"Aaron?" Again, the weak holler, hoping he'd come running.

No reply.

There was enough light to see the deck was empty, but the wan halo from inside the house stretched no farther than a few feet onto the lawn. She made out the approximate shape of her garden, eyes adjusting, but saw no figures out there.

She tried again: "Aaron?"

No reply.

Too late to go back. No chance she could take an intruder by surprise through sneaky reinforcements.

Kate placed one foot on the first step downward. Tried a fresh approach: "Ollie? Is that you out there?"

A smirk in the dark.

She sped up her descent, checking both sides of the stairs, spotting only the things she hadn't tidied away from days past—toys and other detritus scattered around the lawn. A misplaced spike of embarrassment at the mess fluttered in her stomach.

"Ollie, please show yourself," Kate said, finding a thread of steel to her voice. She kept it even, not loud. Not threatening.

"Hey, Katie-Kat."

Kate jumped and whirled to her left, braced for a blow. There was nothing.

Okay, definitely not *nothing*. But no direct attack.

Ollie Swag, at the corner of her house, ushered Aaron along. Although not gripping him with the strength of a woodworking vice, Ollie kept him secure in an embrace. Half shrouded in shadow, they occupied the spot where Aaron had accessed the crawlspace, which didn't strike Kate as a likely coincidence. Now wasn't the time to analyze it, though.

"I got a thing in my head, Katie," Ollie went on, advancing. "And I don't know what to do with it."

Kate could have screamed, hoped neighbors came running. Surely the fire service was on its way. Cops too, probably, since the truck looked like arson. She had to buy time.

"What's in your head, Ollie?"

Emerging from the half-shadow, pale and unsmiling, Ollie rapped his forehead with his knuckles. "You come back to me after a year and a half. You take my money. And you make me look like a total douchebag to my boss, who, by the way, wanted someone else to visit you. If I wasn't here having this chat, the three of us, you'd be in a van with a bag on your head, travelin' just below the speed limit for an appointment not many assholes walk away from. You know why?"

Kate anchored on Aaron's imploring eyes. "It's okay. I'll do whatever you need."

"That's good, Katie-Kate. Very good. See, it wasn't some lucky streak you fucked me with, was it? You hadda know all about that score, those dogs. They rigged the races, babe, and you're the patsy they got running back and forth for 'em."

"I promise, Ollie. It's not like that."

"You're a threat, Katie. To me, and to anyone else in this city runnin' a book."

He took a knife out of his sports coat pocket, a short, stubby blade, too dark to reflect even a small amount of light on the body or the serrated top edge. Only along the very peak of the blade where it had been sharpened did a thin line of silver glint through as he passed beneath the kitchen window. It made Kate think of the knife block on the corner counter, stocked with blue, red, purple, and green knives, all sharp enough to remove a fingertip or possibly an entire digit. She should have snatched one on the way out. Another dumb move.

"Ollie." Kate froze for a second, backing away as Ollie moved the knife closer to Aaron. "Please. Whatever you want from me, it's yours."

"Anything?"

"Anything."

Ollie licked his lips. With more light on him, the sweat was obvious. His hair was lank, his eyes alternating between hollow and lecherous.

"I checked the cameras, Katie," Ollie said. "I figured maybe you're meetin' your handler out there. But instead… Instead, it looks to me like you're thinking about dickin' with my Betsy."

He calls his Trans Am Betsy?

"You gonna tell me, Katie-Kat." Ollie edged closer. His knife was so close to Aaron, the boy couldn't take his eyes off it. "Tell me why you were messing around near Betsy, playin' with gas cans around your car. Tell me who the fuck is feedin' you fixed races, too. But the car, babe. What are you doing near my car?"

"I'm not near your car, Ollie." Kate extended her hands in what she knew was a futile attempt to mollify him, but couldn't help it.

"You're still a danger."

He came closer.

Kate shuffled away without turning from him, but slower than he advanced. The space between them shortened. She had to get to Aaron, if only to touch him.

"You don't need Aaron," she said. "Please, I'll do whatever. I'll tell you what you want to know."

Ollie's eyelids hung heavy as if he were drunk, a sneer dragging shadows over his jowly face. "What were you going to do to my car, Katie-Kat?"

She backed into the handrail, feet clattering the mess she'd left. Plant pots, two trowels, a—

A chance.

"Listen to me very carefully," Kate said, keeping Ollie's attention on her but easing one hand low, her ring finger curled over her little one, her forefinger flicking at Aaron. She risked a glance at him and saw he was focused on her hand—his tic, performed by his mom. He'd know she was talking to him. "What can I do to make this right, Ollie?"

The man was close enough for Kate to smell the alcohol on him, as though he'd been trying to drown out the voice, the urge to do what he was doing. At his core, Ollie might've been a decent guy, could have been better if he didn't succumb to his more rotten edges—his obsession with Betsy being the most obvious. But there were other hints at his corruption too, in his open dealings with prostitutes, his leery half-come-ons to Kate, the way he may as well drool when a hot woman walked by.

None of that mattered. All Kate saw was a man holding her son, using him to bend her to his will. To punish her.

Not him, though. It wasn't *Ollie* punishing her. He was only the vessel. Like Endo had been. A power trip demanding mischief in exchange for help, then throwing a tantrum if it didn't get its way.

No wonder it targeted children. Perhaps in its nature, it was a child itself. She was more certain than ever now: whatever it was, it had a consciousness. Willpower. And it demanded obedience.

"What can I do to make this right?" Kate asked again.

Ollie's teeth showed, his grin like an abattoir of decaying meat. "You know what, Katie-Kat. Gimme some names.

We'll send some interested people round. Show 'em what we think about cheats in this city. Then... then, Katie, we talk about Betsy."

Kate's left hand rested on the spindle part of the handrail. "I'll do that. But Aaron has to go."

"No chance."

"Are you listening?"

"Yes," Ollie said.

Aaron nodded so faintly anyone but his mother would have missed it.

Kate squeezed her ring finger over her little one, then pointed straight out with her forefinger. "Bite hard, then duck."

Ollie's face scrunched up. "Pardon?"

Aaron bit Ollie's hand. Really clamped down on it, drawing a scream from his captor. At that instant, Kate dropped to her haunches and leaped across the lawn, then up, having snatched the spade left in place after killing the bird. For once, her sloth-like approach to tidying the garden had landed her a tiny advantage.

Aaron stretched himself downward, but Ollie's damaged hand grasped for him, the knife hand flailing in confusion.

Kate brought the spade around.

Ollie seized up, a statue, staring vacantly at the incoming tool, as though confused about its very existence. The metal end clanged off Ollie's head and sent him sprawling. With a jolt, he released Aaron.

Kate wielded the spade like a bo-staff and shouted, "Aaron, run. Go get help. I'll deal with this."

Aaron took off toward the side gate at a sprint, concentration dominating his features more than fear. He had an important job to do, and he wasn't going to mess it up.

Ollie got on his hands and knees, dabbing his head where

it was bleeding. He looked at his hand, dazed, as if waking from a dream.

"Ollie, I'm sorry." Kate set her stance, holding firm between the prone man and the direction in which Aaron shot off. "You weren't in your right mind."

"If I wasn't in my right mind before," Ollie said, "how d'you think my mind is after you brained me with a fuckin' shovel?"

It was only now she realized he'd held onto his knife, his fingers molded around it, pushing himself up with his fist.

"I'll hit you again if I have to."

"Heh-heh." Ollie creaked to his feet, blood soaking the right side of his face. "Jesus, Katie-Kat. You got some balls. I ain't sure if I should be turned on or runnin' for the hills."

During every moment in which she'd been afraid, Kate had virtually shut down. She'd lost count of the times trembles and shakes had dominated her limbs. In this standoff, between a fat psycho and her son, she felt like a grizzly bear encountering a challenge from a moose. Sure, he had that blade, but she had the reach.

He stepped toward her. Just once.

She shuffled back. "I'm warning you. I'll do it."

"Catch." Ollie threw the knife.

He was no ninja, though. The weapon tumbled end over end. It was so pathetic that Kate almost laughed. Only it wasn't intended to fly straight and true into her esophagus. It was a distraction. And it worked.

Ollie lunged too fast for her to swing. He nullified the makeshift weapon with one hand and punched her full in the chest with the other, wrenching the spade from her. She dropped onto her back and rolled away in a panic.

Disoriented, ignoring the pain from the strike, Kate scrambled to a crouch, snapping her head left and right to see where her enemy was coming from.

He was fat and strong. Heavy, using his weight. It wasn't a direct route. He circled her, weighing the spade, the brow over his right eye swelling. He barely seemed to notice the blood draining into it. Perhaps whatever was controlling him, *influencing* him, forbade any such feeling.

"You hit me," he said.

"You had a knife at my boy's throat."

He shrugged. "Fair enough. I wasn't making a point, anyway."

Ollie dashed forward, the spade arching from behind him at Kate. It made him clumsy, slow. Sufficient delay for Kate to leap aside.

But he was faster than he looked.

He righted the spade and shoved it toward her, tripping her as she made for the house. She landed almost flat on her face, grazing her hands to break her fall.

Survival instinct took over. She pushed backward on her butt and elbows. It was lucky she did, as the blade clanged down on the concrete where her legs had splayed a second before.

She came up against the bottom step to her deck.

Ollie snarled, pissed at having missed her, and hung the spade out to the side, ready to slice at her rather than another cumbersome hammer blow.

Kate had nowhere to go.

He swung. The spade split the air.

Ollie halted and so did the tool. Again, that confused expression, as if he was surprised to find himself in this place, in this time, in this position.

He jerked upward. Coughed. Choked out a noise like a man about to vomit. Then blood jumped from his mouth.

Kate lowered the arm, which she hadn't realized she'd raised, looking Ollie Swag up and down. He was floating, his feet off the ground.

She blinked, eyes adjusting.

Sal was positioned behind Ollie, manipulating his movements. He heaved the big man aside, limbs still rubbery in their attempts to get free. As the angle improved, the garden fork in Ollie's back became plain.

Sal had stabbed him. He'd saved her life.

He dumped the fat bookie unceremoniously to one side, the fork still embedded in his back.

Kate jumped to her feet and threw her arms around Sal. "Thank you, thank you, thank you." She kissed his cheek, his neck, squeezing him tight.

Only, something wasn't right. Sal didn't respond. Didn't hug her back. It was like embracing a mannequin. He didn't tell her it was all okay. No confirmation the cops were coming, even though the approaching sirens were more than the fire department.

She disengaged. Her savior still didn't react. His eyes were hooded, his mouth slack, a man asleep, only upright and conscious.

"Sal? Where's Aaron?"

Sal took something from his pocket. Fired it up. His special lighter. Much like the one Kate bought from the gas station, except better.

The flame never goes out.

But why…?

This wasn't Sal. If he were a stranger, she'd assume him high on meth, his dead eyes otherworldly in the lighter's flickering glow. Then, looking past Ollie as he writhed with the implement in his back, she found Aaron.

He wandered toward her in a daze. He was drenched.

And there was a smell. A chemical smell.

He said, "Mom? Sal said I should wait, but I didn't want to."

Sal showed a glimmer of emotion. Humor. No, more

than that—victory. A smug winner, getting one over on a rival.

"It wasn't Ollie," Kate said.

The vein on Sal's head bulged, eye twitching. His skin crawled the way Endo's had, and as Kate focused on the flame, she recognized the odor.

Gasoline.

Her little boy was drenched in *gasoline*.

Then Sal did the worst thing of all. With the lighter outstretched, he moved toward Aaron.

CHAPTER THIRTY-THREE

Where Ollie Swag had radiated manic anger, confusion, and even a sadistic glee at imposing himself on Kate, Sal displayed all the emotional attachment to his actions that a shark would. The same dead-eyed blank slate, the efficiency with which he moved, and the likelihood that he would not —or could not—listen to reason.

Ten yards from Aaron, Sal wielded a flame that even a stiff wind couldn't extinguish. And no matter how loudly Kate yelled Sal's name, he barely flinched.

Mercifully, he progressed with an ambling gait, like a rotting zombie in some TV show, willing his body onward as it disintegrated around him. It gave Kate a chance to get between him and Aaron.

First, though, she diverted to where Ollie Swag lay with the pitchfork in his back. His extremities still flopped about, his mouth uttering groans that might've been words or simply the death rattle of a condemned man. With no thoughts except for protecting her son, Kate snapped back into the mental state she'd summoned when killing the blackbird; necessity meant doing something she hated. And what she hated was planting her foot on Ollie's back, grasping the fork by the handle, and pulling.

The metal tines sucked at Ollie's flesh. He keened, boggle-eyed, pushing with hands lacking any strength to arch away from the pain.

Kate fought the revulsion, reminding herself this man had threatened her son with a knife—*without* being possessed by some malevolent force. It took less than two seconds to free the garden fork, then another one to position herself between Sal and Aaron.

"Don't, Sal." She held the fork before her, an old-times villager fending off a witch.

He kept on coming, lumbering. Those dead eyes seeing nothing but their objective.

"Run, Aaron!"

"I can't," Aaron replied.

"Why?"

"He said he'd kill you if I ran."

"He'll kill *you* if you don't."

Aaron burst into tears, a tantrum as much as fear. "I don't want you to die too! I can't let you, Mom. I need you."

Sal shambled closer, the skin on his face dancing with whatever had buried itself within. Or Kate's perception of it. A connection between her and it. Sal's mouth spread into an approximation of a smile; an affectation. Unlike Ollie, who'd been happy to punish her for a perceived slight, Sal was acting, and acting badly.

"This isn't you, Sal." Kate matched a limping sidestep. As Sal swayed back to his original path, she intercepted that too. "I'll use this, I promise."

The bad-actor grin stretched. A voice, not unlike Sal's but stained by an oily undertone, croaked forth. "Good enough."

So that was its plan. She would kill Sal or Sal kill Aaron, a dilemma that would haunt her, whatever the outcome. *This* was her punishment. The thing taking over their lives didn't care who died, who got hurt, as long as it penalized Kate for her disobedience, for taking without reciprocation.

Sal plodded another step, a forced effort, as if wading through mud.

"Both of us run," Aaron said.

"He'll keep coming," Kate said.

At her own words, uttered without thinking, the truth dawned on her, the reason she didn't scoop up Aaron and flee, screaming into the night for help. If they escaped tonight, ran from this lethargic version of Sal Cantero, the entity, the buddy, would execute their sentence eventually. It would not let them go.

She had to stick that fork in Sal.

"Aaron, go!" Kate ordered. "I'll be right behind you. I promise."

Aaron touched her lower back, a child pawing for attention. "I can't."

But subtlety was a death sentence.

"Go! Go now, baby. This isn't Mr. Cantero anymore. It's that thing, that buddy, it's making him do this."

Aaron shifted from his spot, occupying Kate's peripheral vision, but she didn't dare face him. He seemed cowed, seemed to understand.

Sal pivoted toward the boy, raising the lighter.

Aaron turned his back. "You'll die if I run."

Kate retracted the fork for a better thrust. "I won't die."

Then Sal howled. His skin tightened, the ripples gone, while his hooded eyelids opened wide. The grimace was real, not an inhuman creature attempting to ape emotion. It was Sal, the original Sal.

His face snapped back into that mask, that facsimile of

the man she knew, the man she'd kissed, the man she now realized she wanted in her life. Had this been virtually anyone else, she would have shoved the tines into them already.

"He's there," Kate said. "He's fighting it. Sal, can you hear me?"

"No Sal…" came the reply from inside Sal's body, the slick, guttural noise approximating his voice.

"We're going." Kate lowered the fork, although not all the way. "If he can do that, you don't have complete control. And I don't have to hurt him."

"You will." Sal's free hand darted out and grabbed the fork right below the spikes. "Getting easier." That shark-stare intensified, as if it was feeling something. Not an authentic emotion, but perhaps an achievement, chipping away at Sal's will. "You kill…" It lifted the fork and rested the points on Sal's chest.

"No." Kate applied no pressure, but the flame still flickered, and Aaron remained in play, covered in gas. "Please, Aaron just go!"

Aaron's face contorted, that ball of frustration she'd seen in him when he couldn't explain.

Why won't he run?

"I can't go," Aaron insisted, as if reading her thoughts. "It won't let me. You'll die."

"Choose." Sal's body pushed against her, forcing her back, closer to Aaron. "This body. Or that one." It tilted the lighter Aaron's way.

Having experienced the buddy's influence, the strength of its suggestions, Kate now understood what she hadn't when begging Aaron to leave: it was taunting him, pushing him to stay, anchoring him to his mom out of fear of losing her. Logic didn't factor into it. The buddy made him truly believe Kate would die if he left.

Whatever was controlling Sal ran out of patience. "Then I decide."

Sal's body shoved the fork at Kate, using the full strength of its vessel to pin her against the house, the fork's handle flush to her chest, right where Ollie thumped her. And Sal was a strong man with a laborer's muscles. Kate was powerless against him.

Aaron, having been unable to run from the scene, darted the other way, toward Ollie. He came back halfway and stood rooted to the spot, ten feet from Kate and only six from Sal. She thought he'd frozen in terror. Only now, he was holding the knife Ollie had dropped.

While he couldn't depart, he clearly didn't need to remain inactive.

Kate could smell the gas from where she was pinned. "Aaron, don't. He'll burn you…"

"Decision is made." The thing inside Sal jabbed the fork's handle in Kate's windpipe, making her gag, winding her and dropping her to the floor.

He switched the implement around. The fork-end pointed at Kate. While she gasped for air, he thrust the tool and stabbed her in the thigh. The tines cut through her leg into the soft ground beneath. Pinned in place, she couldn't even scream in pain, lacking the oxygen to summon it.

Sal advanced on Aaron.

Kate looked down at the fork, not completely skewering her flesh as she'd feared. The first and second spikes had torn her skin on either side, drawing blood, securing her to the hard-packed dirt by the crawlspace. But it had missed what little meat hung on her bones. Either the creature was a great aim and was toying with her, or she'd lucked out at being skinny enough that it bypassed anything vital. That didn't stop the lesser wounds from being acid-painful.

She gripped the fork in both hands, pulled up to dislodge

it. This hurt even more than when it went in, and she still couldn't scream, couldn't breathe. It may have missed most of her muscle, but it slashed plenty.

Aaron.

Kate had to protect her son. Whatever she had to endure, he was the only thing that mattered.

She screwed up her face, turned her fingers into steel coils, and lifted. Every inch of the metal grated against her flesh as she extracted the impalement.

Now free, she gulped at the air and dragged herself forward, through the throbbing and bleeding. Her leg wouldn't work properly, so she couldn't stand; while the gashes hadn't disabled her, they'd inflicted more damage than a deep graze. Even if she could stand, she was too weak to use the fork as a weapon.

Her vision blurred. She saw enough, though.

Sal, shambling toward Aaron.

Aaron, standing his ground. So terrified of losing another parent, he'd rather die himself.

I don't want you to die too! I can't let you, Mom. I need you.

"Get away from him!" she cried. "Punish *me*. Take *me*."

Sal loomed closer to Aaron, even as the boy backed up. "Take, but no give."

"I never asked for you." Kate gained on him, slithering faster than he was clomping.

"You did." Its voice was still Sal, but had mutated into that of a snake, a *sssssth* to its tone. "You assssked for me."

She hated that it was right on a technicality. She had stated more than once she wished she could take it from Aaron. It must have heard her pleas.

She said, "I don't want your favors, I don't want your predictions. I just want you gone!"

Sal extended the lighter toward Aaron.

Dragging herself inch by agonizing inch, pushing with

her good foot, Kate wasn't going to make it. A chasm opened in her chest and she wailed in grief, pre-empting the death of her baby boy. The infant she'd nursed, comforted, fed, and raised. The shaggy haired little cherub, the sweetest kid she'd ever met.

Sal stopped short of the knife's dull point.

Aaron closed his eyes, the blade held up as if that would fend off fire. "Leave my mom alone."

Sal's entire body stiffened.

What is he waiting for?

Sal snapped the lighter shut, dousing the flame. He grunted—a foiled animal. Then he reversed his route to where Kate had dropped the fork.

"What...?" Kate almost begged for an explanation, but the rush of adrenaline shooting through her was too much. She even wanted to *thank* the entity for sparing Aaron—that was how screwed up she felt for that instant.

"I took it back," Aaron said.

"What?" The shock brought the pain in her thigh lancing through her again. Tears brimmed in her eyes, but she fought them back, confused about Aaron's statement, yet understanding precisely what he meant. "You did *what?*"

"Last night, you took it away from me, to help me. But it's mine again."

No, no, no, no, no. What was he thinking?

Sal slogged toward her, having collected the fork. He'd stabbed her with it once, as the screaming gouges testified, the damage inflicted to incapacitate her and force her to watch Aaron burn. But the way he held the equipment now... she was certain he'd drive it through her skull.

She heaved herself to within a few feet of Aaron. "Throw me the knife."

A narrow chance, a minuscule one, but she needed to take

it. Her wound was unlike any pain she'd felt before, but she wanted to live. Couldn't let Aaron watch her die like this. Hated to leave him alone in the world, with only people like the J-Js to raise him. But they were still better than her parents.

Sal's approach had grown steadier, less shambolic, as if the thing controlling his body was winning the internal battle.

Kate said, "If I don't make it, Uncle Jonathan and Aunt Jennifer will take care of you."

"No!" Aaron yelled. "I'll do whatever you want, but don't kill my mom."

The Sal-creature looked at Aaron, and in that oily voice said, "Must... follow... rules."

Sal halted within striking distance of Kate.

Aaron rushed at her, arms open. "Mommy...!"

Kate batted him away, hard. He flew back onto the grass, away from any stray blow.

The fork raised. Sal was that shark again, a shark with worms under his skin.

One chance...

Kate thrust the small blade at Sal's leg. She was inches short of stabbing him.

The fork came down.

Kate squeezed her eyes shut.

Two loud bangs crashed through the night, forcing Kate's eyes to open. Instinct made her jerk aside.

Sal dropped to his knees, the garden fork relinquished, clattering to the ground less than a foot from Kate. The words someone shouted took an age to register, yet she knew they made her safe.

"FBI, freeze!"

The two FBI agents, Ruiz and Richardson, approached with their guns extended, taking in the scene: Sal, down;

Aaron, rushing toward his mom; Kate, bleeding as she hugged him; Ollie on his front, status unknown.

"What happened here?" Ruiz demanded.

Sal was on his knees, staring at Kate, his skin smooth, his eyes glistening. "I'm sorry," he said in his own voice, before collapsing on his side.

PART FOUR

NO SURE THINGS

CHAPTER THIRTY-FOUR

After uniformed cops from both the City of White Plains PD and a patrol duo from Westchester County flooded the scene, they secured the property and tended to the injured. One officer declared he'd contact the coroner to deal with Ollie Swag, who had died from his injuries. The fire department, meanwhile, neutralized the gasoline, which Sal had lugged over from his garage, carrying it past his blazing truck—now extinguished—and intercepting Aaron as the boy ran to him for help.

Kate still didn't know if Ollie had been prodded into action by a force that seemed to influence as much as control, although it had needed to step up its game with Sal. Clearly, its power over humans was not unlimited, hence its preference for Kate to *want* to torch the Trans Am, before she snapped to her senses and the entity threatened her instead.

It was Agent Richardson who shot Sal—once in the shoulder, then lower in his back—but he didn't die. At least, not on Kate's lawn. While the half-dozen uniformed officers worked under direction from a detective who'd arrived out of Westchester County PD, the paramedics stabilized Sal on his side and carted him away on a gurney, regaining consciousness long enough to track Kate's gaze as he left.

"We'll be with you soon," she said.

"Don't," he croaked in reply. "After what I did…" He faded away, and then he and the paramedics were gone.

A second paramedic team stemmed the bleeding from Kate's leg, fired it full of morphine and, after an examination, the guy in charge recommended they take her to the hospital. Such nasty cuts should be stitched, and she'd need painkillers if she hoped to function as a regular human being. While he went to work strapping it up, another paramedic checked Aaron over.

Once the cops established jurisdictions, Ruiz took the lead—a courtesy from the WCPD detective since Kate was the subject of a federal investigation.

"Hey, Kate, listen," Ruiz said in her soft-yet-tough *trust me* voice. "I appreciate this is difficult, but I need to speak to you."

Kate kept on staring at the same spot. "Where did you come from? Were you watching the house? I'd have thought someone in your position wouldn't do that kind of thing."

"I don't. Colleagues do. They were following Oliver Smith, AKA Ollie Swag." Ruiz set her foot on the second step to the decking, where Kate had been sitting for too long, and leaned an elbow on the raised knee. "We saw you'd been in contact with him, and he's known to be into racketeering, amongst other things. So, we put a tail on him. He pulled up in your street. Our guy isn't dumb, so he called me. I got here, and we all heard the screams."

"Is your partner okay? I don't see him around."

"He's never shot anyone before, never fired his gun outside the range, so he'll get counseling. He's on leave effective immediately, though. We have procedures where shootings are concerned." Ruiz wiped a hand down her face. "Your official statement will go to the cops, but why don't you fill me in on your side of things?"

The paramedic had almost finished strapping Kate's leg. It was numb and although the nature of the bleed suggested the assault slashed no major arteries and avoided the bone, a trip to the hospital couldn't be avoided. Not to mention the psychological toll.

"Sal saved us," Kate said, unsure why she led with that. Unsure, too, why she said it when Ruiz would've known what she saw wasn't a man saving a woman, yet in her heart Kate believed it. Sal's body only moved falteringly because he didn't want to harm them, was fighting back against that urge. Any faster, and either Aaron would be a blackened corpse or Kate would be sluicing Sal's blood from her hands.

"Saved you?" Ruiz said. "How?"

"Ollie Swag came for me." Kate should wait for Jonathan, maybe plead the fifth. After all, gambling through an unlicensed bookie was a crime. Not a federal one, she thought, but still a crime. "I won some money from him. He wanted it back."

It bothered her that she'd slipped into lying again with such ease, and this lie would take little to disprove. The transaction was digital, not a briefcase full of cash.

"This isn't an interrogation," Ruiz said. "You and Aaron, you've been through so much. If we can help, please talk to me."

Kate looked over at Aaron, whom she'd reluctantly handed over to the paramedics to be sure he had ingested no gas, or got it in any cuts, or suffered injuries beyond the bruising received when Kate deflected him from trying to help her. She worried, now, that they'd been separated for other reasons—to assess whether she was a risk to her own son, and to take him from her if the answer was yes.

She didn't know where the next lines came from, perhaps

thinking like Jonathan, pondering the story he might concoct to get a client off. Reasonable doubt, even if the feds didn't buy it.

"Ollie Swag was behind the insider trading."

Ruiz placed her foot on the floor and hooked her thumbs into her pants pockets. "That so?"

Kate hadn't thought it through, could only hope to mitigate any questions with ignorance. "I don't have the full story. I don't know how it works. He gave me the tip. I talked to Endo." The story coalesced on the fly, stronger than she'd hoped. She let it run. "Endo came with me to verify it. When he was satisfied, when Endo said it looked like a legit —" She stuttered at the word she was about to say: *bet*. "When Endo said it was a good call, and he was investing a bunch of his own money, I borrowed cash from Ollie and joined in. Better than a finder's fee."

"Why you?" Ruiz asked.

Kate shrugged. "Ollie heard I wasn't into sports betting anymore, but that I worked with traders. He had a tip and wanted to get in on the action."

Ruiz nodded along.

"I didn't realize it was illegal until you arrested me."

"Huh." Ruiz glanced at the paramedic who, to his credit, hadn't batted an eye at the conversation. "Endo didn't express any concerns?"

"He seemed… tense, but no. Not directly. When you questioned me, I panicked. Made up that stuff about the dream, and… I'm sorry, Agent Ruiz. I'm sorry I didn't come clean. But as you said, Ollie Swag works—worked—for some dangerous people. I couldn't expose him. He was blackmailing Endo, which I guess pressured him into killing himself, and then tonight he threatened to take Aaron away if I didn't find someone else to do more illegal trades. He had a *knife*."

Ruiz rubbed an eyebrow, bent over into the paramedic's eye line. "Can I get a minute with Mrs. Mallory?"

"Her leg is pretty messed up," the paramedic answered. "I gotta get her to a consultant soon as we can. See if surgery's needed."

"Are you done for now?"

"Sure, but I'm taking her right away."

"Do I need to go in an ambulance?" Kate asked. "I'd prefer to drive myself."

"On that?" The paramedic pointed at Kate's leg.

"It's just the left one. I have an Auris."

"But still…"

"It's fine." Kate tested her leg by pressing a foot to the ground. Even through the morphine, she detected a throb where the spikes had gouged her thigh. It would hurt soon. "I want to come home as soon as I can, and I can't afford a cab. I want my own bed."

This was actually the honest truth. Her money was still tied up and her winnings wouldn't arrive until the banks opened tomorrow, and she hated the thought of overnighting in a hospital.

The paramedic didn't like it, a big huff of a sigh suggesting she was a fool. "You'll need to sign a waiver."

"Then I'll sign a waiver," she said.

Ruiz gave a pleasant but demanding smile. "Looks like I have a few minutes."

"Sure." The paramedic eased Kate's leg onto the step so it was level with her hip, and she leaned against the guardrail. "I'm right over here if you need anything." He rose to Ruiz's height and said, "No stress. No strain. Okay?"

"Okay." Ruiz watched him depart, then sat beside Kate's foot. "I'd love to believe you."

"It's true," Kate said.

"Except it isn't, is it? You and Endo were running that

trade from Hetherington's before Mervin Corney put a stop to it. That's the first part that doesn't add up."

"No, wait." Kate spun the event into the tumble dryer of her mind. "That wasn't his money. He wanted to meet Ollie before—"

"Shush, Kate. You have time to invent a coherent story before I make this official, so just think good and hard about it. Also, consider telling me the truth. You'll find I'm one of the more sympathetic people at the Bureau. Which brings me to my second point."

"Which is?"

"That throughout all this, you've been more concerned with your son than me. Than jail. You are hiding something, Kate, and we leave nothing to chance. We will learn everything soon, and we'll be able to prove it. All of it. I don't want to go hardball on you, but I can't help you if you don't talk to me."

Does she know more than she's saying?

She half expected the answer to download from the ether, to pop into her head, but without the buddy riding with her, she had to plow her own furrow.

"You researched that LaPaul guy," Kate said. "The banker who started making unbelievable trades suddenly."

"I did."

"His son committing worse and worse behavior as he went. Both eventually killing themselves."

"Correct."

"And you're pushing me because this sounds like a similar situation."

Ruiz's expression remained unchanged. "On the surface, sure. This is a similar situation. Unexplained shorting of stocks on a kamikaze trade. A child going off the rails." She twitched her head toward Ollie Swag's corpse. "Death as things get hairy with the SEC."

"What do you hope I'll tell you?"

Ruiz blew out a loud lungful, shifted onto the step below the one on which Kate's leg rested, and drew closer. "In all honesty, I don't know. I wish I did. But we both know this isn't a low-rent bookie throwing tips around. And if you had an insider, you'd have confessed by now, unless it's family. And we can't connect you, Endo, Marcus, or Ollie to anyone with knowledge of the operation. There is absolutely no way you could have known about it. Not without help."

"You want to believe it's something other than criminal."

Ruiz stared. The lines on her face hadn't been apparent before, but as Kate studied her, the surrounding hubbub of law enforcement and medical personnel doing their jobs faded. It was just the two of them. Kate, conscious of the morphine-dulled throb in her thigh, and Ruiz, a woman in her early forties who had appeared to be in her mid-thirties when they first met, but now—talking around things FBI agents could not discuss if they wanted to advance in their careers—she could have been fifty or older.

"You need this," Kate said. "You need to know there's more."

Ruiz said nothing, just hardened the crinkles at the corners of her eyes. Waiting, hoping, Kate thought, for the confirmation she yearned for. More broken by her past than any functioning federal agent could afford to be. How much had she hidden from her employers? Or was she playing Kate? A superior poker player, using her pain to crank Kate open like a tin can.

"I looked you up," Kate said, erring toward Ruiz's hurt being real. "Your sister."

Ruiz turned away for the first time. A long blink. Then back to Kate. "It's not about her."

"It is. You might not believe me about the dream, but if you can prove what I did was somehow… supernatural…

like you think that LaPaul thing was… you can be sure your sister still exists. Somewhere."

"Whatever you want to say, Kate, I'll listen."

Kate reminded herself of how the buddy had told her Ruiz was desperate for proof of the afterlife. Only, she couldn't use it to benefit herself. Heck, she might incur the buddy's wrath simply having voiced it to Ruiz, but the agent hadn't seemed particularly rattled. Perhaps she knew a Google search or similar would turn up a news story that named her. It wouldn't be hard to check. If she continued down this road, the entity currently inhabiting Aaron might demand a big favor, or a small one, depending on how events panned out. Kate almost wished she still had the buddy with her so she could ask.

That wish brought their biggest problem thundering back to her: Aaron remained infested. And that was what it felt like—an infestation, a parasite or symbiotic entity attached to its host. She had more ideas about that, but needed to talk them through with someone who wasn't a federal agent. It was the main reason she wanted to drive alone, even though she expected to regret it.

"If my son is fit to be moved," Kate said, "I'd like to go to the hospital now."

CHAPTER THIRTY-FIVE

Ruiz could only watch as the paramedics attempted to talk Kate out of driving herself to the hospital. However, the local anesthetic wouldn't impair her ability to use the wheel, and the dead leg wasn't needed in the hybrid vehicle, so there was nothing stopping her.

While Ruiz paced amid the various lights and the many investigators from the fire department, local PD, and the neighborly lookie-loos, she placed a call to ASAC Dougherty. Didn't matter that it was late. The assistant special agent in charge for New York City had demanded updates every hour, minimum, an arbitrary deadline he'd set after learning of Richardson discharging his weapon. The shooting was right-eous, Ruiz had assured him. But now Kate's story of Sal Cantero saving their lives could land Richardson in a less comfortable interview with the FBI's Inspection Division. She briefed the ASAC on Kate's version of events and expressed her opinion that Kate was being far from truthful.

"Why would she lie?" Dougherty asked.

"Can't say at this stage, sir. But I know there's more going on. We just haven't snagged on it yet."

A nasal sigh puffed from the phone, followed by what Ruiz interpreted as a grumble. "Inspection Division is sending someone to speak to Richardson, and they'll pick up with you as soon as they get done with him. Might be the morning now. They'll need to interview this Mallory woman and her son, too."

"Of course."

"I don't want the two accounts to clash, Ruiz. When ID presents to the SIRG guys, I expect it to be a formality, the way it should be. Am I clear?"

The Shooting Incident Review Group would evaluate evidence from the Inspection Division, who were responsible for investigating when any FBI agent discharged a firearm. They held the final say over whether Richardson did the right thing in shooting a man in the back. Ruiz had witnessed it and was absolutely sure that the only reason she wasn't the one suspended was because Richardson was faster on the draw. Sal was poised to kill Kate Mallory, the garden fork a deadly weapon in his hands. In her mind, the spikes were traveling forward, directly at Kate's head, when the bullets entered the man's body. No time for a warning. Imminent threat to life. It was righteous, and Kate was covering for Sal Cantero.

"It could be an abuse cycle," Ruiz said. "If we can poke holes in her credibility, make her tell the truth, we should get the result."

Another nose-breath sounded, less harassed than the sigh moments earlier. "I'll get Hadid and Walowski to push ahead with that angle. Tie it in to your fraud case."

"I can do it tonight, sir."

"This isn't your strong suit, Ruiz. You're a good investigator, but—"

"We have established a connection. I think she was about to open up when she put the shutters down."

A pause. No sigh. No deep breaths or grumbles. Considering the risks of letting Ruiz go it alone, no doubt due to the incident that got her stuck on medical leave until she transferred to the SEC liaison position.

Ruiz said, "I'll record everything, sir. I'll talk to her one-on-one, and make sure there's no hint of a threat, and nothing anyone can point to as witness tampering. Or coaching."

"You're sure?"

"I can break what she's hiding. Richardson will be fine, and we might get someone more substantial than a single mom who made a couple of bad decisions."

This time, Dougherty's pause was much shorter. "You have until morning, Ruiz. Then I'll have to replace you. This isn't your beat. You get that, right?"

"I do. Thank you, sir."

Ruiz hung up, surveying the scene, drifting to her car as the quiet, studious work of documenting everything continued. From the soggy, charred wreck of the Ford truck, to the CSI team suiting up to detail Ollie Swag's demise, and the two federal agents hanging back—the pair who'd been surveilling Ollie Swag and brought Ruiz and Richardson out to this placid suburb. None of it shook the unsettling churn that had gripped Ruiz since Kate mentioned the bombshell confirming the presence of the impossible.

Her sister.

Her twin.

The other half of Ruiz's soul.

How had she known?

I looked you up…

"No, you didn't," Ruiz said aloud, although there was no one nearby to hear her.

The only way Kate could learn about Julietta Ruiz would be if someone in the Bureau told her. And it was a tight circle at that. No news outlets ran with her name, and those who had inquired were informed of the fallibility of rumor and conjecture, and the senior editors reminded that ongoing cooperation between the FBI field offices and themselves hinged on no falsehoods being printed, spoken, or otherwise transmitted. And it wasn't simply to respect a mourning agent's privacy.

People's lives were in danger.

No, Kate could not have known about Julietta's death or the reasons behind it. And she surely could not have surmised the depth of feeling Andrea Ruiz still fought to keep going every single day. Lighting candles, praying, seances, even tarot. None of it brought the peace she sought.

But Ruiz suspected if Kate could offer that one thing, explain how she knew about Julietta, it'd be the same source that had given her the foreknowledge of Villiers going under. Then, maybe, Ruiz could either nail the mole inside the bureau, or she'd finally speak to Julietta again, directly, *knowing* she'd hear rather than just hoping.

She'd read the files on Brian LaPaul several times, noted how loose ends were left to dangle, and now she had the chance to tie them to Kate Mallory. It didn't matter that Ruiz could never sell that to Dougherty. She needed it for herself. Then she could press on with merging back into the Bureau, finally at peace.

At her car, only a dozen yards from the driveway, Ruiz watched Kate emerge from her property, the paramedics having loaned her a crutch, although they still accompanied her, giving her Auris a disdainful glance before surrendering to her will. She got in, secured Aaron beside her, and backed out onto the street. She spotted Ruiz, and the pair regarded one another as Kate drove past. And then she was gone.

Ruiz hoped the woman came to her senses soon and

spoke openly. She didn't want to charge her, didn't want to pull the woman's life apart.

If Kate didn't play ball, though, exonerate Richardson and prove to Ruiz the truth she'd suspected all these years, then Ruiz would have to sacrifice her for the cause. Because nothing was more important than life and death.

CHAPTER THIRTY-SIX

Four years ago, Kate had broken two toes, so she was adept at using crutches, the technique resurrected like riding a bike. With the ambulance waiver signed, partially because she wasn't sure her insurance covered a non-emergency ambulance ride, she gave her initial statement to the detectives and they released her from the scene. She headed around the outside of her house—not allowed back inside until CSI relinquished the property—opened her car and folded herself inside. Aaron got in beside her. He still smelled like an empty gas tank.

The firefighters had used the same kind of shower usually reserved for chemical spills and said they were lucky; if he'd remained covered in the fuel much longer, it might have burned him. He was also lucky none had gotten in his eyes, nor snuck into his mouth and down his throat. The WCPD detective had permitted a change into PJs, too, so they allowed her to head to the hospital under her own steam.

Kate pulled out onto the street busy with blue and red lights, her view lingering on Sal's husk of a truck, then on Special Agent Ruiz seated in her own vehicle, before driving away, leaving it all in her rearview mirror. "Is it here? With us?"

"I think so," Aaron said. "It's always here."

"Is it satisfied with Sal getting shot?"

"I can't say."

"Why?"

"Because if I ask, I'll have to do something I don't wanna."

Of course you will.

"About what happened back there," Kate said.

Aaron concentrated dead ahead. "I know. I should have run. But I couldn't, Mom, I—"

"That's not what I mean. I mean, I saw it was afraid."

Aaron's brows knitted together. "Afraid?"

"Yeah." She shone a mirth-free smile. "When it was about to set fire to you. I told it to get out of me. I'm guessing at that moment, you wanted it out of me too."

"I thought it. Wished for it to come back to me. Out of you. So you didn't have to put up with it anymore."

Kate didn't think she'd ever loved that kid as much as she did in this moment. There were nicer situations where her love had bloomed hotter, more all-encompassing, but this was different. It wasn't an unconditional love, either, gifted to most parents around the world; this was a more grownup love, a pride in her son. And, if she was brutally honest, pride in herself; she'd raised this selfless child, after all.

She, and Craig.

No time for mushy stuff, though. She needed to voice her hypothesis while it was still fresh.

"It stopped," she said. "When it moved from me into you. Whatever was controlling Sal switched from struggling to kill you to coming after me."

Aaron was on the same wavelength. "It was scared to die."

"Meaning," Kate said, "I reckon we've learned two things that could help us."

Aaron shook his head, looking out the window. Back to his mom. "It's trying to tell me stuff. But I don't want to know. I don't want to say them. I don't want to think them." He bashed the sides of his head with his fists. "No, no, leave me alone."

Keeping one eye on the road, Kate held Aaron's hand nearest to her. It was all she could do. "Easy, baby. It's okay. Just breathe. Imagine nice thoughts. Drown the uninvited ones out."

He inhaled and exhaled deeply, his bottom lip wobbling.

"It's scared again," Kate said. "Because we know its secret without it telling us. Two secrets, actually."

"What secrets?"

"How it transfers between bodies. If the person infected by the buddy wants rid of it, and someone else is willing to take it, it doesn't have a choice in the matter. It just moves over."

Aaron again gave the hypothesis some thought. The scenario had happened twice, so Kate expected he'd accept that. He nodded.

"Second," Kate said, "we know it can be killed."

"How?"

"You saw how it acted when it went into you? Then turned on me?"

"Sure."

Kate had now picked up the signs for the hospital, relieved to see them as the immobile leg throbbed again. Pain would soon follow.

She said, "If the person it's hiding in dies, I think the buddy dies too."

Aaron's face lit up as if she'd told him Christmas was coming early, tomorrow to be precise. She'd been wrong about it flinging Endo's body at her to execute her, the aim imprecise. Perhaps that was why it took to influencing her, tempting her to burn Ollie's Trans Am instead of scaring her into it.

"The buddy wants to live," Kate said. "If it's inside me, and I kill myself, it can't bother anyone else."

Aaron paled, his face twisted. "NO! You will not kill yourself, Mom. You won't leave me like Dad did. You can't do that. I won't let you."

"Aaron—"

"You can't take the buddy out of me if I don't let it go. So you won't be doing that. Never. I'll never let you have it."

"I didn't mean me." Kate's elation from moments ago at her son's gesture curdled into torment at his panic, his outburst. Even without the buddy coming into their lives, he'd been bottling up a ton of issues, something she should have noticed and dealt with. She'd circle back to that as soon as she could. "I meant… I don't know. I'll take it until we find someone to put it into."

"Like someone who's already dying?"

"Maybe."

Aaron again fell silent as he thought her plan through. Then he fixed her with the expression of an adult explaining something awful that a child overheard on the news. "No, I will *not* do that. You'll do the gambling thing. Your disease makes you ill. Makes you want to use him more."

"I won't, Aaron, I promise."

"You promised Daddy you wouldn't either. But you did. And you did it this week too."

As Kate merged with traffic on the road that would take her to the nearest hospital, she wanted to cry. Wanted to reach into her chest and massage her heart, to tell it Aaron wasn't holding onto a supernatural entity because she was such a weak, selfish bitch, or that his father had died because of her.

Even though it was true.

The absence of trust was justified. She'd gambled so many times this week, using the buddy to enhance their lives, then refusing to perform the task demanded in return.

"I promise," she said. "I won't ask for it back until you're ready to give it. Okay?"

Aaron's bottom lip came out again, this time without the wobble. "Okay."

They drove the rest of the way in silence, only breaking when Aaron asked, "What about a bad person?"

"What do you mean? Like a criminal?"

"It's a curse, so why not? Trick them into taking it on."

A *curse*. Sure. It made as much sense as a demon or genie, or some dark angel corrupting the host inside and out. Kate almost answered right away that infecting an evil person was a good idea, was already considering what form that trickery might take, but a spark inside her stopped it. "If we give it to a bad man—or woman—it's still powerful. A bad person will use it, and won't feel guilty about paying the price. Especially a criminal."

Aaron looked dejected, his idea shot down. "Even someone on death row?"

Again, Kate's knee-jerk thought was that he was correct. But after considering it, she had to disappoint him once more. "Passing it to a condemned man on death row sounds sensible, but even gaining access to a prisoner like that will be almost impossible." It wasn't a case of showing up and saying, *Hey, can I get some one-on-one time with Joe McSerial-Killer, please?* "Then getting him to take it is another matter. After that, if we succeed, what if the buddy tells him how to escape? Or feeds him an appeal defense, or blackmail for a judge, or—"

"Okay, I see. I'm dumb."

They pulled into the hospital grounds. "Oh, you're not dumb, baby. We just have to find another way."

"There isn't one."

"How do you know?"

Aaron tapped the side of his head. "Because he told me. Sorry, it just came out."

Kate found somewhere to park and killed the engine. "What's the price?"

Aaron stared at her hand. Tears spilled down his cheeks. "I'm sorry, Mommy."

Kate sighed, resigned to the fact something worse would, indeed, happen if she refused. She moved her hand to his.

He lifted it. And bit the skin next to her little finger.

She clamped her free hand over her mouth, stifling the howl that would have escaped her throat had she not prepared herself. It was nowhere near as painful as a pitchfork through her thigh, but still no picnic.

He let go. "Sorry."

"It's not your fault." She rubbed her hand, the indentations remaining, but he hadn't cut her. "Let's just head inside. Get my leg fixed. Check on Sal. Then we'll decide what to do next."

CHAPTER THIRTY-SEVEN

It seemed word had gotten around the hospital that a stupid woman had refused an ambulance ride, despite having two holes in her leg. They rushed her through the ER to an examination room where one Doctor Lafayette had already received notes from the paramedics. Kate had never known efficiency like this, but as the morphine was wearing off faster and faster, she accepted the privilege gratefully. Meanwhile, Aaron made himself comfortable on the folding cot they provided, although he could not sleep. He watched, instead.

It was only after the doctor removed the dressing, staunched Kate's blood flow with a tourniquet, and propped her leg up, that the reason for her celebrity treatment showed itself: Special Agent Andrea Ruiz. She must have followed them at a distance and spent the last hour or so getting up to speed.

She slipped in while Dr. Lafayette was out prepping what she'd need for a longer-term fix. Stitches, a soft cast, and painkillers.

"I'm not speaking to you without a lawyer," Kate said.

"Then let me talk." Ruiz observed Aaron watching her

328

cross the room. She sat on a plastic chair on the opposite side of the bed to Aaron and spoke quietly. "Sal Cantero is in surgery. Initial thoughts are the second bullet didn't hit any vital organs, but they need to check nothing got nicked. The one in his shoulder may be more problematic. A ligament got damaged, which is… painful. And might limit movement for some time."

"For a long time," Kate said, forgetting about her lawyer vow.

"He confessed, by the way. He's going to prison. Ten years, maybe more."

"He won't. I won't let them put him in prison."

"Well, it's not federal jurisdiction, you understand, but if you give me a reason, maybe I can intervene. Ask them to think about it in a different light."

"Isn't my word enough?"

"No." Ruiz made her face stern, her tone hard. "My friend, a federal agent, shot a man in the back to protect you and Aaron. I know what I saw during the exchange, and I know what I saw after. I know a crime scene. This idea that he was… What did you say he was doing with the fork? Because it looked like he was making to stab you with it."

"It was an accident. He got it free, and the momentum made him lift it like that."

"And your boy covered in gas?"

"Ollie did that. Before Sal saved us."

Ruiz sighed, dipped her chin, then met Kate's eyes. "That's even more full of shit than your dream scenario. Ollie Swag had no gasoline on him, while Sal stank of it; the fork was in Ollie Swag's *back*, so I'm not buying that you pulled it out to save him, then you accidentally fell on it, only for Sal to yank it out at the exact moment we came along. It's like a preschooler's lies about how the paint got spilled. And let's not forget Cantero himself requested a tox screen."

"A what?"

"He asked me—and I'm paraphrasing from memory here, but I'll try to get it right. He asked us to help him understand. 'Why would I try to burn a little boy like that? Why would I want to kill Kate?' He said all that in front of witnesses. Doctors, nurses, cops, and me."

Kate closed her eyes and lay her head back, wishing for the doc to return and kick Ruiz out. Yet, there was more going on. Something more the FBI agent wanted. "Why are you telling me this?"

"Because," Ruiz said, "I want to understand why a woman would protect the man who tried to murder her son. Give me something. Tell me how you got that information. About the short trade and why there's a dead loan shark on your lawn. I need to figure out why there are so many parallels between your insider trading and that of a dead stockbroker with a dead mentally ill son. Because it seems to me, the longer this goes on, the more people die. Soon, it's not only small-time hoodlums the world has to mourn."

Kate said nothing, searching for a reason to trust Ruiz, but found none. She was about to speak, but Ruiz cut her off.

"And let's not forget about my sister. Don't give me that crap about looking her up, because that isn't true either. You're a liar, Kate. And it needs to stop. Now."

Kate never considered herself a dishonest person. But she didn't hold herself to a higher standard than others. She understood the need to shield her family, herself, from those who might not believe her. If she'd been entirely honest at any point before confiding in Sal, her friend Tammy would have deemed her mad, the J-Js would have judged her an unfit mother, and the authorities—local or federal—would have labeled her a danger to herself and her son. After all, this had only started because she wanted to protect him. To grasp why he was behaving so badly.

And now she knew, had she behaved any better? Even without the buddy goading her?

"I'll tell you everything," Kate said. "Every impossible detail. But only after I've spoken with Sal. Alone."

Ruiz looked at the door. It remained closed. Back to Kate, skimming over Aaron, who'd been trying to listen and probably heard everything.

"Suppose I say yes," Ruiz said. "How can I be sure you'll hold up your end?"

"Because I'm tired. And whether you believe me or not doesn't make it less real. It won't help us get free from it, but it might give you what you need. But first, I have to make things right with the people who are victims too."

Dr. Lafayette returned with a nurse and stood still in the doorway. "What's this?"

"I'm leaving." Ruiz rose and made for the door, pausing only to say, "Okay, deal. As soon as he's awake, he's yours."

* * *

Ruiz spent her downtime at the hospital going over the research into Brian LaPaul and adding to it remotely thanks to a fast Wi-Fi connection in the cafeteria. There was no set filter on NCIC, ViCap, OneDOJ, or any of the criminal databases that allowed her to search for crimes with confluence of illegal enterprise out of thin air combined with a decline in the wrongdoer's offspring. The only one that came close was a CompStat entry.

This database was unlike the others in that it used pure numbers to discern crime patterns. One entry showed that, in 1996, a child aged fifteen was convicted of kidnapping a classmate and torturing her with cigarettes, a felony which led investigators to uncover a litany of other violent incidents in his history. Looking into the files themselves, Ruiz found the boy's mother had helped conceal his proclivities.

Ruiz only snagged on it because the woman named in the statistics was Honor Shackleton, a minor celebrity in the 90s. She was a single mom whose wealthy husband dumped her for a much younger model, and went on to build a small business empire from her garage—a revolutionary mop of some sort. Admittedly, it was a short-lived revolution, one that never made her product a household name, yet she was briefly worth more than the husband whose libido struck a fatal blow to their marriage. Her arrest for destroying or concealing evidence in a crime—namely, several assaults and other violations committed by her son—ended her sharp rise and, combined with the financial frauds she initiated, she remained behind bars today. Her son's file was sealed.

Looking deeper, Ruiz found Honor Shackleton had often facilitated the boy's wishes by buying off the victims' parents, others through lawyers who bullied the cops into dropping the charges, and using those same lawyers to slam the parents with a defamation suit should they utter a word. Some had tried to press the issue, but they had ended up with more problems than an assaulted son or daughter. The police arrested one complainant following a tip-off regarding child pornography on his computer.

Ruiz looked up the court filings, and skim-read thousands of words, picking up on key phrases from the son such as, "I had to do it, or my mom would have had to beg my asshole father to help," and, "I don't know how I came up with the idea, but it was mine," and, "Mom said we'd be rich, and I'd get my share." The one that stood out was, "If I didn't hurt them, the business would fail. We'd be back to square one."

The similarities were undeniable. Sudden success. A child

acting in a depraved manner. All crashing back to earth when the truth came out.

With eyes begging to sleep, Ruiz soldiered on, searching LexisNexis for news stories dating to the 1980s where people got rich quick, only to be brought down by violent crimes committed by their children.

Why only children?

She guessed she could pick up the search again when she was less fried. If this proved to be an earthly explanation like a hacking syndicate or a more fantastical story of some twisted wish machine, both fit with what Kate had been going through. Only, if it was a foreign power or criminal group behind it, surely they'd have made a connection between Kate and the paymasters by now. And that didn't explain Kate protecting Sal Cantero. Ruiz knew what she'd seen, and she'd seen a man about to ram a garden fork into a woman.

Whatever the conclusion, it wouldn't help Richardson. Wouldn't help her get back on top with the Bureau. It could ease her pain, though. The fantastical version would at least cease her trying to itch that phantom limb that had been her twin.

She could let go, finally. Even if she failed in her career, there'd be a life to live.

"What the hell am I thinking?"

Not for the first time, Ruiz worried she was genuinely insane. A lot of agents hid psychological flaws from the bureau shrinks, eager to get back to work, to prove they were promotion material, and plow on through the mental pain. Ruiz had compartmentalized Julietta, but now the door was open. She might not be able to hide it much longer if Kate didn't prove to be the real deal.

"Agent Ruiz?" said a uniformed cop, having approached across the cafeteria.

Ruiz looked up from her screen and rubbed her eyes. "Hi."

"The woman you asked us about? She's awake. She's asking to see the suspect."

* * *

Kate had set the alarm on her phone to wake her when Sal's surgery was due to finish—four hours after Aaron fell asleep. Her leg had been stitched and was bound tighter than before, and she would have to traverse the hospital in a wheelchair with the aid of an orderly. Her insurance covered her for the lease of crutches and a self-propelled chair, and Dr. Lafayette recommended a night of observation before taking a decision on a second 24 hours. Kate had accepted the first night without question—it allowed her somewhere to leave Aaron —and permitted a limited amount of morphine to ease her to sleep for a few hours.

Having woken to her low-volume alarm, calling a nurse resulted in little sympathy and insistence she remain in bed. As Kate struggled to get her legs over the side and reached for her crutches, the nurse called an orderly to help. Kate directed the young Indian man, who had a pleasant manner and an overhanging gut, to take her to Sal Cantero's room. She rode in a wheelchair, providing horizontal support for her leg, after the pair of cops on duty had been made aware of her visit.

"You sure?" the female officer said. "He banged you up good."

"It wasn't him," Kate said.

The female cop nodded.

The man said, "We can help, y'know? You don't have to cover for him. What he did, ma'am…"

He didn't finish the sentence, just handed Kate the card

for a charity called Better Lives and delivered a thoroughly modern male smile.

The orderly rolled her inside Sal's room, where her neighbor and friend lay on his side, facing her, one hand cuffed to the rail. His eyes were half-open, drowsy. He blinked as she advanced. The orderly stopped two arm lengths from the bed, applied the brake, and departed, closing the door behind him.

"Hey, Sal." Kate sensed the hollowness of her own words but wasn't sure how to overcome it.

Sal blinked again. "Kate." He was hoarse, croaky, but it was his own voice.

"I need to know what it was like. What you were seeing?"

"I can't." His eyes drooped closed. When Kate made no move to leave, they creaked open, his mouth twisting down in a fashion that could have been an exaggerated sad clown, or grief combined with physical pain. "I was flooded with images. Lookin' at my truck, the flames, I'm searching around for more fire extinguishers, and then Aaron comes running at me, crying for help and…"

He ran out of steam. Short, sharp breaths while he gathered himself.

"I got these flashes. My wife, my daughter. All I needed to do was burn Aaron, and I'd have them back in my life. I'd learn what Maria had been thinking, and Bella would be with me. I'd be a daddy again."

That chimed with Kate, with what she recalled from her experiences. The infestation, she was certain, could only make a person do the worst things within certain boundaries. It had to present Endo as a threat, cause Kate to feel unsafe in his presence, persuade her to kill him. When she did not, when she wrested control of her emotions through logic and knowing what Aaron had described, it made Endo act instead. Elevated his emotions, punched specific triggers within him.

If she hadn't experienced Aaron's problems, she might have plunged that knife into Endo herself. The vulnerabilities inside Endo, the triggers, had amplified and sent him plummeting to his death. Likewise, it zoned in on Sal's weakest link to the living world.

"I don't know how it came to me, Kate. I don't get how I fell for it. But when I approached Aaron, I was somehow holding the gas can I use for the lawnmower. I started thinking about it, but then I saw you. Like a memory. Hurtin' Bella. Like I just sensed it. *You* were responsible for the crash, not Maria. And taking Aaron, through fire, would bring her back. It was... like a trip, a hallucination, but... real. Real, like I'm talkin' to you now."

"It looked like you were resisting," Kate said.

"Not... exactly." Sal moaned, rolled his head aside as if he was about to vomit. He didn't. He needed some deep breaths before resuming. "It was like blackouts. I was thinkin' stuff. Seeing how setting fire to Aaron would work, then I'd be thinking about Bella, and when I came to, Aaron was soaked. In your yard, I kept flashing back to how you were responsible, how hurtin' you, eye for an eye, would give me Bella. I didn't see what I did."

"It realized it couldn't make you do it just by tempting you, so it..." Kate envisioned the scene again. The strides, slow and even. Like someone coming back from a serious injury, re-learning how to use their legs. "It took you away, your consciousness, put it with what you want most in life, and when you were out of it, not looking, it moved your body." She trawled her memory of the skirmish, forced herself to look at it with detachment, and she came back to its manner, its frustration. It was obvious now.

"This thing... it was learning to walk as a human. It had

never resorted to this before. It was controlling you. Making you act."

"It's almost a relief to wake up with this on." Sal jangled his handcuff. "Means I can't hurt anyone else where I'm goin'."

"You wouldn't hurt anyone, Sal."

"I wanted to hurt you *both*. Even when I *didn't* want to. I knew it wasn't real, but I chose to try, anyway. Because, if there was even a 0.01% of a chance to hold Bella again... It was worth it to me. To kill Aaron, to kill you."

"You didn't, though."

"I can't tell if I tried, or if I let the blackouts do it."

Kate didn't see it that way. Maybe he didn't remember the moment he cried out, trying to break free. Whatever he said, though, Kate held nothing but pity for him.

She said, "Any parent would do anything for one more day with a dead child."

"Even kill a woman? Pull out her guts, dance in the blood?"

"You tried to fight it, Sal. I have no doubt, you—"

"Not hard enough—*Aaagh!*" His head and shoulders arched and his face turned red. He strained, some internal pain flaring.

A nurse ran in and started fussing over the monitors and machines, checking Sal's pupils, ignoring his insistence that he was fine.

The nurse was joined by colleagues, including a doctor who pointed at Kate and said, "Get *her* out of here."

Kate thought her rude, but had no chance to respond as she was being wheeled backwards, the orderly having returned with the commotion and removed her to the corridor. "Time to go back to your room, ma'am," he said as he pushed her back the way they'd come.

It was pointless objecting, but Kate was about to anyway,

when she ceased forward motion before a woman in a pantsuit.

Ruiz. "Well?"

"Ma'am?" the orderly said.

"Two minutes," Kate replied.

The man set the brake, then retreated a respectful distance.

"You got your time with him," Ruiz said. "It's your turn. Tell me what you've been hiding and I'll do my best to help you."

"Sal goes free."

"Damn it." Ruiz half-turned, running a hand through her short hair.

"I knew you'd stiff me."

"I bluffed you. Now I'm raising the pot."

"Whatever. You still went back on the deal."

"No." Kate hated herself for this, but it was necessary. For herself, for Sal, for Aaron. "I'll tell you everything. When the time is right."

"Tell me something now."

"No."

Ruiz fixed on her, a menacing demeanor she'd held in reserve until now.

"What do you *want* from me?" Kate asked, a flutter to her voice. "You want to believe so badly?"

"No one knows about Julietta, Kate. The only logical explanation is you got a tip-off from inside the bureau, which I doubt. But if it *is* a mole, I want to nail the son of a bitch, because it's probably the same person who gave you the Villiers tip. But as I said, I doubt it. The circle around Julietta was small, and I trust them all. You see, Julietta was my twin. My *identical* twin. She was driving *my* car because hers was in the shop. Picked it up from my parking bay. They were after *me*."

"Who were?"

"A syndicate of Russian diamond smugglers. Tens of millions of dollars at stake. They'd already tried to buy me and I'd refused. And they knew I was the lead agent. They ran her off the road into a parked truck on the freeway. She didn't stand a chance." Ruiz swallowed, her voice hitching. "It was supposed to be me. And you know what I did?"

"No."

"I stayed on. Through it all, I stayed. I bottled up all my grief and anger, and I went at them full throttle. We had them a month later. That's how close we were. But then, when one of them was laughing at my dead sister, mocking me, I snapped. I beat him in that interrogation suite, and two agents had to haul me off. Repressed guilt, rage, whatever. That bastard got away with killing her."

"He went free?"

"Went to prison on a RICO rap, but not for my sister's murder. That's still unsolved."

Kate's chest ached, empty and echoing, her husband's death still not resolved to her satisfaction. She could barely imagine what it must be like to lose a twin without closure.

Ruiz said, "It tipped me over. Almost a year of therapy before they'd consider letting me back in, and only then behind a desk. Now... I have a chance to move on. To figure out what to do with my life. If I can just... hear... the truth."

"But I don't know the truth."

Ruiz's shoulders rose, her arms tense. She blew out her cheeks as her shoulders dropped. "What is it, Kate? A spirit? Is it you? The dreams you mentioned?"

She wanted more than Kate could give. Thought that proof of the supernatural was confirmation her sister was happy, at peace in some afterlife. She could lie. Not for her own gain or convenience this time, but to give comfort to

Ruiz, get the agent off her case; she could insist Ollie was the source, and let the Organized Crime people piece it together.

Kate shook her head. That didn't help the immediate problem.

She injected steel back into her tone. "Sal goes free. Then you get what you want."

"*When* did it start?" Ruiz asked. "At least tell me that. When did you notice the change in Aaron? I can track back then. Maybe look into other crimes, things done by other people. I can make the bureau and the cops understand."

Kate had decided the *when* didn't matter. Nor, really, did the *how*. But hearing Ruiz ask about it, almost directly challenging her to snitch on Aaron's supernatural passenger, the question burned inside her.

"No." She set her face to stone.

"I'll believe you, Kate. And I'll help. I promise, I'll help, but I can't release your friend."

Kate wanted to talk about the buddy, about the unexplainable predictions, how she believed it to be more than an infection of psychic powers and even the proof Ruiz was searching for. She resisted, though. Using that might invoke demands for a return favor. But if Ruiz saw it as a personal attack, any lingering sympathy she had for Kate would evaporate.

"Just make sure Sal isn't charged, please," Kate said.

"It's the County's jurisdiction, not mine. I'm only a witness."

"And I'm the victim." Kate couldn't hold her cool much longer. The only reason she didn't shout her last words was their proximity to sick people behind doors and glass. "While they keep Sal locked up, I'll be getting him a lawyer."

"They won't release him if they can show he's dangerous."

"He isn't."

"Lots of domestic abuse victims side with the abuser."

"Then you need to persuade them your initial version of events was wrong. I'll keep my promise to you."

"And Richardson is screwed," Ruiz said.

I'll tell you life exists beyond ours, Kate wanted to shout, to promise Ruiz would hear what her grief-addled brain demanded. But not yet.

Ruiz added, "You'd let the agent who saved your life get hauled over the fire to protect the man who tried to kill you?"

"I'll talk when Sal is free." Kate pulled out her phone and checked the time: four a.m. "I'll call my lawyer in two hours. Once you get Sal released from custody, I talk. In full. You don't, my mouth stays shut."

Kate was blowing smoke, and she knew it. Ruiz knew it too. But she would strive to equip Sal with the best representation available. As she sat back and allowed herself to be wheeled back to her room, Ruiz's comments about Richardson coiled inside her. How much of the problem would come down to the shooting?

If Sal had not been attacking Kate, an FBI agent had shot an innocent man.

When they reached her room, a different complication arose. Aaron was awake on a nurse's lap, sobbing. He saw Kate and ran to her, avoided her leg, and hugged her tightly, all without speaking or making a sound.

"He woke up, and you'd disappeared," the nurse said, rising from the cot where she'd been comforting him. "I assured him you'd be back soon."

"Thank you." Kate held Aaron, kissed his head, and only disengaged while the nurse and orderly helped her into bed.

When they were alone, she kept Aaron close, lying beside

her. He still hadn't uttered a word. Was this what life was to be now? Led by fear? Fear of every minor mishap being blamed on these experiences?

She wondered if even years of therapy could unburden them. Tonight's events were going to hit her like a truck soon —once she stopped long enough to consider them. If Kate wasn't affected by PTSD, then surely Aaron would be. In many ways, he'd had it worse, not least because he was a child.

They needed to find a way. She needed to fix it once and for all.

"Do you remember when you first used the buddy?" she asked with another kiss to the top of his head.

"The day after my birthday. It was my wish. To make you proud with my schoolwork. To show my teacher I wasn't a baby."

He couldn't simply have wished it to life. There had to be more to it.

"Three weeks ago," she mused.

"Yep."

"You wouldn't kill me if the buddy asked, would you?"

"Of course not, Mom. I promise, I wouldn't…"

"The bigger the question, the bigger the favor, though."

Aaron remained perfectly still. "I think so."

"Do you understand what it means to spend money to make money?"

"Is that another gambling thing?"

"Kind of. But not in this case. If you spend ten dollars on something, then sell it for twenty, you've made ten dollars. You understand?"

"Sure."

She had a theory that teetered on the verge of insanity, but she didn't want to frighten Aaron, or accuse someone unnecessarily. It could have been nothing, but she had to try.

"I need to ask the buddy one last thing—"

"No, Mom, no more gambling. No more. I can't."

"It's one thing. One question. A yes or no answer. That'll just be a small thing, won't it?"

He mulled that over for a second. "What is it you want to ask?"

"Aaron… Did Daddy kill himself or was it an accident? Then we can all move on."

Aaron went silent, staring into space as if in some sort of trance. Then his brow creased. "Mom?"

"Yeah, what is it?"

"The answer is no."

"That's it? Just no?"

He nodded, his bottom lip wobbling, tears glistening. "I don't know what that means, Mom. Did Daddy kill himself? Did he do it by accident? How can both answers be no?"

Kate had dreaded this. Perhaps dreaded it more than learning Craig had chosen to take his life.

No.

That tiny, two-letter word changed everything.

"It's okay, baby." Kate hugged Aaron close, nuzzling into his soft, shaggy hair. "Whatever it means, whatever the favor it demands in return, we'll deal with it."

But Kate knew exactly what it meant. She just needed to work out what to do next.

CHAPTER THIRTY-EIGHT

Having discharged herself from the hospital by mid-afternoon, Kate settled Aaron back home and cooked a meal of canned hearty vegetable soup. She added slices of fresh, crusty bread, the loaf brought over by concerned neighbor Susan in more sedate skin-tight running gear than usual, as a kind gesture to welcome her back. Kate then secured the babysitting services of Jennifer for the post-dinner-through-bedtime shift, and traveled to the sanctuary that had served her well to date.

When Kate had originally stood at the lectern in the community center, her first meeting weeks after Craig's funeral, the space yawned before her like a cavern, full of hostile faces staring at her, waiting for her to mess up her words, stumble over them, and she'd have to run, weeping at her failure. After she fended off the grief and summoned the courage to speak, it had not been that way. Everyone was welcoming, gentle in their encouragement. And, although the stage-managed scene continued to fray her nerves each time she addressed the room, there was something about those fraught moments in the buildup that appealed to her. It was not until today that she pinpointed the reason.

Today, she knew what she had to say.

"I used to be scared, showing up here and talking. But I kept coming back. I don't know if that's something the reverend planned or if he likes people up high, speaking to fellow gamblers like they're a flock or something. It's the rush. The charge. The twitching of muscles, of wishing I hadn't eaten before showing up. It's the same as when I would place a bet using unearned credit. A thousand bucks on a sure thing."

The memory of that sensation tugged at the corners of her mouth, but shame wilted the smile.

"Only, if I'm honest with myself, and we try to be honest here, my anxiety urged me the other way. Suggested there was no gamble to be made. No *sure things*. Because if the sure thing was real, gambling wouldn't be the ultimate rush. Risking your livelihood. Your well-being. Your marriage."

She wasn't certain if she should continue on this tack, but she'd rehearsed it on the way here. Needed to unburden herself.

"Because that was what I risked that final time. Not money. We weren't super-rich, but even a middling lawyer who spends half his sixty-hour week on community services earns a decent income. Yet, whatever I spent, we couldn't have repaid, even in installments. Unless he quit his philanthropy and concentrated on money, money, money. And I had nothing to offer, of course, not in the current economy. So, I staked my marriage. And I lost."

Kate had transferred her hands to the sides of the lectern without realizing.

"It's a source of pain for so many, and with good reason. It's a dreadful thing to be thrilled by. The lure of riches.

Because the key is control, isn't it? To only take the parts you need. Small increments. Soon, you're there. Where you demand to be. That one last big score, and you don't need the gambling anymore. Until you find something else you value more than winning. But by then, you've lost the stake that matters most, and you finally—*for real,* this time—wake up and vow to never, ever place another bet. You look back at the wreckage you've caused and see it's too late."

Slow footsteps echoed. A solid clomp… clomp… clomp. The sole audience member stepped out of the shadows where he'd been listening, where he said he was most comfortable. As she progressed through her speech, her unburdening, he made himself seen in the circle of light cast by the scant fluorescent tube overhead. Hands clasped behind him. Heavy, expensive shoes. Pristine pinstripe suit. Silver fox hair.

"Is this a confession, Kate?" Jonathan asked. "Because if you're confessing to a crime, something not related to the case I've been hired for, attorney-client privilege won't apply."

That wasn't strictly true. "I think perhaps you forget, Jonathan, that I didn't simply turn up at law school, find it difficult, then quit after a few months. I completed two years of study before Aaron came along. And maybe it *was* hard. Maybe you're right, in a sense. Yes, I did jump at the chance of having a baby and taking a break and not risking failure. Allowing Craig to furnish me with a house and a life. But the fact is, I loved that life. We decided, together, that I'd postpone my studies, probably have more kids later, because it worked. It worked for us. It was what we wanted."

"Until you flushed it away with your selfish impulses."

"With my addiction, yes. Craig didn't want to risk another child until I controlled that side of me. I hadn't even realized it was an illness when I was earning money in Reno. It was a job. And my time at Cornell, living fast with Craig, that was a distraction from it all. Our trips to casinos on vacations and long weekends kept me in check. It was only when Aaron started school and I was idle at home that it rose inside me again. It snowballed. I didn't notice until it was too late."

"Until you gambled your marriage."

Kate stood exposed up there, as if aware of a sniper in the rafters. She'd thought the elevated station might give her the courage to push on, but she was faltering.

Jonathan folded his arms. "What *is* this about, Kate? I did what you asked. Your home is released back to you from the CSIs. Jennifer is straightening it up." It was a barb, a dig at her again, since she'd already tidied the mess the police had left, although it wasn't much to begin with. "I'm glad that smell's gone, by the way. Shame about the gasoline lingering."

"Did you sort Sal out like I asked?"

"Salvator Cantero? The guy who attacked you? Yeah, we assigned a lawyer to him. He can afford it. I mean, what is *this*? Here? Is this why you needed Jennifer to watch Aaron? To show me you're putting in the effort to be a decent mom?"

Kate set aside the passive-aggressive comments and returned to her mental script. "All this time, I thought you were better than me. Better than Craig. One minute I'm slogging my guts out at night school to live up to him and prove I'm the equal of you and Jennifer. Then Craig wants to divorce me all because I tried to play catch up. Sneak a few thousand dollars onto a credit card, and... Well, you know how that all turned out. Craig... if he hadn't died, we'd have lost everything. Because I had to push it. Push it beyond what we could afford to repay. Otherwise... it wasn't gambling."

"Are you here to confess something more than weakness? Because I can fire you as a client. In fact, I'm doing that right now…" He took out his phone, fumbled it, blinked fast as he pulled up the messaging app. His fingers stuttered on the screen, hesitant. Then they went to work.

"What are you doing?"

"Texting my partners to make it official. You're no longer my client, Kate. Too many lies. And now a conflict of interest."

"You think this counts?"

"It's family business. Brings us into conflict. Opposing sides, so to speak." He completed his message and tapped the send icon harder than the other words. "Your two years at law school taught you about confidentiality. To be clear: Anything you tell me from here is not privileged."

Kate leaned toward him, resting her upper body on the lectern. "What do you think I'm here to tell you?"

Jonathan put his phone away, although it was clear he'd activated another app, a voice recorder. It didn't matter since she'd already set up her own means of recording the session.

He clasped his hands behind him and pulled his shoulders back, chest full. "Did you kill Craig?"

Kate almost smirked, but the rawness of losing her husband resurfaced even now, over a year later. "You know I didn't kill him, Jonathan. Because *you* did."

Yes, or no, Aaron… Did Daddy kill himself or was it an accident?

No…

"The buddy," Kate elaborated. "That's what Aaron calls it. A source of knowledge from… Well, there's no way to tell what it is exactly without paying a price. But I thought one question was worth it. We asked if Craig killed himself or if it was accidental. The answer was, 'No.' Aaron didn't understand. A straight-up *no*. But I got it. *No* to both means it was not an accident where Craig got sloppy. And it wasn't suicide after the absence of hope consumed him. Which meant his death was intentional."

Kate lowered her voice, deepened it, her eyes narrowing at the man before her.

"Craig was murdered."

Jonathan maintained his shoulders-back, chest-puffed-up pose, adding a frown. "What the *hell* are you talking about, Kate? Are you okay, because if you're having some sort of an episode—"

"Add to that the timing of Aaron doing well at school," Kate pressed, "right after you threw him that party... a special gift... And none of the other kids who attended had shown behavioral issues. I checked. It came from you, Jonathan. You passed on the infection to him. He wanted help, and you didn't need the gift anymore. It transferred from you to him."

Jonathan disengaged his hands and spread them in front of him, his mouth working like a guppy before he managed, "Kate, I have no clue what you mean. Who's Buddy? What did I give Aaron? Is he sick?"

"That's why you won so many cases. Why you had that hot streak and pulled the massive corporate win out of your ass, the one that sealed your promotion to partner. You had a friend. All along. Giving you brief hints, tips, nothing so big that you couldn't cover up the favors you had to do. Adults can work it out more easily than kids. More faculties, more experience with life. You take only what you need and then pay the fee. Small ones. Because in legal arguments, that's all you need."

"This is bullshit, Kate. You're hallucinating. Too many opioids—that's what you're on for your leg, isn't it? You OD-ing here?"

"That last case," Kate said, undeterred, the pieces slotting together like the closing stages of a jigsaw. "You were losing that case until you uncovered the bribe made by the plain-tiff's team to a key witness. That collapsed everything and you walked out stinking of rose petals. So much that they couldn't ignore your successes."

Jonathan was laughing now. Short, forced bursts. He turned a half-circle and back again. "Are you accusing me of something? Something unethical? Or illegal? Because it sounds like you're ranting about... What? A friend slipping me intel illegally?"

"But something as big as making partner must have come with an enormous price," Kate said. "What was it, I wonder? It compelled me to kill a man for a hundred grand. When I refused, it forced despair on the guy, made him dive out a window in front of me. Then, just twenty-some thousand meant I had to commit arson. When I resisted that, too, my son nearly died. What's the cost of a promotion to partner? Of a—what? Ten-million-dollar pension?"

Jonathan had stopped the pretense of laughter and hadn't blinked in a while.

She said, "Was the price killing your own brother, perhaps? Then you struggle with the guilt. Don't use it again, refuse its gifts for a year and a half. Then, maybe uninten-tionally, you pass on the presence to your nephew who's struggling at school?"

"You're crazy," Jonathan said. "A total and utter loon. And I don't mean that flippantly." Jonathan took out his phone and showed her the screen where—yep—he'd been recording their conversation. He thumbed the app off. "We haven't always seen eye-to-eye. But you're still family. I'll get you help."

He scrolled through his contacts and moved the phone to his ear.

Kate snatched up her crutches and stilted her way down the single stair to the floor, and hobbled toward Jonathan.

She hadn't thought this through, except to hide her phone, propped by the foot of the lectern, and to stream and record their exchange. He hadn't confessed, though. For the benefit of his own device, she suspected. But now it was off, she hoped to push him over that precipice, to threaten her, to imply it was him, Craig's murder having been confirmed.

"Think of Aaron," she said.

"I *am* thinking of Aaron." Jonathan retreated from her, the person he was trying to call not answering. He hung up.

She continued after him, worried they were moving out of range of her phone, although they'd still be on camera if he attacked her. "Did you think of him when you stripped him of his father? Your brother. For a bag of gold?"

Jonathan threw up his arms, rounded on her, his face beetroot red. "Please, Kate. Stop this! It's getting embarrassing. You're fucking cuckoo. I don't plant some spy in my opponents' camps and sift through confidential information. I do my *job*. Me and my team. We uncovered the paper trail through hard fucking work. Something you've never grasped."

"Don't lie!"

Both were shouting, plenty audible to reach her phone.

She said, "You didn't have a spy. You had something in your corner that no one can fully understand. Sal called it a genie. Like some trickster that tempts people with what they desire most in the moment, then forces them to do whatever it finds amusing. Frankly, I think we should just call it a *demon*."

It was the first time she'd used the word out loud. She'd preferred *infection*, *infestation*, as if it were a disease compelling the victim to seek out highs, to demand lows as compensation. But it *was* a conscious entity, something aware of what it was doing, feeding off the misery and pain inflicted by its return favors.

"You had a monster on your team," Kate continued when Jonathan didn't reply. "You used its predictions to advance your career, small enough increments to hide the price tag it demanded. But when the last one—directing you to that bribe—landed you the partner position you'd been chasing, it claimed the ultimate sacrifice. Craig."

Jonathan swallowed, his face having paled from bright red to a sickly gray.

"What did you do, Jonathan? He called you and Jennifer to say he'd left me. A chance to get him alone. How did you do it? Shake his hand with yours coated in shellfish remnants?"

"Kate..." Jonathan sounded choked, something stuck in his throat, like it was swelling, the way Craig's must have bulged, closing his airway after ingesting traces of his most severe allergen.

"Just tell me the truth!" Kate yelled.

"*I* didn't uncover that bribe," Jonathan said. "And it certainly wasn't some... demon. No ghosts, no goblins, no leprechauns. It was *Jennifer* who spotted it. *She* tracked it down."

Kate's entire body turned to ice. She took a crutch-assisted step forward. "Wait, what?"

Jonathan kept his distance, backing away the same number of steps Kate advanced. "There's no secret ceremony. No psychic tricks like that dream you lied about. Just hard work. We put in the hours. And as with many of my break-throughs, Jennifer pointed me in the right direction."

Jennifer...

Did you know, I was like his paralegal when he worked from home?

He said, "She uncovered the bribe. She was my rock. All along."

"Oh, God." Kate diverted from Craig, clumping as fast as

she could on the crutches, pleading with some higher power that she wasn't too late. "I got it so wrong."

"Where are you going?"

"Home," she said, desperation grabbing her chest and dragging her along. "Aaron lied to me."

CHAPTER THIRTY-NINE

Kate could barely think as she hurtled home. She observed no speed limits, her good foot only easing off the accelerator long enough for her to check junctions, while her injured leg burst with occasional pain at the bumps and hard corners.

The painkillers—opioids—were secured in her medicine cabinet. She hadn't dared risk dulling her senses until Jonathan was safely under lock and key, which meant the pain had resumed a couple of hours ago. Limited pain due to the tight strapping, but it flared every few seconds.

Despite the speeds, the skidding, the flashing by of lights, Kate must have been in a daze, as she remembered little of the journey when she pulled into her drive.

She got out, struggled with her crutches up to her front door, and pushed into her house, calling, "Jennifer? Aaron?"

"In here," Jennifer replied from the living room.

Trying to calm her breathing, to push the panic away, Kate headed for the woman's voice. Lungs working overtime, she nudged the door open and prepared herself for whatever might confront her—physical violence, the body of her son, a snarling, slobbering demon dog. Sweat coated her from head to toe.

She lumbered inside the room.

Jennifer and Aaron sat side-by-side. Aaron leaned on her, his hand down the side of a sofa cushion, Jennifer holding an open novel, only a dozen or so pages read.

"Hi, Mom," Aaron said.

Jennifer gave her a simpering smile. "Hope you don't mind. I know it's past his bedtime, but…" She showed Kate the book's cover: Artemis Fowl. "It's one of those we got him for his birthday. He said you don't read with him very often, so I thought it'd be nice."

Kate's mouth was dry, and not because of yet another passive-aggressive judgement on her momming abilities. She worked her tongue to produce a trickle of saliva. "Are you okay?"

"I'm fine, Mom," Aaron said. "The book is way different to the movie. It starts in Vietnam and Artemis is a total badass— Sorry, I mean, he's cool."

"I was talking to Jennifer," Kate said. "Jennifer, are *you* okay?"

Jennifer looked baffled. "I'm fine. Of course, I'm fine. Why wouldn't I be?"

Kate's palms sweated on the crutch handles, the sleeves over them supposedly preventing slippage in these situations. "Aaron, please take your hand out from there."

All three cast their gaze to the sofa cushion in which Aaron had wedged his hand. He did as requested, sitting upright with one leg folded under him.

He waved at her. "Like this?"

Kate said, "Lift the cushion."

Aaron paled, shook his head. "It's okay, Mom. I'll go to bed."

"Move. The. Cushion."

"Please don't, Mommy."

Jennifer watched the exchange like a tennis match. "What's going on here?"

"Aaron, step away, please." Kate pointed one crutch at him. "You don't have to do this."

Jennifer's brow furrowed, unable to disguise her puzzlement at Kate's actions. "What is this?"

"Pleeeeeaaase…" Aaron's face looked like it might cave in on itself. "I was going to. But I couldn't."

Confused, growing impatient, Jennifer put down the book and shuffled aside. She shifted the cushion and stared at what tipped over, having been wedged between the two pads.

Before Kate could react, before Jennifer asked the obvious question about what was going on, Aaron lunged and snatched up the knife.

It was from Kate's ultra-sharp set, the ceramic blades that looked so much like toys. The one in Aaron's possession, held two-handed, was the twelve-inch purple blade, pointed at his aunt.

"Kate?" Jennifer said. "Is this more of those problems we talked about?"

"You lied," Kate told her son, ignoring Jennifer for the moment. "When you said you didn't listen to the buddy. When you said all you asked was the yes or no question."

Aaron was crying, trembling, although the knife was steadier than his legs.

"You knew the price as soon as you heard the answer," Kate said. "The buddy knew you wouldn't kill anyone close. Knew I'd help you resist anything like that and fight the consequences. But the person who murdered your dad?"

Jennifer touched her throat, shocked.

Kate let the silence hang, focused on Jennifer, ready to

throw herself forward if Aaron attempted to use the knife on her.

Within seconds, Jennifer was shivering with a different kind of fear than Aaron's. Her lips parted, but she didn't speak.

"Don't try to deny it," Kate said. "The creature Aaron is carrying around doesn't manufacture monsters. It reveals the true monster inside a person. Strips away their restraint, and points them at the most severe subject it can get away with. It's like a challenge. It's a bored thing. A demon, a ghost, a force of nature we can't possibly comprehend. It knows the future, so nothing surprises it. Imagine how tedious life would be if you knew every little step in advance. So, I think it changes things that it can't predict. Gives the host choices it can't see. Because knowing the future changes the future. Interfering with things changes the future. It's the only time it can't know. That's why it tries so hard, to make us do things we know are wrong. It doesn't know for certain if we will or not. Right now, it's laughing its ass off inside Aaron, or wherever it physically waits, watching and waiting to see if he does it."

In the smallest fieldmouse voice Kate had ever heard her use, Jennifer asked, "Does what?"

"Kill you." Kate sidestepped, using her good leg to be sure she didn't fall. Her thigh burned. "And I expect it specified a knife, not poison."

Aaron's nod was as small as Jennifer's voice.

Kate said, "The manifestation of inner evil is only visible to the focus of the creature's amusement. Seeing the target crawling with infection, making us feel like what we're doing is justified."

Aaron made a strangled squeak in his throat, scared to speak. "I can't see anything wrong with Jennifer."

"You don't need to." Kate was closer to Aaron than Jennifer, listening to the sounds of the house. "She killed your dad. That's enough."

The fish tank filter burbled closest to them, the washing machine muffled in the utility and, possibly, a person's soft footfalls. Someone else was present. Jonathan had gotten in his car as Kate departed the community center. She assumed he'd come here too and was listening from the hall. She hoped he was.

"Jennifer was bad to the bone all along," Kate said. "She had no intention of doing anything other than stripping me of all her brother-in-law gave us. The house, a child that was one thing she couldn't achieve. But when they made Jonathan's position as partner official, and she no longer needed the buddy, you wished for the sort of help it offered. It passed from her to you."

"If I kill her," Aaron said, "we'll be free."

Jennifer shrank back into herself, imploring Kate in silence. No denials. Nothing like the protestations her husband spouted.

"No," Kate said. "We won't be free. We'll be trapped. Like Aunt Jennifer was. Dropping hints to her spouse about his cases. Spotting things in his paperwork. An unofficial secretary for years, she could slip something in there. Evidence of the bribe in that big case, of facts misaligned, which would send Jonathan's investigator or Jonathan himself, the right way."

Jennifer's breath hitched once, twice, like the start of a panic attack. "I'm so sorry. Whatever you think of the things I was forced—*forced*—to do, I never meant it to go to Aaron. I'd never do that."

"No, it was just the right moment. Your satisfaction with the outcome, along with Aaron's pleading for help. Those two things, you no longer needing it, him needing it, made it cross over."

"So…" Jennifer rubbed the back of her neck, stuttered a few times. "It was a creature?"

"An entity. Demon. Spirit. Ju-ju from beyond. We can't say precisely, but— What? You thought it was all you?"

Her glazed look conveyed concentration, focus on memories, working out if Kate was right. "I thought I had a magical power. That I had to even out the good with some bad—"

"That you were special?"

Jennifer snapped back to her usual bearing. "Well, yes. I'm sorry if that sounds conceited, but yes. Jonathan and I, we do far more good than bad. But now you're saying it's a… thing. A creature that passes between people?"

"It seems that way. And it won't leave you alone. It'll keep on coming, offering snippets to help along the way."

"It tricked me." Jennifer snorted in derision, squinting as if about to demand to speak with the manager. "Fine, if it helps, I'll take the monster back."

Aaron scuttled a couple of steps toward her. "No! It made you kill my dad!"

Jennifer again seemed more offended than cowed, scared now she'd been caught rather than guilty for her actions. If Aaron picked up on it, there'd be no stopping him, not with the buddy's finger on the kid's emotional scales. But Kate could not bear the prospect of him living with murder. She was close enough to knock the knife from Aaron's hand with one crutch if she had to. She leaned her weight on her good leg in preparation, hoping she wouldn't need to hurt him.

"If you just let me alone," Jennifer added, the silence seeming to unnerve her, breaths so quick she was almost hiccupping, "I promise I won't use it. I'll confess what I did to Craig. I'll go to jail." She nodded erratically, eyes manic, flashing to the knife with every other word. "Everything will go back to how it was. It'll be okay."

"How did you do it?" Kate asked. "How did you murder my husband?"

Jennifer shut her eyes, geeing herself up. "Prawn tacos." Again, her breath hitched, a hiccup of guilt. No, not guilt. Regret at being caught out. "When Jonathan got that call, he ran out to the office right away. Jumped at the chance to sort out the paperwork, even though he wasn't officially assigned. So I went out. I ate some prawns, something spicy to hide the smell."

"Then headed to my husband's motel?"

Jennifer nodded, that aura of shame radiating. "In a baseball cap and a hoodie, like some street urchin. I drank a beer too, but made sure the prawns went on my lips. When Craig opened the door to me, I pretended to be drunk, and kissed him."

Kate couldn't stop the images from cascading through her: Craig, opening the door; confused at the person before him; Jennifer, luring Craig into a false sense of security, appealing to his caring nature, before slobbering poison on him.

"A seduction routine?"

"For what it's worth, he rejected me." Jennifer switched to that angelic simper again. As if she'd made everything right with her words. "I ran away, embarrassed. But the damage was done."

Kate could not be sure if Jonathan was recording this. It wasn't a slam dunk that he'd turn on his wife, although given the severity with which Craig's death hit him, she would put odds on him turning her over in a heartbeat.

"Mom?" Aaron said.

"Yes, baby?" Kate said.

"I saw Becky's face go weird before I hurt her."

"Okay."

"Aunt Jennifer doesn't look weird. I don't think she's who I'm supposed to hurt. I... I got told it was her, and I just wanted to."

And, Kate thought but didn't say, Jennifer was reasoning with them. Ollie had explained himself too, and he displayed no bugs under his skin, either.

No physical changes.

"Meaning she isn't the monster," Kate said. "She isn't the buddy's target."

Meaning...

Someone had snuck in. Someone Kate assumed was an ally.

"Jonathan?" Jennifer said. "He knows I'm here."

Kate turned from Aaron, staggered on both legs and crutches for the living room door, praying she'd get there in time. Kate wouldn't see the skin ripple, and she didn't need to. This wasn't how the curse worked.

The door flew open, slamming into Kate and knocking her on her butt. Agony thundered through her thigh, and the crutches tumbled away.

"Is that you?" Kate said, her uninjured leg propelling her backward.

First, a gun rounded the frame, followed by Special Agent Ruiz. "Nobody move. Kate, are you both okay?"

Better than Jonathan.

"You got all that?" Kate asked her.

"Yes. I got everything."

"Mom..." Aaron said.

"It's okay, baby, she's with me."

* * *

But *was* Ruiz with Kate? She still hadn't decided. Even as she stalked into the living room, gun pointed at the floor, matters still weren't clear.

For the longest time, Andrea Ruiz had yearned to communicate with her sister. Had attempted the stupid things like ouija boards and the scams like psychics and spiritualists, which she expected going in would yield nothing, and she was not wrong; all actions a kick-ass FBI agent should shun. Perhaps if she hadn't bottled everything up in favor of nailing the gang to the wall, she'd have reacted in a healthier way, found the closure she needed. In the end, snapping the way she had, the dominos had toppled. Losing her position, and the crushing sense of failure that drilled inside her, did nothing except assault her mental health further.

With Kate, she hadn't wanted to believe it, but there were too many coincidences. Kate herself had been on the verge of admitting it several times. She'd only held back in order to extort Ruiz some more, to push her away. The woman demanded her ill-gotten money, her killer of a neighbor set free, and—for some reason—her brother-in-law and lawyer, Jonathan Mallory, arrested for murdering her husband.

She'd live-streamed what she promised would be a confession. When that turned out to be a damp squib, Kate set about Jennifer Mallory, running around White Plains like a decapitated chicken searching for its missing head.

Before departing the hospital, Kate had outlined her plan. That would be her final request, then she'd spill all. Ruiz had refused until Kate gave her something. Any morsel that could help. Even a hint of what she was going to reveal, what she knew about a world beyond ours, somewhere the dead might live on.

"All I can say," Kate had relented, "is that we tap into knowledge we shouldn't be able to see. It's almost impossible to resist. I'll lay it all out, blow by blow. But first, you have to do this. With me."

Ruiz had not accepted out loud what Kate said, partly because she didn't want to be heard on her makeshift wire colluding in the fantasies of a disturbed woman—which was how the FBI brass would interpret it. In fact, she told Kate it was nonsense, again primarily for the recording but also to get Kate talking.

Instead, she'd promised Ruiz would see. She'd understand once they set up the stings. Off-mike, Ruiz had stated they should go to the police, a murder like Craig's falling outside her scope, yet there were exigent circumstances here. Kate was her witness, her informant, and trusted no one else. If they stuck to that, they could prevent a judge barring any recording from evidence.

Kate said nothing more about the situation. Ruiz had guessed much of it, anyway, and as she listened to Kate conversing with Jonathan in the community center, she'd cemented the notion in her mind. Those instances she'd found, they all matched. It all made sense.

An entity like Kate described filled in the gaps in all those cases.

A spirit. A genie. A demon.

When Kate ran out of the hall, having concluded what Ruiz caught onto seconds before her, Ruiz had to get to Kate's house. She'd been parked a block from the community center, so kept Kate in sight as she sped dangerously fast, arriving at her street too late to stop her blundering inside.

Ruiz should have called it in as a suspected home invasion, but she'd followed her instinct and rushed into the property with as much stealth as she could muster. She listened in the hall, taking in all she could, hoping her recording app would be sufficient to both pick up the confession and submit as evidence. A personal phone might not wash with a judge if all Ruiz's breaches of protocol came to light.

Ruiz was still a witness, though. An FBI special agent, albeit one with a career break due to a psychiatric order. It should have been irrelevant, but a defense lawyer might bring it up. Even if the judge struck it from testimony, it'd be there, hanging in the jurors' minds.

There was no doubt here. Jennifer Mallory, in her confession, corroborated Kate's story. The demon, the genie, the spirit—it was a real thing. Or perceived as real by more than one party, anyway. In that hallway, the words beat at Ruiz's brain, swelling inside her skull.

Kate had held it back, this thing, this power. Jennifer, too. She'd used it and she'd benefited, and in contrast to Kate, she'd carried out its orders without hesitation. Even her husband's brother was expendable.

What if it got into the head of someone truly dangerous? A serial killer? A terrorist?

That kind of unlimited insight could yield a way into the White House, the plans for a nuclear weapon, how to obtain the materials required. It could show the right or wrong person the correct place to set a conventional bomb where it would go undetected until the President happened nearby.

The threat was so severe, Ruiz could not allow it to go unchecked. She had to act. Even if she lost her answers, never learned if Kate knew more than she'd said. It was—to coin a political cliché—a national security nightmare. And it had been living within these borders since at least the 1980s.

Cutting it off here was the best thing. It might even drive Ruiz back to the position she'd earned. A place in the field, chasing down more terrorists than financial bully boys.

So, there, in Kate's living room, holding them all under the barrel of her gun, Andrea Ruiz was ready to do her duty. Whatever the price.

* * *

As promised, Kate had given Ruiz everything. Between the streamed conversation with Jonathan and this stand-off, all Kate had experienced was on the table. Yet, back at the hospital, when they set up the initial sting, Ruiz had—predictably—expressed the notion she did not believe Kate. But it wasn't a scoffing dismissal. She'd even perked up when Kate said she could prove it, and prove her brother-in-law killed her husband. Kate believed her own lawyer was a murderer. It wasn't official FBI business, certainly no warrant involved, but a civilian voluntarily calling her?

Ruiz said she'd make it work. Now she was here, having listened to Jennifer's confession and, with luck, recorded that too.

Ruiz swept in, the professional approach of someone who'd practiced this a hundred times. It didn't seem likely she drew her gun often, but Kate understood FBI training was intense, muscle memory sowed into agents from the start. Ruiz had cocked the weapon, and kept Jennifer covered with her finger outside the trigger guard, gliding sideways toward Aaron, as Kate assured the boy, "It's okay. She's with me. We can trust her."

Ruiz held out a hand. "I'll take the knife, Aaron."

"You have to accept responsibility," Aaron said.

Kate bit back the pain, levering her working leg under her and pushing up. Her back slid up the wall. "She will, baby. She'll go to prison for what she did—"

"Not her, Mom. You."

"Me? Take responsibility for—"

"Her skin is crawling, Mom," Aaron said.

An ear-splitting BAM filled the room as Ruiz discharged her gun. Jennifer's throat burst at the front and her right side. She flopped on the couch, blood geysering several feet;

the bullet must have destroyed the carotid artery on its way out.

Ruiz reshaped her stance and angled the gun on Aaron, who still held the knife. Her speech slurred as she spoke. "She was a threat to national security. An attack is imminent. Tell me what I need to know, or I will not hesitate in taking you both out."

CHAPTER FORTY

"You have to take the blame, Mom," Aaron said, the knife relinquished to Ruiz, then subsequently placed on the coffee table. "For shooting Jennifer. Confess to killing Dad. Blackmailing Endo into killing himself. Threatening Ollie Swag before killing him. All of it. You tell the cops it was you, and the killing ends here."

"It won't kill you," Kate said.

Ruiz's gun switched to Kate.

Aaron said, "It doesn't feel physical pain." These weren't the words of a ten-year-old. They were being fed to him, downloaded into his brain to recite to the grownups. "It can hurt me, take an arm or a leg, or make my back stop working. And Agent Ruiz will kill you if you don't confess everything, and she'll plant the evidence, anyway."

Ruiz had been lucid when speaking about national security. That must have been how the buddy touched her, how it made her shoot Jennifer—the certainty that killing her protected Ruiz and the country as a whole. Took advantage of the woman's sense of duty. It was as if she'd been paused, a similar expression to the one Sal had worn when he was in that coma-like netherworld. The gun, aimed in Kate's general direction, faltered, the barrel dipping.

"Give me the buddy," Kate said.

"No, Mom, I can't. You... you'll get sick again."

Ruiz's body spasmed. One word, slathered in that oily undertone: "*Choose*."

"I'm ready to die, Aaron," Kate said. "I won't let it keep a hold over you."

"I won't let it hurt you either," Aaron insisted.

"If I die, the buddy dies. And it can't kill you unless I let it."

Aaron looked up at Ruiz, mouth agape, a million options racing across his face, not one of them palatable.

"I won't let it kill you," Kate said, "and it won't kill me if it's inside me."

Ruiz firmed her grip on the gun, lucid again, yet determined to end this threat to her nation. "I'll shoot you right now."

"Why not Aaron?" Kate asked, every ounce of her soul screaming at her not to say it. "Why can't you threaten him?"

Aaron, too, winced. Only a fraction of a second later, he calmed. He probably didn't know why, but he was no longer afraid.

"He can't be a threat to national security," Kate said. "He's just a little boy. Ruiz wouldn't harm a child, not after what she lost. And there's nothing you can hold over her to make her zone out long enough to take control. She's come to terms with her loss, even if she doesn't realize it yet. Sal hadn't. He was still making bargains to resurrect her. Ruiz just wants closure."

Ruiz's eyes hooded over again, and her voice, laced through with the buddy's, said, "Then die."

Ruiz shook off the drowsiness of the entity's influence and shored up her shooting stance.

Kate said, "Do it, Aaron. Trust me. I can handle it. Do it now. I'm not confessing. If you don't do it, I'm going to die, and I'm not coming back."

Aaron stomped his foot, as if a tantrum was brewing. "No. I won't do it, and you can't make me."

"Baby." Kate waited for his attention, and fixed on him. "I understand it now. I get what it's doing. And I can beat it. I swear to you, the biggest, most important promise I've ever made, I need you to send it to me." She barely needed to prompt him further, but added, "Trust me, baby. It's for the best."

It was like a gentle breeze. She hadn't picked up on it when the buddy first transferred into her, but it felt familiar all the same.

Ruiz froze.

Kate launched forward in two massive hops. Indestructible, she tackled Ruiz at the waist. The gun flew onto the sofa and the two women slammed to the floor, every movement shocked through with agony.

In a near echo of the confrontation with Ollie Swag, Kate yelled at Aaron to, "RUN!"

This time, he did so, casting a worried glance between Jennifer's corpse and his mother grappling with an FBI agent, before hurrying out.

Kate threw an elbow back at Ruiz. The agent grunted, but absorbed the blow and shoved Kate away. Ruiz slammed a heel into Kate's bandaged leg, and the worst pain since she pulled the fork out crippled her. An animalistic howl escaped, but she kept on fighting.

Still on the floor, Kate swung her good leg at Ruiz, but the agent parried it, landing a punch in Kate's gut. She doubled over on her side, breathless, and stars burst as the world fell sideways. Ruiz's follow-up to her face landed hard.

What chance did Kate have? A civilian against a trained FBI agent?

"Can't kill me," Kate said.

Inside her head came the reply, *No need to kill. Just hurt. Cripple. Teach a lesson.*

Ruiz flipped Kate over—again flaring the wounded thigh —and put a knee in her back, applying a choke hold banned by law enforcement across the majority of the country.

Aaron reappeared at the door. "Mommy?"

Kate couldn't speak, the constriction too much. She reached out to him as he inched inside the room.

"The neighbors…" Aaron said. "They're all outside. They're acting… weird."

Something approximating laughter resounded about her brain. *Window.*

"Window," Ruiz croaked.

Ruiz's body twisted Kate around, releasing a few pounds of pressure, enough for her to arch up and view the street through the large bay window.

Nosy parker Dorothy in a dressing gown and slippers; Susan, the fitness freak from the next house down; a man whose name Kate didn't know but thought he worked for the council; a muscular guy in workout gear, Bob-something, who lived next to Sal. All of them, shambling toward the house in the same lilting gait as Sal when he was under the influence.

Ruiz will not kill Aaron, the entity delivered to her, *but one of them will be weak enough to obey. When you black out, that is what will happen.*

The full pressure dropped back on Kate, her vision darkening at the edges. She found the strength to tip Ruiz over, both locked in an embrace on their sides, spooning in her final conscious throes.

Aaron's small, timid voice penetrated the funk. "Mom?"

Kate forced her eyes to focus on where it came from. And there, right before her, Aaron had lifted the knife from the coffee table. He was holding it out.

Ruiz clocked it too.

"Me," Kate choked out. "Kill... me."

Aaron shook his head.

"Trust... me."

Ruiz's grip tightened.

Aaron thrust the knife toward Kate's neck. A killing strike.

Ruiz spun them both away, and the blade missed. The movement loosened her grip and Kate jammed her wrist into the crook of Ruiz's elbow and pushed. She gasped for air, but the spell wasn't broken yet. They struggled.

Aaron checked the street. "They're coming!"

"The gun, baby." Kate was weakening. The gamble of making Aaron try to kill her had worked, granted her a reprieve, but this phase was the buddy's doing, its interference with the future. It couldn't foresee the outcome. In fact, Kate might have had a better idea of how this would pan out: she could not hold out against the superior fighter for long. "Get... the gun."

Aaron scanned the room, searching, searching, finding Ruiz's service weapon.

He cannot fire a gun. He's too small. He cannot help you.

He went for it, Ruiz unable to break away from Kate. His little hands lifted the gun from the couch, straining, even compact pistols far heavier than they looked on TV. And although a snub-nose model, it wasn't some compact purse gun. It was a model Kate was familiar with, academically—a SIG Sauer P238. Although she hadn't fired a gun in over a decade, she knew how to work it.

Aaron's wide-eyed terror took on an extra dimension as footfalls sounded from the hall.

"Give it to me," Kate said, straining hard against Ruiz.

She still had one arm pinned beneath her, the other holding off Ruiz's choking arm.

Aaron didn't know what to do.

Kill an FBI agent, and you will be jailed.

Yes, Kate thought in response, *but there's another way.*

She pulled her wrist away from the arm Ruiz was pressing toward her, resuming the choke. It was the only way to reach out for the gun.

Although Ruiz yanked her back, Kate dug her heels in. She felt the thigh wound tear as she resisted, but it was worth it.

Aaron put the gun in her hand.

"Eat this, you asshole." Kate shoved the barrel in her mouth and pulled the trigger.

Aaron screamed, "MOM!"

Ruiz released Kate.

The whole house was stuck in a time warp, Aaron taking half a step forward to prevent his mom from killing herself, Ruiz blinking, watching her arms grow slack from holding onto Kate, as if waking from a troubling dream. Nosy Dorothy and Bodybuilder Bob shuffling into the room.

And Kate Mallory, lying on the floor with a gun in her mouth, having safetied he pistol before squeezing the trigger. For the first time in years, she was thankful to her parents for something: an education in firearms. Their greatest gift to her.

Most Sig Sauer guns had a double trigger firing mechanism, similar to a Glock, but the P238 was smaller, a concealed carry weapon chosen, presumably, because a financial crimes special agent was unlikely to need anything bigger. If anything at all. It also came with an external safety instead of a de-cocking lever, which meant when the hammer fell, it did not blow the top of Kate's head off.

She just didn't decide to flick it on and, therefore, stay alive until the last second.

That she meant it, that she would die for her boy's freedom, she figured it couldn't be foreseen. No way for the buddy to anticipate if she'd been willing to die all along.

"Knowledge of the future alters the future," Kate said, aiming what was fast becoming a mantra at the thing that was too scared to die. "You can only see it if folk aren't aware of you seeing it, and if you aren't guiding things."

No reply.

"What the hell did I *do*?" Ruiz said, pushing herself away from Kate.

"It's releasing you," Kate said.

Dorothy, too, seemed to be waking up, scrutinizing her surroundings. "Where am I?"

"Umm…" Bodybuilder Bob came around.

"Could you do me a favor?" Kate asked pleasantly, holding the gun toward the couch. "Take Dorothy home? She came wandering. I think you spotted her and brought Susan along to help."

Bob considered that for a moment, closed his eyes for longer than a blink, and when he reopened them, he must have played out the scenario. Dorothy conceded, too, holding the big man's arm as they withdrew from the room. It was possible the buddy was helping influence them, but Kate wasn't sure. It had gone silent on her.

"We have to get your leg looked at," Ruiz said, on her knees and checking Kate over.

Blood swamped the dressing.

"Forget it," Kate said.

"I heard it all." Ruiz attempted a kind, open expression aimed at Aaron, but the boy focused on his mom. "I get it now."

"Do you?" Kate pushed through the pain of her bleeding

leg into a sitting position. The stains showed through the bandages, warm blood trickling down her leg. She still held the gun and thumbed off the safety. It was ready to fire. "I don't think you can understand. Not really."

Aaron sleepwalked over, fully aware, and sat beside her. "Don't do it, Mommy. Please."

"Do what?" Ruiz asked.

"Shoot herself for real," Aaron replied.

"No, you've won. I mean, I went through it on the wrong end. I knew—I just knew—you guys were a threat..." Ruiz spotted Jennifer, lying dead in her pooling blood. "Even though you'd warned me what happens, I shot her, because if I didn't, she'd take us all out with a bomb. I don't know how I thought that, but... if it's what you say." She tore herself away from the corpse. "You won. You stopped it."

"For now," Kate said. "But the only way to kill it, to stop it spreading to someone else... is for me to die, too."

CHAPTER FORTY-ONE

Ruiz tensed. Every muscle, every organ, her vision blurred—both figuratively and literally. She could not let Kate do it. But nothing she'd said was untrue.

"Everything we've talked about absolves Sal of any wrongdoing," Kate said. "No matter how bizarre it sounds, you'll fight for him. Won't you?"

"I will," Ruiz said. "But you don't have to do this."

"How else does it end? And I've been through the death row scenario, the cancer patient, and plenty of others."

"Me. I'll take it." The offer gave Ruiz goosebumps. And something else. Something she couldn't pinpoint. "Let me."

"And end up stumped on a case one night, and the buddy offers the answer? But you can't act because then you'll owe a favor. If not, you'll have to live with knowing the answer to some case but being unable to solve it. Do you really think you'll be able to resist?"

"Or worse," Aaron said. "It sometimes tells you the answer anyway. If you use it, you have to do whatever it says."

Ruiz allowed the hypothetical scenario to grind away. She

375

didn't want to agree, but saw the logic. "Knowing the bad guy, and where to find him, what evidence I need…"

Kate gritted her teeth, obviously in pain from their fight. "If you got the chance to convict the men who ran Julietta off the road… could you say no?"

"What if I didn't resist it?" Ruiz asked. "What if I just stopped instead?"

Aaron cuddled into his mom and she put her free arm around him, tears brimming in her eyes.

"The buddy has to die," Kate said.

"What about Aaron?" Ruiz checked the window, half-expecting reinforcements she should have called for prior to storming in here. "I don't have a career after today. I shot an unarmed woman. My sister isn't saying hi anytime soon, and I—"

"No," Kate said.

"Why are you so desperate to die?" Ruiz demanded. "I'm a better candidate to take it with me. Murder-suicide is a scandalous legacy for me to leave, but at least—"

"I killed my husband." Kate's skin pulled tight around her eyes and mouth, her neck all but webbing with the strain of saying that. "Jennifer might have committed the crime, but I'm the one who drove him there. Made him leave. This… me, taking the buddy on… and dealing with it… I can't be responsible for someone else dying over my mistakes. This balances things out. I get to do this one, decent thing in my life. And… he's better without me. Without this thing inside."

This thing… Did she mean the monster or the addiction? Or both?

Aaron dragged himself from her, hit her in the arm. A little boy, distraught that his mom could contemplate leaving him over… what? Some guilt-ridden sense of justice?

He was as angry as he was scared. "Aunt Jennifer would

have found Dad anyway, Mom. If she had to kill him, she had to kill him. That night, or another." He squinted in frustration. "*It wasn't you.*"

Kate obviously wanted to hug him, to give in, to comfort her son. Confusion screwed up her eyes, unable to decide. Unable to leave her boy, yet unwilling to forgo the responsibility.

"Give it to me, Kate," Ruiz said softly. "It's the right thing to do. And I need it."

"This thing," Kate said, her expression falling back to that single-minded determination from moments ago, "this force, whatever it is, it isn't proof of anything."

It was Ruiz's turn for tears. Sudden, overwhelming, high-pitched and babbling. She'd identified that unknown something that piqued with the goosebumps.

Peace.

Ruiz said, "At least I know there's life beyond this world. If there's a human soul, and we're not just meat running around for the amusement of things like the evil bastard you're holding onto, then maybe—"

"Maybe, what? You get to end your suffering? What did you do, lie to your FBI shrink about your suicidal thoughts? Waiting for an opportunity to die?"

Was that the demon—the buddy—feeding her that revelation, or did she work it out? Because the answer was yes. She did lie. But there'd been no repeat of that urge. Until now. Until the prospect of dying for something more than ending her pain appeared.

"Like you have?" Ruiz shot back. "Lied to everyone? Yourself, your shrink, your kid? Just bottled up these feelings, until now you have a genuine excuse. Don't for a second think I don't see it, Kate."

"I wonder, did your colleagues know about that?" Kate

said, as if ignoring Ruiz. "Is that the real reason you ended up in a field office attached to the SEC?"

Ruiz stared back, no attempt to reply.

Kate said, "That's it, isn't it? They didn't trust you wouldn't be reckless. Put your safety at risk and go out on a high. A hero. And who knows, you might just get your biggest wish."

Ruiz held still, rivers trickling down both cheeks. "It should have been me, Kate. Unlike Craig, it should have been me who died. *You* dying doesn't balance anything. This... *this* is what sets the balance straight."

* * *

Kate brimmed with aches—not just the stabbing pain from her leg, but in her body, her throat, her gut. The buddy was delivering information. Truths.

She won't be reunited with anything. She will die. She will suffer.

And me?

No reply.

"I understand," Ruiz said. "I wish I didn't."

"There's no way I could live with myself if I did that," Kate said. "Condemning you to what might be a blank void. While me, I... I have done nothing but hurt people. I screwed over my husband, endangered Aaron, used Sal and Jonathan and plenty of others. I have to do this one good thing. Something unselfish that *helps* others instead of hurts them. Take Aaron. I trust Sal more than Jonathan."

Aaron was sobbing. His tears soaked her sleeve that supported his head. "Mommy..."

"I'm sorry, baby. We must be strong. We have to be—"

"NO!" He sat up sharply. Jumped to his feet. "I won't let you." He ducked and snatched for the gun.

Kate whipped it away from him.

In doing so, she swiped the weapon into Ruiz's orbit, and the agent moved for it. Kate shuffled back and pointed the gun. It seemed weird, even in that moment, to threaten a woman who wished to die.

Still, Ruiz raised her hands and retreated from Kate. "Okay, easy."

Sirens whined in the distance.

"We don't have long," Ruiz said. "Give me the buddy. I can beat it."

"I can't…"

"You're wrong, Mommy, you *are* strong enough." Aaron paced a half-circle around the two living women. He looked and sounded so grown up, so sincere. He squinted at Kate as if trying to explain an ill-thought-out idea, the narrative of a dream. Only, he'd obviously thought this through while he was lying beside her. "I thought you weren't strong enough for this, but you are."

Kate tried to move to him, to hold him, hug him, and her leg reminded her of its condition, a blast of fire coursing out of both wounds. She kept the gun close in one hand and held her thigh with the other.

Wet. Bleeding profusely.

"You don't need to give it away," Aaron said. "You can hold it off, Mom. You can beat it."

Kate fought through teeth pressed together so hard they felt ready to snap. She hissed with an intake of breath. "What if I can't?"

"Your sickness makes you do things that hurt people. But you don't want the buddy to get more powerful. That's already a good thing. And saying you might leave me, or die, or whatever, you don't want to do it anymore than I want it. Maybe it's easier, but I think if you wanted to do it, really, really wanted to, you'd have gone already. You're strong,

Mom. If you fight, and just tell it no, you'll win, I know you can. I wouldn't have sent it back to you if you didn't want to beat it." He sniffed, wiped tears with the heels of his hands. "Please don't leave me."

"I'm not strong enough."

"But you were, Mom. After Dad died, you took care of me. You stuck to your promise. You beat it back, like you beat back the buddy when it wanted you to kill that Endo man and burn the bad man's car. And it'll be there, all the time, to remind you—if you gamble or do anything with the buddy's favors, something worse will happen. Even worse than a divorce. Don't you *see*?"

One stage of recovery from addiction was surrendering to a higher power. For some people, that was God, or the deity of a person's chosen religion. For others, it was fate, and how the addict needed to control it, force it to become what they wanted by bending it to their will... by not giving in to the urges. The buddy, a constant reminder of her weakness, could be her higher power.

Aaron stood before her. "You don't have to die, Mommy. Not until you're an old lady."

Ruiz glanced to the window, the sirens louder. "If you're not passing the demon to me, at least give me the gun. They'll shoot you dead on sight if you don't surrender it."

All Kate's mistakes shuttled through her, all her weakness, all the times she caved to temptation, those dark moments where she calculated how many pills it would take or how to make swerving into a bridge look like an auto accident. Not just this week, from that basketball score to the multiplier on the dogs, but before then, before the buddy infested their lives. A huge ball of guilt and hurt and empathizing with how hard Craig had strived to cure her, how she'd failed him. Failed everyone who tried to help.

Aaron was right. She'd spent all her time trying to solve a

puzzle, to purge them of their adversary. What if the answer wasn't eliminating the problem, but accepting it?

She'd held her addiction in check for the longest time. Her need to protect her son, to ensure she never hurt him the way she hurt Craig, had gifted her the strength to overcome it. She didn't need the meetings, except around major sporting events that everyone was talking about. But even then it was a balm, something to soothe her, not a necessity. Since she buried her husband, she hadn't been remotely tempted.

Not until the sure thing.

Except now, the sure thing was more than a gamble, more than placing a risky bet. It was a sure thing that the buddy's help was a curse, a worse option than ignoring it, a cast iron certainty she'd hurt someone, should she succumb to its offers.

"Be my mom again," Aaron said. "Like you have since my buddy started causing trouble. You've done everything for me. Everything to protect me. And even people you don't know too well. How can you think you aren't strong enough?"

Kate lowered the gun and handed it back to Ruiz. The agent accepted it cautiously, a hand on Kate's shoulder.

"Are you sure about this?" Ruiz asked. "I'll do what I need to."

She'll burn…

"It's my burden now," Kate said. "I'll keep it under control. For Aaron. For me. And if it tries to punish me for it, it knows I'm willing to die to protect others."

"You'll be stronger than me." Ruiz holstered her gun and snapped the clasp over it. "I can still remember what it was like. So I'm going to jail for what I did."

Aaron was holding the knife again. By the handle.

"Aaron?" Kate said. "What are you doing with that?"

He didn't answer.

If she could stand, she'd have moved to him, checked his face for blemishes, for rippling skin, and prepared for him to use the blade on either her or Ruiz, or—the final option left a gaping black hole in her chest—on himself.

But he wasn't a zombie version of Aaron. He just looked frightened.

"Aunt Jennifer killed Dad," he said, placing the knife beside his aunt's bloody corpse. "Could we say she tried to kill us too?"

PART FIVE

11 MONTHS LATER

CHAPTER FORTY-TWO

Aaron blew out his candles and the gathering of kids and grownups cheered, Kate the loudest of all. She didn't expect her joy to feel so much like relief, and chalked it up to having got this far without another incident.

After opting to go play some more and save the cake for later, Aaron ran off with his three friends—all boys at this age—and took them to the bottom of their lawn where Sal had unveiled the new tree house that morning with a ribbon-cutting ceremony. They didn't have as far to run as they did in the old house, but it was a pleasant enough space. Easier to manage and only a few plots down from the house Kate and Craig had lived in for a decade. When it came up for sale so soon after the FBI dropped the charges against her, Kate couldn't resist—their former house was haunted by more than the lingering presence of the buddy. The new place took a little getting used to, but even downgrading to two bedrooms and an office, a smaller overall footprint, and a garden half the size, it was still much nicer than "making do."

Sal, Tammy, Bodybuilder Bob, and Susan from down the

road all watched on as Kate removed the candles and cut into the cake, slicing through the number 11 with ease. She handed out the slices to much thanks, and wrapped others for the boys to either munch on when they got done repelling zombies from their fort, or to take with them and top up their sugar high on their parents' time.

It was far from an extravagant party. Just enough for Aaron to enjoy, now the gossip and teasing had largely died at school, and kids were no longer afraid to be his friend. The three he played with today were his hardcore circle, a unit of like-minded children a touch younger than their ages. Tammy had said it was nice; they'd grow up together, mature together, and—with luck—remain friends for a long time.

Kate accepted the compliments on the cake, baked with her own two hands, and snuck away with a slice and a fork to the person who'd remained alone on the decking—a construction similar to her previous one. Like the rest of the property, it was just a bit smaller, but solid, and served their needs.

"Hi, Jonathan." She handed him the plate, a paper napkin underneath. "I'm glad you could come."

He gave a tight smile and took the plate, balancing the fork on the side, but didn't eat. "He looks happy."

"He's a resilient kid."

Jonathan stuck the fork in the cake but laid it on its side. He watched the small gathering. "How much does he remember?"

"I don't know. Bits. He knows there was something we can't talk about that made him do things. That forced his aunt to... Well, we both know what she did. A ghost, he calls it now. The therapy helps him stay straight at school. And at home. Thank you for that, by the way. I think she's got a better handle on PTSD than Dr. Patel."

Jonathan had recommended Dr. Sheila Pasternack, for both Aaron and Kate. With Kate's glowing recommendation, Sal had also opted to avail himself of her services. His business had bloomed since the previous year's violence; when the media hailed someone as a hero, it served as free publicity. That he was able to publicly declare forgiveness for Grant Richardson, and that he did not hold the agent responsible for the wounds that still hobbled him, drew political pressure for the Shooting Incident Review Group to demand only a light reprimand and a phase of retraining before resuming his duties. Sal still grew frustrated at his shoulder's limited movement and the need to take a sit-down rest every couple of hours, but he was convinced his physio regimen would see that off in time.

"How have you been?" Kate asked.

"Working. The other partners were very understanding. Most of them. A couple were a little put out that they'd promoted the husband of a—quote—*psychopath*—end quote." He shook it off. "She wasn't always like that."

"I know."

"She was always ambitious. Always supporting me. I had no idea what she was doing. I mean, so many times, I'd benefited from some piece of research she landed me with, I told her she was wasted. Wasted simply helping me at home, but she didn't want the responsibility of a permanent post. I guess I know why now."

"Too many return favors."

They hadn't spoken since the day after Jennifer died, other than a brief FaceTime call on Christmas Day. They'd exchanged text messages around other holidays, but the wound was too raw. Kate had reached out for today, as she knew Jonathan missed his nephew. A true emotion in what she'd often written off as a shell, as a man using Aaron to remain close to his late brother. Returning to them, in their new home, must have been difficult.

"I'm still not convinced," Jonathan said. "Even if she believed it and you believe it… doesn't make it real."

"It's okay." Kate made her attention linger on Jonathan, but someone else had arrived via the side gate. "All you have to worry about is staying in Aaron's life. He misses you too."

Jonathan frowned briefly, having not expressed such an emotion, but didn't correct her. It was clear to Kate that he'd been happy to watch the party, if not mingle with commoners, and that she'd done the right thing inviting him. And she didn't need a demon feeding her that information.

"I have to say hi to someone," she said. "But stick around after, okay? Aaron'll like that."

Kate descended from the deck and made for the grownups who'd shown for the event. Of their immediate neighbors, only Dorothy was absent, preferring not to attend a child's party full of strangers' screaming offspring. At some point that morning, though, she'd dropped off a card and a small present comprising Gummi Bears and sherbet, but hadn't hung around to be thanked.

"Hey, this is nice," Tammy said, collaring her as she made for another slice of cake. "I did the same thing for Chris's seventh. Gave him the choice: big party or a better present. He chose the present and six pals." She winked. "Worked like a charm."

"How's Hetherington's?" Kate asked. She'd kept in touch with Tammy via the cleaning team's WhatsApp group, which she'd never left despite not returning to work with Dev and the others, although it was mainly used for exchanging memes rather than talking shop.

"Same old." Tammy shrugged, popping her eyebrows toward Sal as he chatted with Susan and Bob. "How's it going there?"

Kate's cheeks warmed, and she caught Sal's eye, where the pair lingered a moment before Kate returned to Tammy. "Slowly. But we're giving it a chance. He's getting back to his old self, and I'm ready to think about dating again. It's... well, you know what it's like bringing a new man into your kids' lives."

"Yeah, but I don't over-analyze it like you."

She knows you're fucking him.

Kate didn't care if Tammy guessed that she and Sal had taken the next steps in their relationship. It wasn't a revelation, just not something she wanted to discuss at her son's birthday party. Over cocktails or a bottle of wine when they were alone, maybe. But not here. If anything, it was an open secret in the street already. All anyone had to do was watch how Susan no longer leaned into Sal, how Kate and Sal made those small, intimate gestures—the touches, the sly looks, the lingering glances that melted into grins that told the world this pair understood things no one else did. It was irrelevant what Tammy knew or didn't, thank you very much.

Tammy had spotted the newcomer who'd arrived while Kate was talking to Jonathan. "Who's that? I know her? I *feel like* I know her."

The woman had stuck to the edge, near the house. She was waiting to be admitted, to be acknowledged, plainly awkward at having intruded. In casual jeans and a plain top, she wasn't on duty. Her first informal interaction with Kate.

"That's Andrea Ruiz," Kate said.

"Right. FBI lady. Arrested you that time, yeah?"

"That's right, she did." Kate picked up a spare slice of cake. "I should say hi."

As she passed Sal, Kate brushed her free hand over his ass. He almost dropped his crumb-laden plate. Susan caught the public display of affection and giggled, almost as surprised as Sal. He blew Kate a kiss.

Kate delivered the slice to Andrea Ruiz, who shook her head and touched her stomach.

"It's a party," Kate said. "Calories don't count at a party."

"Is that a fact?" Ruiz said.

"I thought everyone knew that. Don't they teach you *anything* at FBI school?"

Ruiz accepted the cake and tucked in. Her "mmm," suggested she was glad Kate pressured her into it.

"Thanks for stopping by," Kate said. "I wasn't sure you'd come."

"There's not much in the way of conflict now." Ruiz surveyed the scene. "You're not even living in a crime scene."

Kate wasn't ready to joke about it yet, and it showed.

"Sorry," Ruiz said. "I mean, this place is nice."

"It was time. And it's done Aaron the world of good. Getting out of there. The nightmares stopped almost overnight."

Ruiz nodded, as if that was the most natural thing she'd heard. "How about you? You coping?"

"Some days, it's difficult. It tries to offer me scraps of information, but I'm handling it. So far so good."

"I'm still looking into it. In my spare time."

Kate had too, but Ruiz possessed far more resources. "Anything look promising?"

"Just history. Nothing we can use."

"Like what?"

"Like more details on the stuff we guessed already. How spirits like this have served as cautionary tales. In some Middle Eastern cultures, they call it a djinn. The stories of that demon eventually morphed into the genie, held in a lamp and, over hundreds of years, into that Disney character who sings and makes merry. It might also be a part of Norse legends, like Loki."

"Isn't that a superhero thing? Like Tony Stark and Thor?"

"They have their roots in gods and demi-gods. I mean Thor and Loki, not Iron Man. Loki was the trickster in the comics and films, and that's what he is in the myths. He'd promise one thing, deliver it, but there'd always be a twist, a price to pay."

Kate recalled that Aaron had explained the origins of some of his favorite superhero characters, but she had paid little attention—the frenzied babbling of a child relaying information he deemed of great importance while she'd prepared dinner one evening.

She said, "Yeah, I get that. Makes sense that people recycle old stories, old characters, and give them a modern spin. There's more contemporary fiction based around the things you've said. Like that story of a box with a big red button turning up in a suburban home—where you press it and you get rich, but someone dies in exchange."

Ruiz nodded along as if she'd come across that one too. "But no solutions. Everyone in those stories seems to end up worse off than before."

"Because they give in to selfish temptation," Kate said. "I haven't. Yet."

"What's the latest?"

Kate tried to laugh, but it came out strained. She checked that no one was listening, scanned the garden for the boys lost in their fantasy battle, an imaginary siege surrounding the tree house. "I woke up a couple of weeks ago to a list. In my head. Football teams, ranked the way the league would pan out. Right before the season started. First to last, in order. I knew the best online odds for 'guessing' correctly."

"Pretty high?"

"20,000 to one."

Ruiz whistled. "That's life-changing money right there."

"But I didn't go for it. I didn't even find it difficult to reject." Kate again focused on Aaron, on the happy little boy and his friends. At eleven, he was on the verge of teenager-dom, ready for a phone this coming Christmas, and a whole unknown world to discover. She had to savor moments like this. "You know, it's weird. It's the little things that are hardest to turn down. Those niggling complications when I'm in class, I can zone them out, keep the dam from leaking. The personal is even tougher. Telling me Aaron is hungry, or he's upset about being bullied at school, or that Sal is on his way over, so I better change out of my sweatpants."

"How is he? Sal?"

"He's healing. Working hard with the physiotherapist. How about you? Moving on? New job."

"Me and Richardson, yeah, we moved on together. We picked a cold case unit."

Kate gave a *huh*, then, "The FBI has a cold crimes section?"

"Yes, even the FBI can't boast a one-hundred percent record. Old, unsolved federal crimes that might link to current ones. Like sudden, suspicious wealth combined with deviant behavior or a psychotic break in a loved one—or themselves."

Kate was glad to hear it. Ruiz's intent was clear. "You're using FBI resources to investigate this djinn? This demon?"

"Me and Richardson. Although he's more Scully to my Mulder. But he was grateful for Sal's testimony. There was enough to exonerate him, but suspicion about his competence stuck around. He'll build on our new posting and move on when he can."

"So we might find a solution."

"Or other ghosts and ghoulies that might be out there."

They lapsed into silence, watching the party—the kids playing, the adults chatting. Kate checked on Jonathan, who seemed to do the same, his cake half-eaten.

"How do you do it?" Ruiz asked. "Keep on top of it?"

"My law studies have come in handy. I'm now finding technicalities to tap into the buddy's thinking. Like those hints that something's wrong with Aaron, I can—realistically and fully believing it of myself—tell it I would have sensed that anyway. It slows down after I get one over on it. I just wonder if, in time, I might absorb it into myself. Dilute it and banish it for good."

"Like an infection."

Kate had thought about it a lot. "It's difficult, but I am coping. When I weaken, I remind myself that I'm depriving it of power by forging my own path. If not, I'll die eventually, hopefully as an old woman."

"And so, too, will it die," Ruiz said, sounding almost like one of those storytellers of old legends. Maybe she'd read too many lately.

"Unless I find a way to destroy it. I'll never pass it on."

Another lapse into silence was broken only by Ruiz growing uncomfortable. She hadn't come here as an FBI agent, or even as a friend. There was unfinished business, and it felt like an unburdening. A tying up of loose ends before she could move on to new pastures.

"You went to Endo's funeral," Ruiz said.

"A vacation to Hawaii for Aaron. And I got to say goodbye. It seemed only right after what we did."

Kate still didn't feel right about squaring away the blame for the trade on Ollie Swag's shoulders. It was sufficient to drop the charges against Kate and Marcus. The assumption was that whispers in the criminal underworld had made it to Ollie's door, a leak from within the agency that they would look into but never find. Kate's cooperation helped, and that Marcus piggybacked on her short trade meant it wasn't a big enough crime to prosecute. As part of that deal, Marcus had agreed to remain under digital surveillance for some time, in case the supposed mole reached out to him, which allowed him to keep his license to trade as a free man.

Agent Ruiz made contact officially-unofficially all the way along—officially in terms of her logging the visits for her boss, but unofficially due to the matters they discussed off the record. A new, unexpected friendship had taken root, albeit gradually. Still not comfortable enough to call themselves girlfriends, but being able to show up today was almost as big a step as when Kate first slept with Sal.

Initially, Ruiz had been reluctant to go with Aaron's idea of having Jennifer painted as a complete psycho who went bat shit when Kate confronted her about Craig, but it wasn't far from the truth. Ruiz wasn't in her right mind, and it was indisputable that Jennifer had killed a man rather than resist the buddy's demands. When they looked into her movements more intricately, they found her on CCTV in the vicinity of two other unsolved murders—both homeless people who'd burned to death as they slept in their tents. It seemed unlikely they'd ever prove beyond a reasonable doubt that it was her, but it was enough for Jonathan to believe it, and to let Ruiz live with the fact her finger had pulled the trigger.

And despite what he'd said up on the deck, Jonathan knew the truth. He knew it now. For a while, he was adamant that other, more earthly matters were driving Jennifer. That perhaps she and Craig were having an affair, and the kiss was accidental. But the new evidence, the information showing it was Jennifer who'd insisted he defend the homeless guy accused of burning his friend in his tent, and that Jennifer was belatedly identified as present… combined with Kate's tale of how the buddy worked, he had to accept it. Just not on the surface. Perhaps his therapist would help. One day, Kate, Jonathan, and Aaron might even be a family again.

"So, what's next?" Ruiz asked, following Kate as she led the agent—her friend—toward Sal and the neighbors.

"No one knows what's next," Kate said. "Except, well…" She allowed a tiny laugh, but killed it quickly. Still not ready to joke.

Ruiz, to her credit, didn't smile.

Use me or release me. I will find a way through.

- You won't.

It wasn't a conversation as such, but Kate had started to think of its efforts that way. From the big plays like a final league tally, to the smaller, harder-to-reject snippets, if she could not destroy it, she would suffocate this thing within her.

Release me.

- No. You die when I die.

I can tell you what's next.

"I'm not interested in what's next," Kate said aloud, which drew some looks from the gathering.

It's important.

"Now is what's important." Kate addressed the group who listened as if she were giving a toast. "People, family, this moment. I don't care about the past right now. And the future will be a surprise. We'll make it our own. And we'll take whatever it throws at us."

Not interested? Not even the accident Aaron is going to have on Tuesday?

Sal said, "Here-here," and his arm moved around Kate's waist. He called, "Hey, boys, you got cake waiting!"

The racket of four eleven-year-olds sprinting and shouting for cake drowned out the buddy's offers, kept that door closed. And so it went.

Temptation she would have to live with. She had until Tuesday to either reject what it offered, or nullify the favor it would demand. That was for tomorrow, though. Today… well, she would see what today brought.

Release me. Unburden yourself.

- No.

As Kate kissed Sal on the cheek and Aaron made barfing sounds while grinning at the pair of them over his cake, only one thing was certain: She could resist the buddy's lure for at least one more day.

FROM THE AUTHOR

Thank you for reading my book. I hope you enjoyed it. If you would like to receive more stories free of charge, sign up to the reader group with the link or QR code below.

www.jordan-bach.com/fans

You will not only receive a digital copy of every short story I write (once they are ready), you'll also stay informed about new releases, giveaways, and special offers.

It goes without saying, but I'll emphasize it anyway: **your email address will never be shared or sold**.

Alternatively you can follow me on my Amazon page, Book-bub, Goodreads, or head over to Facebook and search for "authorjordanbach".

In the meantime, if you have a couple of minutes, a review on wherever you like to leave reviews would be appreciated - your preferred book retailer, social media, Goodreads, or even your own blog. They really do help new readers find authors' work.

NOVELS BY JORDAN BACH

Best Buddies

Your son's invisible friend is not imaginary…

Reflected Dark

Are you a killer? Or are you something worse?

Harmony Four

Four murders. Every four years. Forever. Until now.

NOVELLAS:

In the Barn

Even the innocent can only be pushed so far

REFLECTED DARK
Are you the killer? Or is it something worse?

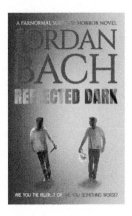

When his lover's murders start meeting grisly ends, the cops find Robert's DNA and fingerprints at the scenes. With cast-iron alibis and no memory of the killings, how can he be guilty? Could some entity conjured from his rage be responsible? And can he ever hope to control it?

Search your online retailer or scan the QR code below

HARMONY FOUR

Four murders, every four years, forever. Until now.

When a new sheriff learns his town prospers because of a four-year killing cycle, he sets out to prove the local superstition is nonsense. But, if it is not nonsense, he has a duty to protect. To fight. And to save the town without losing everything.

Search your online retailer or scan the QR code below

Made in the USA
Monee, IL
25 March 2023